SARAH
MUSSI

Here be Wizards

THE SNOWDONIA CHRONICLES
BOOK THREE

SARAH MUSSI

Here be Wizards

THE SNOWDONIA CHRONICLES
BOOK THREE

shrine
bell

www.shrinebell.com

Here Be Wizards
Sarah Mussi

First published in 2020 by Shrine Bell, an imprint of Vertebrate Publishing.

Shrine Bell
Omega Court, 352 Cemetery Road, Sheffield S11 8FT, United Kingdom.
www.shrinebell.com

Copyright © Sarah Mussi, 2020

Sarah Mussi has asserted her rights under the Copyright, Designs
and Patents Act 1988 to be identified as author of this work.

Cover design by Nathan Ryder – www.ryderdesign.studio
Map illustration by Simon Norris
Author photograph © Roger Bool
Typesetting and production by Cameron Bonser

A CIP catalogue record for this book is available from the British Library.

ISBN 978-1-911342-34-2
10 9 8 7 6 5 4 3 2 1

Production by Vertebrate Publishing.
www.v-publishing.co.uk

Shrine Bell and Vertebrate Publishing are committed to
printing on paper from sustainable sources.

MIX
Paper from
responsible sources
FSC® C018072

Printed and bound in Great Britain by Clays Ltd, Elcograf S.p.A.

Dedication

**To Myrddin Emrys, Welshman,
Mage and Magician of All Time**

*In local tradition, it is said that Carmarthen be a town that
was built up around a sacred oak tree. It is said that that oak
marketh the spot of the birthplace of the mythical magician
Merlin and guardeth the place whereunder a portal opens
unto Wales's magical realm of Annwyn. It is further claimed
that the origin of the name Carmarthen, or Caerfyrddin,
cometh from Myrddin, the Welsh name for Merlin Ambrosius,
Myrddin Emrys.*

*It is said that Merlin hath made a prophecy regarding
this ancient oak.*

*'When Merlin's Oak shall tumble down,
Then shall fall Carmarthen's Town.
When Merlin's Oak be treated kind,
Then Heart's Desires ye shall find.'*

From *The Legends of Wales*
Unknown

THE PATHS

-of-

ANNWYN

AVALON

WILL-O'-THE-
WISP MARSHES

TWRCH TRWYTH TOR

UNICORN'S BLUFF

MERLIN'S GLADE

MERLIN'S OAK

RUN-TO CAVE

And so it begins ...

21 June

At the Witching Hour Upon the Eve of Midsummer

The girl turns her face to the summit; above her the air shudders.
Heart pounding, blood hammering, she steels herself. 'I will do
this,' she mutters. 'I will have him or I will have my revenge.'
Then she shouts:

'Imperium Magis!
Wild water roar!
Sky pour down thy stinking pitch!
Sea mount up in fury!
Dash all voyagers to bits!
Lightning strike, thunder bite!

Perish all on rocks this night!
Fire find fire, blaze and burn!
As I now suffer, take your turn.
By darkest arts and deadly sin,
Let this unholy work begin.'

High above her, a helicopter veers off course. Its lights plunge out. Steel grates and plastic melts. The engine falters. The pilot screams. Thunder roars. Out of nowhere, a wild wind blows. Ahead, the sheer face of Clogwyn D'ur Arddu appears. There is a sickening lurch. Rain slashes down.

The plummeting starts.

The shrieks of the people on board are drowned out in the tempest.

Act One

Midsummer's Eve

'Here there be Wizards, wise and fair:
One tall and young with golden hair,
One old and bowed with many a care,
One cruel and wild: O Heart's Despair!
But looks deceive. Beware! Beware!'

One

I'll follow you, I'll lead you about a round,
Through bog, through bush, through brake, through brier.

Puck in *A Midsummer Night's Dream*
by William Shakespeare

As if by instinct, I halt. Something's wrong. Flashes of light sear across the horizon. Then comes the boom of thunder.

I scan the slopes for cover. Another roll of thunder crashes out. The rocks tremble. I take stock: storm; lightning.

Not good.

I'm halfway up Snowdon and way too exposed. Do I turn back or carry on?

Don't get me wrong, I love a good summer storm. The

thrill of lightning; the fun of counting the seconds to see how far away the storm is; the crazy drum of thunder.

TBH, I love it better from the safety of my window seat, in our old farmhouse, all cuddled up with a hot chocolate. Not so much up here, high above the upper pastures. A target for any chance lightning strike.

Or not-so-chance.

Sigh. I'd really wanted to get up to the Devil's Bridge.

The storm rumbles closer. Definitely not good.

I mentally flick through the safety guidelines in the *Mountain Rescue Volunteer's Handbook* (AKA Mum's Bible):

Caught out on a mountain in a thunderstorm:
1. *Look for cover.*
2. *Avoid trees or large stony outcrops; instead head for cracks and crevices in natural rock faces.*
3. *Move to sheltered overhanging rocks and be sure the scree on the slopes above is not loose.*
4. *Failing finding cover, lie down flat and stay there until the storm has passed.*

The first fat splodge of rain hits my cheek. Lie down flat? In sheep poo? And prickly thistles? Really? You've got to be joking. I'll climb higher and search for cover.

But before I have time to move, the sky rips open. A spear of purple-blue, volcanic orange, then intense white slashes down. Lightning strikes the slope just metres above me, igniting a stunted hawthorn. *Flipping heck! That was close.*

No time for Plan A.

OK, you win, *MRV Handbook*.

I drop flat on to the turf. And my face lands on hard nobbles of sheep poo. Great. So much for a romantic visit up to the Devil's Bridge to tell Henry how much I love him. (DB is where we first kissed, so my utterly-best-ever dreamy-happy-place.)

I lie there thinking, the heat of the burning scrub above me, the rain pelting down. *That hawthorn was the tallest thing around here. So if I stand up, I'll be next.*

Still going up to the Devil's Bridge, Ellie? Get real.

Not Going To Happen.

Rubbing my cheek free of the sticky sheep poo, I roll over to see where the storm's coming from.

I shield my eyes from the battering rain and peer out.

In the distance, a blanket of white spreads across the sky. It's nowhere near dark yet. It never gets totally dark at midsummer up here. But a grey storm cloud is blowing in from the west. It blackens the sky, making it feel much later than it is. I glance at my phone: 6.47 p.m.

5

Something silver flickers in the rolling billows of cloud. Lights? They appear to be heading towards me, though they're mostly obscured. I tilt my head up and squint into the pouring rain. Something *is* speeding this way, quite fast. A plane? Helicopter, maybe? I sit up properly to get a better look. Whatever it is, it seriously needs to gain height. I go all goosebumpy. *Don't they know about the huge cliffs dead ahead?*

A sheet of cloud folds over the moving object. Its lights blink out. Engines stutter. A shiver runs through me. Whoever's up there is in trouble.

Trouble!

A sixth sense sends tingles through my skull.

A dark bird swoops out of the sky, trilling out a note of alarm.

Danger!

Instinctively I roll sideways and drop back to flat. There's a crackle of static. A flash of light, then an almost instantaneous boom. My heartbeat shoots into overdrive. FLIPPING HELL! The mountain seems to shake. Rain *waterfalls* down, totally drenching me.

An outcrop of stone just above me splits in two! SPLITS IN TWO! A boulder crashes down, right where I was lying.

Oh my God.

That was just centimetres away. I could have been smashed to bits!

I throw my head back and breathe. *My ears! The noise!* That was louder than a bomb going off.

I was lying right there!

My legs tremble. My insides are squishy jelly.

I could have been splattered!

I glance up and get hit square in the eye by a massive raindrop.

There are more stones up there. I must move. NOW. I roll on to my tummy and start to squirm away. My legs are so shaky, they hardly work.

That rockfall ripped a gash right down the mountain.

Thank God I rolled away!

I think fast. *Lightning strike, boulder crashing down, dark bird swooping. All those things are weird. Something's up.*

Something weird.

I stop crawling and sniff the air. Rain, earth and ... what's that smell? *Magicke?*

Surely not?

I mentally check through the requirements for magicke.

Water. Rain. (Splatting me in the eye.)

Fire. Lightning. (Setting fire to random hawthorn bushes.)

Earth. Rocks. (Tumbling. Squishing. We won't go there.)

And the racing air.

Could be magicke, then.

Oh my God! I'm out on Midsummer's Eve and there's magicke about.

Definitely not so good.

Stay calm, Ellie.

I seriously need to get out of here. I check the skies again. It's magicke all right. Maybe I can make a run for it back down the mountain … Another rumble of thunder dies away. The struggling cough of an engine takes its place. I look up. The silver flickering is visible again, speeding much closer. It is a helicopter, and it is in trouble. It's way too low. It's going to crash. *Oh my God, this is the kind of thing that happens when there's bad magicke about.*

'WATCH OUT!' I scream. 'FOR GOD'S SAKE, TURN BACK!'

Poor visibility. Torrential rain. Rolling clouds.

Ancient Magicke.

And the evil Black Cliff of Clogwyn dead ahead.

Just waiting for a blood sacrifice.

Two

I want to stand up and wave my arms around, signal the pilot to turn back. But I'm stuck flat on the ground getting drenched. Some evil power is guiding the magicke. Must be. And I'm a target too. If I try to interfere, it'll totally come for me. So how can I warn them? I wish I had a radio. I pull out my mobile.

No coverage.

One text (from earlier).

George

You about, Elles? Fancy a magical evening together?

Great!

George never misses a trick to let me know he's available. (His is a very long sad story of unrequited love. Mine is not.)

I pull off my high-visibility vest. Since my experience last winter, my mum insists I wear one when I'm out alone on Snowdon.[1] I know, don't say a thing. Anyway, apparently, like with whales, you can see high-vis vests from outer space. Now I'm grateful for mine. I quickly slip out of the sleeve holes and wave it above my head.

If it wasn't so serious, I'd laugh my head off. Like, who is that weirdo lying on a sopping wet, sheep-pooey hillside waving a high-vis thingy about? Ha ha. Ignore it.

But it's the best I can do, because I haven't got a flare.

Never Go Out Without a Flare. That's another of Mum's rules.

Note to self: since Mum is a trained Search and Rescue Volunteer, DO WHAT SHE SAYS.

But I was only going up to watch the sun not-setting on the longest day of the year ... and the evening was bright ... and the sky was blue ... and love was in the air ... and I wanted to feel near to Henry ... in our special place.

How the heck was I supposed to know I'd need a flare?

I should have known better. Here on Snowdon, weather conditions can change in the blink of an eye. Being out late without any emergency stuff is stupid.

---

1. You can read all about it in my story *Here be Dragons*, but basically I went out in a snowstorm and my mobile went dead. Fabulous. I nearly died – BUT that's how I met Henry, LOVE OF MY LIFE and part-time dragon. No, correction: part-time gorgeous handsome amazing boy (LOVE OF MY LIFE) and most-time dragon.

And just to underline that point for me, the storm really gets going. The temperature plummets. Icy hail bullets down. Like tiny daggers, it stabs my skin. I cover my face with my hands. Thunder shakes the mountain. Sheets of lightning, tridents of jagged energy and buckets of rain slash downwards. All over me. Soaking wet. Wonderful.

The silhouette of Snowdon flashes bright and blinks out.

And the helicopter keeps on going – straight at the cliff face.

I shield my eyes. I try to listen to the engines, praying they'll make it. But everything's drowned out in thunder. I peer upwards, trying to locate the helicopter. I can't make out anything except lightning.

Then there it is!

It lurches out of the skies and down towards the mountainside. It's trying to gain height before it reaches Clogwyn, but instead it's losing power.[2] I hold my breath. I bite my cheek. *It hasn't a hope in hell.*

I hate Clogwyn. Its cliffs are so deceptively high; its darkness swallows everything. *Why don't they try to land?* They say the King of the Underworld, Gwyn ap Nudd, created Clogwyn to tempt climbers to try their strength. And fail. And die. And then he drinks their blood and chases them into the Otherworld. Nasty guy.

---

2. Clogwyn is Clogwyn Du'r Arddu, or the Black Cliff of the Darkness.

The air smells thick with evil right now: dank wet herbage and burning hawthorn. Another burst of thunder rolls across the range. The evening shakes. A fork of lightning outlines the helicopter against the darkness of the cliff.

I press the palms of my hands into my eye sockets. In the blackout behind my hands, I still see the after-print of the flash.

Please don't let the helicopter crash. Please, dear Snowdon, please.

Scared to look, yet knowing I must remember every detail, pinpoint the exact crash site, anything to help, I peek out.

For one moment, I see clearly: the helicopter lit up in a halo of blue light. In that space of silence before the thunder comes, I hear the engine finally falter and cut. The blades flicker and the helicopter descends straight into the shadow of Clogwyn.

The rocks ring out in horrific triumph.

And a burst of volcanic orange erupts into the darkness.

As suddenly as the storm starts, it stops.

An eerie stillness descends. Everywhere's gone gloomy.

I sit up. I scan the slopes. All is desolate. I shiver inside my wet clothes. I pull out my phone again. Battery life's OK, but still no coverage. I reread George's text. I wish he was here. No way to text him.

A helicopter has just crashed into the cliffs. I must get help.

No one can have possibly survived. *But what if someone has? What if they need emergency life-saving first aid?* I'm a trained volunteer mountain-rescue first-aider. I must race up the mountain and help them myself.

I've no idea how I can help. They may be really, really, *really* badly injured.

But I'm the only one who knows they've crashed. Possibly.

I do a quick mental calculation: how long will it take me to get to George's cottage? A good forty minutes. How long will it take me to get up to Clogwyn? Only fifteen. I check the sky. Let's hope the storm is over.

I start running uphill.

Ha ha. The storm immediately picks up.

Rain slices down. Lightning strikes out. Oh God. I duck. One bolt – just behind me. *Breathe in. Jeez, that was close. Just let me get to the crash site. Please, Snowdon.*

As I run, I pray and I make a plan. *I'll administer any kind of help I can. Henry, please protect me. I'll take photos if my battery lasts. Mighty Snowdon, hear my prayer. I'll record details. Then I'll head to George's place. Please, universe, give me a break.*

My sides ache. I hope the crash won't be too terrible. *Not burning bodies. Run. Get there and assess the situation. You can report to emergency teams then.*

But what about the magicke?

My lungs burn. A lightning bolt stabs through the darkness. My breath cuts short. A shrub in front of me crackles into flame. I fling myself sideways. I cough. The air smells of bleach and smoke. *Breathe.* I send *another* prayer up to Snowdon. *Please, please, please protect me.* I get back up on my feet. I run up the mountain again, spluttering.

A mountain that reeks of magicke.

A mountain covered in treacherous boulders.

In a crazy evil storm. Brilliant.

Inspirational.

I am tearing through bracken, hurtling as fast as I can towards a dangerous, awful, hideous crash site, where I'm probably going to be able to do absolutely zero, except get myself struck by lightning. *Are you nuts?* a small voice says. *This is madness. Turn back while you can.* But no, it's as if I've been caught in some malignant force field. I can't – even if I wanted to.

I pull my phone out of my pocket again. There might be a bit of coverage higher up. Snowdon is tricky. You might get a signal on one spot and absolutely zilch a metre away. I keep one eye on the coverage bar, the other on the terrain in front of me. Running across a mountainside is tricky too. The last thing I need is to fall and twist an ankle.

I glance from the phone to the sky. Lightning alert! I drop flat, just in case. I wait until the lightning strikes somewhere else. As you do. Then I'm up and racing on again.

And I run as I've never run before.

I fling myself through furze and heather, plunging up the slopes.

Ahead another ball of fire explodes. The mountain rings with a sharp terrible booming.

What the heck was that?

I pause. Check. Pant. Listen. The wind's right at my back, fierce, howling. Up ahead, Clogwyn is lit in angry flames.

Go.

I weave in between boulders – zigzag, leap, twist. Sloshing my wet, wet clothes.

What if the helicopter has totally exploded and set everything on fire?

Can magical hellfire melt stone?

A wailing, shrieking sound tears past me. *Christ, what was that?*

The only way to reach the crash site is to cross the next slope and make it to Clogwyn by the left side of the llyn.

I topple a pile of rocks, kick on turf. My lungs can't take this. No clean air. That sickly smell of magicke. Chlorine and bleach and frankincense.

A pain in my side stabs deep. *Keep going.* Gasping, coughing, chest burning.

Just make it there and see what can be done.

I slip. I'm so wet. I fling my arms out in front of me. I hit the mountainside, keep tumbling forward.

Lightning zaps overhead and strikes the spot I'd been on just before I fell.

Holy crap.

Snowdon, thank you. Thank you.

Then through the darkness, I see it. About thirty metres above me to my right, a high black-sided cliff standing out against the sky.

Clogwyn Du'r Arddu.

Nearly there.

I splash through swamp. *So cold.* Water slops over the tops of my shoes. *Ignore it. You're soaked anyway.* I flounder uphill. *Go diagonally across the mountain; make for the bottom of the cliff.* Grey slate. Dark sky.

Wildfire.

And the boom of thunder.

Three

Up ahead, the red glow of huge flames lights the way. I can smell burning debris. Plastic. Rubber. *Yuck*. Still no coverage on my phone. I try to take a bearing, and then glue my eyes back to the ground beneath me.

Stay calm, stay focused and don't trip up.

As I round the last curve ahead, a blast of thick smoke hits me. I start to cough again. I drag my T-shirt up over my nose. *Carbon particles. Double yuck.* Embers swirl at my face. They're flipping hot. They burn my skin. *Ouch.* Rain stabs the singed patches. Terrific. Away to my left, flashes of light outline the huge silhouette of the mountain.

My chest hurts REALLY badly. My breath comes in gasps. The stitch in my side is agony. I'm drenched to the bone. Shivering and sweating all at the same time. And I'm here in the shadow of Clogwyn. The place I hate most in the entire known world.

Wonderful.

On the far side of the llyn is the crash site. It's so ferociously hot, I can't get any nearer. I can't see how anyone's survived. The helicopter must have crashed straight into the rock face, then dropped in a mangled burning furnace to the bottom.

Turn back, Ellie.

I've wasted precious time. I should have gone straight to George's. The terrain's mental. I'll have to climb through gorse and rocks to get any nearer.

Turn back, then.

Go for help.

But there might *perhaps* be a survivor collapsed nearby, maybe? Someone who got out of the craft before it exploded. I must make sure. Report back accurately. Tell the rescue team …

Thunder booms off the cliff face. It echoes in great shadowy symphonies and crashes away down the slopes.

The foliage around the lake blazes, despite the rain bucketing down. That's weird. Everywhere around me burns incandescently.

The wind howls like a pack of wolves. Somehow, above its wail, I think I hear someone screaming. A shrill crying, whistling off the rocks. I must be brave. *Go closer; get as near to the fire as you can; search the wreckage; look for survivors.*

I scan anxiously around the margins of the lake. Flames, all flames. They're spreading round the lakeshore too. If I can get round to the back – through all that bog and sedge – I might have a chance.

Or I might get cut off.

I look at the water. There are many terrible stories about this lake. This is where the Afanc lives, apparently.[1] For a brief second I think of Rhiannon – best friend, best enemy, bestie of besties, best daft rich kid, best totally infuriating airhead. Best ANNOYING stupid-clever whinge-bag. She told me things about the Afanc – though I'm not sure I believe her.

But what if it's still down there, looking up through the dark water with staring eyes – watching every move I make?

A wave of heat hits me. Its energy is all dark magicke. I'll go around the far end of the lake. Just to double check for survivors, then I'm out of here. I prepare myself.

---

1. The Afanc is a lake monster from Welsh mythology. Sometimes it resembles a huge crocodile, sometimes a beaver, sometimes a dwarf-like creature, and sometimes it glows like a demon. Whatever it looks like, it is HIGHLY UNPLEASANT AND FATAL. AVOID IT.

I know what I'm about to see will haunt me. I tell myself it is not about me. It is about life and somebody's might be saved.

I watch the flames fanning out around the far end of the llyn. The wind is howling in from the north now. The whole of the mountain will go up unless it changes.

OK – get in behind the lake and out again before the burning bracken traps you.

I pull my T-shirt over my mouth and nose to shield my breathing, leaving only a small space for my eyes.

Carefully, very carefully, I creep forward, trying to avoid shards of red-hot metal lying treacherously on the lakeshore, trying to fend off a carbon rain of ash.

Soon I'm round the edge of the lake. Above the wind, I can still hear the wailing. *Maybe someone is alive?* The sounds are coming from the far side of the crash where the flames are at their fiercest. I must pass by the tail end of the helicopter. I don't like getting into the lake. (With the Afanc and all that.) But right now it's the lesser of two evils. I wade a little bit into its chilly waters and on to the slippery unseen stones below its surface. Very cautiously, I inch past the crash site. The whole place is smoke. The heat is so intense. So bright. *Nobody can have survived.* Molten metal, burning fabric, oil, petrol.

I pull the T-shirt even tighter over my nose. Still I hear wailing behind the wind. I step deeper into the water until it's up to my waist.

Past the crash site. Blink. YAY, I did it! For a moment the wind drops. There it is again – that distinctive wailing cry.

There is somebody!

And they are alive!

I was right!

It sounds like the crying is coming from inside the cliff. *The wailing wolves of Clogwyn?* My heart pounds. *Stay focused. Is this some kind of trick from that demon of the cliffs, Gwyn ap Nudd? A cry luring me in?* All the tiny hairs on my scalp tingle. The indigo sky above deepens. Nothing seems to penetrate the shadow of Clogwyn D'ur Arddu.

This is midsummer's night, when the walls between the worlds are paper-thin.

I glance at my phone. Still no coverage, but I have two bars of battery left. I click on the torch app and shine it around into the darkness.

Flames from the crash site dance up the walls of Clogwyn, like great dragons breathing fire. The wind drops. Overhead a flash of lightning shocks everything into stark silhouette. Then all light blinks out and I'm plunged into an even darker gloom. The cliffs boom out a thunderous reply. The noise drowns out the wailing.

I peer into the blackness. A glow of orange lights up shale and towering stone, looking like the entrance to the Underworld of Annwyn, filled with the flames of hell. The dreaded kingdom of Gwyn ap Nudd – Lord of the Underworld, Great Wizard of the Dark Art of Necromancy.[2]

Tentatively I move forward, torch pointed at the ground. In the lull after the crack of thunder, there's the crying again, now coming slightly from my left. I shine my torch around. Rock, debris, burning reeds, shifting shadows and some kind of a buggy or bundle.

And the crying.

Closer. Sharper.

Coming from the seat thing.

A child?

I try to make it out. I must be mistaken. *Surely nothing can have survived?* The buggy shape is like a kid's car seat.

And something is strapped into it.

A little kid is still strapped in its seat!

Could it have been thrown clear of the helicopter on impact?

Carefully I negotiate my way towards it. Huge flames

---

2. Gwyn ap Nudd is HORRIBLE. I'll tell you more about him in a bit.

flare up from the main fire and race towards the screaming shape. I struggle forward, smash my shin on a rock and start to choke on the fumes. I'm so glad I came. If I hadn't, that poor creature would have been burnt alive. Still might be. I need to act fast.

Flames block my way. I jump through them. 'I'm coming,' I yell. I pray that my soaked trousers and T-shirt will protect me. 'Don't worry, I'll get you!' I reach the seat and turn it over.

Yes, strapped inside is a child!

And it's alive.

Oh God. Thank God!

'It's OK. It's all going to be OK!' I shout.

Four

The kid screams and screams.

I don't know how badly injured it is – *he* is. At least I think it's a he. I want to pick him from the seat and clutch him to me. This is why I struggled on! The safety belt is stuck around him.

He was calling me to him.

'OK, I'm going to try to get you out of this harness,' I say. But my first aid training clicks in.

Check first. Perhaps he's injured. Only move him if absolutely necessary. Getting him away from the fire *is* necessary. I pick up the whole seat, intending to move it some metres away. It's bulky, cumbersome and HEAVY. I stagger under its weight and put it back down. The kid wails.

'Shush,' I say. 'It's OK. I'm here.'

I shine the torch into the seat. Curled up in it is a scrawny wailing creature, about the size of a toddler. He's so blackened and splattered with debris I can hardly make out if he's injured or not. Part of a blanket tucked around him has already caught fire. I pull the blanket off and stamp on it, then I drag the seat upright and haul it after me. Carefully I start to retrace my steps.

Another streak of lightning bolts right down. Striking exactly where I'd stood a moment before.

Crikey!

I'd better be mega-mega-careful.

Another crack of thunder booms off the cliffs, and the wind changes.

A wild westerly blows in from the far end of the lake. The flames that I'd thought wouldn't block my exit flare up around the far shore. My jaw drops. *I must hurry.* I fumble to unclasp the child from the smouldering seat. The belt webbing has melted and fused. The kid reaches out to me, whimpering and crying.

Get the kid out and round the edge of the lake before the fire closes in on us.

The flames race greedily forward.

Hurry. Hurry.

I'm not going to do it. Flames a metre high blaze at the

margins of the llyn. The wind fans them onwards.

The seatbelt is STUCK!

I yank at it. The child clutches on to my hair and pulls. 'Don't,' I say, wincing with pain. 'I'll get you out, I promise.'

He screams right into my ear. I flinch. Eyes watering, I pull and yank at the belt. I glance back at the helicopter. There's no hope anyone else has survived. It's a miracle he did.

It's going to be a miracle if I survive.

I curse the straps – how can they be so tangled? I give them one almighty yank. Suddenly they break and I stagger back.

The heat of the fire is scary. Even a few centimetres closer is unbearable. Some demonic force seems to be fanning the flames. They simply burn in the air, living off nothing! *Unnatural. The fires of Gwyn ap Nudd?* My throat goes dry. I try to swallow.

I've got to get us both out of here.

I look around wildly. The flames are everywhere. *Everything* is on fire.

Dear Snowdon, please don't let this fire be straight from the Otherworld. Please don't let it be from Gwyn ap Nudd.

I steady myself. *Just get out with the kid. Gran will know what to do about everything else.*

27

But how do I escape?

There's very little bracken around this side of the llyn to burn, but the flames seem to suck energy out of the actual stones.

Pick up the child. Do something.

But then what? What if he's hurt? Has broken bones? Is burned all over?

I should be calling rescue services.

I *must* pick him up and do something.

Now.

Through a break in the storm clouds, I see the evening star shining. I imagine Polaris, the pole star, somewhere up there, and Draco weaving his dance in the sky. *Is this your doing?* Another of the White Dragon's tricks?

I glance down at the boy. He's stopped crying and is curled tightly in his tattered seat. He looks up at me.

'Gonna be all right, buddy,' I say. Poor kid. *Were his parents in the helicopter?* 'Gonna get you out of here.'

He blinks. His hair is singed and blackened.

'This might hurt a little bit,' I say. 'But I've got to get you to a safe place.'

On Midsummer's Eve, nowhere is safe except Granny Jones's (George's gran and our nearest neighbour on the mountain).

But there's no way back round the lake now. The fire has cut me off.

My heart thuds. *What if this is the White Dragon's work?*[1] *He hates me. I know it. What if he has magically teamed up with Gwyn ap Nudd?*[2]

And is he trying to burn me to a cinder too?

Despite the heat, I break out into a cold sweat. *Stay focused. Just get yourself and the boy to Gran's.*

Just don't get spooked.

Or what if it's Sheila's witchery?

Sheila is evil. She wasn't always. Once she was my pal. But she swore if she couldn't have Henry, no one else would. So far, she's winning.

Some friend.

If it hadn't been for Sheila, I might be with Henry right now.

Stay focused. Do something. What would Gran recommend? She knows every herb on the mountain. She knows how to ward off evil.

Think, Ellie. Think.

Flowers? Herbs?

I remember my charm. Of course! *My magical silver charm.*

---

1. More about the White Dragon in a bit.
2. Gwyn ap Nudd burnt all of the Fae Lands to a cinder when the lady of his choice refused his wishes. Imagine burning down all of Fairyland just out of spite.

29

Quickly I pull the chain with its pendant out from around my neck.

The child starts wailing again – shrill, unnerving, like a cat in pain.

'I'm sorry,' I say. 'I've just got to try to make sure we're safe.'

I hold my charm up to the sky. 'By Bloudewedd and Y Ddraig Goch, by the power of the Lady of the Lake and all things good,' I yell, 'if this fire is fanned by enchantment, I counter it. I defy it. I banish it to whence it came.'

Nothing happens. It's almost as if the flames roar all the louder. There's a crackle as they eat up the sedge by the border of the lake.

I bite my lip. The fire's cutting me off from the water's edge!

A thought starts to form.

Use the lake to get away.

Use it now before the fire cuts that exit off too.

'HENRY,' I scream, 'if you can hear me, send help!'

Then I take a deep breath, bend down and scoop up the scrawny kid, as gently as I can. He screams and entangles both fists firmly in my hair. I ignore the pain and the pulling.

I run.

I run as fast as I can, clutching the kid to me. I run to the shores of the llyn. I run through the fire. The heat sears up. I plunge into the cold, cold water. My breath cuts short. My limbs go numb. The floor of the lake drops suddenly and I'm out of my depth.

Kick out. Save yourself.

I gulp air. I pray the Afanc had no family. I pray that Rhi actually did destroy it.[3]

I pray that the child can survive the chill of the water after all his trauma. He suddenly feels very heavy. I flip over on to my back, clutching him to me, and using side-stroke I cross-chest tow him, like we were taught in swimming class. He screams and grabs at me. At least he's breathing. I tighten my grip for fear he'll drag me under.

I kick hard with my feet, pushing myself along, guided by the stars. I head out across the lake, over its bottomless depths, away from the fire.

Right over the lair of the dreaded Afanc.

---

3. You will have to read Book Two, *Here be Witches,* to find out about that.

Five

The waters lurk deep and dark beneath me. I clutch the child tight. The burns on my hands throb. It's hard to hold him steady. He starts a weird mewling, as if he's calling out to someone.

'Shush, I'm sorry. It's going to be OK,' I croak out.

Please make it OK, Henry.

I feel a sucking at my back, as if something in the water has reached out a shadowy hand and is plucking at my T-shirt. It's cold. Icy. If I don't fight back, I'm going to freeze and sink.

Frantically, I strike out into the dark water. I'm out of breath already and bone-tired. I keep whispering to the child, 'It'll be OK. It'll be OK.'

The child keeps up his mewling. Perhaps his burns are hurting too? Perhaps I'm holding him too tight? *Just keep kicking, Ellie.*

I glance back to where we just stood. The whole area is on fire. Huge flames, two metres high. They consume the entire stretch of land between the lake and the cliff.

I got out just in time. Thank you, Snowdon. Thank you, Henry.

I tip my head back. Cold water in my ears. Maybe I'm a third of the way across the llyn by now?

If I can reach the far shore, we'll be OK. I twist my head to look back again. I get water in my eyes. Blurrily, I watch the flames. A haze of dark smoke swirls up and forms a massive cloud. I blink. The child tightens his grip and lets out a horrific cry. As if he really is calling out to a world beyond our own. *I'll be OK. I'll get help. I'll save you. Breathe. Conserve strength. Just keep going.* My mobile will probably be ruined. Crap. It was a new one too. No chance of calling anyone now. I'll have to go cross-country, all the way to Gran's. I hope I've got the energy.

'It'll be OK,' I whisper again to the child.

The drag on my back gets much stronger. I kick harder. But I'm so weak. My arms ache. These llyns are rumoured to be bottomless. *Even if Rhi killed the Afanc, what else lurks down there in the cold endless water?*

I twist my head again, willing the far shore to be closer. All around me, a swell is forming. Like a giant hand stirring a giant pot, the swell spins and speeds.

And instantly I'm caught in a whirlpool.

The wind changes again. The cloud of smoke mushrooms towards me. It forms a hideous demon face ... a face blackened with soot ... a face I've seen before.

Gwyn ap Nudd. King of the Otherworld, Dark Sorcerer of Annwyn.

I knew it. Cold shoots into my bones. Icy. Numbing.

I don't want to die. Not like this. Not after everything I've been through. Not with the child.

The smoke starts to choke me. I feel a trembling in the pit of my stomach. I can't kick any harder. I can't go on.

What would Mum say?

'Hypothermia, darling.'

It's just hypothermia and fatigue, I tell myself very sternly. *You're OK.* It'll take twenty minutes before it fully disables you and your cells start dying (*Mountain Rescue Volunteer's Handbook*, section 43). Nothing to worry about. Yet.

But I can't breathe.

And there's a whirlpool sucking me in.

Kick harder.

Thick smoke everywhere, stinging my chest. And it's so cold. Move your arms.

Gwyn ap Nudd? My mind can't take it. My heart pounds. My throat closes up.

Keep the circulation going.

Pray the little one survives.

I can't move my right arm. I've got to hold on to the child. My hands are agony. If I drop the child now, there will have been no point in any of it.

The great whirlpool twists around me. I kick. Hard. Harder. *So heavy.* The centre of my mind goes blank. My brain is closing down. I don't know what to do. The current is way too strong. The kid is gripping on so tight.

I don't know what to do.

I tip my head up and imagine the stars behind the thick smoke. *Oh Henry, if you are there somewhere, even if your spirit is out there, stay with me. We've got this far.*

I feel a warmth stealing along the veins of my body. Of course it could be what's called *thermalisation*, but I choose to believe it's warmth from Henry's heart.

He loves me.

He loves me so much he'll send me help.

I know it.

I won't give up.

I kick more fiercely. I feel a cramp in the calf of my left leg. I kick anyway, through the cramp, trying to believe that everything will be fine.

Kick. Pray. Hold on to the child.

Miraculously, the pull of the whirlpool lessens. The choking smoke dissipates. I feel the icy fingers of the swell slipping, and I know that if I can keep on kicking, I'll reach the far shore.

And then my back and neck and head scrape shingle.

Shingle! I made it!

I scramble to my feet, holding the little one closer than ever. I take a moment to check that he's still breathing. His face is pale in the starlight. I'm amazed he seems fine, not freezing like I am. Then I'm sloshing forward in my trainers with my jeans dripping.

I drag myself towards Gran's cottage. I don't care that I'm treading burning embers underfoot. I'm so wet and cold they don't stand a chance!

I make for the curve of the upper pasture.

About half a mile.

Thank God it's all downhill.

And there it is. Gran and George's cottage.

Legs trembling. Arms dead. Shoulders aching. Hands raw. Exhausted. Gasping. Hot. Cold. I make it.

I MAKE IT!

Six

The cottage door flies open. A wave of warmth and summer sweetness floods out to greet me.

'Ellie!' shrieks Gran. 'Holy spirits! Get inside!'

George is suddenly at my side. 'Elles,' he says, 'what's happened?'

'Please take care of him. Don't let him die … ' I hold out the soggy dripping bundle.

George steps forward, and seems to be about to dangle the child upside down, as if the only way he can think to hold a baby is by its feet.

Gran swipes the child off him, almost aggressively. 'Don't you touch it,' she warns. Then she turns sharply to me. 'Where did you get this?'

I blink. *What's wrong?* Then I sway, suddenly dizzy.

'Don't bother to answer her,' says George. 'Sit down first.'

He guides me to a chair.

'How long has it been with you?' Gran's voice escalates.

'He's a boy,' I whisper.

'Shush, Nan,' says George. 'We'll have the full story later. Ellie needs to get dry and warm; she's shaking.'

I feel tired to the bone and as soggy as wet tissue.

Gran tuts and grumps. She holds on to the child (who seems to have gone quiet and limp). She bends over him.

'Is he OK?' I ask.

A newsreader announces something from the TV, her voice fractured and faint.

' ... *breaking news ... remote and treacherous ... a helicopter ... lost contact ... radar ... '*

'Is he going to be OK?' I whisper again.

' ... *bring you updates as soon as a clearer picture emerges. Access is only possible on foot ... four kilometres or a two-hour hike over very challenging terrain ... three people feared lost ... '*

'Is that where you've been?' demands Gran.

' ... *rescue services have not been able to approach the area ... raging thunderstorms ... burning ferociously ... '*

I nod. I think so.

' ... *over 700 metres above sea level ... '*

'And what on earth induced you to go out of doors on Midsummer's Eve?' says Gran.

I look at her. I try to think. *Why is she so cross? Why did I go out?* I shrug my shoulders. But I do know. I'm just too shy to tell her. I'd hoped – wanted – to somehow feel closer to Henry – on Midsummer's Eve when the walls between the worlds are thinner. I'd just wanted to get up to the Devil's Bridge ...

'The threat of wildfire is making the task of getting personnel and equipment to the site very difficult ... potentially dangerous ... '

George hands me a large crocheted blanket. Outside, everything goes silent. No birdsong, even though it's still twilight.

A spooky feeling races up my spine. 'The child *is* going to be OK, isn't he?' I ask Gran again, my heart racing.

'You really should get out of those wet things,' George says.

'Please tell me, Gran,' I plead.

'The child will be fine,' answers Gran in an odd voice.

'Hey Elles,' says George, 'I tell you what: you strip off and rub yourself dry with a towel; I'll get you one. Then I'll run a hot bath for you.'

I nod and shiver. A hot bath sounds really good. I look wistfully at the hearth. Normally there would be a fire burning there, but with the heat we've been having, there isn't even a pile of logs. 'I was nearly struck by lightning,' I try to explain. 'And I had to swim Llyn Du'r Arddu.'

'Get that bath going then, Siôr,' says Gran, 'and Ellie, follow me.'[1]

George races out and is soon back with a fluffy white bath sheet.

'But the child will be cold too,' I say.

'The. Child. Will. Be. OK,' says Gran in a tone that means *that is the end of the matter*. Then she pulls me into her little parlour.

I strip off my wet clothes. Check my phone. Ruined. Gran hands me the towel. I shiver. Outside the wind picks up. There is still no sound of thrush or blackbird. Weird. Instead I hear the wind whistling round the house.

I dump my wet things on the slate floor. Gran offers me an additional blanket. I wrap myself up, but I still shiver and shiver. 'I think I saw the face of Gwyn ap Nudd in the smoke,' I whisper.[2] The wind whistles louder. Gran doesn't answer. I can't seem to get warm. My teeth chatter. I tremble. The shivering gets worse. It's as much as I can do to stutter

---

1. Gran always calls George *Siôr*, which is the Welsh version of *George*.
2. Gwyn ap Nudd is a great warrior wizard with a berry-blackened face. Shiver and shiver some more. He's really scary and the leader of the Wild Hunt, which comprises the white wolves of the Cŵn Annwn plus their hag, the hound mother Mallt-y-Nos; Gwyn ap Nudd's infamous hound, Dormarch; and a monstrous beastly boar called the Twrch Trwyth. Gwyn ap Nudd rides a wild black stallion and commands the Fae Folk of the Otherworld. He allies himself with the Pookah and all who seek power through Necromancy and Ancient Black Magicke.

out, 'You s-sure the k-kid'll be OK? Sooo cold … been in the water … '

Gran still doesn't answer.

A tremor of fear starts on the crown of my head. All the little hairs on my neck prickle. 'Gran?'

'Shush. That one is not at risk. His type never is. 'Tis you who have been poisoned,' says Gran in a weird way. I look up at her, puzzled.

Poisoned?

Normally she'd be fussing and dialling 999 or rushing up and down with a zillion potions; hugging the child, doing her best. I just don't get it.

'Poisoned?' I say.

'A moment, Ellie,' says Gran. She goes back into the front room. I watch as she strips off the sodden blankets around the child.

Something is terribly wrong. She hasn't even checked him.

The child seems to unfold in front of my eyes. He's huge! No wonder he was so heavy. He doesn't seem much the worse for wear, though. There's not a scratch on him! Plus he's not looking at all cold.

Gran checks his breathing as she wraps him up in a fresh blanket. She takes a potion bottle off her dresser and then she's back.

'You've done a miracle,' she says to me, 'though I'm not sure you should have ... Now drink this.'

I frown. *What does she mean?*

Gran forces a spoonful of some foul, tangy herbal concoction at me. It stops my tremors and almost immediately a relaxing warmth steals through my veins.

'The chilly waters helped you,' Gran says, putting the stopper back into the bottle. 'Give me your hand.' She examines my burnt fingers. 'This is not good, Ellie. Follow me.'

Still salivating to get rid of the awful taste in my mouth, I follow her back into the front room, towel and blankets clutched around me.

'Now look at this.' Gran unfolds a corner of the blanket covering the child. Beneath it is nothing but the perfect pink flesh of the boy's lower leg. Not a scratch, not a weal, not a burn; not a singe, even; no bit of redness at all. 'It's just as I suspected' – she points to a pallid weal across his face – 'only the mark of exchange ... ' She pulls a thoughtful face, then takes down one of her colourful Indian paisley shawls and swaddles the child swiftly and tightly.

Instantly he wriggles and moans. 'Careful, Gran,' I say.

'That child, if child it be, will be fine, for a while. The colours will hold it. Now you must get into that bath and stop the poison from spreading or you'll catch your death of cold.'

'The colours will hold him?'

'Yes,' says Gran. 'The Grey Lands are named so for a reason.'

'And what poison?'

'The touch of the damned.'

She's lost me. *I start to panic. I don't understand. Damned? Poisoned?*

'Won't you call the police,' I whisper, 'and tell them the child's safe?'

'All in good time,' says Gran. There's a shadow in her voice that scares me more than ever. 'We don't know yet what this child is.'

'Bath's ready,' calls George from the back room.

As I slip into the foamy water, I suddenly think what a strange thing *that* was to say.

We don't know yet what this child is.

Not *We don't know yet* who *this child is.*

The warmth seeps into my bones.

Poisoned.

Touched by the damned.

My throat goes all tight.

Gran is scared. And Gran never gets scared.

Despite the warm water, I shiver.

Something terrible must be happening.

Seven

By the time I've had my bath, got into a huge knitted jumper of Gran's and put on one of her mad velvet skirts, and borrowed George's just-in-case phone and put it on to charge, George has cut some great chunks of fresh bread. He's laid them out on the table with veggie spread, some homemade hummus, grated carrot and fresh sliced tomatoes. Gran's new fad is to be completely vegan. What does George think of that? Don't ask. Gran is throwing together a salad of parsley, radish and lettuce that she's just brought in from her vegetable garden.

The bath warmed me, but I've pulled on one of George's tracksuits under the mad skirt too. My hands still hurt. A lot.

George must have been out to bring in wood, as a fire is now crackling in the hearth. I huddle up to it and pull a blanket around me. George disappears into the kitchen and comes back with a tray of steaming bowls full of veggie soup. He plants everything on the dining table, then darts back into the kitchen and reappears with a massive pot of tea and pours me a cuppa. They are both so thoughtful: a lit fire (these flames seem friendly, thank heavens) and food …

'I don't take sugar,' I say as I see him ready to put one humungous spoonful right into my mug.

'Quite right, Ellie,' says Gran. 'After your adventures, you need something much healthier.' She points at the salad. 'Now, while that child was contained by the shawl, I contacted the emergency services and the rescue team. I've not told them a thing, just made enquiries. They say they know nothing yet of the fate of the people on board the helicopter, or who they were, but when they do, they'll make an announcement. So now you need to tell us everything.'

I'm strangely weary, like I really don't want to go back over any of it again. *And why didn't Gran tell them about the child?*

George hands me the cup of tea, 'Get outside that,' he says, and then, 'Why didn't you call me?'

'I wanted to,' I say, 'but you know Snowdon – no coverage.'

Gran nods her head knowingly. 'Of course not. Tonight will be much worse than usual.'

'Nan, stop being so wise-old-womanish,' says George. 'If you know something we don't, then just tell us.'

I check George's phone, now with my sim in. She's right. Nothing.

''Tis Midsummer's Eve,' says Gran, as if that is the answer to everything. 'There will be no coverage, not for the whole night. Not anywhere out on Snowdon. For tonight the Fae Folk are abroad. That's how it is and how it always will be. Now I want the full story – for there is something in this matter that I don't like.'

'Oh, you mean like Ellie nearly getting struck by lightning and burnt to a toasty crisp, and then facing death by drowning or hypothermia?' says George.

'Fiddlesticks!' snaps Gran. 'Ellie wasn't in any danger from those things. She's a mountain girl – an odd storm or a hill fire or a mountain lake can't hurt her. The only danger she was in was from that.' Gran points a gnarled finger at the sleeping boy. 'And its sort – creatures of the damned.'

'What?' I say.

'Hey Nan,' says George, 'I know you're not keen on kids, but that's a bit harsh.'

'First things first,' Gran continues.

What does she mean?

'Tell all, Ellie,' she insists.

'Gran,' I say, 'you're freaking me out. What's wrong with the child?'

'Trust me,' she replies, 'I must know all first.'

So I shelve that last weird comment of hers (for now) and tell her everything, from how the storm suddenly came to the thunder and lightning, and how its malice seemed to be directed straight at me. I tell her of the helicopter crash and the flames that had a life of their own. She pokes the fire at this, peers into the swirl of smoke and cinder, and her shoulders slump.

And then I tell her more about the child and how he became so flipping heavy, especially when the waters of the llyn started to drag me down ... and then I describe the dark cloud and the face of Gwyn ap Nudd and the whirling thing at the centre of the lake and how I prayed to Draco and Snowdon and Henry ...

When I finish, there's silence.

Gran gets up. She fusses about. She takes my teacup. She swishes the tealeaves around at the bottom of the cup. She turns them over into the saucer. She spins the handle three times until it points at me, then knocks another three times on the top of the cup and mumbles something, I think it's 'May I come in?' (As you do.) Then she tips the cup over and peers deep into the pattern of leaves inside.

George and I share a look. Gran has done this so many times it's almost normal behaviour.

Almost, but not quite.

'It's worse than I thought,' she mutters.

The windows rattle as the wind outside seems to change direction yet again.

''Tis a blessing you prayed to Snowdon,' she adds.

'Is it OK to speak normally?' asks George. 'Or shall I fetch a piece of plumbing or the odd bit of steel clothes rail?'[1]

'Look,' Gran says, pointing at the tealeaves.

The wind rises, battering on the slate walls of the cottage. My hands are suddenly alive with pain. I see huge, menacing, black masses of air in my mind, piling up in the teeth of a rapidly rising storm …

Stay focused, I order myself.

'Look!' Gran repeats.

Obediently, we look at a great clump of damp tealeaves on the bottom centre part of the cup.

---

1. Iron and metal is believed to repel, contain or harm ghosts, fairies, witches and other malevolent Otherworldly creatures. Words spoken through iron or copper cannot be caught by the wind and whispered to enemies and spies. We did a lot of speaking into odd bits of plumbing during our adventures in *Here be Witches*.

'That is not a good omen,' she says. She pokes the fire again and adds, 'In fact, it is so bad, there is nothing, absolutely nothing, I can do about it.'

'What's the bad omen?' I say.

'The tealeaves, you noodle,' says George.

'But what do they mean, duh?' I say.

'It's not cool to say "duh" any more,' says George.

Gran glares at us. We both straighten our faces. George pretends to be interested and picks up the teacup.

'What about this?' says George. 'You missed that.' He points at a single grain of tealeaf near the rim.

Gran snatches the cup back from him and examines it closely. 'Ah! At last, some help!' She peers and peers as if she can hardly believe there may be a good omen in the leaves after all.

I officially give up. I'd really like to know what's going on, but I just feel too weak.

''Tis the marker,' Gran says, her voice rising. 'And it's showing us the way.'

Eight

'The marker?' asks George.

'The way to where?' I add.

''Tis the stone,' says Gran.

'The marker stone on Snowdon?' George guesses.

'That's right; the standing stone way up there on the mountain.'

'You mean the Menhir of Mawr?' I ask.

'That same one,' she says.

'But what does it *mean*?' asks George.

'And what about the child?' I glance over at the huddled shape beneath Gran's shawl. I want to trust her, but surely she doesn't intend to just leave him there like that?

'If it involves the Menhir of Mawr,' says Gran, 'then it is beyond my seeing powers. Someone will have to go up the mountain and ask the stone what it is that we need to know.'

The air grows colder. I shiver, listening to the wailing of the wind outside. I don't want to go out there again.

'Someone will have to go up the mountain,' Gran repeats.

No. Not me. Please not me.

I want to stay here, safe inside Gran's cottage.

'OK,' I mumble. 'But not now. I'll go – tomorrow … maybe.' I look at George hopefully.

'You must go *immediately* – tonight!' Gran explodes. 'As soon as I've prepared the charms. After tomorrow, the stone will not say a word! It's tonight on Midsummer's Eve that it will speak—'

'But,' interrupts George, 'Ellie is exhausted. And with all those fae things around, it won't be safe.'

'Nevertheless – perilous as it is – she must go, as soon as she is rested,' insists Gran. 'I'll find Ellie a herbal restorative that will fortify her for a while.'

'Well, she can't go alone.' George looks at me from beneath a massive eyebrow frown.

So Come With Me, I mouth.

George grins. The frown disappears. 'I'll go too, and take my new Fiskars X27 Super Splitting Axe.'

Thank you, George.

'And I will defend Ellie from all Fae Folk, fair or foul.'

So hopelessly gallant! I roll my eyes at him. 'I hope you're not thinking of taking the Fae Folk on,' I say.

'But have you seen it?' He smiles. 'I ordered it online – just in case, you know – as you have a habit of destroying all my best axes. So if we are going off on more adventures, I'd better order another one, right away – in advance. I rather fancy the Hults Bruk Kalix Fell … '

I sigh. I've had to admire George's new axe every time I've been to Gran's cottage – Every Time – ever since he got it delivered, not to mention watching him trawl through a thousand different websites beforehand *and* listening to him weigh up the comparative virtues of endless axe choices before he decided which one to go for.

'Rest assured,' George adds, 'the Pookah will not get past my well-tempered steel!'

'The Pookah?' I ask.

'Yes, you know – the Fae Folk of old Wales. Goblin-like, elvish, beautiful and devilish. Considered to be bringers of both good and bad fortune. They like to steal the brightest and the best of teenage kids away to their lands forever.'

'I might like to see Fairyland,' I say.

'Fairyland is no more,' Gran says. 'The Fae Lands have been scorched dry by the fires of Gwyn ap Nudd. Now they have become the Grey Lands. The Pookah now serve Gwyn ap Nudd. Don't ever eat or drink Pookah fare,' she warns randomly.

Just as I am about to start asking more about the Pookah and the Fae Lands, a number of things happen.

Firstly, it seems like the child cries out. Secondly, Gran snatches back the teacup and looks into its depths once more. Thirdly, the wind blows down the chimney with such force it scatters burning embers out into the room, across the sofa and on to the carpet.

George jumps to his feet and stamps out the glowing cinders.

Gran, with a furious curse unlike any I've *ever* heard her utter, picks up the poker. It's been in the fire for a while and is white hot. Gran marches over to the sofa, where the child lies moaning in his sleep.

For one horrible moment, I think she is going to plunge the burning poker down into the sleeping child.

And she almost does!

But she seems to catch herself mid-sweep. Instead of thwacking the iron down, she tips the white-hot end upwards and lays the rim of the cool end vertically on the child's beautiful forehead.

The child reacts as if he *is* being murdered!

There's a shriek like all the demons of hell let loose. The child's eyes fly wide open. From corner to corner, from side to side, from upper lid to lower lid, his eyes grow black.

Totally black.

There is not one bit of iris or pupil – no light reflects from those bottomless holes – no whites, no browns, no blues.

Oh my God. What has Gran done?

'Get back,' warns George and picks up his axe.

A shiver goes over me; a trembling worse than all the chills of the llyn starts in my bones. My hands scream in pain.

And then in the brief silence, the child speaks. In vile, poisonous tones, somewhere between the sound of a hissing snake and the squeak of a rusty hinge. From the child's mouth pours a language fetid and toxic.

And I cannot understand a word of it.

It's not English.

It's not Welsh.

It sounds abusive.

And it's deeply scary.

George drops his axe in shock. It clangs ominously on the stone hearth.

My heart pounds. I realise my jaw is clenched so tight

my teeth are grinding together. Plus I've raised my arms in the shape of a cross to defend myself.

'I have you now!' hisses Gran. Her voice is cold and hard. A chill wind runs through the room, stirring the curtains and making the fire splutter anew.

'Holy smoke!' says George. (It's an annoying new phrase he picked up from an old movie – his latest fav expletive.)

'Ellie, bring me one of my bracelets – that iron one,' Gran commands. She points to a rack on the wall where a number of beads and bracelets and charms hang. The 'iron one' looks like some kind of open ring thing that you might find in a museum under the section marked Iron Age or Paleolithic Torture Ornaments.

'And the chain beside it,' orders Gran.

I grab both and pass them to her.

As quick as a flash, Gran wraps the chain around the child's arm.

That makes everything a lot worse.

The child screams, ear-splitting caterwauling, as if the chain is red hot.

I throw my hands over my ears. 'Stop it!' I yell at Gran. 'You're hurting him!'

'What's going on?' shouts George. He picks up his axe and stands ready again.

I've never, never, ever seen Gran so stern, so cruel. From the look on George's face, he hasn't either.

'There is no time to explain,' says Gran, 'but I have caught this one. The colours won't be strong enough, but the metal will hold it whilst I prepare a portal.'

'What do you mean?' I shout. 'A portal?'

'We are in much, *much* deeper trouble than I thought,' says Gran. 'You were right, Siôr, to mention the Pookah.' She turns on us dramatically. 'This is no child you see lying on the sofa, but a changeling that the Pookah have sent.'

Nine

'A what?' yells George. 'A changeling? I don't get it!'

But deep in my memory I remember stories of children taken by the Fae Folk and goblins being left in their place. Well, not goblins, exactly – but a troublesome spirit in a child's form – creatures that bring nothing but illness and misfortune with them.

'I don't understand,' I squeal back. 'How can it be a changeling?'

I remember something about portals too – magical places that open up between Fairyland and our world – so children can be snatched and changelings left in their place.

'Ellie,' says Gran, her face set like stone, 'this is Midsummer, when all portals between the worlds are unlocked.' She holds the poker, ready to lay it across the child again. 'It is said in legends that when the Fae Folk – not the Tylwyth Teg, but the Pookah – are given the opportunity, they will pass through those portals to snatch the unwary and imprison them in the Grey Lands.'

There is a distinct drop in temperature despite the fire. The room grows icy. Shadows seem to scuttle into corners and build and writhe. A wind flaps the curtains and instantly Gran crosses the room and snaps the curtains shut.

I shiver and draw the blanket tighter.

'What happened to the Grey Lands?' I ask.

'The King of Annwyn, Arawn, was overthrown by the black arts of Gywn ap Nudd,' starts George. He seems to be reciting from memory. 'Because of a prophecy, to protect his usurped realm, Nudd wanted to destroy a changeling child, Arawn's heir, who was being protected by Nimue, the Lady of the Lake.'

Gran nods and motions him to continue. The temperature drops even further.

'The Lady Nimue refused to hand the child over. So in his rage Nudd burnt Annwyn, AKA the Fae Lands, to ashes. Till today he has kept the realm blackened and in cinders.'

Instantly I flash back to Gwyn ap Nudd's darkened face, swirling in the billows of smoke.

'Tell her the prophecy,' prompts Gran.

'Well, Arawn's memory is apparently revered in a traditional saying: "*Hir yw'r dydd a hir yw'r nos, a hir yw aros Arawn*", which means "Long is the day and long is the night, and long is the waiting of Arawn." This is what Gywn ap Nudd fears most. The return of Arawn or one of his blood.'

Gran looks at George and gives him an approving nod. 'Good, good,' she murmurs. 'You are starting to understand.' Then she continues, 'But you forgot to add the prophecy states that Arawn's heir can only defeat Nudd with help from the Mortal World.'

Ah! So that's why Gwyn hates humans, I think.

'And because of this, the Pookah, the servants of Nudd, will snatch children and replace them with one of their own whenever they can. They send those snatched children to serve Nudd in a life of misery in Annwyn. This pleases him: to subject the children of men to a life of slavery in his land of ashes – if they are lucky – and it serves to remind us of this realm, not to interfere with his.'

'And if they are unlucky?' I ask.

'Then the child will become sport. Sport for Gwyn ap Nudd's own amusement, to bait and hunt and kill. Nudd likes to hunt – especially the children of men. It keeps his skills sharp. For he knows that into his Grey Lands will one day come those who will aid a son of Arawn, and together they will destroy him and the kingdom of Annwyn will be seized back. Any human who enters there does not survive long.'

'Holy smoke!' says George again (annoyingly).

'So I must seek a way to bind this changeling, and if possible return it to the Grey Lands tonight while the walls are thin,' says Gran.

'But what about the poor child they've taken?' I add.

'It will be hard to release such a vulnerable little one from the hands of Gywn ap Nudd,' she says. 'He will perch the babe on his great steed and transport it everywhere he goes with his Wild Hunt, until it is of age to serve or be hunted.'

Everything now makes sense. The reason why the child did not burn in the crash; the strangeness of its being thrown out of the helicopter; its attempts to drown me; its calling out to the Afanc … I realise now that's what it was doing!

'Sadly,' says Gran, as if she can read my thoughts, 'when the helicopter crashed into Clogwyn on Midsummer's Eve, shedding innocent blood, it smashed open an unlocked portal.' She makes a weirdy pagan sign to ward off the Evil Eye with her hands – fingers all twisted, something like the hand-horn corna, but held upside-down. She points the sign at the fire, and adds, 'That portal under Clogwyn has always stood half open.'

I know that's true. I've felt its dark energy hanging in the shadow of those cliffs ever since I can remember.

'And now Gwyn ap Nudd can come and go as he likes on our mountain.' Gran shakes her head.

'So a kid from the helicopter has been taken?' asks George.

'Yes,' says Gran, 'but that is not the worst thing.'

'Not the worst?' George cries. 'I can't think of anything much worse.'

'You'd better tell us,' I say.

'If any more of the Pookah get through the portal, anyone not yet an adult is at risk, including both of you. At any time, the Pookah may touch you on the left shoulder and if you're caught unaware, unguarded, you will be whisked into the Grey Lands and replaced by one of them. Slowly, slowly, if the portal stays open, they will creep through and spread. All around you may soon be those who are not what they seem.' Gran stares wearily at the floor.

Even George seems weighed down.

'From now on, trust none of your friends. Believe no one. Create a secret code between yourselves, so that you will know if one or the other of you has been taken. And if you find yourself in a land of ash, know that you have been snatched into the Grey Lands. Know that the Pookah have taken you and you must find a way to survive without eating or drinking anything they give you.'

'You said "unguarded", Gran. How can we guard against them?'

'Always have metal touching your skin. The Pookah cannot abide metal. It bites and burns them. And of all metals, they hate iron and silver the most.'

I think of my charm on its chain around my neck. It saved me. I bless my grandmother for passing it down to me. I bless Gran for keeping it safe. I raise my hand to my throat and run the slim chain through my fingers.

'Why exactly can't you eat their food?' says George.

OMG, George and food!

Gran sends him a stern look. 'Fae food is enchanted – it can cure any illness you have, and some have sought it to cure themselves of dread diseases by eating it – but it can enslave you too, like a terrible drug. You may forget yourself and be unable to return to this world without the help of a mage or the like.'

George goes to the table and makes himself a HUGE sandwich. He stuffs it full of salad and falafel and hummus, and with his mouth full (I know, totally GROSS), he says, 'A mage?' Then he sees me looking. 'Just topping up in case,' he explains between ginormous bites.

'One who has been ordained as a wizard,' says Gran. 'One who possesses a Book of Shadows and can use High Magick.'

So many thoughts are whizzing through my head. The Menhir of Mawr, an open portal, a changeling, the Pookah, a wizard, the Grey Lands ...

'But what about the child they've taken?' I say again.

'I fear that that child is already lost.' Gran shakes her head very sadly. 'He should have died in the blaze anyway, though that is little consolation. It would have been better perhaps if he had. The Pookah will have saved him from that fate, but now, poor thing, he is held hostage in the Grey Lands – in the hands of Gwyn ap Nudd. And they will surely have fed him already, for he is too young to know to refuse their fayre.'

'That's awful,' I say. Poor little thing.

'But maybe there is something ... ' mutters Gran. 'I will ferment some fruit in an eggshell, which may start the change-back process. Then I'll need to roast a hen ... That will be a start... but someone would need to snatch the child back ... You must know that your task is not to rescue him, but to understand this new threat sent down on our mountain and to—'

Gran stops and turns up the radio.

'Wildfire from the site of a recent crash is now spreading down the mountain at an alarming rate …'

'Hark at THAT!' shouts Gran. 'This fire is no summer mountain fire!' She beats the poker on the flagged floor in emphasis. 'You mark my words! 'Tis fae fire fanned from the Otherworld by the breath of Gwyn ap Nudd himself, sent to destroy us all!'

'But the boy?' George insists.

'Poor child, he is lost. We must harden our hearts and forget about him. Unless great Merlin can come again to this world, there will be no wizard strong enough and no magick high enough and no love selfless enough to save him.'

'But what about us?' I cry in alarm.

If George was taken, I couldn't bear it.

Gran jumps up and snatches down two more iron bracelets, hanging from the pegs on the wall. 'Put them on,' she orders, her face set and grim. 'Anyone who is still young can be taken.'

George and I reach for the bracelets.

Gran's face softens. She breathes a huge sigh of relief and

says, 'Thanks be to the Lord. Neither of you has yet been touched.'

George looks at me and raises his eyebrows.

Stop it! I mouth back.

Ten

'Now, be very careful. Do not remove the iron,' Gran instructs us both. 'I will give Ellie a draught of pure power water that has flowed through the Llech Ronw to give her strength and to counter the poison that this changeling has laid upon her.'[1] She hands me a small, stopped bottle. 'Drink it all.'

I gulp down the draught. It tastes really clean, like super-filtered water. It's cool too, yet it burns my throat and warms my chest like neat spirits. My burnt hands start to itch like crazy.

'I will make charms that may last this night,' continues Gran. 'But I have not tested their strength against sorcerers, and I am no wizard to meddle in the magic they have.'

---

1. In the Fourth Branch of the *Mabinogion* (the story of Math ap Mathonwy) you can learn all about the Stone of Llech Ronw. Have tissues handy cos it's a sad story. ☹

She keeps casting worried glances at the covered child. George puts his axe in a backpack.

Is it me or does the air fill up and spill over with a weird dark energy?

'Go to the rack, both of you, and take down three chains each, the strongest you can find,' instructs Gran. 'Place one around your neck and one around each ankle. Do this now, before you do another thing.'

Chains, metal, iron. Protection. George and I kept safe. I race to the rack; why didn't we do this before?

'Oh God, chains and changelings,' moans George. 'Just when I thought Ellie and I could have a nice relaxing Midsummer's Eve stroll, skipping through golden pastures and holding hands under the moonlight.'

I frown at George – like that was ever going to happen.

George puts on the chains, shaking his head quietly. 'Good,' says Gran. 'You will have to go soon and go quickly. For on Midsummer's Eve all eyes will be wide open and watching you. Many will try to trick you if you are not purposeful. Stick to the paths always, for Druids and saints have trodden them and there still lingers some power in their footsteps.' She crosses herself and makes more weird pagan signs.

'Yes, it is Midsummer's Eve,' sighs George. 'We get it.'

Gran takes no notice; she's watching the changeling. It's awake, and watching her back. It stares at us all with baleful eyes. It wrenches at its chains, then lets out an unearthly wail and casts murderous glances at Gran.

I shudder. That thing gives me the creeps. *And to think I carried it all the way back from Clogwyn.*

'You are going to be OK, aren't you?' I ask Gran. 'Alone with … it?'

Gran looks unsure. 'I'll light the holy fires,' she says.

'You *are* going to be OK, *aren't you, Gran?*' I repeat.

Gran looks suddenly so frail, so old. She doesn't answer. Instead, she goes to the ancient dresser and takes down jam jars filled with dried flowers. 'St John's wort, vervain, trefoil, rue and rose petals,' she murmurs, as she scoops out teaspoons of them and loads tiny cloth-sewn pouches for us.[2] 'And clover for emergencies.'

Then she paces around, placing garlic on the windowsills. She throws a bunch of sage into the grate, which starts to smoulder and smoke.

'Protect us … ' she mutters. 'Protect us … '

I know what she's doing. She's trying to defend herself from the changeling … from the fires …

---

2. St John's wort is always gathered on Midsummer's Day, apparently. Cos it holds the power of the sun. The other flowers (vervain, trefoil, rue and roses) are also powerful, especially if you want to see into the future, or so Gran says.

'Maybe we should stay?' I suggest.

'Much better you go – as soon as all the preparations are finished,' she replies. 'Take these to ward off evil eyes.' She hands us the amulets filled with the dried flowers. 'And may the Ancient Ones protect you.'

She busies about a few minutes more, then shoos us both towards the door.

'Make haste and be away,' Gran says. She checks the amulets are securely tied around our necks. 'You must be sure to catch the witching hour and knock upon the stone at midnight. I have much to do ... ' she mutters on. 'Catch the black cockerel, light the bonnefyre[3], roast the bird, crack the egg[4] ... '

'Talk about things being cracked,' sighs George.

'Get to the crossed paths by the stone and observe the signs ... ' She looks up at us. 'You two should be going right now.' She adjusts the cloth pouch of dried flowers

---

3. In Wales it is called *Gŵyl Ifan, or Gŵyl Ifan Ganol Haf* (St John's of Midsummer), in worship of St John the Baptist. People used to stay up at night and make three kinds of holy fires to counteract the fires of hell: one of clean bones and no wood, called a 'bonnefyre'; another of clean wood and no bones, called a 'wakefyre', because folks stay awake by it all night; and the third of both bones and wood, called 'St John's fire'. Gran is the only person I know who still lights these fires.

4. I heard a changeling story about a woman whose toddler was stolen by the Bendith Y Mamau (probably another name for the Pookah). She was given instructions by a magician of how to get her baby back. She had to remove the top from a raw egg and stir the contents, then go to a crossroads at midnight during the full moon and observe Gywn ap Nudd on a Faery Raid in order to confirm that her son was on the horse in front of him. Lastly she had to get a black hen and roast it over a wood fire until every feather dropped off. Then the changeling would disappear and she could return the next night and snatch back her child from Gwyn ap Nudd. Long story, but I think Gran is going to have a go at doing something similar.

around my neck for the umpteenth time and kisses me on the forehead.

'But first,' says George, 'you have to eat this, Ellie.' He presents me with a doorstep of a sandwich. Huge thick pieces of veg and fakon bulge up from inside it.

'Great,' I say, 'thanks, George.' George might not be super-refined, but he's definitely very kind, as well as being fit and handsome in a golden Viking sort of way. I'm just saying that impartially, of course. I only have eyes for Henry ... But if I did have other eyes, I'd certainly look twice at George. 'Now, if you could get me a knife,' I say, 'I can cut the sandwich into manageable pieces that will actually fit in my mouth.'

George heads back to the kitchen. As he opens the door to the back room, off the kitchen, I hear the dryer going.

'George is right,' says Gran. 'Eat it slowly, but move fast. Better not to be hungry with the Pookah about.' She presses a bag of small bony things wrapped in a tea towel into my hand. 'Here are the runes. Cast them when the time is right and use the dish cloth. I will take care of the changeling until the stone has spoken, and I'll let your mother know you are with us. Then we will know what we will know'.

'Oh-kay,' I say.

George returns with a bread knife and cuts my sandwich in half. All its contents promptly fall out.

I glance over at the child. It seems at last to have fallen asleep again – a fitful, tossing, whimpering kind of sleep. As I watch it, I remember the crash and the burning and the way it held on to me. I shudder in horror.

'Let its poison go,' murmurs Gran. 'Think of the other poor child.' She crosses over to the dresser and rubs her hands with herbs. 'To have lost your family all in one go, and find yourself stolen away into the Grey Lands.'

'I'll get him back,' says George, suddenly all flashing eyes and big heart. 'I'll save him or die trying.'

Eleven

A little before ten o'clock, the two of us have left Gran's cottage far behind and are heading up towards the Pass of Arrows. I'm back in my still-damp jeans and a jacket of George's with a daysack on my back. We're making good headway and aim to arrive at the Menhir of Mawr, the wizard's Oracle, by midnight.

'What do you think it's all about?' I ask. 'I mean, what's the bigger picture?' I've had enough to do with magic to realise this is just the start of something.

'Don't know,' says George. 'But Nan's been restless all day. And muttering to herself a lot. I asked her earlier if all her mumbling was a sign of the onset of dementia, and she clipped me round the ear with a wooden spoon!' George rubs his ear sorrowfully. 'It hurt a lot.'

'Did she say what was disturbing her?'

'In fact, I think she's *broken* my ear,' says George dramatically.

'Don't be stupid.'

'Nobody cares,' moans George. 'You would kiss it better if you cared.'

'I'll kiss it better,' I say, 'if you tell me why Gran was so disturbed today.' George's face instantly lights up.

Big mistake.

'I take that back,' I say. 'She didn't clip your ear at all.'

'Do you blame me for trying?' he asks.

I can see this conversation is going nowhere. I shove my hands into my jacket pockets and stride up the slope.

George catches up. 'OK,' he says. 'She just kept muttering, "It will not be over till it is over," which though logical was not very illuminating.'

'She means Henry, I suppose,' I say.

'I guess so,' says George. He pulls a rueful face at me, meaning *it's always about Henry, isn't it?* 'Sometimes,' he adds, 'I wish it was more about me than him, but we won't go there tonight.'

I'm glad, though a part of me aches for George's sake. He's so kind and strong and ready to lay all of himself on the line. He's been a true friend and totally there for me. I can honestly say that I love George more than anyone else in the world, but just not like *that*. Who knows, if there had been no Henry, perhaps it could have been different. Sometimes when I see the way Rhiannon makes her big puppy eyes at George, and the way he smiles back at her, I feel … well … almost possessive. I can't be possessive, of course, because I have Henry. My love for Henry is 100%. Maybe it's because I just don't think Rhiannon is the right person for George.

It's not jealousy, is it?

I'm sure it's not.

I don't want to be jealous of George, because that feels weird.

I pace on up the slope, wondering.

I remember the time when I thought George was dead. He lay ice-cold on a bed of stones on the top of Cadair Idris. My heart lurches at the memory. It's as if I am there again, reliving the panic, the despair.

I think of what life might be like without George.

As if telepathic, George squeezes my arm.

'It'll be OK,' he says. 'It's always OK when we're together, isn't it?'

And it is! That's the crazy thing.

I round the next shadowy ridge. A halo of silvery moonlight struggles to shine through swirling clouds.

I wish I could let George know how much I really do care. I stop on the pathway and turn to him.

'I would love you if I could,' I say, 'if I was free to. I mean, I *do* love you – you are my very, very, very best mate ... '

He sends me a puzzled look. 'Hey,' he says, 'I know the score – you don't have to make anything easier for me, Ellie. It can't ever be easy for me, so it would be useless to try. I will always love you whether you love me or not – whether you love someone else or not. Whether you are here with me or far away.' He pauses. 'Whether you are alive or dead.'

Oh God, I don't want him to love me that much.

'Loving you gives me purpose in a way you wouldn't understand, maybe,' he finishes.

I look into the grey shining shadows. I bet I would. Henry gives me that feeling all the time.

'Plus it was only a teeny-weeny little kiss-snog for a poorly ear – not a marriage proposal, you know.'

And that puts me in my place. With a heavier heart I trudge on. Some people might think to have two fit, gorgeous boys in love with you would be fabulous. But it's not. It's just sad and makes me feel bad.

Above us the sky is deep indigo with pale-lemon edges, as if the sun is not yet far beyond the horizon. Overhead an RAC helicopter breaks the silence. On its way to the crash site, maybe. The air is tinged with smoke mingled with the scent of wild herbs drenched by the storm.

I find it hard to believe everything Gran said. But the way that storm came out of nowhere and did its worst and then disappeared was pretty spooky. Those bolts of lightning that seemed directed at me; the way those flames crackled around the lake and fanned out purposely in my direction.

And the changeling Pookah child.

Oh God, I hope Gran is OK.

We'd better hurry. I speed up, taking the next slope at a pace far too fast. Cold air hits my lungs and I gasp for breath. A stitch starts in my side.

Through the darkness I see the upper edge of Clogwyn, and to my right is the steep slope that falls away towards Ffestiniog.

I stop and rest on a large boulder. Gradually my breathing calms down. I take long deep lungfuls of mountain air.

And then I smell it.

Far away.

Bleach and burning.

We make it to the Menhir of Mawr.

Out of breath, covered in sweat, the two of us lean up against the standing stone. We suck in breath. The smell of smoke is much stronger up here. My sides ache and my legs feel wobbly. I bend over, trying to ease the stabbing sensation in my ribs.

We mustn't waste time. Snowdon is burning.

'Now what do we do?' I gasp.

I'm not sure George knows. I don't think he was listening much to Gran's instructions.

I'm wrong.

He's even jotted it all down.

Note to self: never underestimate George.

He pulls out a folded Post-it from a small book in his back pocket and reads:

1. Go to stone.
2. Knock on it at midnight.
3. Ask it what the omen in the tealeaves means.
4. Throw runes if needed to get a clear answer.
5. Note carefully what happens – especially any terms that seem to be set.
6. Come home.

'What does "terms that seem to be set" mean?' I ask George.

George makes a *don't ask me* face and says, 'You know Nan – she's totally mental, but possibly always right. I am possibly not always right. So I don't really know. I think it's best to just follow her instructions anyway, and not second guess her.'

It's true: Gran has a spooky way of getting things totally correct. So as I catch my breath, I mentally go over her instructions.

'Do we ask the stone straight out, then,' I say, 'when we get to point three?' I'm not sure. I feel it needs a bit of ceremony – or at least a 'hello' or something.

'Guess so,' says George.

'Should we speak to it in some special way? Or put our hands on it, or walk around it three times widdershins or something? Give it a bit of ritual?'

'Let's walk around it three times – not widdershins, though.'

'Why not?' I say.

'Keep to sunwise. We don't want to wake up bad spirits.'

I shiver. Definitely not.

I check my phone. Midnight.

We put our hands on the stone. Slowly we circle it three times sunwise. Three times we knock, as we go.

'Halloo,' we call. 'Speak, O Ancient One.'
The wind howls.
The moon vanishes behind a dark cloud.
And we are plunged into deep shadow.

Twelve

Nothing happens, except I nearly trip up on a tuft of grass.

We wait. Only the wind howling. Only the moon shadows racing.

'I think we should do something else,' I say. 'Summon the elements or something.'

'Good idea,' says George. 'Let's touch the sky and ground, air and earth.'

'Don't forget fire,' I say.

'No,' he says. 'Not with what's gone on tonight. We can touch the burns on your hands – that will do.'

I hold out my hand. 'Be gentle.'

George touches the burns. They sting and start throbbing anew. 'By the power of fire,' he says.

I lick my finger, reach up and touch the wind. I feel it

sharp against my dampened skin. 'By the power of air,' I say.

I touch the still-damp hemline of my jeans. 'By the power of water.'

I bend down and put my finger to the ground, digging it slightly into the earth.

Something sharp slices into me. 'Ouch,' I say.

'No,' says George. 'Not ouch.'

'By the power of earth,' I gasp, my sliced finger hurting.

Soil sticks to my fingertip, but I don't care. I must remove the splinter and nurse the pain. I pull out a section of something and put the pad of my finger to my lips, blood and soil and grit and all.

I suck at the pain and feel the gash with my tongue.

'This is not my evening,' I wail.

'Let's look,' says George, 'but don't forget we're halfway through a ritual. We should knock on the stone again now, before the midnight hour passes, and ask it what the tealeaf omen means.'

'It was a piece of glass or something,' I say.

I show him, a sharp-edged piece of glass about the size of a broad bean. *How come there's a piece of glass right here, beside the stone? Some stupid hiker must have broken a bottle or something and left it here.*

I am about to silently curse them, when I see it's actually a shard of mirror.

OMG!

Memories flood back to me. *It was here! Three months ago. Where we smashed the witch's mirror and broke the spell laid over Snowdonia.*

'George,' I whisper, 'it's the mirror – the one that once belonged to the Lady of the Lake.'

George and I, back to back by this very stone, fighting off the hordes of Sheela Na Gig and all the other cursed creatures that the White Dragon had woken.[1]

'Put your hand on the stone,' George says. He takes my wrist.

'OK,' I say and reach out. As I put my hand on the stone, blood oozes from the tip of my finger and smudges down its stony surface.

A buzz of raw energy surges through my finger, through all the burning and wetness, up my arm, across my chest and through my ribcage … until it seems to strike down on the centre of my back.

I stumble. I blink. George looks at me, his eyes narrow.

'The stone is alive!' I shriek.

---

1. The White Dragon, AKA Oswald, is horrible. He's the mascot of Wessex, the territory of the West Saxons. Legend has it that the White Dragon will not cease his attack on Henry, the Red Dragon of Wales, until he has finally conquered him and Wales as well. I pray to the stars above that will never be.

'Ask, Ellie! Ask!'

I'm reeling from the force of the pulse. *Breathe*. I try to remember the advice Gran gave.

Tonight. Midsummer's Eve. All of the things that have happened since I first met Henry …

My mind seems wiped.

Henry, the Red Dragon.

'Ask it!' yells George. 'It's you – it'll speak to you.'

'What is it?' I say to the stone. 'What's wrong? Why the storm, the fire, the changeling? Why did you send an omen out in the tealeaves?'

There's a shivering around us, as if a giant hand has stirred the air overhead and passed its fingers through the bracken. The ground seems to shudder. A wild wind wails above – round and round – and a small tornado rises directly above the stone.

I bite my lip. I hold my breath. I am suddenly afraid. There is a power in this stone way beyond anything I've ever felt.

Will it speak?

And if so, what will it say?

The whirlwind above the stone collects dust, sucking debris, dirt, leaves and gunk upwards. George takes a step back. He lays his hand on his axe. 'Something's up, and I don't like it.'

I get a distinct sense of vertigo, as if the world is spinning.

Then I hold up the shard of mirror.

Big mistake.

And look into it.

Bigger mistake.

The surface of the mirror shines, as if it reflects light from unseen stars. I don't see my face in it at all. It's weird to be so suddenly erased. I look into its depths, hardly believing I'm not there. A rush of déjà vu. I peer closer. *Really nothing?*

Just an eye looking back.

I jolt away.

Then look back again, ashamed at being so spooked.

It's not entirely dark. A huge misty range of mountains zooms in at me. They're covered in shadow and snow, above them moonlight skies. They're strangely familiar.

It's as if I'm on a plane, flying through time zones. My heart starts beating faster. In the far distance are tiny pinpricks of light: dawn is breaking on some distant horizon.

The little lights pull at me, tugging at my eyes.

George shouts. He sounds very faint. I can't quite hear him.

I should have known better.

Note to self: if you find a shard from a witch's mirror buried by a standing stone, a wizard's Oracle, on Midsummer's Eve and if you look into it, after you've shed living blood on that same stone, you really should expect anything.

Stupid.

The vertigo makes me feel nauseous.

As if I'm going to faint.

As if I'm falling into the mirror.

I try to stop myself.

But it's too late.

I'm sucked towards the pinpricks of light. Lightheaded. Dizzy.

I lose my balance.

Whirling lights.

Giddiness.

'Help!' I cry.

I fall forward. The shard of mirror seems to expand. Somewhere in the periphery of my vision, I see George with his axe raised, as if he's about to smash something.

I see the stone towering against the night sky.

I hope to hell I'm going to be OK.

And then the darkness closes over me.

Thirteen

In Which Ellie Finds Herself to Be Lucky and Unlucky

For a brief instant, the mists clear.

I see the shape of the dragon winding up towards the Pole Star.

Then I know where I am. I look around. Strangely it's a hot, sunny afternoon. I'm lying on springy grass, high up on the mountain, near the Devil's Bridge. The peak of Snowdon towers above me, smoking pink in the afternoon sun. I can hear the call of birds way overhead. A fresh mountain breeze strokes my face and tugs at my hair.

'Isn't it fabulous here?' says a voice I know and love.

My heart pounds. *Can it be him?* I turn my head.

'Henry?'

It has to be. This is like a replay of something I can't quite remember.

And there he is, right beside me! Lying on the heather, his arms thrown wide. He's as impossibly handsome as ever. His thick chestnut hair has bits of bracken stuck in it. He's smiling and smiling.

'Is this some kind of dream?' I ask.

He rolls over and gives me a great big bear hug.

'Yeah.' He laughs. 'And no.'

I hug him back, scarcely believing it's really him.

'OK,' I say, grinning. 'Is this a game?'

If he's not bothered by the fact that we're lying on the grass on a hot afternoon, high on the mountainside, even though it's midnight on Midsummer's Eve, why should I be?

'I can't believe it,' I say.

'I know,' he replies. He kisses my forehead and we flop back on the turf, arms encircled around each other. He uncurls a hand and grabs mine. And we just lie there, all tangled up, and so, so close, staring up at the blue, blue sky, twining our fingers together.

I decide I'm not even going to try to understand what's going on. I'm going to forget about flames and changelings, forget about the Pookah and the helicopter. It's all absolutely nothing to do with me. Rubbish and nonsense. Just a crash on the mountain. I've been listening to Granny Jones for far too long – because now I'm HERE, where I've always wanted to be: out on the mountain with Henry.

Behind us, over the peak of the mountain, a dark cloud starts to form. I look up at it, puzzled. Something massive is swelling at its centre.

'Do you think it's going to rain?' I ask.

Henry just pulls me closer. A rush of electricity burns through me. *Here I am with Henry! I've found a way to be with Henry again.*

And Henry as a boy. A Henry I can hold hands with!

It's all too good to be true.

I disentangle my arms, only to throw them around him again. I squeeze him so close. I feel his heart pounding against mine. 'What I don't understand,' I say, 'is here, in this place, you're a boy again. I thought you were unable to change shapes – after the High Magick of Merlin was broken last spring?'[1]

'This place is older than any magick,' says Henry. 'We call it the In-Between Place but it has another name far more ancient. Its laws were forged long before either Merlin's High Magick or the Olde Deepe Magicke. I could tell you more of its history, for this place is from the Before Time, the Time of Dragons, and why here you can find your Heart's Desire and be with the one you love ... for this land is ruled by the Heart, and those that love and are truly loved in return may find their way here, by accident or by design ... but that would waste our time and we may not have much longer to be together ... '

---

1. You can read about it in Book Two, *Here be Witches* – but honestly, I thought I'd never meet Henry again as a boy.

Tears rise, sudden, fierce. My eyes prickle. My throat closes.

'Time in the In-Between Place is always limited for the living.' Henry's voice is tinged with an unbearable sadness. He tries to smile.

I swallow back the tears.

'Don't cry, my Ellie,' says Henry, hugging me. 'For this unexpected meeting has warmed my heart and made me hope there will be more unlooked-for happiness.'

I bury my face in his shoulder and hug and hug him.

'We will be together again one day, somehow.' He kisses and kisses my brow.

I tighten my arms around him, hold him tight and tighter.

I'll never him let go.

I'll stay here with him forever.

I press my lips into his neck, willing it to be so. But already I can feel a subtle shift in the atmosphere. The grey cloud has moved over the peak and is creeping down the mountain towards us.

'That's not a raincloud, is it?' I say. Another weird feeling of déjà vu sweeps over me. I shiver despite the heat. *Of course it's not a raincloud.*

Soon we'll be swallowed up … soon we'll lose our way … lose each other in its darkness …

'It's starting again, isn't it?' I say.

The déjà vu gets stronger. I untangle myself and sit up. 'I can't bear to lose you over and over.' I clutch his tunic, my grip like iron.

Henry sits up too. He encircles me in his arms. 'O stars above! Why can't we have longer?'

The sunshine fades. The birds stop singing. I'm right. I knew it was too good to be true.

'If I have to go back to my world, I need some answers,' I say between gritted teeth.

'I'll tell you everything I know,' says Henry.

'What do I have to do to always be with you?' I say.

Henry smiles sadly. 'I don't know that ... I wish I did.'

The shadow of the cloud skims over the bracken towards us.

'But let us be quick – tell me how you got here this time,' says Henry.

'I found a shard from the witch's mirror, the one we smashed at the Menhir last spring. The Lady of the Lake's mirror. The one I used to be with you before. Anyway, I cut myself on it. Then I looked into it, and found myself here. It still works! I'll look into it again ... '

Henry draws back, then leans forward again and kisses my forehead. 'Yes, do that. The mirror calls me when you look into it. I can't explain exactly how – but, yes, it works... '

He looks intently at me, focusing his attention, demanding I focus mine.

'What is it?' I say.

'We are in peril,' he says. 'Tonight a spell was cast by one who understands witchcraft. A blood sacrifice was made on the Clogwyn Cliff; a portal opened. Those that live in the Grey Lands can now pass into your world, but this is against the order of High Magick. Merlin sealed all portals to Annwyn, except one, which he keeps secure, defended day and night by his own powers.'

I try to focus. *A spell. A sacrifice. An illegal portal. Got it.*

'Through this new portal has come magical fire from Annwyn, fanned by Gwyn ap Nudd. This much you know. This fire will not stop burning until it meets a greater fire.'

Magical fire. Unstoppable. Not sure I *want* to get that.

'I've seen the fire,' I say. 'It hurt me.' I show him my burnt hands.

He takes my palms to his lips and kisses them. His breath is sweet and cool on the burning skin. Weirdly the weals of angry flesh seem to grow paler. And I swear the pain fades.

'How did you do that?' I say.

'What?'

I shake my head. It's not important. 'Tell me about the fire.'

'That's about it. Until the fire is out, and the portal closed, Gwyn ap Nudd will come and go as he pleases.'

I take that in. The fires will burn down houses and land.

People will die or be maimed. Wild things will be roasted alive.

'And the Pookah,' I say, 'will snatch kids, I know.'

'Yes, changelings,' says Henry. 'Anyone who has not yet achieved adulthood is at risk.'

I nod my head. 'I've met a changeling already. Granny Jones is with it right now.'

'Ah, Mother Jones.' Henry smiles fondly. 'I'm glad she's caught at least one of them.'

'But what can be done?' I ask. 'How can the fire be put out and the portal resealed?'

'Enchanted fire must be fought with fire just as powerful,' repeats Henry.

I remember the lines carved into the fireplace in Halfway House: Fight Fire with Fire.

Something about these words nags at me.

'So what can we do?' I ask.

Henry is starting to fade. He looks awful, ill almost, sort of bleached out and washed away.

I. Won't. Let. Him. Go.

I try to hold on. His grip loosens. His hand starts fading out of mine.

... fight fire with fire ... my hand ... his hand ... fading ... my burns fading ...

His kiss.

My burns.

His sweet cool breath.

Fading …

He's a dragon.

'DRAGON FIRE!' I scream. 'You're a dragon. Can your fire quench the flames?'

'I wish it could … true dragon fire can quench anything … ' Henry's voice too is fading.

'THEN QUENCH IT!'

'If I could, I would seal my fire into one of these stones and let you carry it back to launch at the flames of Annwyn …

'DO IT!' I yell.

'But here in the In-Between Place I can only be a boy.'

'Isn't dragon fire a greater fire?' I demand.

'And in the Mortal Realm, I am buried full fathom five … '

'BUT IF YOU WERE FREE?' I scream.

'Until the battle between the White and Red Dragons is resolved, I will never be free. Oswald will quench my fire with his ice.'

'THEN YOU MUST STOP FIGHTING!' I shout. He's moving away from me so fast. 'CAN'T YOU JUST STOP FIGHTING OSWALD AND CALL IT QUITS?'

Henry laughs, faint, sad.

Swirling mist closes round us.

I find myself grasping at thin air.

No. Don't leave.

HENRY!

His voice drifts through the haze. 'One or both of us dragons must die before the curse over us is lifted ... before we can stop fighting ... Dragons don't die easily ... it is fated thus in the stars. It may be that I am the one who has been marked out by Death ... '

No.

That can't be!

If Death takes him, he will be lost forever ... They can never stop fighting.

'IS THERE NOTHING AT ALL WE CAN DO?' I imagine Snowdonia blackened and smoking ... maybe further than Snowdonia ... down to the coast and into the whole of Wales ... wider and wider ... People ... businesses ... homes ... lives.

'SOMETHING?' I shout. 'SOME HOPE? SOME WAY TO DEFEAT OSWALD?' *Think, Ellie. Think.*

For a moment the mist clears. I see Henry speeding away from me. How did others kill dragons in the old stories? Perseus? Heracles? Tristan? St George? They used swords.

'WHAT ABOUT A SWORD?' I shout.

For a second Henry grows clearer.

'TO KILL OSWALD WITH?' I add.

94

'Who would wield it?' sighs Henry's voice like the rushing wind.

'BUT CAN MAGICAL SWORDS SLAY DRAGONS LIKE IN THE OLD STORIES?' I stick doggedly to my point.

He seems to nod.

'DO YOU KNOW OF SUCH A SWORD?' I yell.

Henry is almost gone, quite transparent; his outline is like condensation on a window pane.

'There was one once … '

'I'LL FIND IT,' I holler. I'm on my feet, struggling through the mist after him.

Only his voice remains.

'I'LL FIND ONE. I SWEAR I WILL. I PLEDGE MY LIFE TO IT.'

'No,' whispers Henry. 'That promise will take your life for that of the dragon's … '

I think that's what he says.

'I DON'T CARE!' I shout. 'I'LL FREE YOU. I'LL HELP YOU DESTROY OSWALD IN WHATEVER WAY I CAN. I SWEAR MY LIFE ON IT.'

And then he's gone.

I try so hard to hang on, to stay still, but a tugging starts.

'HENRY!' I scream.

My voice is swallowed up into the nothingness.

Fourteen

'HENRY!'

I come down to earth with a bump.

George is shaking me.

I'm trembling all over.

'Hey Elles,' George says. 'What happened? You just went mad weird back then.'

I blink and look up at him. 'Don't know,' I mumble. But that's not entirely true. I know it was the piece of mirror, and somehow I got through again to the In-Between Place and found Henry.

And somehow I lost him.

It takes a moment. I squeeze my eyes shut, tell my heart to stay in one piece, tell my throat not to close so tight.

I must find the sword. Help Henry. Save Snowdonia. Stop the fires.

I grab George's arm. I should tell him. I gulp and say, 'I saw Henry. He needs help.'

'You spoke to HENRY?' yells George. 'When? How?'

'Listen, dragon fire can put out the flames … the fires on Snowdon … but until the White Dragon is dead, Henry's fire is useless.'[1]

My ears are ringing. I can't think straight. 'We've got to get a sword to kill Oswald!' I say.

'Take it easy,' says George. 'Ellie, you're not making a lot of sense.'

I suck in a deep breath. 'If we had a magical sword, we could slay Oswald to lift the curse over Henry, then he could save the mountain – if he could put out the fire with his fire … ' I'm starting to sweat.

'OK, calm down, Ellie,' suggests George. 'That's a lot of "ifs".'

'Dragon fire will quench the fires of Annwyn!' I say.

'But freeing Henry?' says George. 'How easy will that be?'

'You got a better idea?'

'Find another dragon?'

I can't help it. My eyes fill up. I don't want another dragon. I want to free Henry. 'I don't know another dragon,' I mumble.

---

1. The spell cast by Merlin curses the dragons to stay forever at war, forever incarcerated under Dinas Emrys, until they can both find love in their hearts. Unfortunately, Oswald, the White Dragon, has a heart devoid of any gentleness.

'Let's carry on asking the stone, shall we?'

'I know we can free Henry.' I blink my eyes and swallow. 'We just need a magical sword, that's all.'

'And a way to dig up the dragons, *and* a way to slay Oswald without getting killed ourselves. *Plus* how do we get a magical sword?'

My shoulders slump.

'Hey Elles,' says George, 'I'm only saying how I see it. Don't do that sad thing. Please? Look … if we have to find a sword, we will … I was just saying – just hoping – there might be an easier way.'

'I don't know an easier way.'

'OK. We'll find a magical sword and whup that White Dragon with it. OK?'

I nod.

'Any bright ideas about where to get this sword, then?'

I shake my head, but then have a thought. 'Not unless we can find the Isle of Avalon again and ask the Lady of the Lake … She forged Caledfwlch.[2] All the old stories say she did. And Caledfwlch is the most magical sword ever.'

'Yeah, she did. That's true.' George pulls out the small tattered book again from his back pocket. 'Time to double check.' He reaches his phone and touches the torch on.

---

2. AKA Excalibur.

'You swiped that off Gran!' I say, recognising the title, *A Study of the Flora, Fauna and Inhabitants of Annwyn.*

George smiles, then reads out, '*The Lady of the Lake lives on the Isle of Apples, also known as Avalon, in the Kingdom of Annwyn …* ' He skips some pages and continues, '*The magical realm of Annwyn can only be accessed through one portal.*'

'Yes, Henry told me that,' I say.

George carries on reading. 'Via Merlin's Oak?' he says.

'George,' I say, looking up at him, 'you will help me get the sword, won't you?'

'Do I have a choice?' asks George.

I shake my head.

'OK, so I'll help you get the sword … but we came up here to ask the stone what was going on, so maybe we could do that now?'

'Thanks,' I mumble. I love George. I put my arm through his. 'Really, thanks.'

'So let's do it,' says George.

'We should use these runes Gran gave me,' I say, 'Apparently we throw them and depending how they fall, they'll give answers.'

George groans. 'More hocus-pocus! Why aren't things simple? Why can't we just ask our questions and get straightforward replies?'

99

'She gave me a tea towel as well,' I say, 'to throw them on.'

'As you do,' adds George. 'OK, but if we only get a recipe for spaghetti, we can try something else, I suppose.'

I spread the cloth out on the ground by the Menhir, place the pebbles on the cloth in a pile and turn three times sunwise. Then I press the palms of both my hands flat against the side of the standing stone.

High above me, the moon sails on a bank of violet blue. In the west, rosy light stretches tight across the horizon. Midnight clouds hang over distant valleys, shining in cream and pink. Overhead, Polaris blazes out. I look straight up, acknowledging the presence of the great dragon.

'Bless this Midsummer's Eve, Mighty Draco of the Skies,' I say, then I turn to the stone. 'O Oracle, o magical Menhir of Mawr, please answer my questions.'

The wind sighs through the bracken. A gust whips up the slope, bringing the smell of wild thyme, fresh, heady, enchanting.

As if in my head, I hear the stone reply: *Ask your question.*

My heartbeat shoots into overdrive. *OMG!*

'What is the meaning of the tealeaves tonight?' I say. 'Where can I find Merlin's Oak and how can I get through into Annwyn to find the Lady of the Lake? Will we get the sword and will we be able to defeat Oswald – and how exactly? Will Henry be able to put the fire out?'

'Elles,' says George, 'that's not just one question, is it?'

I shoot him a *sorr-ry*.

George stands on the opposite side of the stone and reaches his arms out. 'If we're going for multiple questions, then … ' He places his hands on the stone too and asks, 'How can I help the lost child? And get Ellie to notice me?'

Night herbs perfume the air. I give George a big *not now* pinch. Then I bend down and pick up the runes.

The stones lie smooth and warm in my hands. They feel almost soft to the touch. I get a sudden irrational desire to put them in my pocket and not throw them at all.

'Be careful,' says George, 'the stones are tricky. They don't always show what is or what will be, but only parts of it. They don't warn you if you misunderstand their meaning.'

'I know that,' I say.

I do know it and I don't know it.

'Please answer,' I whisper to the Oracle. 'Even if only the question we came to pose – the meaning in the tealeaves.' Then I crouch and scatter the small, round pebbles on to the tea towel.

And as I throw them, I think of Henry, buried beneath

Dinas Emrys, fighting his worst enemy, dispirited for eternity. It's the cruellest kind of torture.

I pull my thoughts away from him, trapped there beneath the heavy soil.

Stick to the present problem, I tell myself.

But I can't seem to stop my mind wandering … *How can I have Henry back … as a boy … just for me … just as he is in the In-Between Place …*

Please, stone, grant my heart's desire: let me be reunited with Henry.

Together forever.

I let the runes go.

A bruising silence descends. High above the cliffs, a black dress of darkness clothes the slopes of great Snowdon. Shadows from its peak condense around us.

Midsummer's Eve is when the Olde Deepe Magicke is very near. If I do one thing wrong it will break through and overwhelm us.

I shiver.

Please answer my question. Please help me to read the signs correctly. Stone of Stones, guide your lesser stones to send the right message to me.

The Menhir of Mawr seems to grow taller. Around it the shadows lengthen.

And I hear that voice again, deep inside my head:

The terms of this quest are as you have wished them, for I can see into your heart. You must risk all for love, even unto the peril of your life, for so you have sworn on this night upon this stone.

Once and once only will I tell you the terms set for your mission to succeed:

ALL MUST BE ACHIEVED THROUGH THE MEETING OF THE HEART'S DESIRE. ALL ELSE WILL REAP THE HEART'S DESPAIR.

A jolt of energy passes over my heart. For a moment I think I'm going to faint. I reach out and clutch at George.

'What is it, Elles?' he says.

'The stone spoke.'

'Steady on. Hold on to me.'

'It was a warning.'

'Don't worry about that right now. Just remember what it said.'

I nod.

'We'll get back to Nan's; she'll know what it means.'

I'm really dizzy. I steady myself on the stone.

'The runes on the tea towel,' says George, 'what about them?'

I can't look down. 'Don't know,' I say.

'OK, no worries. We'll forget about them.'

I balance myself against the stone, trying to get a grip, trying to calm myself down. I try box-breathing like Mum showed me – rule number whatever in the *Mountain Rescue Volunteer's Handbook*.

After a bit, I feel better.

George scoops up the rune stones. 'We should go,' he says. 'If I hold your arm, will you be OK?'

'I think so,' I say.

ALL ELSE WILL REAP THE HEART'S DESPAIR.

What did it mean?

I need to think. I'm so dizzy.

Did I mess up the question with my longing for Henry?

We should have figured out the rune stones. They might have revealed something important.

Too late now.

'You good?' asks George.

I nod. Somehow.

'Feel you can you tell me any of what the stone said?'

'It said: "ALL MUST BE ACHIEVED THROUGH THE MEETING OF THE HEART'S DESIRE",' I mumble.

I miss out the rest. I don't tell George how my question went all wrong.

'What does that mean?' says George.

'Don't know.'

I don't know whose Heart's Desire the stone meant. I only know that my Heart's Desire is to see Henry again, to be with him somewhere like the In-Between Place – but in a way that will never fade – forever and ever. I don't tell George that, for obvious reasons.

'Ohhh-kaay,' he says. 'Nothing about the tealeaves or a portal or the sword?'

I shake my head. And we stand there, waiting for the right moment to leave.

'I guess Meeting the Heart's Desire must be the meaning of the random tealeaf – the one Nan thought was a ray of hope,' says George.

A ray of hope?

I bite my lip.

Not when *ALL ELSE WILL REAP THE HEART'S DESPAIR.*

Fifteen

I tilt my head and look up at George. He's silhouetted against the dark sky. In the distance an iron-grey mist creeps up the mountain.

I shudder as I remember the dark cloud in the In-Between Place.

George wheels round. An acrid scent wafts up at us.

'Holy smoke!' he says.

'That's so not funny. It really could be smoke.'

'Let's get out of here.'

I look at my finger where the shard of mirror cut me. Just a smudge of blood and a raw soreness. I feel for the splinter of mirror wrapped in a scrap of plastic in my pocket. *If only I could get back to Henry. There are so many questions I should have asked him.*

George peers into the darkness. 'Let's get back to Nan's.'

Suddenly I really, *really* want to be at Gran's really, *really* badly. I can feel a foul thickness in the air as if some horrible magic is reaching out, searching for us.

The choke of smoke. The scent of bleach and ashes.

'Yes, let's go,' I say.

George puts his arm around my shoulder. 'It'll be OK, Elles,' he says as we step out.

The mist creeps nearer, swirling up at us in thin ragged wisps. I breathe in. I shiver.

It IS smoke.

'You look pretty awful, though, like you've seen a ghost.'

'Something like that,' I mutter. *How can it be smoke? Has the fire from Clogwyn spread up here already?*

We push forward, crossing down the slopes away from the Menhir of Mawr until we hit the Ranger Path.

The smoke is thicker there. It has a strange after-smell that lingers in my nose and at the back of my throat, almost like chlorine.

Suddenly I know it's not just smoke wafting over from Clogwyn.

It's the scent of Annwyn's flames. Something's on fire and it's from lower down the mountain.

Alarms bells ring inside my head. 'George, something's not OK,' I say. A chill slithers down my spine. My knees go super-weak. 'This fire is from the Grey Lands, that means it *thinks*; it's got a brain; it *knows* what it's doing.'

George stops short, brings his head up and appears to be listening.

I turn and start running down the mountain. 'Gran's house!' I yell. Terrible premonition. It all makes sense. The changeling incanting its foul spell. The portal opened at Clogwyn. Gran lighting the holy Fire of Bones.

The fire knows! The fire is alive! The fire is intelligent!

The fire was being called to Gran's cottage!

George catches me up. 'Ellie!' he yells. 'Slow down.'

'NO!' I shriek. 'It's Gran!' I have no breath to talk. I wave my hand frantically at him to follow.

The path ahead is steep. I run. And run. And leap down shadowy slopes, trying to avoid dark shapes of rock.

We must get to Gran's.

The fire is targeting Gran's place. I know it. It's going to kill her, stop her from helping us; it's going to free the changeling. It's been timing us, creeping slowly over the dips and slopes, trying to keep downwind. All the while set on one object: Gran's cottage.

As we top a curve in the landscape, we see the devastation below.

'Ellie!' screams George, raw panic in his voice.

Red, angry, blazing. The dark silhouette of the building. Flames metres high, on the path leading there, stalking forward like some hideous fiery figure. The fires of Annwyn licking the night sky.

Together we race, tripping and sliding on the grey slate slabs, tangling our legs in the mass of gorse and heather. Smoke burns my lungs. I run. I gulp in great, hot, thick gusts of it. Bitter. Toxic.

Bleach and acid.

Chlorine and dust.

I drag my T-shirt over my nose, but the smell is in my mouth, in my chest. My teeth are vibrating with it.

I run. George runs. My tongue grows dry and sore.

'Gran will be OK?' I shout hoarsely at George, my statement turning into a question.

Of course she'll be OK. Gran is clever. Gran is wise. She understands these things. She has knowledge. She'll know how to protect herself …

'She'll know what to do,' George yells back.

But he doesn't sound sure.

I think of Gran lighting her three holy fires on three corners of the property. Three corners protected.

But what about the fourth corner?

Gran was working on the idea of the trinity.

It comes to me like a blast of dust in the eyes. Painful, blinding.

Gran knew this fire was evil.

She was calling on the trinity to save her cottage. That's why she put garlic on the windowsills, the bunch of sage burning in the grate … she was placing protections. To defend herself from the changeling … from the fire … she sent us away … she knew … she was getting us out of the house …

And it's my fault. I brought the changeling to her place. It saw she was a Wise One and called out.

The fire will try to destroy her … lest she destroy it…

The trinity of the three fires will not be enough to fight fire with fire. Only dragon's fire can … The Olde Deepe Magicke is elemental – it will find the missing fourth corner … it will get in behind Gran's charms … it will come from the direction least expected … It will creep along, behind the woodsheds, yet spare them – not letting one piece of kindling betray its evil intention – then up through the herb garden, blasting all her precious herbs before they can be used against it … then it will strike from the back of the cottage!

The back!

That is where the choking smoke and the evil flames from the Grey Lands will get in!

I think of the changeling child and the way its eyes turned so dark. I push my legs harder. I brace myself against the vertigo of the slope and run down the mountain until my heart pounds. A violent sweat breaks out across my forehead. Rivers pour down my neck.

George shoots past me in great strides, leaping bracken and boulders.

Nobody can keep up with George when he's going at a full sprint. I try, but soon he is well ahead of me. My cut finger is throbbing. My eyes are fixed on the mountainside beneath my feet. *Dear Snowdon, don't let me take a false step, wrench an ankle, twist a ligament.*

Don't let me fall.

Something tells me to stop.

I skid to a halt.

The rocky ground gives way to a stony scree that goes straight over a small cliff.

Oh my God. *Thank you, Snowdon.*

Keep focused, Ellie. Stay alive.

Thank you. Thank you.

It's one of many small cliffs that border this path. Small but deadly. It could have easily sent me to my doom.

Keep going.

Stay focused. Stay alive.

I skirt the cliff carefully, so not to dislodge any more stones that could take the path out from under my feet. I know this mountain.

More haste.

Less speed.

The smell of burning grows stronger. The sky glows incandescent in puff-balls of sulphurous yellow. Heat radiates upwards. The whole horizon vibrates a dull cadmium orange. A bright fan of flames spreads out. The path turns an evil gleaming neon lemon.

And I know that the fire has already reached Gran's cottage.

And I pray to God poor Gran is still alive.

Sixteen

I tear past cliff edges, round bog and briar, across knolls and through tufted outbreaks of sedge and saxifrage. I'm on the homeward stretch.

Dear God, let Gran be OK.

Nestled in the curve of the mountain below, above the lambing pastures, a horrific sight greets me. Flames dancing in demonic fury.

And the heat!

I stop short.

Blink.

Granny Jones's cottage glowing, totally ablaze.

Everything. Everywhere. White-hot.

That lovely, cosy cottage with its warming fireside, its thick rugs.

Flames metres high.

The wooden table where we sat and ate so many times, the little loft room where Davey slept, George's bedroom, the henhouse, the kitchen garden ... all of it crackling, roaring upwards in hideous flames.

How can Gran's charms have failed so badly?

I smell the acrid stench of burning; hear the screech of rafter and smack of slates as they fall through flames and hit flagstone floors ... *All her Rod Stewart LPs ... her scarves ... her velvet shawls ... her famous kitchen with its herbs and potions ...*

All burning.

I stop for a second, reeling. Then I'm racing like the wind.

Gran?

Where's Gran?

Desperately I scan the lane and the stone wall ... Maybe she's on the little lawn that leads to the woodshed ...

No Gran.

No figure watching in horror as her home burns.

The unthinkable begins to dawn.

Gran is inside ...

'NOOO!' I scream.

I'm flying down the track in the dark, whipping around the outbuildings and crashing through smouldering shrub and flying embers.

The fires from the Grey Lands are burning Gran alive.
Where's the changeling?

In some weird aberrant way, I don't wish it harm ... I'd save it if I could, even though it's a fae thing sent to betray us.

'Help me, Ellie!'

It's George.

As fast as I can – legs like rubber, chest on fire, eyes smarting, coughing, panicking – I catch up with George.

He's trying to heave open the back door of the cottage. It seems to be locked from the inside.

The heat is unbearable. I don't know how he can stand it.

'Fetch another axe or garden spade,' he screams. 'I can't let go of this or the door will snap back. Make sure you have iron on your skin, or the flames will roast you!'

George has wedged his best axe between the door and its frame and it's taking all his strength to keep the crack open. The iron is protecting him, staying cool even in the face of fire.

And it's Magicke. Evil Olde Magicke. The Pookah from the Fae Lands. Gywn ap Nudd and his wildfire.

All set on killing Gran. *They timed us ... they sent the flames ...*

They concealed the taint of carbon ... they hid the roar of the furnace ...

They know she threatens them.

They know we threaten them.

I wrap the chains tight around my wrist and race to the tool shed, jumping bundles of smouldering hay. I scoot round piles of kindling. Over the hiss and screech of burning, I hear something. Faint chanting.

I stop and listen.

There it is again. The shrill voice of Gran from inside the burning kitchen, chanting the Druids' prayer:

> 'Dyro Dduw dy Nawdd;
> Ag yn nawdd, nerth;
> Ag yn nerth, Deall;
> Ag ... '

Thank you, Snowdon. Thank you. THANK YOU.

Gran's alive!

Gran's fighting back! She's trying to defeat the flames.

'Hang on, Gran!' I screech. I get to the doorway of the tool shed. I can see a glowing light inside. A bale of straw in the corner is on fire. The great logs piled at the back are hissing. But there it is, George's second-best axe and a shovel, hanging up on a beam. *The fire can't touch the iron.* Heart pounding, I grab both of them.

As I turn I hear a terrified clucking. *One of the hens trapped in the shed?*

That's odd.

They don't come into the toolshed.

Maybe when their henhouse went up in flames, one sought shelter here?

The cluck comes again, a weird high pitch to it. My chain with its stars and moon charm is icy against my chest.

It's a trap.

A voice inside my head screams, *GET OUT!*

GET OUT OF THE SHED NOW!

Oh my God. The flames can mimic sounds, confuse me, lure me in ...

I race to the door before it shuts and magically locks itself against me. *This fire is alive ... can think ... is trying to outwit us ... has magical powers ...*

I start chanting the Druids' prayer too:

> 'Dyro Dduw dy Nawdd;
> Ag yn nawdd, nerth;
> Ag yn nerth, Deall;
> Ag yn Neall, Gwybod;
> Ac yngwybod, gwybod y cyfiawn;

Ag yngwybod yn cyfiawn, ei garu;
Ag o garu, caru pob hanfod;
Ag ymhob Hanfod, caru Duw.'[1]

Just in time, I'm back through the doorway, axe in hand. The whole shed bursts into wild angry flames behind me. The clucking stops.

There was no hen.

Thank God, I can still hear Gran chanting. Back to George. By the time I arrive, he's got his hands around the door, pulling hard.

'Smash the axe into the door,' he yells. 'I'll use mine too – together we can do it.'

But suddenly I know better.

Above George's shouts, I can hear Gran's voice getting higher and more intense, chanting and chanting.

'No,' I say, 'leave the first axe to hold the gap. It's made of iron – it'll counter the magic.'

The chains we're wearing are stopping us from getting burnt alive right now. Gran can last a while yet. She's in the kitchen –

---

1. Grant, O Ancient Ones, Thy protection;
And in protection, strength;
And in strength, understanding;
And in understanding, knowledge;
And in knowledge, the knowledge of justice;
And in the knowledge of justice, the love of it;
And in that love, the love of all existences;
And in the love of all existences, the love of the universe.

she'll use all those cast iron pans to protect herself.

'You smash the panels with this one. Create a space for us to get Gran out, George. The Fae Folk can't stand iron … ' I pass him his second-best axe.

George nods. He leaves his best axe wedging the door open and raises the other above his head, bringing it down on the back door.

I close my hand over my silver charm. I start chanting the only thing I know will work: '*Dyro Dduw dy Nawdd.*'

The wood splinters and groans, then seems to close back around the axe head. George yanks the axe free with superhuman strength and brings it down again. I can hear him muttering to himself, 'You will not have my grandmother – you cannot have her.'

I raise my voice and yell out, '*Ag yn nawdd, nerth!*'

George strikes the back door with his axe, over and over, while I take out my silver charm and hold it up. I swing the shovel and chant and walk a circle around the cottage, again and again. I stop by the lean-to, still chanting, and grab boxes of nails. I throw them at the fire, time after time, and chant and chant.

At last the wood on the door yields.

'Stand well back, Nan!' shouts George, and with one mighty kick he slams into the back door.

The panels smash. A wall of fire springs up in their place, but George leaps through it.

I squint through the smoke and embers. *Don't lose guard. Don't stop chanting.* George's shape flickers in silhouette as he sprints towards Gran. George looking like a Viking, yellow hair tossed back, shoulders broad and strong, tall and impossibly beautiful.

> 'O Snowdon, protect George.
> Protect Gran.
> Dyro Dduw dy Nawdd;
> Ag yn nawdd, nerth.'

George kicks aside burning debris. He strides through the fire. The flames fall away from him, as if he has some power beyond their own.

I blink in awe. I've never ever seen George looking so powerful. I pick up the dropped axe. Its handle burns my hands and I drop it, fast. I drag my iron bracelet up over part of my hand and try the axe again. *Iron. Iron will protect me. Henry has kissed my hands. I will not be burned.* I must help get them both out, before the fire develops some new trick.

'By earth,' I yell, and kick soil from the plant pots through the doorway. 'By air,' I holler and blow as hard as I can.

'By water.' I spit at the flames and they hiss back in anger. 'And by holy dragon's fire!' I conjure up an image of Henry blasting flames in full fury. 'Avaunt ye!'

I see George and Gran for an instant, still trapped inside the building.

'I command you to stop,' I yell, my voice wobbly, shrill. Then I plunge the axe into the flames and chant the Druids' prayer yet again.

The flames hiss and turn blue. They send up a screeching shout, furious …

But defeated.

The instant the iron makes contact, they drop back.

George snatches Gran to him, pulls a great Le Creuset casserole pan over his head and a steel colander over Gran's, and turns to run towards me.

I hang on, holding the axe in place, chanting, 'By earth, by air, by water, by dragon's fire, by the power of Snowdon, by the great dragon Draco … '

In one swift movement, George jumps through the doorway, Gran in his arms. The axe is too hot for me to hold any more, and I let go. The flames flare up again, venomous, rageful, and instantly snap back to form a wall of heat.

But Gran and George are out.

They're out!

They're safe!

I throw my arms around them.

Together, the Power of Three.

'It is the fire of Annwyn,' Gran mutters weakly, coughing. George helps her away from the door, until we are standing in her back garden at a good distance from the devastation.

As if in spite, the flames tower even higher than ever above her cottage. They form the outline of the great king of the Otherworld, Gwyn ap Nudd.

''Tis your flames that have stolen the beauty of Fairyland and turned it into the acrid, ashen-grey land it has become,' calls Gran. 'Avaunt ye!' She removes the colander from her head, thanks it, holds her hand up and curses the flames in high ancient Welsh.

I think she says, 'The blood of Arawn is upon you. The curse of his sons shall undo you. The waiting is over.'

And as the flames twirl into the night, they take other shapes, ghastly forms: beautiful elfin creatures that twist into ashy grey goblins with evil eyes; a huge boar with tusks that drip blood-red embers; white-hot wolves which devour the cottage.

The cottage Gran was born in; the cottage where she's lived all her life.

'Twas the little thing, the changeling child, that called the fire,' moans Gran.

'Where is it?' I say, suddenly panicky.

''Tis gone,' says Gran. 'Gone back to the Grey Lands.'

'YESSSS,' the flames hiss. 'Yesss, we have taken back our own, but now we are here, we will stay here and burn your land to cinders, for we curse you and all that are yours.'

We sit on the mountain slope behind the back garden, inside a circle of pans and axes, the rest of the nails, a fantastic array of cutlery, a cheese grater, the colander, a soup ladle, a metal toast rack and an egg slicer – all emptied from Gran's pockets. Gran picks herbs from the mountainside – selfheal, vervain, trefoil – and presses them into her burns.

'Let's see you fight this fire,' the flames snarl. 'Prepare yourself. Ashes to ashes and dust to dust. As it is in the Grey Lands, so will it be in yours. For we are the wild raiders of Gwyn ap Nudd; we are his hunters and none shall stand against us and survive. We are awake and cannot be lulled asleep again. This fire will not be doused – not until all of you, and your sacred mountains, are cremated for eternity.'

Act Two

Midsummer's Day Morn

Whet the bright steel,
Sons of the White Dragon!
Kindle the torch,
Daughter of Hengist!
The steel glimmers not for the carving of the banquet,
It is hard, broad and sharp pointed.

From *The Saxon War Song*
by Sir Walter Scott

Seventeen

Rhiannon's dad's hotel stands on the road into Llanberis, its stately entrance flanked by two Gothic urns. Once upon a time, carved stone dragons stood there. The urns remind me of how very dangerous everything can get.

I mean it.

And I need to remind myself of it. Often.

That. Fire. At. Gran's. Was. No. Joke.

The two stone dragons from the hotel entrance were pulverised. By magic. Imagine the strength needed to smash through stone and concrete, as if you're crumbling crackers. That's the kind of power the Olde Deepe Magicke has. I've seen it at work right here, only last Christmas. Right in front of my eyes. No kidding.

I give the urns a wide berth. Even the spot where those dragons stood still thrums with bad energy. Magicke is like that. You have to be uber cautious. It leaves footprints.

Soon Mum and Gran and George and I – and our border collie, Ceri – sit in the conservatory of the hotel. The telly in the reception is on the news channel. A reporter is interviewing a fireman, their voices just audible in the background. Gran has ordered herbal tea for everyone and is fussing over the fact that these days they don't use rosemary in infusions, as they should. As if she's forgotten she was nearly burnt to a crisp less than a few hours ago. When Mum pops out to use the bathroom, Gran demands we update her on what happened up at the Menhir.

There's really only time for the headlines.

Dragon Fire Can Quench the Fire Of Annwyn.

Henry Can Do That.

When He Is Freed From the Curse of Fighting Oswald.

When Oswald Is Defeated.

Like Dead.

Which Can Be Done With a Magical Sword.

Possibly Caledfwlch.

Which Can Be Found in Avalon in Annwyn, the Otherworld, AKA Fairyland. Possibly.

If We Are Really Nice to the Lady of the Lake.

But We Need a Portal To Get into Annwyn.

And There Is Only One Left Open – Called Merlin's Oak.

'Then what are you waiting for?' asks Gran. 'More cottages to be burnt? Innocent folks to be consumed by fire in their beds?'

'We don't really know how to get going with it all,' I hiss.

'Take the portal. That seems OBVIOUS.'

Is it my imagination, or is Gran a bit snappy?

The interviewer on the telly asks, *'How fast can fire spread?'*

'But the sword … ' I venture.

'Get into Annwyn and ask Nimue for it, of course,' says Gran, as if we're all stupid. 'The Lady of the Lake in Avalon.'

'OK … But where actually is Merlin's Oak and how do we actually get through it into Annwyn?' asks George.

'Merlin's Tree is in Carmarthen, you foolish boy!' snorts Gran.

Yes. Definitely snappy.

'Which you would know if you'd *actually* done your Magical Arts homework.'

Ah, so Gran has been schooling George in the Magical Arts …

'We've got helicopters and engines out, but reaching and evacuating the outlying cottages is proving challenging … ' says the telly.

'Erm,' says George.

'Some of the mountain lanes are now impassable ... and winching cottagers to safety through burning undergrowth poses ... '

'But how do we get through it?' I ask, hoping for some details.

'Take. The. Portal,' says Gran, rolling her eyes.

OK. Step. Away. From. The. Grumpy. Old. Lady.

'But ... ' whispers George.

'Use Merlin's Oak in Carmarthen,' repeats Gran. 'And don't try Clogwyn. Never use a Pookah portal.'

'Pardon?' says Mum as she returns from the bathroom.

'My insurance offices are in Carmarthen,' says Gran swiftly.

Mum looks seriously stressed. 'I don't even know where my insurance papers are, let alone the brokers' offices.'

'Try not to worry, Mrs Morgan,' says George. 'It'll be OK.'

Like obviously it won't.

Mum, if anything, looks even more stressed. Ceri lies on the carpet beside her. She won't even wag her tail, but looks up at me with sad, accusing eyes.

'Firefighters fail to curb extremely aggressive flames ... ' The telly shows pictures of Snowdon, all dark behind bright fire.

'I'm sure they'll stop the fire before it gets to the farm,' continues George.

He's such a big liar.

'… *flummoxed emergency services are not able to predict* … *the fire's unusual behaviour* … '

I bite my lip. Our farm lies on an outer flank of the lower pastures, about half a mile downhill from Gran's cottage.

Totally in the line of fire.

Not funny.

'… *daybreak may bring a clearer picture and allow services to* … '

I *know* the fire *will* get to our farm long before the fire engines, if it wants to. Because by the time we'd got to our place, woken Mum up, got her and Ceri out of the building, and explained how this REALLY was Very Serious and she needed to come with us Right Now, the flames could be seen racing across the upper pastures heading *absolutely* for the farm. I swear I could hear them laughing as they sent embers ahead on the wind.

What I'm praying is that the fire will realise we're not there, and forget about using up its magical energy to burn the whole place down. But those flames are spiteful. My eyes start to grow hot. *My laptop, my clothes, my new quilt and my little room* …

Stop it. It's more likely to happen if the fire knows it'll upset you.

It's just a room, just a quilt, and it's a mercy that there are no sheep any more. It's a mercy Mum is here and Ceri's safe with her. The fire can burn itself to hell and back.

I think of the livestock we once had and start shivering. The way that last attack by magicke slaughtered all our darling lambs. Those foul white wolves.[1] We'd been hoping to restock the farm, but Mum's been so busy with Snowdonia Tours and her volunteer rescue and ranger work (and Jeff) that it's been one more thing left undone. Maybe it's also because neither of us has had the heart.

All those poor darling woolly little lambs.

The tears spill out and roll down my cheeks.

I brush them away. *Stop crying.* Gran and George have just lost everything. Their whole life was up on the mountain. They're not in tears.

George shoots me a worried look. 'You OK?' he mouths.

I shake my head.

'Need a cuddle?'

I nod.

George sits down beside me and puts his arm around my shoulders.

He's lost everything and here he is, still thinking about me when I should be comforting him. I wish I *could*

---

1. All that happened in Book Two, *Here be Witches*. You could read about it there. But it comes with a warning: Readers Might Find This Upsetting.

comfort him, but my lip is trembling and I feel so weak. I lean my head on his arm and just sniff.

'Well, Gran,' says Mum, forcing a smile, 'it looks as if you and I will be living in luxury at this hotel for a while.'

'I hope the insurance is going to pay for it,' snaps Gran.

'The website says they will,' says George.

Bless George. Since we got Gran out and collected Mum and arrived here, he's done nothing but soothe burns, check insurance, book rooms, order endless cups of tea, coordinate with the fire service, stay positive. He hasn't complained once, though it must be about four in the morning by now.

Gran looks shaken. Her face is ashen white. All she's done is sit there and twist her handkerchief round and round her left index finger.

'My cottage,' she murmurs, 'my little cottage.'

I don't have a clue what the insurance will cover – if they'll rebuild Gran's cottage or just pay her a lump sum or do neither …

I just pray the flames don't reach the farm. I pray they won't reach Llanberis and seek out this hotel and burn Rhiannon's family fortune to bits.

But I know they will.

They're coming.

And we have to do something.

Those flames won't stop.

You heard Gywn ap Nudd.

He'll never stop.

It suddenly dawns on me – right now, they're on their way, burning through sedge and heather, slipping in smouldering cinders past gates and houses, slyly wafting their sparks on the breeze over streams, never stopping, just hiding … planning … whispering their curses …

They'll burn down everything.

Everything we care about.

And they won't be happy.

Until they roast us all alive.

Not unless we do something!

'George.' I grab his arm. 'We have to do something NOW!'

Those flames will spread over the whole of Snowdonia.

Further.

And further.

This is what they've planned.

All along.

To burn down our whole world.

Eighteen

Before George can answer me, Rhiannon bounces into the room. Rhiannon in the sweetest little pair of millennial pink PJs ever seen. I swear she's even got make-up on!

She falls upon my neck and kisses me, over and over, saying, 'Oh my poor darling. Oh my poor Ellie. Oh my bestiest bestie. Oh no! This is so DREADFUL! Oh poor darling George! OMG! *OMG!* I am so going to have a noodle stomp.' (A noodle stomp is what Rhiannon does when she doesn't know what else to do. I think it dates back to some event in her childhood when she spilled her pot noodles on the floor. She was so upset she ended up having a tantrum, stamping on them because they weren't Oreos and you couldn't just pick them up and dust them off or something.)

'Oh my poor GEORGE!' wails Rhiannon again. 'You've

got NO HOME. You're all HOMELESS!' He isn't homeless – only temporarily unhoused. Plus he is not *hers*.

'Oh Georgie, you poor, poor, poor, POOR thingie.' And then she shoves me aside and falls on George.

I look away. *Think, Ellie. Is there any other way of putting out the fires?*

Rhiannon is draping herself all over George. (I notice he is smiling. Humbug.)

I bite my lip. I can't think of any other way. And I want to free Henry more than life itself …

'We must all practise calmness,' says Rhi.

We must get the sword … and free Henry so he can put out the flames.

'Guru Google says: *Just close your eyes and let it go. Let it go. Let it go … '*

Because the flames are not going to stop.

They're going to burn and burn until everything is gone.

'*Let it go, let it go,*' sings Rhi as if she's in a Disney movie. She wafts her arms about. She's into mindfulness at the moment. I know. Don't say it. OK, DO say it.

INAPPROPRIATE TIMING.

But how can we get to Carmarthen? And where exactly is Merlin's Oak?

Rhi leaves George for a moment to give me another hug.

I swear she smells of expensive perfume. When she heard we'd all arrived (even though it was stupid-o'clock and we were all in TRAUMA), she must've got up, washed and dried her hair (she's even straightened it), sprayed Chanel number something or other, put on her best PJs and made herself up.

Ohmygod, she's got false eyelashes on too.

And now George is smiling! And being Mr Nice Guy with her.

Such a pushover.

That's the thing about George. He never really tells Rhiannon how it is with him. Sometimes I think he actually *likes* all that pink attention. Sometimes I think he might even fancy her back. Deep down he might truly care about her. Then he comes to me and says how embarrassing it is when Rhiannon flirts with him, because (as I should know) I am the only one in his heart and all that.

Plus she is really, really pretty.

It's a long story. Short version is: Rhiannon has been falling all over herself for George, flirting with him, ever since they first met. She possibly, actually, might even be in love with him. But Rhi being Rhi, it's hard to tell. And George has been running a million miles in the other direction, but not very fast.

In fact, v-e-r-y s-l-o-w-l-y.

New thought: *Perhaps he hasn't been running from Rhi? Perhaps he secretly wants her to catch up?*

This thought is very disturbing.

Not because I want George for myself. Obvs.

But because he Actually *Is* Mine.

What the heck am I thinking?

Stay focused on the fire.

I shake my head and order myself to stop thinking about Rhiannon and George.

Which is difficult.

To be fair, maybe Rhiannon is genuinely sorry for George (on top of the flirting). There are dark circles under her eyes. Since the events of last March, a lot has changed wth her.[1] Maybe she actually has some idea of what we've both just been through. Unlikely, though.

George smiles and puts his arm round her. Puts His Arm Round Her. *See what I mean?*

'Don't worry, Rhi,' he says. 'As long as you have a smile for me, I can face anything.' (See what I mean times a zillion?) 'And if you can sort out a room for Nan and Mrs Morgan at a cheaper price for a longish stay, we'd all be very grateful.'

---

1. You can read about the events in *Here be Witches*.

'Very grateful,' calls out Gran. Then she yawns. Poor Gran, she must be exhausted.

I realise I'm exhausted too, and it's already beginning to get light. Neither George nor I have slept a wink.

Mum sees Gran yawning. 'Let's go and see if they've found you that room yet. You really must get some rest.' She takes Gran's arm and steers her towards the reception area.

Rhiannon raises large limpet eyes at George. 'But what about you, George? Won't you be staying here too? For a very, very longish time? I have a room, which won't cost you anything if you don't mind sharing ... '

I can see her mind ticking away. Clear as sunlight, she's thinking ...

George has no home now.

George will need a home.

My dad has a hotel.

George can live at my hotel.

I can see George whenever I like.

I can even have him as a roommate.

That will save him masses of money.

George will be really grateful to me.

George will be so grateful to me, he'll give me lots of his time and attention.

TOTALLY LOTS.

GCSEs are over ... Summer holidays are coming ...

Gratitude is only a few steps away from love ...

Blah ... blah ...

'Ellie and I have to go on a mission for a few days,' says George.

Thank God!

George slowly detaches Rhi's arms from around his neck.

(Too slowly if you ask me.)

BOOM!

All the clogs in Rhiannon's scheme jam.

'*Go on a mission?*' screeches Rhiannon.

'Yes,' says George. 'There's something going on and, well, you know ... ' His voice trails off.

Rhiannon's face grows as dark as thunder.

'GOING ON?' she screeches again.

George nods, pulls a *sorry, yes, I'm afraid so, I hate to disappoint you* face – all down at the lip and scared, raised eyes.

Rhi doesn't miss that. 'YOU'RE GOING, WITHOUT ME?' She turns to face me, her eyes flaming. 'HEY ELLIE, WHAT'S THIS?! GOING OFF *WITHOUT YOUR BESTIE?*'

The force of her attack is like being shoved in the chest.

'It's going to be tough, Rhi,' I say. 'Probably a lot tougher than last spring.'

'LAST SPRING WAS NOT TOUGH AT ALL!' she counters, tossing her hair back. 'WITHOUT ME, WHERE WOULD YOU ALL HAVE BEEN *LAST SPRING*?'

Her eyes are staring balls of dark fury.

'DID I GET IN THE WAY *LAST SPRING*?'

'Well … ' I say.

'*EXACTLY!*'

'But, Rhi, you're forgetting about the wolves,' says George quietly.

'And the witches and Sheila and how they swore their revenge,' I say.

Rhiannon shudders. Her voice drops. 'I haven't forgotten,' she says more quietly. '*But wherever you're going, I am going too.*' She narrows her eyes, folds her arms and threatens to get shrill. 'I have a right to come. I've proved myself.'

Which is true.

George shrugs and looks at me.

I take a deep breath. Rhi did help last time, but she didn't help as well. Plus someone ought to be here watching out for Gran.

'You could help us,' I start, 'by taking care of Gran and letting us know what she suggests—'

That's as far as I get.

'FORGET IT, GIRLFRIEND! TELL ME WHERE YOU'RE GOING!' demands Rhi.

'Fairyland,' says George, already giving in.

'*FAIRYLAND?!*' screams Rhi in an ear-splitting wail.

'Shush, you'll wake the guests,' says George.

I'm more worried the flames will hear and cut our route off before we can get out of Llanberis.

Those flames can think. They can speak and they can plan ...

I lean forward. This is serious. Rhi has to understand. 'We're going into Fairyland,' I say. 'But it's not the Disney version. It's not like a kiddies' picture book. It's not even called Fairyland any more. It's called the Grey Lands. Because it's dry and harsh and burnt up and hostile. And since the days of Merlin, it's lost all its beauty.'

'*Into Fairyland,*' she whispers, utterly ignoring everything I've just said, as only Rhi can. '*Will there be Unicorns?*'

I curl up my nose and frown. *Is she serious?*

'*I've always wanted to see a Unicorn,*' whispers Rhiannon. Stars shine in her eyes.

'I don't know what there'll be,' I say quite truthfully. Though I seriously doubt there'll be Unicorns frolicking about like a whole fae herd of My Little Ponies.

'That! Is! It!' she says. 'I'm *definitely* coming!'

'You're not listening,' I say. 'The whole of Fairyland has

142

been desiccated by fire, and now there's nothing there but acrid soil and the stink of bleach and smoke.'

'Don't care,' says Rhiannon. 'You want me to come, don't you, George?'

George looks at me.

Traitor.

'It won't be easy ... ' he starts to say.

'That's just Not Good Enough!' she says. She eyeballs me and tosses her head back. 'George says I can come!'

I open my mouth to protest.

But Rhi doesn't give me a chance.

'I'm COMING!' she yells. 'Whether you like it or not!'

Nineteen

'Just don't tell Sheila!' Rhiannon hisses as she starts making her Packing-For-Fairyland list.

I'm not very likely to tell Sheila anything. I'm highly unlikely to speak to her *ever* again.

'She came round her yesterday, all fake nails and highlights in her hair, like last spring didn't happen. And she asked what *you* were up to.'

I widen my eyes. Not good. Sheila never pays friendly visits without some dark motive.

'I told her I didn't know,' Rhi adds.

My borrowed phone pings.

A random number flashes up in the messages app.

+44 7967 843521

Did you like the makeover I organised for George's cottage?

Whaaat?

> **Ellie**
> Who is this?

So spooky. We were just talking about Sheila. I bet it's her. I send a text to her phone too.

> **Ellie**
> Get a life.

My phone pings almost immediately.

> **+44 7654 111156**
> Yours is next. Suck it up.

I breathe out. *It's definitely Sheila.*

She can't leave us alone. I'm not even going to acknowledge her existence.

My real friends are right here.

Rhi and George.

Let it go.

Yes, let it go. Guru Google is right.

I look over into the reception area at Gran, wondering

if I should tell her. As if by telepathy, she turns her head, nods and beckons me over.

I join Gran and Mum, putting my arms around them. 'Have they sorted you out rooms yet?' I ask.

Mum grabs hold of my arm. 'I don't need to stay here,' she whispers, 'unless Gran wants me to keep her company. I can go and stay at Jeff's.'

Long story. Mum's in love with Jeff. He's in love with her. He wants to move away from Snowdonia and keeps getting fantastic job offers all over the world. Mum's always longed to travel. Jeff won't take the jobs, because Mum can't go with him. Why?

Short answer: me.

I squeeze her shoulders. 'You can do whatever you like, Mum,' I say. 'Whatever you feel best doing.'

Gran tuts a little and says to Mum, 'With the greatest respect, I do not need you to stay, my dear. I will be decidedly happier by myself. I lived alone for many years before George came to live with me, and in fact I prefer my own company.'

'I know,' says Mum, 'but you've just been through a terrible ordeal.'

'We could meet up for supper tomorrow?' suggests Gran. 'And you could get off to Jeff's house now? This fire has been very upsetting. But nothing will get any better by us sitting here. It's so late … I mean early. It's already morning. I'm sure our insurance policies will cover everything. Do try not to worry. We should all go to bed and get some rest, if we can.'

I kiss Mum on the forehead. I know Jeff will take care of her.

'What about you?' Mum asks me.

'I've got Rhi and George,' I say, 'and we are meant to be setting off together for a few days, for a holiday, now our GCSEs are over. It was all planned,' I lie. 'I just forgot to tell you.' Mum raises an eyebrow. 'So don't worry – get to Jeff's and let him take care of you.'

'Where are you off to?' asks Mum, giving me the once-over as only she can.

'Just to Carmarthen,' I say (after all, that is not a lie). I do not add: then I'm going to find Merlin's Oak and step through its portals into the Grey Lands. Where I'm going to encounter, at the risk of my life, apparently, magical forces that will have serious yet unknown outcomes. All this to save my beloved Snowdonia, and possibly the whole of the known world.

Obviously, I don't say that.

'Oh, how lovely!' says Mum, 'I've always loved Carmarthen.

The coast is so lovely there. Beautiful beaches. Is Rhiannon's father going there on hotel business?'

Gran nods approvingly.

I dodge the answer. 'I'll be fine,' I say. 'I always am. I'll keep in touch.'

Mum looks at Gran. 'Does this trip have your approval?' she asks.

Gran nods again. 'The child has to go,' she says, then raises her eyes and fixes me with a steely look. 'Beware of the changelings,' she repeats. 'Do not underestimate them. I have taught you what to do. Make sure you check. You must leave the iron behind. Raw iron cannot cross. Remember what I said, touch none of their fayre, *none* – or you will fall into a deep sleep and forget yourself, or wander forever lost to the Mortal World. And NEVER use a Pookah portal.'

Mum mouths, 'Does she need the toilet?' and rolls her eyes as if to say, *The fire must've sent Gran a bit doolally.*

'Make sure you follow to the last letter everything I've said,' Gran finishes.

I give her a kiss on the cheek, by way of an answer, and hug Mum goodbye.

Then I rejoin Rhi and George.

'So it's settled,' says Rhiannon, in full bossy mode. 'I'm going with you. I'll get Dad to tell the chauffeur to drop us down there when he's going for supplies, or even if he's not. Dad is such a sweetie-pie, he'll do anything I say. We can go this afternoon. You two can get a bit of rest before then – while I pack. You can snooze in my apartment. But not "together", OBVIOUSLY.' Rhi wags her finger at us.

She looks so happy. *How can she be, when everything is so awful?* I shake my head. But sleep, YES. I need sleep. Maybe Rhi just doesn't understand. *Those flames have burnt down our homes and are coming for hers next …*

I remember Gwyn ap Nudd's hunters' words: *'None shall stand against us and survive … '*

Suddenly I get a feeling that I won't survive … I go cold. Like someone is treading on my grave. I remember my pledge – to free Henry or die trying.

What if I really do die trying?

What if I don't come back?

What if none of us come back?

I turn to Rhi. 'It's dangerous,' I hiss. 'You need to *really* know that. There will be no one to rescue us in Fairyland.'

Rhi rolls her eyes, as if to say: *And? So?*

I look across at Gran again for reassurance, but the sofa's empty.

I can't see Mum either. She must have left for Jeff's already. Then I catch sight of Gran. She's being ushered towards the lifts by a hotel steward.

I take out the little phial of stardust that Henry once collected for me. I carry it with me everywhere. He told me stardust offers the gift of forgetfulness. By brushing your brow with it, all melancholy fades. If you anoint your eyes before sleep, you wake refreshed. No sad memories cloud your mind. Your heart is free and your cares forgotten.

I race after Gran.

I don't need the stardust. I'll never want to forget Henry, however painful it gets.

I reach Gran. The lift door opens and she steps in. I hold the closing doors and say, 'If anything happens to me, or any of us … ' I press the phial into her hand. 'It's stardust. Use it. Help everyone.'

Gran looks so weary. She nods, takes the phial and raises her hand in a pagan blessing. 'Don't you worry about us … '

I think she's going to say, 'Just come back safely.' But she doesn't. Instead she looks terribly tired.

'Gran?' That footfall on my grave again.

Gran summons up a smile. 'Your farm won't escape, you know. But other farms may – if you succeed.'

The lift door starts to close.

'They're depending on you ... '

Our farm won't survive ... my childhood ... my window seat ... the flowers in spring ... the snow in winter ...

I swallow hard.

I need Henry.

I need him so much.

I go over to the reception and sit down out of view on a high-backed sofa. I pull out the shard of mirror.

The mirror that can open up the way to the In-Between Place.

I unwrap its protective plastic.

And I look into it.

Twenty

In Which Ellie Finds Herself Upon the Devil's Bridge in the In-Between Place

Of course he's waiting for me.

Up there again by the Devil's Bridge.

How did I know he'd be there?

How did he know I'd come?

But that is just the way it is, here in this In-Between Place.

I see him from far away.

Waiting on our spot.

Our lonely romantic spot.

On one side, the mountain falls away hundreds of metres to Llanberis Pass. On the other, it tumbles down a cruel slope of rock to the icy waters of Llyn Du'r Arddu under Clogwyn.

I shudder as I look at the place, remembering the helicopter.

But there he stands, his thick chestnut hair bright in the summer sun.

I run uphill until my lungs are bursting. *I need him so much.*

He's here, waiting for me. I can hardly breathe.

'Hey Ellie,' he says. 'Here we are!' He laughs as if he's won a bet with himself.

I gasp, catch my breath. Words come rushing out in a great splutter. 'How long have we got?'

I'm learning. In this In-Between Place, time never lasts.

'Don't know,' he said. 'I never know.'

I breathe.

Henry is smiling and smiling. 'It's so good to see you.'

I don't answer, I just fling my arms around him.

We stand there holding each other so tight. Quivers run through me. If only it could be like this forever.

'I love you so much,' I whisper.

Henry pulls away. His face looks troubled. 'I love you too,' he says. 'That's the hardest part.'

What does he mean?

'Are you sure you really want to be with me forever – whatever it takes?' he asks.

I breathe out, slowly. *Just breathe, Ellie. Just take in what he's saying.* But my mind is exploding, fireworking, high jumping.

Hoping he's found a way ...

'I don't think you really know,' I say, 'how much I long for that.'

'There may be a price.'

A price? With one toss of my head, I dismiss any price as too high.

'Don't care,' I say.

He sighs. A gust skitters over the surface of the rocks below us. A little shower of powderiness eddies around my feet.

'You have no idea, do you?' he says.

I probably don't.

'Ellie, you can stop. You can forget the quest. There's still time.'

I look at him. Now I'm laughing.

'I thought I should give you a choice … '

'I choose you,' I say. 'Forever, whatever.'

He laughs as well. 'I choose you too, but that's not the choice I meant.'

'I know,' I say, 'but it's the only choice I make. Whatever leads me to you.'

We both stand there. Kind of embarrassed. Kind of excited. Kind of scared.

Henry sighs as if he's just remembered something he'd rather forget. 'Then we need to talk. I don't want to scare you, but … '

He pauses.

'What?'

'If for any reason, I'm the one to die in order to end the curse … '

'Don't say that.' My stomach lurches. My throat dries up. I grip hold of him. 'That can't be,' I say. 'Tell me that won't happen.'

Henry bites his lip. 'Well, just in case, we need to figure out how to stop the fires from Annwyn.'

'If you die, I won't want to live.'

'But others will, Ellie,' Henry tells me gently.

He's right. We must try to stop the fires if we can, whatever happens.

'Are you saying we need a Plan B?' I ask.

Henry nods.

'OK.'

Mentally, heart on hold, I go through the *No Henry Plan B*:

Solution 1: Get another fire-breathing dragon as George suggested?

Problem: Don't know any – except maybe could locate one in China? (All nearer ones seem to be extinct.)

Solution 2: Steal fire from the Greek gods, like Prometheus did.

Problem: Do Greek gods still exist/have fire? And where is Mount Olympus?

Solution 3: Store some of Henry's fire for future use.

Problem: How? Can you freeze-dry fire? What about canning it?

Problem solved: Henry is not allowed to die. Heart is allowed to beat again.

But I ask anyway, 'Could you store some of your fire in a tin can?'

Henry laughs.

'I'm serious,' I say.

'I can breathe fire into stones. That's about the best I can do.'

'Would that work?' I ask. 'Would it be possible to get the fire back out of the stones to use against the flames of Annwyn?'

He pauses and thinks about it. 'Yes, if you could crack the stones open.'

'So will you store some when you can?'

'But how will that help?' asks Henry.

'If you stone-tin-can some fire and we both die, I'll tell George to crack open the stones. At least then we'll have done our best to stop the flames burning forever.'

'OK. I'll store some fire in advance, under the mountain.'

He looks away from me towards Clogwyn.

I follow his gaze.

A darkness is forming under the cliff. We must hurry.

'Why did you suddenly think that maybe you might not survive?' I ask.

'There are things you don't know.'

A cold river runs through me. Icicles form around my heart. 'Tell me.'

'I can't.'

'Please,' I say. 'I'm frightened.'

The darkness swells, mushrooming out towards us. Blood starts pounding at my temples.

'Listen,' he says, 'I'll mark the stones with the sign of fire.'

'The sign of fire?' I say.

'Yes.' Behind his smile, his eyes are full of pain.

The looming darkness swells closer.

'Tell me everything,' I say. 'Trust me. Whatever it is.'

I want to be a part of it, whether it's sad or dangerous or anything.

'Trust *me*,' he says. Henry's grip tightens on me, until my hand feels crushed. 'Remember,' he says. 'Tell someone about the firestones.'

The darkness is nearly upon us.

I crush his hand back. I don't want anything to separate us. Henry puts his arms around me, presses me to him. He holds me tighter and tighter, until I can hear the hammering of his heart.

'We must try to bear whatever happens,' he whispers.

'It's not going to end badly, is it?' I whisper.

Henry braces himself. 'To crack the firestones open you'd need a hammer.'

'Or an axe?' I ask.

'The fires will be easier to quench at their source. Like turning off a tap. So ... '

'Like over there at Clogwyn. Where the portal opened.' I point at the Black Cliff of the Darkness.

Henry nods. 'Yes! Exactly.' He looks at the cliff with renewed interest. 'Three stones should do it. One above Clogwyn, over there.' Henry points to the top of the cliff face where the Ranger Path runs.

'OK.'

'The second stone at the bottom of the cliff.'

I look up into his dark eyes. Big mistake. A wild giddy feeling explodes inside me. I swallow hard.

As above.

So below.

So mote it be.

'We're not going to need them, you know,' I say. I glance back at Clogwyn. The darkness is dragging itself closer. It's starting creeping up the slope behind us.

'And the third stone?' I ask.

'The third could be thrown at the cliff as hard and as high as possible, I think.'

'You aren't going to die, anyway,' I say.

Clogwyn. Sheer cliffs. Shrouded already in darkness. It's impossible not to imagine falling off them, striking stone, twisting and spinning out into space. Falling to a broken death.

Suddenly the darkness is upon us.

With a rushing force we're pulled apart.

And now I'm really falling.

Falling and falling.

And Henry is gone.

Twenty-One

We only just make it out. By the time we hit the road, flames have already crept down the rail track and set fire to outlying cottages. The fire service are in full swing evacuating the west end of the village, putting up road blocks and stopping all traffic. But we make it.

We drive out of Llanberis, up towards Pen-y-Pass. Snowdon lies smoking on our right. The windows of the minibus are shut tight, even though the air is stiflingly hot. High overhead, emergency helicopters whir. The radio is on, but no news updates yet.

I try to peer through the haze, to get a sense of how far the fire has spread and how bad the damage is, but it's all dense and opaque. Like some weird wall of grey air.

Please, dear Snowdon, don't let the fires burn down everything.

Up ahead, through the thick smoke, I'm sure I can see something: a dull orange glow down the mountainside. I squint uneasily. It's hard to make it out, but I'm pretty sure behind all that haze, huge flames are speeding down the slopes.

Racing towards the road.

Trying to cut us off?

A fire engine rockets towards us, sirens blasting. The pass ahead is still open, then.

'Rhi,' I say, 'is there any way we can speed up? I think the fire is trying to close the pass.'

She goes a bit pale, raises her eyebrows, widens her eyes. 'Driver! Go faster!' she orders.

The driver, Huw, puts his foot down and takes the curves at dangerous speeds.

'What are we going to do when we get there?' asks George from the front seat. He seems calm, though his knuckles are white from gripping the side rail. 'We need a plan.'

I pray Huw knows these roads well.

'Let's just get there,' I say and point at the charred black mountain, the billowing clouds of soot, the DEFINITE fiery glow of flames.

'Apparently Merlin's Oak is famous. It once stood on the corner of Oak Lane and Priory Street.' George checks his phone. 'According to Google, it's going to be a three-and-a-half-hour drive.'

Rhiannon glances nervously at the driver again and gives him a prod. 'Huw, keep going!'

'Doing my best,' he grunts.

A traffic alert suddenly blares out from the minibus radio: *'The A4086 and A498 are currently experiencing wildfire threat. Emergency services advise drivers to avoid journeys along these roads unless absolutely necessary.'*

'Keep going,' repeats Rhi.

George reads from his mobile: *'Merlin's Oak used to stand in the centre of Carmarthen. Legend has it that Merlin, King Arthur's famous wizard, placed a protective curse on it. He foretold that Carmarthen would "drown" if the oak was ever removed, and some even said a curious, pointed notch in the tree was the face of Merlin himself, caught in the cleft – pinned there by the magic of his lover, Nimue, the Lady of the Lake.'*

He stops. A strange expression knits itself across his brow. He shakes his head slightly. I don't like that look.

'The tree was poisoned in the 1850s. It was then removed from the town when someone set it on fire at the end of the 1970s.'

Fire! What if the tree was set alight by the flames of Annwyn trying to get out?

And what if the fires are still there, waiting when we get in?

A shudder runs through me.

'Apparently Carmarthen suffered its worst floods ever sometime after that,' adds George.

I peer out into the dim afternoon. We're through Nant Peris. The glowing looks bigger *and* nearer. I can still hear helicopters.

If only we hadn't delayed.

The driver's going fast, though. We might make it up to the pass before the flames get there. I hang on to the seat in front of me. *Stay focused.*

Now, Merlin trapped in a tree?

I don't buy it. Merlin wouldn't have let anyone stick him in a tree, unless he'd wanted to. I don't think Nimue would do it to him either. She was lovely to us and helped us *because* of Merlin.

We skid round a bend. My heart rate shoots up. *Holy crap! That was a bit scary!*

But I suppose the legend must have *some* truth in it …

George takes a deep breath. 'I was just looking up dragon-slaying in Gran's book too … '

'And?'

'It might not be as simple as it looks … '

'Tell?'

'We might need to find a wizard to wield the sword.'

'Why?'

'Only wizards are dragon lords, apparently … '

'So?'

'Only dragon lords can slay dragons.'

My heart drops to the floor with an ALMIGHTY clunk.

'So even if we can get into Annwyn and find Nimue and get her to give us the sword, we might still be no nearer freeing Henry!'

'Yeaaah … ' says George slowly. 'Seems so … Yeah … so finding a wizard is going to be a bit … challenging … Merlin was the last great wizard, apparently. Seems as if there's nobody else we can call on. Except Gwyn ap Nudd, of course. Joke! Sorry, not funny. Totally not funny. There just aren't any wizards left nowadays. Nowhere. Not even in Fairyland, maybe … it seems … '

No wizards?

No dragon lords?

A sudden gust of soot billows down at us. Thick. Black. Choking. Can't see a thing.

The driver mutters, 'Damn smoke,' and brakes sharply.

I lurch forward into the seat in front. The driver swears as we slide over a scree of cinder. We round another bend on two wheels.

Rhi screams.

That was a twenty-metre drop we just missed! My heart goes crazy. *That gust of soot knew what it was doing!* Rhi is as white as a sheet.

'Holy smoke!' yells George.

Yes. It Is Still Annoying.

'Seat rails,' George hollers. 'Hold on to the seat rails. They're made of steel.'

I cast a glimpse in the direction of the summit of Yr Wyddfa and pray, 'Dear Snowdon, help us to save you. Help us to get to Carmarthen. Help us to find a wizard.'

We round the next curve and there in front of us are colossal, mammoth, Brobdingnagian flames.

Ultra, uber, unbelievable monsters.

I'm not kidding.

All across the tarmac, from verge to verge, the road is on fire, white-hot and bubbling.

'Miss?' asks the driver.

Rhiannon shrieks.

'Just speed across it,' George says. 'It won't have time to set the wheels alight.'

'Miss?' repeats the driver.

'Yes,' whispers Rhi, 'do what he says.' She glances behind us. The road is dense with smoke. It's now or never. 'Yes,' she repeats. 'Do it.'

The driver puts his foot down. There's a weird traction and a stinking smell. *What if we get stuck? We'll be roasted alive inside this van.*

The minibus stalls. The driver starts the engine again. The gears crunch. The wheels spin, like they're stuck in mud. The driver rams it down to four-wheel drive. There's a foul smell. The air con seems to let everything through. The minibus pulls forward.

Far too slowly.

Flames jump up at the windows.

What about the petrol tank?!

I hold my breath and pray, chanting the words of the Druids' prayer with my fingers crossed:

> *'Grant, O Ancient Ones, Thy protection;*
> *And in protection, strength;*
> *And in strength, understanding ... '*

The engine revs and revs. The wheels spin, but stick. The minibus moves forward. Just centimetres. The tyres must be ruined. *Please don't let us stop.* Christ, it stinks. *Please keep going.* A tall pine crashes down in flames just where we were. Rhi screams, then coughs, then screams again. We don't look back. All of us start coughing.

> *'Grant, O Ancient Ones, Thy protection;*
> *And in protection, strength … '*

I bite my lip. Rhi hangs on to the seat rail, her knuckles white. George doesn't say a word.

We reach the top of Pen-y-Pass.

We pick up speed.

We open the windows.

The air clears.

It seems we're through.

Oh my God.

It seems we're OK.

For now.

Twenty-Two

Despite stopping in Beddgelert to replace all four damaged tyres, we make good time. It's seven in the evening and we're nearly there.

George directs the driver the last few miles into Carmarthen. I peer out into the everlasting twilight, watching – for any mist, any darker-than-dark haze, any hint of fire.

I've never been to Carmarthen before. The town looks shrouded in overhanging gloom. No smell of the sea. No seagull's cry; no tang of salt air. You'd hardly believe we're near the coast.

Can the fire have reached here already?

Stupid question.

It's not ordinary fire, is it? It can reach anywhere.

The treetops that line the road sway slightly, as if the air is being roughed up by some giant hand high above us.

'A thunderstorm's coming,' says George, 'I can feel it. I was in a bike accident once. We were on a dirt track and there was a terrifying crack of thunder. I came off the bike and broke my arm in three places. Ever since then, I can feel the approach of a storm, right here in my arm bone.'

'Humerus,' corrects Rhiannon, all encyclopaedia-ish.

Of course! The fire can travel by storm. One flash of lightning, that's all it'll take. As soon as we're a sitting target …

'Arm bone,' says George.

George is right. A thunderstorm is coming. I know it, but not in my arms or any other bones. It's obvious – that's what any *intelligent* fire would do. Strike when we think we're safe.

And I can smell it coming too.

Smoke and bleach.

We'd better be very, very careful.

I turn and squint through the rear window again. The lowering clouds are being chased out by a sulphur-yellow, darkening sky. Nasty.

I lick my top lip and shiver. I don't taste salt, just the acrid trace of something like chlorine.

'That storm is coming from the Grey Lands,' I say. 'I can taste it on the wind.'

'You sure?' says George.

Obviously, I am in a car, driving through Carmarthen. There is no normal way I can taste the darkness of the Fae Lands. But things aren't normal, are they? I lick my upper lip again and my saliva burns.

'I'm sure.'

'Are we nearly there?' asks Rhiannon like a big kid. She's dressed in a charming pair of tiny shorts and is putting on lip gloss. She has a make-up bag in her rucksack, which is nuts, but seeing as she organised the transport, I don't say, 'What On Earth Did You Bring That Make-Up Bag Along For, Rhi?'

I know anyway.

George turns and gives her a huge George-type smile. His eyes sparkle, his cheeks crinkle up until his almost-dimples show and the skin folds in cute little ridges over his nose. He reaches out a hand and pats her shoulder. 'We are definitely nearly there, Rhi.'

George is so much nicer than me. Sigh.

I watch the sulphur-dark cloud. It's true we *are* nearly there. And so is the storm.

'What can we do to avoid the lightning?' I say. We won't get anywhere if we have to keep lying flat all the time.

George laughs. He rolls his eyes and weirdly pulls out handfuls of cutlery from his backpack. 'Soup spoons to the rescue!' he yells. Then hands out knives, forks and spoons.

Rhi giggles. She takes a butter knife. 'Namaste to the elements!' she says and does that yoga prayer thing with her hands, but with the butter knife pointing upwards between her palms.

'I know it's nuts! But Nan told me if there's a threat of lightning, keep your hand on a fish fork,' says George.

I smile. Crazy, clever, old Gran. She's thought of everything to keep us safe.

We pocket the cutlery.

I check my borrowed mobile. One more text.

That same random number.

+44 7654 111156

I told you it was WAR. Be prepared to DIE.

I shudder. But I don't respond. Instead I send Mum a text.

Ellie

Love you, Mum. I always will. And I love it that you have Jeff to love you too. Don't worry about anything. Everything will be all right in the end. We just got to Carmarthen.

XXX E

I cross my fingers. I so hope it will be all right.

The minibus turns into a B road.

Please let it be all right.

And we arrive.

~~~~~

The junction of Oak Lane and Priory Street is not spectacular. But it's Merlin's place, where his tree once stood. The oak is no longer there, obviously. To the uninitiated, it's just another junction. If you came upon the place by chance, you'd be none the wiser.

Maybe.

Unless …

The trees on the pavement start to bend in the wind.

Park. We should park. Quickly.

There's a quality that hangs in the air. I can't quite put my finger on it. Streetlights seem to shimmer overhead. The air vibrates with their orangey glow – a certain aura – that pulsing light. It's as if I could reach out my hand and touch something – some other dimension – palpable … illusive.

In contrast, the junction is a white-painted roundabout on iron-grey tarmac. Dull. Prosaic, even.

Please, Merlin, let your magic protect us.

I had somehow fancied the gateway to the Fae Lands would look different. Perhaps a misty rainbow would arch over it, or tiny brilliant lights would bespeckle the air. At the least, the odd extraordinary-looking rock or gnarled tree.

But no, it's just a roundabout.

We pull up.

'Are you certain this is the place?' Rhi asks.

Even as she speaks, lightning strikes. It hits a steeple very near us. Far too near.

Yes, this is the place.

We'd better hurry.

'Nan said the last gateway to the Fae Lands still stands open, for those who know the password,' says George. 'Right on the spot where Merlin's Oak once stood.'

'But do we actually know the password?' I say.

'Ah,' says George, 'that's the tricky bit. The password was lost long ago in the Dark Ages.'

'So what do we do?' I yell.

'Looks like we'll have to improvise.'

Twenty-Three

Just as we unclick our seatbelts, lightning strikes again.

Flames shoot down the church steeple. The smell of burning hits us. *So that's its plan! Thanks to Gran's kitchenware, it can't strike us directly, so it's going to start a fire. Set us on the run. Scare us off.*

I smile, because at least now we know the cutlery is working.

'Let's be quick,' George urges.

'But the password?' Rhi hisses.

Very Good Question.

We drop down from the minibus. Rhi tells the driver not to wait, and she'll call her dad when we want to be collected. I try to remember if Gran ever told us any kind of password. Ever.

The driver is not happy.

'He wants to wait,' says Rhi. 'How much money shall I tell him to put in the parking meter?' She looks at George and then at me. 'How fast does time run in Fairyland? Is one hour there the same as one hour here?'

More excellent questions.

Overhead, thunder rumbles.

Sadly, no excellent answers.

I have no idea of how time will run in the Grey Lands. Will we be gone for a lifetime or only a few seconds?

Will we even get in?

Will we ever get out?

'Not sure, Rhi,' says George. 'I think you should insist he leaves us here. We can always phone him.'

Rhi looks dubious, but shrugs and dismisses the driver. I cast a glance at George. He always seems to think of sensible things to say.

Another searing flash.

The whole sky lights up.

Right beside us, an overgrown shrub crackles into flame.

We run to the centre of the roundabout.

'Holy smoke!' says George.

Gwyn ap Nudd is not wasting time.

George holds up a bit of cutlery. 'Fork off, Nudders,' he hollers.

I shake my head. Not even funny.

I take stock. No oak tree. Not even a random twig. Nevertheless, a roundabout is a circle and circles are magical. And junctions are meeting places, right?[1]

I whisper up a prayer to Draco. 'Dear Dragon, Lord of all points of the compass, please let us through to the Grey Lands. Please don't let the lightning strike us before we're safely there.'

I am just about to add, 'Please let us complete the mission and defeat Oswald,' when I realise that Oswald, being a dragon, might be under the protection of Draco himself. Oops.

We huddle together at the centre of the roundabout. A sea wind whips in. Around us the storm starts breaking.

I repeat the Druids' prayer. George places knives, forks and spoons, plus a shoehorn (?) and a cast iron trivet, in a circle around us. Rhi helps him. I look up Open Sesame Spells on Google.

The lightning does not strike again. Thanks be. Google offers me no insights.

'I think Merlin's magick must be somehow protecting

---

1. In folk magic and mythology, crossroads represent a location 'between the worlds', a place where two realms touch, a place literally 'neither here nor there', 'betwixt and between'. Maybe the In-Between Place is a kind of crossroads or roundabout ...

this circle too,' whispers George. 'Don't like to say it, but some of Nan's soup spoons aren't the best quality.'

I raise an eyebrow.

'Alloy,' he whispers, 'bit cheap.'

'What do we do now?' I say.

'I know,' says Rhi, all super-bossy. 'Let *me* tell you all what to do.'

I roll my eyes. Rhi sees me and scowls.

'I know LOTS about Fairyland,' she says. 'And I LOVE fairies.'

I don't say anything. What's the point? It's not the same kind of 'Fairyland' she knows 'lots' about, is it? But hey, WE HAVE ALREADY TOLD HER THAT.

Instead I scan the sky. If we don't get into the Fae Lands, I don't think we'll survive long once we've left the safety of the ~~kitchenware~~ white circle.

'OK,' says Rhi, 'I think we should all join hands, because there is a synergy in our powers and together we will be more potent.'

Oh crikey! Synergy, is it? And Being Potent!

'Good thinking, Rhi,' says George, smiling kindly at her. 'But keep a tight grip on your butter knife as well.'

Humbug.

But OK. I agree about the 'synergy'.

'Plus if we get through to Fairyland,' Rhi adds, 'we must hold on to each other really, really, really tightly so that we are not separated when we reach the other side. I read that somewhere. Maybe in a Narnia book.'

She's probably right again. I might have read that book too.

Note to self: Give Rhi A Break.

There's an almighty clap of thunder. The wind picks up speed. My hair is blown all over the place, mostly into my eyes. My jacket flaps about madly, like one of those fake silk flame things.

'Holy smoke,' says George, 'this storm's trying to blow us off the roundabout!'

I REALLY do wish he'd stop saying that.

Then, to make things worse, the gale becomes a tempest, which becomes a cyclone, which becomes a tornado, and we're spun sideways. How exciting.

'Join up!' yells Rhi.

We all link arms and get hurricane-bludgeoned and bone-drenched as we try to lean into the wind, to stop it scattering us.

'Now,' says Rhi, 'this is what we did when I was doing witchy practice thingies.'

I roll my eyes again.

'Please,' says Rhi, looking at me. 'I know. But it works and I was trained in this.'

The last thing I need while I'm trying to be nicer is to be reminded of how Rhiannon was once a horrible witch.

'OK,' I say, 'Rhi knows what to do.' (See, I *am* being nicer.) 'Let's do it before we're blown away.'

'Well, we must seal the four corners of our world by making offerings to the four elements. We should take up positions at north, west, east and south in this circle.'

'Brilliant,' bellows George over the wind. 'You've got it, Rhi! Seen Nan do something … same.'

'But there are only three of us,' I point out.

'You'll just have to do two of the compass points then, won't you?' she snaps.

We position ourselves at the three/four points. I dodge about as south to George's north and west to Rhiannon's east, although we are so tightly clumped together that I'm not sure there's much difference.

'Now,' says Rhi, 'we must repeat: "by earth … by fire … by water … by air".'

OK. Looks as if Rhi actually learnt something when she was a witch. I make a new mental note to self: Being Judgemental Is Not Part of Being Nicer. A lone seagull cries out as the wind hurls it shorewards.

A nearby tree in a massive planter bends under the gale. The wind batters it from left to right until all its leaves are ripped off. The planter actually slides across the pavement. The hurricane of air shoves us around too. We stagger forward. We're harried back. A raincloud bursts.

'Quick,' I say between clenched teeth. 'We can't hold out much longer against this.'

Please let Rhi's magic work.

'We must circle sunwise, deosil, around this centre part of the circle,' yells Rhi. 'That's clockwise, by the way. Then we must repeat "by earth, by fire, by water, by air" and turn that into a sort of poem, if we can. Poetry is meant to make the magick work better.'

'OK.' I grit my teeth. 'I'll make up a few lines … anybody can chip in.'

A sheet of lightning sweeps down at us. Right over our heads. We duck. We scream. We nearly scatter.

'Hold firm,' says George.

The lightning breaks up at the edge of the roundabout. The rain pelts down.

OMG. Knees tremble. Pulse races.

We move as solemnly as we can, chanting:

'By earth, by fire, by water, by air,

Open the portal! Hear our prayer!

By air, by water, by earth, by fire,

Please grant us our Hearts' Desire.'

I don't quite know what I'm expecting – maybe a thunderbolt, or an earth tremor. Maybe waves roaring up from the coastline and crashing down on the road, or … hopefully a great portal opening wide in mid-air …

It doesn't have to be that transfiguring. Just something, anything.

Ha ha.

Only the roaring wind.

'I'm sorry,' sobs Rhi. 'It's supposed to work.' A crash of thunder echoes out across the bay.

Suddenly I get a Eureka moment. 'When we're asking for something, shouldn't we offer something too?'

The rain sweeps over us in sheets.

'Like at Halloween … treats, or Christmas … mince pies. I think we should make an offering to open up the portal.'

A shower of spray strikes us – salty, bitter, cold, thin and stinging. The wind spins itself into a fury.

Maybe this storm is a trick.

So we don't see the fire creeping up.

'Please let's hurry,' I shout. I stare around for any telltale flicker of flame.

The row of cottages opposite stare back, stony-faced.

Tall lampposts like giant dentists' probes point down at us with evil intentions. Traffic bollards declare absolutely nothing is out of place and the now-not-so-decorative tree in its wooden planter tries hard to pretend that Merlin's Oak was never here.

Rhiannon drags off a bangle.

I pull out a strand of hair. It's instantly blown away. I take another.

George offers up a tube of Smarties. (OMG, I didn't know he'd got sweets secretly stashed in his pockets!)

We place everything in the circle, but all of it scatters away.

We start the chant again anyway.

A sleek black Mercedes, with tinted windows and polished metalwork, draws up to the roundabout. Its windscreen wipers are a blur of rain-wash. The driver lowers his window, just a fraction, and circles round us. Over and over.

What's he doing?

Weird.

And he's going widdershins.

That's bad.

He beeps his horn and yells out of the window, 'Vandals! Stupid effing kids. Get out of here!'

I suppose we must look pretty daft: holding hands and chanting as we turn circles, round and round in the middle of a thunderstorm, on a public junction. But his attack seems undeserved. The car swerves around the roundabout for the third time in a row. I'm distracted as a curtain of water sheers up from its wheels and drenches us.

Something is wrong.

He seems to drive off … but then turns the car around and with speed heads back, straight at us!

He lowers his window fully.

And through the open window I see the evil eyes of Gwyn ap Nudd, his blackened face, his twisted snarling lips.

Now the earth melts rather than shakes and the skies overhead press down. Gwyn ap Nudd curses in a foul toxic tongue. I hear the engine rev.

A thinning and hollowing out begins.

He's trying to stop us, trying to make us let go of each other.

He's going to drive the Mercedes over the roundabout.

Mow us down.

The car shoots forward.

STRAIGHT AT US.

I flex my jaw.

And suddenly I feel as if I'm shooting upwards, far too fast, and then just as suddenly dropping.

'Hang on!' screams Rhi.

I hold on to her like crazy. *Has the car hit us?* My hands ache as the world washes away. An incredible sense of giddiness swallows me up, as if I've done a thousand spins on a fairground waltzer, fast and faster, dizzy and dizzier.

Then I am plunging, hurtling, at a terrifying velocity.

I feel myself ripped apart.

And then nothing.

Twenty-Four

'HANG ON!' yells Rhi again, then her voice breaks.

'Try to ... ' begins George, and then he shouts, 'Rhi, let go! You're pulling my arm off.'

'It's not me,' squeals Rhi.

A white mist swirls up and funnels around us.

'That was Gwyn ap Nudd!' I yell between gasps of breath.

'ELLIE, YOU OK?' screams Rhi.

The tightening stops me breathing. I can't answer. The tugging makes me sick. 'It's magicke,' I whisper. (I hope to God it's not because the car hit us.)

'Well done, Rhi!' yells George.

'OMG!' screams Rhi.

I send up a silent prayer to the universe: *Let us be OK. Let us be OK.*

Then, like a hand across the moon, the roundabout,

its white circle, the storm, the car and Carmarthen completely vanish.

The three of us are caught in air ... holding hands ... out of breath ... spinning ... toppling.

My head pounds. My heart beats thick and fast. My throat goes dry. I'm drowning in mid-air. I squeeze my eyes tight and hold on to Rhi and George as hard as I can.

The mist starts to thin ... a barren place ... thorns ... sand ... heat ...

Gwyn ap Nudd tried to run us over.

We spin faster.

I can't breathe. I force some air in.

Where is he now?

Can he follow?

Stupid question.

Then the smell. *Ugh!* Yuck! Bitter. Acrid. Dusty. Ashy. Chlorine. Bleach. Smoke. I start coughing. Choking.

My chest. My lungs!

I gasp for breath again. *Hang on to Rhi's hand. We're going to be wrenched apart.* The others are coughing too.

'ELLIE,' shrieks Rhi, 'YOU CAN QUIT BREAKING MY FINGERS!'

I'm clutching her so tightly, my arm is aching with the grip. I daren't let go. But my eyes. *My eyes.*

I can't see a thing.

I've got to wipe my eyes. The stinging is unbearable.

'ELLIE!' screams Rhi again, trying to snatch her hand free.

I must breathe. I gag and vomit into dry air. I let go of Rhi. I reach for a tissue in my pocket. The mirror shard shoots out of my pocket along with the tissue.

My shard!

I wipe my eyes. I cough. Wipe my eyes again. Choke. Wipe my eyes a third time. I wipe and wipe my eyes. The tales are true, then. There is a fae land. *Oh, my eyes. My lungs.* A desiccated land, cursed and burnt to a cinder – scorched, barren and hostile.

Smelling of bleach and acid.

Covered with murderous hostile vegetation.

And I've lost my bit of mirror.

Then I look down.

OH MY GOD!

Razorgrass!

I've heard about it before. I never thought it really existed. Sharp as diamonds. Cold as steel. Don't move. Not. An. Inch. My heart goes all tight and my lips twist up.

Where's my shard?

With my eyes still smarting, I peer out at the acres of

razorgrass. If my shard has fallen into a dense tuft, I'll never get it back. Not if I want to keep my fingers.

I can't see a thing. But I must check the ground, find my shard, avoid the razorgrass.

I pull my sleeve over my hand and wipe my eyes. I wait for the stinging to stop.

Soon I can see. Well, a little bit.

I'm standing underneath the branches of a mighty oak. Shade and light dapple over me. *Where are the others?* I peer into the tree's shadowy depths, trying to see if they are there.

I check the dust around me, hoping to see my mirror shard, hoping it hasn't gone far.

'This must be Merlin's Oak,' says George between coughs. His voice is quite near, maybe around the other side of the great tree trunk.

'George?' I say.

George steps into view from the shadows of the oak. He spits. 'Yuck! Everything tastes so sharp, so bitter.'

I look again for the shard. There it is. Right next to a bit of tissue. I can see it!

THERE IT IS!

Just on the edge of the razorgrass carpet. *Go carefully. Watch. Steady now. Razorgrass can take a finger off before you even feel it.*

Very cautiously, I pick up my precious bit of mirror. I tuck it into my pocket.

I rub my eyes again. They sting. But I can see at last.

'Holy smoke,' George says, 'look at that.'

The landscape before us falls away: ash, cinder, charred earth, silver flora, razorgrass, tiny-thorn trailers, stinging nettles, brambles, flowerless gorse and thick carpets of miniature acacia. *How could this place ever have been Fairyland?* The air hangs thick with smoke, bitter acrid smoke, and the smell of bleach is everywhere.

'Where are the Unicorns?' shouts Rhi as she stumbles round the trunk of the great oak.

Thank goodness Rhi is through too. We're all here. The Merc didn't get us. Phew.

'There *must* be Unicorns!' Rhi wails, picking at the oak leaves in distraction.

Poor Rhi, she is so obsessed with them. I shake my head: Not. Going. To. Happen.

'Hey guys,' whispers George, 'if you listen, you can hear the sounds of Carmarthen through the branches of this tree.'

I pause and strain my ears. He's right. The sound of traffic, of voices, of a dog barking somewhere deep inside the foliage. All really faint.

I look around. The pale, sandy, earthen desert stretches out in every direction, humming under the hot air. Parched soil, shrivelled and filled with sharp stones. The blackened bushes all low, no higher than my waist, but thick with thorns, like the savannah in Africa. Below the thorn bushes, grey-brown tiny-thorn trailers creep across the blackened, cracked crust of the earth.

'I know there are Unicorns somewhere,' weeps Rhi.

'Those are the thorns to really watch out for,' warns George. 'The tiny ones on the trailers. They'll pierce your skin and embed into your flesh. They have a sort of stinging poison that makes the area inflamed. Wherever they hook themselves in, you will swell up until it hurts so much you will want to scratch yourself wide open to stop the pain.'

Great.

That's good to know, isn't it?

Like: Step Away From The Thorns.

Except they are everywhere.

'How do you know all that?' asks Rhi.

'A *Study of the Flora, Fauna and Inhabitants of Annwyn*,' says George, producing the moth-eaten copy from his back pocket. 'I've permanently borrowed it from Nan.'

'What does it say about Unicorns?' asks Rhi eagerly.

George opens the book and starts flicking through its pages.

A sharp breeze stirs the surface of the cracked soil. It whirls up sand into small eddies, and soon the ground is covered in small tornadoes. A funnel of flying dust shoots straight at our eyes.

Swiftly I pull the edge of my hoodie over my face. 'Watch out!' I scream at Rhi and George.

The dust stabs the back of my hand, stinging part of my cheek. *Crikey, that hurt!* I nurse my hand against my lips. *Flipping heck, that really, REALLY hurt.*

'Yeah, I forgot to mention,' says George, 'the book seems to suggest that we should trust nothing – even the wind will attack us if it can.'

Now he tells us.

Utterly brilliant.

I remember Gran and her insisting we talked through pieces of plumbing, in case the wind carried our voices to the ears of our enemies.

'Does it say anything about the wind carrying our words to the enemy?' I ask.

'Probably,' says George. 'I haven't like memorised it by heart or anything, but I definitely think we should keep our plans to ourselves.'

'Will a Unicorn hear me if I call out to it, then?' asks Rhi, and immediately shouts out, 'Coochie coochie coo, Uni Uni Uni. Come to Rhi Rhi.'

'Rhi,' I say, 'shut up!'

Rhi tosses her head defiantly. 'COOCHIEEE COOCHIEEE COOO!'

That's SO mega stupid of her. We need to get the hell out of here now.

Try. Not. To. Lose. It. Ellie.

'George, Rhi,' I say, 'I've got a bad feeling – we should get away from here.'

Rhi and George look at the book. The huge oak tree rustles and brushes its leaves together.

'See,' says Rhi, prodding a page, 'there *are* Unicorns … look there … under U … after T and that Twrch Trwyth thing.'

But her words are drowned out beneath a great screeching. A grating. A crashing. The air shakes. The ground trembles.

I knew it!

A loud horn rings out. Something like a piercing car alarm drills the air. Dust flies up. I start to choke. All over again. The smell of bleach instantly gets much worse.

What's going on?

Instinct takes over. 'Run!' I yell. 'Get to those rocks over there!'

Rhi screams. I grab her hand. 'C'mon. Forget about Unicorns. Run as fast as you can.'

We run.

'Mind the thorns!'

We zigzag past lethal bushes (which actually seem to lean out towards us). George overtakes us and races for the shelter of the rock face. He leaps over the thorns in huge long-legged jumps.

The grey trailers snake out in front of us.

They're trying to trip us up!

They're ripping at our legs.

Jump.

Race.

The earthquake rumbles until the noise is so loud I think my eardrums will burst.

We have to make it to the rocks.

We plunge and slide round the edges of the razorgrass. Dark flecks of ash swirl down at us from a thunderous sky. 'Run, Rhi! Run!'

At last, the rock face.

We reach it. There's a deep fissure in it. We squeeze in, trembling, breathless.

I double up panting. Rhi sobs and gasps and sobs some more. The fissure behind us opens into a dark, shallow cave. I clutch my sides. My chest burns. Rocks and tall shadowy spaces. We huddle together, trying to catch our breath. Rhi sobs louder. 'We gotta be more careful,' I gasp.

The shaking stops. The rumbling dies away. Oddly, the wail of a car horn still seems to ring out. I try not to make a noise (which is not easy when you are all crouched up, coughing your guts up). I wipe my eyes. They sting all over again. The dust settles. We stay huddled together and peer out.

Sticking up out of the trunk of the mighty oak, I see the bonnet and front end of a sleek black Mercedes.

'OH MY GOD!' shrieks Rhi.

'What the … ' George stops mid-sentence.

Shadows writhe across the razorgrass. A wild wind starts blowing. I go cold all over, despite the burning heat. My heart pounds. My nostrils actually feel raw. I pull my hoodie tighter around me. *Thank God we made it to this cave-place.* The horn of the Mercedes is stuck on, blaring out. Through the tinted windscreen, I'm sure I can make out something – someone opening a door. Someone has come through the portal and is out there.

The shadows under the tree flicker and stretch out towards us.

The car is stuck in the portal.

And it's our only way home …

The shadows continue to slither in the settling dust. I catch the strains of a new noise. Somewhere far away, somewhere, someone raises an unseen horn to their lips. It lets out a call, long and low, a hunting cry.

Then comes the sound of other horns, even further away.

They seem to be making a weird kind of music. They seem to be saying, *'Halloo. Hallooo, let the hunt begin.'*

'The portal must be jammed shut,' whispers George.

And I know he's right.

There's no way back now through Merlin's Oak.

Twenty-Five

The dust settles.

The blaring continues.

No one says a word.

The front half of the Mercedes stays sticking out of the tree trunk, like a weird art installation.

'How're we going to get home?' whispers Rhi, breaking our silence.

'I'll get you home, Rhi,' promises George.

'There aren't going to be any Unicorns, are there?' Her face is pale and looks suddenly very small.

I shake my head. 'Sorry,' I whisper.

Rhi blinks rapidly, presses her lips together and staggers to the back of the crevice, sinking down in a heap. All around her, the rocks stretch upwards and close in.

'See if you can comfort her,' suggests George quietly. 'I'm going to stay and keep watch.'

I shake my head. Rhi wanted to come. We didn't beg her to. And she was told. She'll have to comfort herself. I peer out. I'm not being hard-hearted; I just want to be as well informed as I can. If the Mercedes is there, Gwyn ap Nudd must be too. Our survival may depend on our vigilance.

At least we all made it here to this cave-thing – out of sight – before the Merc got through the portal. Fingers crossed we might not have been spotted.

I send up a silent prayer. *Please let us not have been spotted.*

Gwyn ap Nudd will know we're around somewhere, though. It'll only be a matter of time till we're found …

I glance to the back of the cave. Rhi has apparently comforted herself just fine and is changing her clothes!

'I am cheering myself up,' she announces as she rummages for items in her backpack.

'Shush!' I frown at her.

I peer out again at the massive oak, my mind racing. It's obvious what he's up to – Gwyn ap Nudd has summoned his followers with the car horn. I wish I knew more about him. Knowledge is power.

'What does it say in your book about Gwyn ap Nudd?' I whisper to George.

A squee of glee comes from the back of the cave. 'WHAT DO YOU THINK?' shouts Rhi. She giggles and twirls towards us in a long orange velvet gown with gangly sleeves and a high waist.

'Shush!' I hiss again.

'I'VE ALWAYS WANTED TO DRESS UP LIKE A FAIRY PRINCESS,' she trills.

Whaaat?

A hot rush of rage floods through me. *WHY CAN'T SHE JUST SHUT UP?* I place one finger over my mouth and glower at her angrily.

But Rhi just prances about until we turn to look at her. 'What do you think?' she mouths.

'Not very practical.' George shakes his head.

'And I think you've just blown our cover,' I hiss.

Rhi's face falls. 'What's so im-prac-tic-al?' she spits out.

'Number one: we may have a long way to go,' explains George in a whisper. 'We may have to run again, and you'll trip over yourself. Number two: if any sparks from Gwyn ap Nudd's fire hit the hem of that dress, you'll go up like a firework.'

I glance nervously at the oak tree. *He must know where we are now. What's he waiting for?*

'Well. I'm. Not. Changing. Back,' hisses Rhi. 'Full. Stop.

And just because you look like your usual chopping-up-wood-for-your-granny self, I don't have to!'

'Shush,' I repeat again.

'We might come to a fairytale palace and have to answer riddles. Then I will be dressed absolutely perfectly.' She tosses her head and waves a long sleeve at George. 'And if we do, and you insist on carrying that axe and looking totally like a woodcutter's son, I shall have to introduce you as one.'

George's shoulders sink.

An axe?

That's when I notice a new (and rather beautiful) axe, all lumpy in his backpack.

Rhiannon flounces to the back of the cave and sits on a rock, where she starts muttering to herself. She's not actually saying anything coherent, just mumbling, '**Imperium Magis** me a Unicorn.' Over and over.

Oh God! This is not a good start. I turn back to George. 'What do we do?' I whisper.

George points at the tree and the Mercedes. The horn blares on. The razorgrass rattles. The mini tornadoes of dust whirl up and subside. He shakes his head. 'I don't like it,' he says.

I don't like it either. There's an eerie stillness everywhere.

No birds. No leaves quivering on Merlin's Oak. Just the halloo of hunting horns.

My throat goes dry. I feel shaky.

'Pull our hoodies tight over us and head for the hills?' whispers George. He points towards a row of mountains away to the west.

'Is that the way?' I mouth. The thought of leaving the safety of the cave makes me break out in a cold sweat.

He shrugs.

While we're pondering, Rhi joins us. She seems to have calmed down. She sticks her head between ours to look out. 'Let's avoid water. You know, streams and brooks and thingies.'

'Why?' I ask, though the landscape is so burnt up and barren, I don't think that'll be a problem.

'Don't want to get my dress wet,' whispers Rhiannon. 'Velvet doesn't look so awesome when it's all limp.'

George smiles. He puts an arm around her shoulder. 'Hey, sorry for being so negative about your outfit. You look terrific. And you're right. Who knows what we'll encounter.'

I scan the shadows under Merlin's Oak, trying to figure out what Gwyn ap Nudd's next move will be.

What is he waiting for?

Rhi smiles at George. That adoring look rekindles itself in her eyes. She lays her head on his shoulder. 'Thank you. Now I shall introduce you as the hero, if you promise to always be so nice.'

George smiles back. He gives Rhi a hug.

I keep scanning the great tree.

Rhi beams up at George, a big happy smile.

Maybe I'm wrong. Maybe they would make a great pair ...

'Now you have to call me Hero all the time,' George whispers.

'Thing is,' Rhi whispers back, 'I've actually got to look my best, because I've summoned a Unicorn.'

So that's what all that mumbling was about.

Holding on to Rhi, George points with his free hand to a distant elevation in the west. 'We're going to head for that peak. We'll see more from higher up, figure out where the Lady's lake is.'

'When? Now?' I mouth.

George shrugs his shoulders. 'Sooner is better than later,' he mouths in reply.

He's right. I look up at the sky, trying to figure out how many hours of daylight we've got. We ought to go, while it's still light.

Far ahead, above the elevation, the clouds swell and roll

and seem to suck in all the air around them. As silently as we can, we slide out of the cave and tiptoe past Merlin's Oak, past the blaring Mercedes, our eyes darting from the shadows under the tree to the patches of razorgrass.

Nothing stirs.

The razorgrass rattles.

On we creep.

On into the singed landscape.

Twenty-Six

We creep on and on. The sun slides down towards the horizon. A moon rises up on one side. We need to stop and rest, but that's exactly what we shouldn't do. I've met the Hounds of Annwyn, Gwyn ap Nudd's hunting force, before. And as soon as you stop moving, they know. And then they come after you.

Another moon rises over the far hills. And a third follows. In the Grey Lands apparently there's more than one moon! Looks like there's three of them right now. They spiral into a weird sign – a triskele. Not reassuring. Their moonshine is so bright, Gwyn ap Nudd's Wild Hunt will have absolutely no difficulty tracking us.

The air grows chilly. My hands and feet go numb. Darkness begins to creep down from the mountain range. Our shadows grow longer.

It'll be even more dangerous than ever to stop now.

The wind picks up speed. From far away it brings the sound of excited howling. I swallow an ocean of fear. I quicken my pace and stifle a surge of panic. I remember the Cŵn Annwn, those horrible white wolves, the Hounds of Annwyn.[1] And their eerie wailing. They hunt better after sunset. Under my breath, I start to recite the Druids' prayer.

> 'Grant, O Ancient Ones, Thy protection;
> And in protection, strength.
> And in strength, understanding … '

I tell my feet: move faster.

Dodging random tufts of razorgrass and high-stepping over thin-thorned stems makes my legs ache. The constant pressure of small thorns on the soles of my shoes is beginning to allow some of them to poke through. Occasionally a sharp pain stabs into my heel or the ball of my foot. Each little dagger thrust throbs like a hornet sting.

---

1. The Cŵn Annwn, or 'Hounds of Annwyn', are the spectral hounds of the Otherworld. It is said that the howling of these huge dogs foretells death to anyone who hears them. And according to Welsh folklore, their growling is loudest when they are at a distance; as they draw nearer, it grows softer and softer. Their coming is generally seen as a death portent. Just thought you'd like to know that.

Each step is agony.

Oh please let us figure out where the lake is quickly.

It's hard to breathe too. The chlorine stench burns the inside of my nose, right down to the back of my throat. It singes my lungs. Makes my ears ache. I stop and cough. My sinuses feel sore. My larynx raw. My nose flayed. Each breath is laboured.

'Can't we rest?' Rhi hisses.

I sympathise, but I still shake my head.

I don't want to underline it for her, but <u>Gywn ap Nudd is out there with his hounds hunting us</u>. *Can't she hear them?*

Plus there's no way we can rest surrounded by thorns in the howling dark.

Rhi winds her long skirts up and ties them to one side. Her legs are bare. Little tornadoes of flying sand instantly attack her. The trailers with their evil thorns whip out at her ankles.

'Owwww!' wails Rhi. 'My LEGS!'

'Shush,' I hiss.

'I CAN'T SHUSH!' screams Rhi. 'I'M GETTING STUNG TO DEATH!'

'Please try,' I snap.

'AND I CAN'T *BREATHE*,' hollers Rhiannon. 'The air is all DRY and STINGY!'

Poor *annoying* Rhi. Her feet must be absolutely raw.

Those pumps she's wearing can't have kept out anything. But she needs to SUFFER IN SILENCE.

'Keep going,' encourages George. He crosses over and says quietly to me, 'I may have miscalculated distances. That patch of high ground is as far away as ever. It's almost as if we haven't got any closer.'

Great. And just what I was thinking.

'What shall we do?' I whisper.

'I'm spooked,' he admits.

Me too. My pulse is racing. Every hair along my spine is raised. And I've got a V bad feeling it would be very V V unwise to stop anywhere after dark.

'What're you two talking about?' whimpers Rhi.

'Just thinking how we can get to the hills a bit quicker,' I whisper.

'OH GOD YES!' Rhi explodes. 'I vote for that. ORDER ME AN UBER.'

'Shush!' I hiss again. 'The enemy can hear *everything*.'

'We just don't seem to be making a lot of progress,' says George.

'Bit like *Alice in Wonderland*?' whispers Rhiannon. 'I ADORE that book. I'm sure that's what happens to Alice – she doesn't get anywhere, however hard she tries … or something.'

So how do we get there? I point at the hills and throw up my arms hopelessly.

'I think we should take a break,' begs Rhi, 'a LONG, LONG, LONG one and think about it. I'm all itchy and scratchy and stinging and I can't breathe very well and I am going to SIT DOWN.'

Immediately, the twilight is shattered by horns.

Hunting horns that are definitely MUCH closer than before.

'What is the point of telling you to Keep Your Voice Down?' I'm past angry now. 'Can't you hear how close the hunt is?'

She makes a *I am sooo NOT very sorry* face at me.

'We shouldn't stop,' says George, shaking his head, his voice barely audible.

I don't know what to do, or what to say. An icy wind picks up. The temperature drops even further. I shiver. I remember stories of travellers in Fairyland who keep going forever and never get anywhere. I remember stories of those who stop and rest and never get up again.

'And I'm hungry,' moans Rhi.

'OK,' whispers George reluctantly, 'let's make it to that rock and sit and take stock … just for a few minutes.'

'We really should have thought this through ages ago,' says Rhiannon, all snippy.

She's right.

We should have.

But we didn't.

～〉

Well, I've decided.

I'm going to ask some questions.

We all need help, and I need Henry.

So before we reach the rock, I pull out my shard of mirror from its hiding place – tucked into the little pocket of my jeans. I peel off its protective plastic.

And while George is 'taking stock', and Rhi is scratching her legs, soothing her ankles and pulling thorns out of her shoes, I look into the mirror.

Twenty-Seven

In Which Ellie Finds Herself in Halfway House
in the In-Between Place

Before I even blink twice, I am in the In-Between Place.

I sigh with happiness, because I know Henry is here with me.

'Exquisite!' says the voice I've been longing to hear.

I look around. I am once again in Halfway House! Halfway up Snowdon. Halfway between the Mortal World and the Fae Lands.

We're sitting on an old bench in front of a roaring fire. So familiar! Oh God, I remember this from last Christmas so clearly! The room filled with wood smoke. Candle wax burning. The smell of pine logs. Divine.

It's like we've never left.

A blanket is wrapped round both of us. Firelight sparkles off the old slate walls in little dancing flickers. Together we cuddle up tight.

Utterly magical.

'Like old times, isn't it?' he says.

Just what I was thinking!

I look into his dark eyes … and he smiles.

Oh. I. Am. So. Happy.

I smile back, not able to find words. I can hardly breathe, let alone speak. I just smile.

Smile and smile.

'Look at that,' says Henry. He raises his finger and points at the words etched in stone over the fireplace.

Fight Fire With Fire

I peer at the inscription, willing it to reveal its secrets. It was carved into that fireplace long before I met Henry. That's weird, isn't it? It's almost as if the person who put it there knew. As if some destiny hangs over us. Maybe it's something to do with the Shakespeare quote we talked about the last time we were here. What was it again?

> *'Be stirring as the time; be fire with fire;*
> *Threaten the threatener and outface the brow*
> *Of bragging horror.'*

Who is the threatener? I wonder.

It must be Gwyn ap Nudd.

I turn to Henry. 'Gwyn ap Nudd is the one who threatens all of us right now, isn't he?'

Henry pauses. 'Not just Gwyn ap Nudd ... there's still Oswald ... ' He gets up and stokes the fire. Flames race upwards, cinders spark out. Henry comes back to sit by me. He takes my hand and suddenly looks unbearably sad.

'I think we should stop this mission,' he says.

'*Stop?*'

'I had a funny second-sight thing just now,' he says. 'I don't usually get them when I'm in human form.'

'Tell me,' I say, concerned. He looks so upset.

'I saw you. Still and cold. Like a statue made of marble.'

'Did I look good?' I joke.

Henry turns his head away. He doesn't laugh. 'It wasn't *good*, Ellie,' he says very quietly.

'Well, we can't stop.' Right now I'm somewhere in the Fae Lands, all itchy and tired and not knowing what to do. There's no way we can stop.

Henry gets up and paces the floor, from fireside to door to wall to fireside again.

'Just focus with me on how we can threaten Gywn ap Nudd back, will you?' I say. 'The me in the Fae Lands needs help.'

211

Already I can feel that subtle tugging. We don't have much longer.

But threaten him what with?

What is Gwyn ap Nudd scared of? Why is he hunting us? I search my brain and remember the saying: '*Hir yw'r dydd a hir yw'r nos, a hir yw aros Arawn*'; in English: '*Long is the day and long is the night, and long is the waiting of Arawn.*'

Gwyn ap Nudd betrayed Arawn, drove Arawn from his kingdom. And Arawn swore an oath that he or his blood would take the Fae Lands back. Heal it from Gwyn's never-ending fires. Is Gwyn ap Nudd afraid of Arawn, then?

But how can I threaten him with Arawn?

Or Arawn's blood?

Shouldn't be too hard … lol.

Just have to add 'Finding Arawn' to the to-do list.

I look up. *Henry is fading.*

'NO!' I scream. 'What was it you were trying to tell me?'

'HENRY!'

It's no use, he's gone. The fire dies down. The candles snuff out.

The tugging starts for real. Halfway House dissolves.

I never got to ask him why we don't seem to be getting anywhere in the Fae Lands either. Or what we should do …

Or if we will ever be together again.

Like permanently.

Plus what did he mean when he said, '*I saw you. Still and cold. Like a statue made of marble*'?

It sounded scary.

I shiver.

Cold as a statue?

As cold as death.

Twenty-Eight

Time in the In-Between Place appears to take up no time at all.

The others haven't even noticed I've been away.

I steady myself, and try to look like I never left.

I sit tight on the rock. BTW, it is not a lovely smooth granite dome or piece of shiny slate like in my beloved North Wales. It is rough and pointy and uncomfy. Soon the grit from the face of the rock works its way between my fingers and starts to itch. I stand up and pace about. I try not to scratch myself. Then I sit down again.

The others are just as uncomfortable. 'Whose stupid idea was it to head for that hill, anyway?' Rhi complains. 'And why did no one think to bring a sat nav or even a map? You know those *old-school, folded bits of paper thingies*?'

'I know what a map is,' mutters George.

'None of us have got a clue where we're even going!' She throws her hands up in exasperation.

'Shush,' I say.

'It's quite hard—' starts George.

'You're supposed to be a hero, not someone who's finding it "hard".'

'Sorry,' George mumbles.

Rhi shakes her head, scratches her calf and rubs her ankle. 'We need a real hero.'

'We'd better get going,' I whisper. 'Listen.'

They both stop and listen.

Rhi shrugs. 'Nu-thing,' she mouths.

'That's the whole point. When you can't hear the hounds, that means they're very close,' I whisper.

George indicates we should move. Quickly.

'For crying out loud!' snaps Rhi. 'I'm fed up of whispering, and I'm fed up of tiptoeing and I am TOTALLY MEGA fed up of getting all SCRATCHED UP.'

O Holy Mary, Give Me Patience.

'**Imperium Magis** me a REAL HERO – preferably A Knight In Shining Armour On A Horse, so I don't EVER have to tread on a thorn trailer again,' cries Rhi.

No hero appears. Obviously.

But something else does.

Over the brow of the hill they come. Just twenty metres away: a horde of grinning Pookah. Beautiful. Terrible. Slim. Tall. Elfin. Evil.

All carrying bows.

All with arrows drawn.

All aiming straight at us.

I push myself away from the rock and grab Rhi. 'SEE WHAT ALL YOUR YELLING HAS DONE!' I scream at her. Then I shove her ahead of me and shriek, 'RUN!'

Rhi lunges forward, trips on her velvet gown, squeals, whimpers. Then she gathers the velvet up and sprints.

I hover indecisively. The Pookah cheer. They blow their horns.

If I run in a different direction, can I draw the Pookah after me?

'Ellie!' shrieks George.

Over the hill come yet *more* Pookah. Enough to hunt us all down. In every direction.

'Ellie!' screeches George again.

So I run after Rhi and George. Down the crumbling hillside. Dust. Debris. Dirt. Trailers and thorns. Ripped jeans. Ripped skin. Screaming. Gasping.

The air hisses with arrows.

I duck and dodge and skid and scramble.

I hear shouting. It sounds like another human being calling for help. It's not the shrill call of the Pookah. I want to stop and look. *Could be a trick.* The Pookah might be calling out, tricking us into a trap, so that they can pounce, like that hen …

The call comes again, urgent, haunting.

I have to look. I cast a glance behind me. Something is racing away from the Pookah in another direction. I see a flash of white.

Can there be other humans lost and trapped in the Fae Lands?

The Pookah are much closer. They spring towards me: leaping over the razorgrass and paddling the air beneath them; rolling over, only to bounce back on to their feet and high kick towards us.

The silver silk of their clothing flutters like butterfly wings. A dark swarm of pale deadly moths.

Run.

Faster.

I glance at the sky, three white moons spinning, dangerously low, mesmerising, eerie. Instinctively I duck. Then I race on.

I run and RUN.

I fling myself around the spiky acacia-type bushes, round

those deadly slicing tufts, ploughing down the slopes in a flurry of charcoal dust.

Ahead, Rhi and George are moving like the wind. Behind, the hillside rings with terrifying laughter.

The Pookah are really enjoying this!

I have to slow down. Stitch. Pant. Catch my breath. Listen. I hear something howling.

Go again.

In between thorn trailers, zigzag, leap, twist. *What if they catch me?*

Careful! The slope's covered with zillions of trailers. *Don't trip.*

I slide on a pile of pebbles, kick on sand. My lungs can't take this. *No proper air. That smell. Bleach, carbon.*

The stitch in my side stabs deep. *Keep going.* Gasping, coughing, chest burning. I don't let up.

Downhill. On. On. Downhill. I hear something. Crashing. Earthquake?

I glanced over my shoulder again. They're so close. Another arrow hisses by the side of my head. *How can their aim be so poor? Surely their arrows should have hit us by now?*

Perhaps they don't want to kill us?

They like to hunt?

A darker thought: *They want to capture us alive. They want to present us to Gwyn ap Nudd. So he can watch his hounds rip us apart ...*

The Pookah must know Fairyland so much better than us. *Think, Ellie, think!* There must be a reason why they chose this precise place to attack. *They've had all day.*

And why aren't their arrows hitting us?

Are they herding us, corralling us into a trap for some reason?

'Watch out!' I scream at the others. 'May ... be ... a trap.'

The moons spiral ominously in the sky. Dark. Cold. Terribly cold. Keep running.

Then the arrows stop altogether. But the sound of Pookah laughter grows more shrill.

It must be a trap.

Trap or not, I keep going. The soles of my feet are burning-agony. I don't look where I'm running any more. My ankles are ragged, bleeding from slicing encounters with razorgrass. Acid air burns my lungs. My eyes sting.

Huge boulders start to roll past me.

Oh my God. They're launching rocks on us. One boulder comes flying down, bouncing and smashing the undergrowth. It splinters the stones beneath it. It sends up clouds of acrid dust. Slivers of razorgrass swirl in the air. As they fall they slice into my face, the back of my hands. Blood smears into my eyes.

Boulders to the left. Boulders to the right.

They are corralling me.

'Ellie!' shrieks George from down ahead.

Cackling and giggling, hooting and mocking, another rush of stones.

They want us alive.

Oh my God! They want us alive.

I glance behind me. Tall, beautiful, elfin Pookah, laughing and dancing, rolling their stones and clapping their hands.

Then I hear the dogs, the hellhounds. I understand. They are playing with us, waiting until the hounds come, waiting until their master, Gwyn ap Nudd, arrives. Waiting to deliver us up to him. *To certain death.*

I will not be caught so easily. I will not become their plaything. I will not stand before Gwyn and betray Henry or anyone – or do whatever Gwyn has in mind.

I will not.

I will run until I fall.

I race onwards. I close the gap between George and Rhi and myself. I gasp out, 'It's a trap ... '

Ahead there's another flash of white. For a minute I think it's the same white creature-thing that I caught a glimpse of before. But I'm sure it's not. Much bigger.

The white thing moves swiftly towards us, all hazy in

the moonlight. *This is it! We are being driven straight into the arms of some terrible creature.*

George has hold of Rhiannon's hand and is persuading her to jump over something.

Soon I see what. Swamp. Sinkholes. Quicksand. Surrounded by trickles of thick slimy water. And pale dancing phantom things.[1]

And that huge white thing still waiting on the far shore.

'We'll never cross it,' wails Rhi.

'STOP!' I yell. 'LOOK!' I point at the white thing.

'We must. No choice,' George yells. 'I'll attack it when we are over. While you two run!' He pulls out his axe.

We have to cross it or sink in the mire and die.

'Put your feet where I show you,' George instructs Rhiannon.

'I CAN'T,' wails Rhi.

'Yes, YOU CAN,' I holler.

Pale as death, Rhi does as George says. I wait as long as I can. There are not enough footholds for us all to cross together.

When Rhi and George are partway across, I leap from submerged rock to submerged tuft. The balls of my feet

---

1. I remember now: Corpse Candles are 'fairy fires' set by the Pookah. They lead lone travellers off the beaten track to a marsh where the lights are extinguished, leaving the traveller lost. In some parts of Wales, it is also thought that the presence of a Corpse Candle predicts that a funeral will take place very shortly. Ha ha … guess whose.

blaze with thorn poison. Football-size bubbles rise up through the swamp waters and pop, releasing fetid, foul fumes into the twilight, which plume and just as suddenly snuff out. Tricking the eyes. Leaving blackness, blindness.

And the huge swaying white creature stays there waiting, waiting.

Is it Oswald freed from the lair by some fairy magic? I squeeze my eyes tight just for a moment. *Please don't let it be Oswald.*

But instead of a monster, I begin to make out the shape of a plunging, rearing horse – and on its back a pale rider.

My heart jolts. *Death? A funeral in waiting? Henry's premonition?*

But no …

It's not Death. It's a knight? Gleaming armour reflects light from the silvery moons.

Yes, it's definitely a white knight.

A KNIGHT!

What is a knight doing in the Fae Lands?

George makes it across the last sinkhole.

He did it. We can too.

Rhi tries to follow, misses a foothold, screams and trips.

A huge foul thing springs out at her. It's BIG – a kind of flying bat-snake.

'HEEEELP MEEE!' Rhi screams.

The bat-snake whips its tail around Rhi's waist and drags her downwards.

Ohmygodohmygod.

'HEEEELP ... '

OHMYGOD. I watch, unable to do anything. Unable to even think. The thing poises the end of its tail, where a huge scorpion-like sting arches up. OHMYGOD, it's going to sting Rhi and drown her!

The White Knight swoops down on his charger and hurls a lance at the bat-snake. The thing drops Rhi, the lance sticks into the mud and the knight sweeps her to safety.

Thank God. Thank God. Thank God.

I leap and scream and jump and nearly miss my footing ... and there is the White Knight again – a steady arm reaching out to help me too.

'Ahoy! Ahoy!' he calls to something behind me.

I look back, over the treacherous swamp. On the far side the Pookah are milling. Not laughing and cartwheeling any more. But seething in rage. Arrows flying fast and furious. 'Spawn of Arawn, they are our prisoners!' screech the Pookah.

'Yes, but then *I* came and thwarted you!' the White Knight replies.

'Hand them over! We will fight you for them!'

'You will have to catch us first!' taunts the White Knight. He tugs down his visor, pulls his lance out of the swamp and wheels his horse about.

The Pookah howl in fury, spouting obscenities in a torrid rush of their toxic tongue.

'Don't worry,' says the White Knight to us, 'I have no intention of fighting them. But we must hasten and speed away. The Pookah cannot traverse any swamp. Their kind cannot cross running water. But they will seek a way round.'

I breathe a huge sigh of relief.

'Foolish imps! They thought the Will-o'-the-Wisp Marshes would entrap you.'

Scooping Rhi up on to his saddle, the knight heads for a distant tor at full gallop.

George and I follow as best we can.

Behind us, the frustrated wails of the Pookah fill the air.

Twenty-Nine

Beside the tor of rock, we halt. In the gathering darkness, the White Knight dismounts and helps Rhi down.

'Alight, fair maid,' he says quietly. He looks left and right into the darkness, then gallantly bows to me. 'My apologies that my steed could not bear us all.'

I smile. I'm so glad to be away from the Pookah, I really don't mind.

'Thank you. Like SOOOOO much! For saving my life,' says Rhi. 'I'm Rhiannon, by the way.' She does a really showy curtsey and offers him her hand.

'What was that thing?' I ask

'You mean the water leaper? It is an evil creature that lives in that swamp.'[1]

'Right,' I say.

---

[1]. I later found out it was a Llamhigyn Y Dŵr. I hope you never have the misfortune to meet one.

The White Knight bows to me again, then kneels down before Rhiannon, takes her hand and raises it to his lips.

'And you are … ' prompts Rhi softly.

'Ah,' laments the White Knight, 'I wish I knew.' His voice was small, sorrowful and barely audible. 'I do not even know if I am from an honourable line or am entitled to be a knight at all … yet please allow me to be ever at your service.' He kisses Rhiannon's hand and hangs his head.

'How come?' whispers George.

'All I can tell you is, I set out upon a great quest … perhaps … I think … but I am not sure.'

In the moonlight his horse moves off a few steps, searching hopefully for forage amongst the rocks.

'OMG! That's awful!' Rhi looks horrified. 'Were you like … an abandoned child?'

'I do not know.' The White Knight slumps down on a rock and removes his helmet.

A cascade of dark curls surrounds a boyish face. Large dark eyes, pale thin cheeks. Definitely not any older than us. Sixteen max. More like fourteen, maybe. He lays down his rather oversized shield, balancing it on a stone. Emblazoned on it is a red-cross knight kneeling to a maiden.

'Do you want to talk about it?' Rhi whispers. 'I'm a really good listener.'

The silver stallion moves further off, still in search of edible scrub. George is watchful. In the far, dark distance I hear horns and the baying of the Cŵn Annwn.

The White Knight hears it too. 'The Pookah will not circumnavigate the swamp for a while, but they are not the only danger that the hunt may set upon us.' He listens for a few more moments with a trained look on his face. 'Those hounds are hunting some other poor creature, luckily for us – unluckily for it, though.' He makes the sign of the hexagram and whispers up a prayer for the poor hunted creature. Then he removes his gauntlets, arm guards and breastplate. He scratches his shoulder and says with a deep sigh, 'I wish so much to unload my heart.'

Rhi grabs his hand. 'Oh, you can tell me anything, and I'll try my hardest to help.'

George claps him on his shoulder in a yo-bro way. 'Thanks for saving Rhi,' he says. 'We were really struggling to cross that bog. We only just made it.'

The boy-knight smiles, sighs, then looks sad and hopeless. 'There is not so much to tell about me,' he murmurs, 'except that I am haunted by the belief that I once had a quest, one of paramount importance, and that I have betrayed everything and everyone I love by being unable to remember my mission.'

227

'Holy smoke,' whispers George, 'that's bad.'

I shudder. I imagine what it would be like to forget all about Henry, forget all about Snowdon burning.

'Can't you even remember a teeny-weeny, tinsy-winsy bit?' asks Rhi.

The boy-knight shakes his head, despondent. He bites his lip and sniffs.

'Can you remember why you can't remember?' I ask.

'Alas, to my shame, I ate fairy food.' The knight hangs his head. 'I rue that day. I do not know why I ate such accursed fayre. I cannot remember who gave it to me or where. I awoke upon a cold hillside and have been searching forever and ever for who I am and what mission I was upon.'

'OMG!' cries Rhi. 'That's SO SCARY!'

'But I believe I am a Knight at Arms, and thus I must pursue the Pookah, who no doubt are the villains that tricked me into eating their enchanted wares. I was hard upon their trail today and luckily happened upon you all. Thus I was able to rescue this damsel in her hour of distress.' He smiles up at Rhi.

'Thank you so much,' I whisper, 'for being there.'

'That is what I do now: hunt the Pookah and thwart their mischief. I have set myself this task until I remember my true quest.'

'Well, we're really glad you were out thwarting the Pookah today,' I say.

'Yes,' adds George, giving the boy-knight a bro-hug. 'You have my undying gratitude and I hope one day to repay you for it.'

'And what may I ask is your quest in these Grey Lands?' whispers the boy-knight.

I shoot a look at George. He shakes his head. But Rhi beats us to it. 'We're looking for the Lady of the Lake.' She leans in towards the boy-knight and whispers, 'Well, *I'm* actually looking for a Unicorn, cos, like, I totally LOVE Unicorns ...'

'Ah, the enchanted Isle of Avalon.'[2] The boy runs trembling fingers through his curly hair. 'I fear you can only find her mysterious lake through magic – and only then when in great need. This I have learnt in my travels since I – you know – forgot everything... I too searched for the Lady, hoping she would restore my memory to me.'

My heart sinks.

'But what about the Unicorns? Do you—' But before Rhi can finish, there's a horrendous roaring and rattling. 'OH MY GOD!' shrieks Rhiannon. 'WHAT'S THAT?'

The silver steed flings up its head and rolls its eyes till the

---

2. Avalon – or as we call it in Welsh, *Ynys Afallon* or *Ynys Afallach* – actually means 'the isle of fruit/ apple trees'; it is the place where the sword Caledfwlch was forged and later where Arthur was taken to recover from his battle wounds. Avalon is where The Lady of The Lake, Nimue, lives, obvs.

whites show. Then it bolts. The boy-knight's shield topples off the rock and spins down the slope. My heartbeat accelerates into overdrive, and practically shoots out of my body into outer space.

The snorting, roaring, rattling gets louder.

George pulls out his axe.

The boy-knight jumps for his shield, but instead sends his helmet spinning.

The roaring rumbling becomes deafening.

Gwyn ap Nudd?

The boy-knight, bareheaded and without his armour, jumps in front of Rhi and draws his sword. George joins him, brandishing the axe.

I stare at George. He is a good head taller than the boy-knight. And stronger and straighter. I swear since we got into these Grey Lands he's changed. He looks ... well ... different. Almost as if he really is a hero from some long-lost folk legend, with his braided golden hair and his shining axe, silhouetted against a dark sky of three moons.

The roaring and rattling gets A LOT LOUDER.

Rhi jumps up on to a big stone. The ground shakes.

'WHAT IS IT?' screeches Rhi.

George points at something morphing in the twilight. I peer into the darkness.

Out of the dusky distance comes a huge creature, charging at an incredible speed. I close one eye as I try to make it out.

What is it?

It looks a bit like a pig.

Only a lot bigger. A LOT BIGGER.

A wild boar, maybe?

Flipping heck! It's the size of a buffalo, with massive tusks. The creature snorts and oinks. Just like a huge fat dirty pig. The air crackles. The ground quivers.

'RUN!' shrieks Rhi.

The beast lets out a roar.

Stones rattle and skid around us.

'No!' orders the boy-knight. 'We cannot outrun it!'

'DO SOMETHING, THEN!' Rhi hammers her fist on the rock beside her. 'OUCH.'

Moonlight catches the tip of the beast's tusks. They shine with an eerie light.

'OH MY GOD!' wails Rhi.

And still it keeps coming.

'Stay together!' George and the boy-knight step in front of us.

'I think it's the Twrch Trwyth,' says the boy-knight.

'OH NO,' screams Rhi, 'NOT THE TWRCH TRWYTH!'

Thirty

Rhi sucks at her knuckles and whimpers. 'By the way, what the heck is a Twrch Trwyth?'[1]

'Do not fear, ye maidens,' says the boy-knight. 'I promise I will defend you with my life.'

I scramble behind the boulder, pulling Rhi along with me. The Twrch Trwyth, if that's what it is, is still about 300 metres away.

George and the boy-knight ready themselves.

'The Twrch Trwyth is one of Gwyn ap Nudd's evil creatures,' I whisper to Rhi. 'It was in George's book – we saw it when you were looking for Unicorns, remember? Gwyn must've sent the thing to get us.'

I remember something else. It's not about the Twrch

---

1. The Twrch Trwyth is a massive, enchanted boar who Gwyn ap Nudd has special powers over. (Or who has special powers over him. Who cares which way round – they are both TO BE AVOIDED.)

Trwyth. Or Gwyn ap Nudd. It's important, though …
it was in some sort of legend or poem …

'Hold hard!' shouts the boy-knight, his hand on his sword.

We ought to be doing something to help. 'We need to use magic,' I whisper to Rhi, 'to find the Lady. Like *now*.'

Rhi clings to me, whimpering.

'Try not to focus on the pig,' I say. 'Let's try to solve the problem – it's a riddle, and you like them. How do we use magic to find the Lady? Come on, you trained as a witch … '

The Twrch Trwyth is much nearer – 200 metres nearer. My palms go a bit clammy.

'HOW CAN I NOT FOCUS ON THAT DIRTY GREAT BIG PIG THING?' yells Rhi.

'There's still time … maybe … if we can only think of what to do … ' After all, everything must be possible in Fairyland. Right? *Ellie, think. Think.*

Rhi tries to peep out over the rock. I haul her back. 'IT'S STILL COMING,' she weeps.

'Then help me,' I say, trying to comfort her. 'What magic could we use to get to the Lady's lake?'

She buries her head in her hands. 'I only know the summoning spell. That's all I ever learnt doing those beastly witchy things, and that's not going to HELP, is it?'

'OK,' I say. 'OK.'

The pounding of the Twrch Trwyth is *unbelievably loud*. Even the big rock in front of us trembles. I clutch on to Rhi. My stomach twists into knots. The tor beside us shakes dangerously. Stones and dirt skitter across the ground. My heart thumps and crashes around in my chest.

Think, think, think.

'Sorry,' whispers Rhi. 'If we still had that mirror of yours – that was once the Lady's – we could probably look into it and say my summoning spell and … '

'THAT'S IT! I LOVE YOU, RHI!'

'Stay out of sight! The Twrch Trwyth is coming straight for us,' yells George.

He's right. Faster and nearer. Sparks fly from its trotters. Luckily (I suppose) there's no foliage left to burn.

It's now or never.

'I'm scared,' whispers Rhi.

I bite my lip. Cracks open up in the ground. The rocks around us look like they'll tumble and bury us alive.

'Let us slay the beast or die an honourable death,' shouts the boy-knight.

Use the mirror.

'I have a bit of the mirror,' I hiss.

'You do?' says Rhi.

I pull out the shard from the tiny pocket of my jeans.

I give it a speedy polish with my sleeve.

Then I turn my back on the dark hills to the west. I imagine the sweet, sweet smile of the Lady of the Lake. 'What are the summoning words?' I ask Rhi.

'**Imperíum Magís!**' she whispers back.

'**Imperíum Magís!**' I say under my breath. 'Show us the way to the Lady of the Lake.' I hold up the shard, hoping it won't just take me straight to the In-Between Place. *Probably best not to look at the reflected stars?* Or at myself ...

Tilting it slightly at an angle, I look into its shiny surface.

Reflected in the mirror, the distant hills look different somehow – lighter, brighter. The moons over them have a pink and turquoise aura.

The ground is shaking so much, it's hard to hold the shard steady. And it's so tiny ... The noise of the pig drowns out something Rhi is saying.

I gaze into the shiny surface of the looking glass again. The hills behind me zoom closer. There's a river lying before them, bright like a silver snake. I take a step backwards. I follow the river with my eyes. The hills whoosh even closer. I catch a glimpse between them of a sea of golden water, lit by the rays of some distant rising sun. I step back a bit more. It's a lake!

Don't look into the sky, Ellie. Don't try to see Polaris and

Draco ... Don't go to the In-Between Place ...

The ground underfoot breaks up.

Rhi tugs on my arm, her face bone-pale, cheeks wet with tears.

Stay calm. I focus on the lake. It grows larger. Over it, stars sparkle, moons glow and the sun shines in an impossible panorama of night and day.

Rhi grabs me.

'QUICK, HOLD HANDS, LINK UP,' I yell at the boys. 'I KNOW HOW TO GET TO THE LAKE!'

The boy-knight turns. Rhi grabs me around the middle. I reach out over the rock and latch on to George. 'HOLD ON TO ME!' I holler.

One hand is holding the shard. The other is holding on to George. Rhi has my waist.

I can't reach the boy-knight.

The Twrch Trwyth is only about twenty metres off. Its huge greasy head glimmers. Saliva flecks whip back from its enormous mouth.

This has to work.

George tries to reach the boy-knight ...

'You go!' the boy shouts at George. 'You take the maidens to safety. I will slay this beast. It is my desire to do so. It will restore my honour.'

The Twrch Trwyth thunders forward and lowers its head, entering into its final charge mode.

It bellows.

Shale splinters from the rocks.

The earth separates in chasms, sending tremors beneath my feet.

It's too late to reach the boy-knight.

'PLEASE SAVE ME!' screams Rhi.

Using the shard as a guide, I step out backwards. '**ImpERIUM MAGIS!**' I call. *Oh God, let this work. Don't look into the stars.* Rhi and George step with me. We shoot away from the shivering rocks, like on a fast-moving walkway, a superspeed travelator, like in an airport. We speed away from the grunting, away from the Twrch Trwyth.

And away from the brave, lonely boy-knight.

It works!

'We can't go without him,' yells George.

I know we can't.

I look away from the mirror. The acceleration slows and stops. We are very near the lake. 'Stay here, Rhi.' I pull her arms off me. 'You'll be safe.'

'DON'T LEAVE ME!' she cries.

But George and I leave her by the winding river as it

joins the lake and step away. *We have to help that boy. We owe him.* 'I'm sorry,' I yell at Rhi and I turn my back on her.

Now the shard of mirror reflects the stony outcrop and the Twrch Trwyth.

'**IMPERIUM MAGIS** RETURN TO THE PLACE WE LEFT,' I say. We speed back, as if on that same fast conveyor belt, skimming over the landscape. Away from Rhiannon. And miraculously arrive back at the stony outcrop again.

The Twrch Trwyth reaches the rocks. My throat closes up. My heart seems to stop. The boy tosses his curls backwards. Brandishes his sword. My chest goes tight. The Twrch Trwyth is upon him. He strikes. The Twrch Trwyth skids sideways, but rights itself.

I can't breathe. I can't swallow.

Please, all ye Ancient Ones who rule over all worlds, help him.

The brave boy-knight turns to strike again, but as he brings his sword down, the great boar raises its maw. Its bristles drip with poison; its teeth glitter yellow-cream in the moonlight. Its tusks – dull like old ivory, sharper than any blade – spear-thrust forward and rip into the boy with a long painful tearing sound.

There's a soft 'oof', like air escaping. A short scream.

The boy-knight is thrown five metres into the air.

His body twists. It hurtles down towards us.

Over the cracked chasms of dried earth. Over the gritty dusty tor of rock.

Straight at us.

George steps forward, as if to catch him.

There's a dull crunch and piercing screams. George is knocked off his feet. They both hit the ground. There's a ghastly cracking. The boy twists. Moans. Blood spurts.

White bone. Red flesh. Soaking earth.

It's bad.

I don't know what to do.

I DON'T KNOW WHAT TO DO.

'NO!' yells George.

Thank God, George is alive.

The grunting starts again. *Get out. We must get out.* The Twrch Trwyth paws the dirt, lowering its head for another attack.

George springs to his feet. *He's OK.* He picks up the boy's limp body. The boy doesn't moan or move. One side of him is totally mangled. He's seriously, seriously hurt.

Trembling, I hold the shard up. *Just get us all out of here. My hand is shaking. Don't drop it. Don't look into the stars.* I reach for George's hand.

Don't drop it.

The Twrch Trwyth charges again.

'Step with me, George,' I whisper.

I hold on to him. I chew my lip. I adjust the mirror, so I can see the hills reflected in it. 'By the power of your mirror,' I whisper, 'help us find you, Lady of the Lake. **Imperium Magis!**' I blink to keep sudden tears back. *Keep your hand steady. Your eyes dry.* I look for the dark silhouette of the hills behind us. *Blink. Don't cry. Breathe. I must steady my breathing.* I start inching backwards. George follows, cradling the boy-knight in his arms. We zoom into the darkness behind us.

The Twrch Trwyth skids to a halt and bellows. The rocks scatter and crumble into a cloud of dust, like chalk crushed by a sledgehammer.

I hold on to George, as if I'm drowning. 'Keep stepping. I'll guide us,' I whisper. My voice, tiny and broken. I step backwards again.

I sniff. I blink away tears. 'A little to the left.' I steer him. My hand trembles. 'A little to the right.'

Oh God, let the boy be OK.

The Twrch Trwyth grows small. We're speeding away from it. Its roaring fades out.

George squeezes my hand.

There is Rhi. We stop. She sees the boy-knight.

Bone and blood. Pale white face. Dark matted curls.

She wails.

'Step backwards with us, Rhi,' I say. 'Quickly. Hold tight to George.'

We step and step. We follow the winding river. The lake in the shard zips forward and there are the hills, whizzing past us on either side; it's like being on a superspeed flat escalator going backwards.

'Is he gonna be OK?' sobs Rhi, her words faint, broken.

I can't speak. My voice closed up tight inside my throat.

And we are there.

Past the dark hills, at the golden lake.

And the Twrch Trwyth has disappeared.

And the boy-knight is not OK.

Thirty-One

Stung by nettles, stabbed by thorns, we stop on a dark strait of barren land. There's a boat a few metres down the shore line. An old wooden barge. There's a line of hills opposite. And a great water in front.

The boy is not moving. His pulse is faint. He's barely alive.

We struggle towards the shore of the lake, carrying him between us. With what's left of his armour on he's terribly heavy. God knows how George held him for so long. After a few minutes, we stand at the water's edge, looking down at a reedy waterline.

Slow waves frill up on the shingle with such tiny ripples they hardly make a sound. The water is clear blue, with no clouds reflected in its depths.

George sits down in the shallows, holding the boy. Rhi and

I examine his injuries. We scoop handfuls of water up from the lake and bathe away the blood. It's not good. The Twrch Trwyth has gored him deep in his side. The flesh burns bright red. It looks almost poisoned. He's lost a lot of blood.

Without help he won't make it.

We wrap whatever we have around the wounds to staunch the bleeding. The boy-knight opens his eyes and whispers, 'I know this place ... dreams ... ' His face twists in pain.

After a bit he says, 'My horse?'

'It ran off,' I say. The horse and the helmet and the shield tug at my memory again. Some poem we studied in school, maybe ...

'A red-cross knight forever kneel'd to a lady in his shield ... '

'Do you think we should take off the rest of his armour?' says Rhi.

That's it! The Lady of Shallott!

'You'll have to do it, George,' says Rhi. 'It's heavy and, like, you know – boy-parts?'

Who was the knight with the shield in the poem?

The water laps the stones in minuscule quivering waves, tinged pink with blood.

The Lady of Shallott had to break the mirror to connect with the real world and the knight.

And there was a price to pay for that connection.

I remember who the knight was!

'If that shield was always yours, then I think you must be descended from Lancelot?' I whisper to the boy.[1] 'If so, I think there's a way to restore your memory.'

But dare I? If I hold the shard of mirror up and break it, like in the poem, I may never be able to see Henry again ...

And I could be wrong. *It might not work.*

I won't do it. I'll keep the shard all for myself. I'm not obliged to help this boy. After all, he was the one stupid enough to eat fae food. It's all his fault. We didn't ask him to 'rescue' us. We'd have got across the swamp all by ourselves (maybe not Rhi, though, to be fair) anyway *and* escaped from the Twrch Trwyth ...

Shut up, I say to the voice in my head. This is a quest, and heroes don't refuse to help anyone. Before I can change my mind, I hold the mirror shard in front of the boy's eyes. 'Look into it,' I say.

Feebly, he focuses.

I snap the shard.

The boy blinks. Then smiles. Tries to rouse himself, groans in pain, blinks again.

---

1. Lancelot was the son of a king. When Lancelot was an infant, his father was driven from his kingdom by his enemy. Lancelot was carried off by the Lady of the Lake, who raised the child in her magical realm. He was a changeling and his true family name was Llwch Llawwynnauc. He was also known as Lamhcalad, or in legend as Lancelot du Lac. He was one of the good guys. I guessed our Lance is one of his line because he bore the same family crest on his shield as the original Lancelot.

'I remember!' he whispers. 'My family, my bloodline, my quest ... ' His words are faint, so weak. 'I am the heir of Arawn ... I am a true knight ... I am Sir Lance the Seventh ... ' He reaches out and grasps George's hand. 'I remember everything. Avenge me ... fulfil my quest ... vanquish Gwyn ap Nudd ... win back Annwyn ... end all the burning ... the Lady of the Lake ... ' He looks up at the clouds and rallies. 'Thank you, fair maidens, thank you for restoring my honour and my memory and my dignity.' He closes his eyes, then whispers, 'Place me in the barge.'

We look at each other. Should we?

'I think we should,' says Rhi. 'It's his last request.'

I gulp. I hope not.

'How can I win back Annwyn?' asks George, as we bind Lance's wounds as best we can and lay him flat on the planked bottom of the barge.

Lance doesn't answer.

'Sir Lance the Seventh, like in Sir Lancelot of the Round Table?' asks Rhi.

'Yes,' I say, 'apparently.' I bite my lip. My voice is hoarse. *The boy is dying, and my precious mirror shard is never going to work again.*

We cover Lance with a jacket. Rhi sniffs and wipes

her eyes. And we sit there not knowing what else to do. I should be tired. We haven't slept. It's early morning now. I'm numb. I can't seem to catch the reality of it. I keep waiting to find out it's a mistake, some nightmare that we might wake up from.

I shudder.

Poor, poor boy-knight Lance.

It's all so horrible.

Plus there's no island in sight. The Lady of the Lake lives on an island, right? The Fair Isle of Avalon. So we're obviously at the wrong lake. I can't seem to care much. Even the thought of our quest seems unimportant. *Lance is going to die. Nobody was supposed to die.*

The sun rises a bit higher. A path of sparkling droplets twinkles in tiny dazzling lights out over the water.

'I think,' says George, 'this can't be the place … '

'It has to be,' says Rhi, looking at George. 'The summoning spell brought us here.'

Lance lies still and pale in the barge. *The heir of Arawn on a quest to defeat Gwyn ap Nudd.*

Dying.

'We can't give up,' I say. 'We must try to find Nimue.'

We don't speak again of Lance, the brave boy-knight. He's far beyond our help now. He doesn't move or moan.

His pulse is virtually gone; hardly there. Only his wound seems alive, red and burning. He's slipped into a twilight zone. A realm that perhaps waits for us all.

Weirdly, we remove our shoes and socks and start wading in the water, as if we can walk all the way along the twinkling path down to the bottom of the lake and find Nimue. It all feels like it's all happening to someone else really. Rhi weeps quietly. George just stares at the path. *We need to find the Lady of the Lake urgently. She might be able to help Lance.* I truly hope she can. She'll want to, won't she – if she raised him or his ancestor? She'll be so heartbroken …

She probably can't help Lance. We'll probably never find her, anyway. Everything is awful.

We keep on wading into the lake. Nothing seems to happen. Except the water gets deeper.

'Maybe we should call out to her,' I suggest.

'Yep,' says George. He's looking very unhappy about voluntarily drowning.

But how should we call out? 'Maybe we just shout out, "HELLOOO, LA-DEEEE OF THE LAAAKE! ARE YOU THERE?" I mean, we can't use the summoning spell or anything, can we? That'd be kind of rude, wouldn't it?'

The others give me weird looks.

'Whatever,' I say, feeling stupid.

Rhiannon suddenly jumps up and down.. 'We're all such loons,' she says. 'I know exactly how to call out to the Lady of the Lake.'

Thirty-Two

Rhiannon flicks a long lock of hair off her shoulder, tosses her head back, raises her chin …

And starts singing.

Her song is in a language I don't understand. I think it's the song she sang to the Afanc. If not, it's very similar. Its tune: perfect, melodious, tranquil. It touches a place in my heart I didn't know was there. A place that sends a tremor of electricity along my spine. I bite my lip to stop sudden tears.

Rhi, you're so beautiful. You've been so strong and helpful, and you have such a lovely voice. And Lance is dying. And I feel dreadful. You always wanted to be saved by a knight in shining armour … but just not like this …

I sniff. My throat closes up.

I'm ashamed. I've never really rated Rhi enough. I hang

my head. I'm supposed to be her best friend, but I've never pushed her cause with George. The corners of my mouth tremble. I haven't been a good friend. And to hear her now, singing such a sad song in this lonely place – sweeter than any birdsong, yet so haunting it could almost call the dead back from the grave …

I glance across at Lance. *I wish it could.*

George is transfixed. He looks at Rhi, his eyes liquid and dark. He catches his breath. And Rhi keeps on singing.

As the last lamenting tones ring out over the lake, a mist descends around us. I call out to the others, 'Stay together!'

The song stops.

'How could I resist such a beautiful melody?' says a clear, fluid voice.

I spin around. The voice seems to come from the centre of the mist.

'I'm calling to you the only way I know how,' Rhiannon says. 'For you showed me how to steady my heart when I sang, and how the power of music is to be used.'

The mist thins a little, and I see the shadowy outlines of the others. There is someone tall and shimmering standing near Rhi.

In the swirling mist, Rhi curtsies to the shimmering form and continues, 'Since we last met, I've sung that song any time I thought of you, any time I needed strength. I remember how you guided my hands when the action was near, and helped me do the most horrible thing I've ever done – to the sweetest music I've ever sung.'[1]

'Do not relive that moment,' says the Lady of the Lake, 'for you only did what you had to, and you cleared the world of a great scourge. Many still say your name with blessings to this day, as they walk beside the streams and lakes of Snowdonia.'

'I am in need now,' murmurs Rhi sadly.

The Lady nods her head. She already knows. The barge carrying Lance has floated to her feet. She bends and touches Lance's forehead, sighs and whispers, 'You have done well to return him to me.'

The Lady lays her hand on the prow, where a swan's head has been carved. She strokes it and nods sorrowfully. Then she pushes the boat into the mist. It drifts out on the swell, further and further into the flood, until it is just a speck and then nothing.

The Lady silently looks after the barge until it's gone. She seems deep in thought.

'Will he be OK?' I whisper. But I'm thinking: *Shouldn't we have dressed his wounds or done something more?*

---

1. This story of Rhiannon, the Afanc and the Lady is told in Book Two, *Here be Witches.*

'It will be long before he is seen again,' she says.

'He was so brave,' says George. 'I'll never forget him,'

'Then he will always live on,' says the Lady.

Now I'm really worrying. *What's going to happen to him?* 'Where's he gone?' I ask.

I bite my lip. I sniff back tears.

'Is he going to die?' gulps Rhi.

'Even though I have mightier powers than any mage, am wiser than any wizard and stronger than any sorcerer, I cannot hold back the hand of Death – if it is Death that Lance seeks. If not, if he wishes to live, there may be a way ... in Avalon, where the barge will take him ... If the poison of the Twrch Trwyth in him can be countered, time will tell. I will do what I can.'

Her voice is so sweet, so sad. Tears well up anew. How could I have doubted her?

'Take heart,' she says. 'All true friends meet again, either this side of the veil or beyond.'

The Lady puts her arm through Rhi's and kisses her cheek.

The mist thins.

Rhi is weeping. George's eyes are as round as saucers.

The last bluish haze clears and we find ourselves on an island that seems to float in the centre of the lake. I can't tell if the water has flowed around us, or if the shore near where we were standing has floated out, but here we are paddling on the lakeshore of a lush island.

We wade out of the shallows. The rising slopes are one wonderful orchard – myriads of apple trees in fruit and flower. The air is balmy. Gywn's flames haven't touched here.

'Sit down upon this grassy bank and I will bring food and drink to refresh you, for I am sure that your journey through the Grey Lands has wearied you much.'

Warning bells: fairy food!

Yet it is offered by the Lady of the Lake, who's befriended us, who'll try to help Lance. Surely it'd be rude not to trust her?

But then look at what happened to Lance! He must've trusted someone too.

George bows. 'Lady of the Lake,' he says, in a tone I've never heard him use before, 'your beauty and the stories of your generosity are still spoken of in our world, and already you have proved them all true. But I have strict instructions from my grandmother that we must neither eat nor drink on this mission. And out of the deepest respect to her, I must ask you not to offer me or my companions such temptation.'

The Lady of The Lake sighs and laughs at the same time, a golden fragile sound, like someone has run a hand over harp strings.

'You have spoken well, O silver-tongued youth, and already I can see a great destiny marked over you. So with the greatest respect to your grandmother – for you are quite right to be wisely guided by her – I will not tempt you further with the many delicious foods I could offer. However, for your grandmother's future consideration, please tell her that some of us do not lace the fairy food with the draught of forgetfulness. Nor do we wish to abort the missions of serious quests into our realm. Nor keep you chained forever in Fairyland. Some of us are to be trusted.'

A terrifying brightness shines around her as she speaks – so dazzling that I clamp my hands over my eyes and shut them tight.

'Nevertheless, I must insist you offer us nothing,' George says.

'OH MY GOD!' says Rhi. 'You've gone super-sparkly.'

I blink. My eyes water. The intensity of her brilliance actually hurts. I think she's trying to show us she has the power to do anything she likes. She doesn't need to lace our food.

'But again out of respect for my grandmother, I hope you will forgive me,' ends George.

'You are forgiven already.' The Lady laughs. The light around her fades. 'But if I cannot offer you refreshment, what can I give you?

'My Lady, at present I dare not ask you,' says George, 'for I fear I may have offended you with my refusal of food. But there is indeed something, other than the care of Lance, that is in your keeping. I would like to ask you for that a little later.'

'By and by, then,' says the Lady, 'you will tell me your Heart's Desire.'

Your Heart's Desire!

The words jar me awake. Her sing-song voice and George's new fairytale way of speaking were beginning to make me feel weird.

The Heart's Desire!

Those were the terms of the quest. Somehow I'd forgotten.

'If I cannot refresh you here on these grassy banks, then I will take you to my cavern, for all things in our realm have ears. There you can safely tell me more of all the goings-on in the Mortal World, and the occasion that has driven you to seek me out in the Fae Lands.'

Does she really need us to tell her anything?

I look at the Lady again. Is she pretending not to know why we've come? Does she not already see our Hearts' Desires? Does she really know *nothing* of our quest? I want to trust her. She's always helped us before, and she's so kind and graceful and beautiful, but now I'm worried.

What exactly did the Oracle mean?

Did it mean just *my* Heart's Desire or *everybody's*?

Thirty-Three

The Lady of the Lake takes the lead. She guides us into woodland. Young silver birches sway around us. The apple trees are larger here and more gnarled. Ahead are bigger, darker trees. She beckons us on with one willowy wave. The white samite of her robe floats around her, like mist swirling off the mountain. She turns and smiles and says, 'Do not be afraid.'

I give Rhiannon's hand a squeeze, just in case.

George sends me a questioning look.

I shrug my shoulders in response.

We haven't got a lot of choice. If we're going to ask the Lady for the sword, we must trust her. I want to trust her, anyway. And Rhiannon doesn't seem even the tiniest bit scared. That's a good sign, I suppose.

So we follow the Lady. The woods get deeper. The trees

get taller. The air gets damper, earthier and more humid. It smells divine. Such a relief from all that acrid dust. There's faint birdsong too.

Far away, darting along tiny paths, I catch the flick of a tail and hear the echo of a hoof. *Squirrels? Rabbits? Deer?* Until now in the Fae Lands we've not seen grass or trees, or heard birds, or noticed animals other than the horse and the great big horrible pig and the bat-snake thing.

We follow on, tripping over tree roots. I look down to make sure I don't go sprawling, I see mushrooms and ferns and little scuttling things.

When we're deep in the forest, the Lady leads us down a flight of dim grassy steps, through a garden of wild weeds that wave and swirl in hazy darkness, until we reach a great cliff. There in its side is a carved door.

The Lady touches it lightly. It swings open noiselessly, and we step into a bright crystal cave. Shimmering images of a lost world, marvellous creatures, beautiful landscapes and magical skies are carved on every wall.

'Sit down,' she says with a smile. 'Make yourselves comfortable. I would like to hear all about your mission. Yet I must judge for myself if it's something I can support.'

'Fair enough,' I say.

We seat ourselves on sumptuous cushions.

'Though I hope you can help us,' I add, 'because in our land – right now – we've got a really bad problem.' I take a deep breath. Best to get it all out while I can. 'Over there, it's Midsummer's, and someone, I don't know who, has opened a portal and summoned fire on to the mountain. Snowdon's burning and Gran's cottage has been destroyed and probably my mum's farm too … '

I cast a look at George.

He's deep in thought.

'And … ' I flounder.

'And someone has released the Pookah,' George adds at last, a slight break in his voice. 'One of them, anyway, who came through and snatched a child and replaced it with a changed creature.'

'Ah,' sighs the Lady. 'Is it so? Gwyn ap Nudd has hankered for a changeling for a long while now … I think I see his hand in this.'

'He's ALL OVER THIS!' chirps in Rhi. 'And he's scary and horrible. And I think he might be in tight with this "Someone Else".' She makes air quote marks. 'It's probably our worst frenemy, Sheila.' She looks at me.

I nod my head. She's dead right.

'So I hope you can help us,' I add. I'm suddenly aware that she might refuse to … that I'd taken it for granted that she would help. *How can she refuse?* I cast the idea out of my mind. She can't.

'In our land, the Land of the Mortals—' I start again.

'I know your land well,' she murmurs.

I blush – *of course* she does. I'm doing this all wrong.

I take another deep breath. 'Right now, like I said, it's burning, and … '

I can't go on. My voice catches in my throat. I think of Henry trapped under the mountain and how I must help him … must help everyone I love … I think of my beloved hills all aflame … all the little wild things and the mountain flowers … all the people I don't even know, robbed of homes and businesses …

My heart starts pounding.

She might refuse.

I bite my lip, press my palms together and tell myself to calm down.

'I understand. All too well,' says the Lady. 'I have seen everything in my crystals.' She waves a hand towards them. The shimmering carvings on the walls melt and reconfigure. There are pictures of Llanberis and Snowdon, and George and me on the mountain, and Gran's cottage in flames.

So she *did* know everything all along.

Was she just testing us?

'Only the fire of a dragon can put out the flames of Gwyn ap Nudd,' says the Lady, straightening up, 'and the only dragon who can do that is buried deep under Dinas Emrys, held there by Merlin's magic. I quite see your problem. The Red Dragon is unable to quench this fire, because he is still engaged with the White Dragon. He will have to kill his rival first and thus break the curse over them both.'

'Yes,' I say, so glad she understands. 'And he can't kill Oswald, or at least he hasn't been able to yet. We don't have much time, so we've come to see you ... '

'Will you help us?' asks George.

'Perhaps Merlin was wrong to bind those two dragons so completely under Dinas Emrys,' the Lady says thoughtfully.

'But he meant it well,' says Rhi. 'Those two dragons were apparently making a right racket and gobbling up girls and all that – which was not really on, you know.'

The Lady smiles.

I Do Not Roll My Eyes.

But Henry Was Not Gobbling Up Girls.

'So you have come to ask of me the sword, Caledfwlch, so that you may slay the White Dragon once and for all, and release the Red Dragon to save your homeland.'

So does this mean we can borrow the sword?

'We only want you to *loan* us Caledy, obvs,' Rhi says.

'You are right to have travelled here to beg Caledfwlch of me – he is the only sword that can do the work.' The Lady points to a niche in the wall of the cave and there, just where the crystal shimmers in a golden arc, hangs a sword. I squeeze my eyes tight and open them again.

I Am Looking At Caledfwlch.

The legendary Excalibur! Glowing with a strange energy. The one sword that can free my beloved Henry. My heart beats faster. There it is! Caledfwlch!

'But I'm afraid none of you can use it, unless one of you is a wizard?' says the Lady. 'Since the passing of King Arthur, Caledfwlch has been very fussy and will only respond to a wizard's touch. He will punish any who disrespects him. Plus, only a wizard can slay a dragon.'

'Why?' asks Rhi.

'Because only wizards are dragon lords.'

George bows his head. 'None of us are wizards, nor dragon lords, yet perhaps we might find someone who is, someone who would be willing to aid us.'

'That is impossible,' says the Lady, 'for Merlin is the only true wizard here, and he has hidden himself away in a cleft tree.'

I don't correct her. I don't tell her that legends in our lands

262

say it was *she* who imprisoned Merlin in the tree … or that maybe if she *really* wanted to help us, she might consider releasing him or having a quiet word with Caledfwlch?

'Or Gwyn ap Nudd,' she muses. 'He's a wizard too, not a High Mage like Merlin, but still a wizard. Though I think he would be in great peril if he tried to wield Caledfwlch.'

Gywn ap Nudd?

The thought of him with Caledfwlch anywhere near Henry makes my blood run cold.

'You see, once, a long time ago, Gwyn sought to take a child from me. That child was Lancelot, the heir of Arawn, Gwyn's sworn avenger. Gwyn wanted to slaughter the child. I had to call Caledfwlch to my defence; the child was hurt and his blood stained the blade. So Gwyn cannot use Caledfwlch without peril to his life, lest he summon the wrath of Arawn down upon him.'

I understand now.

Lance, the heir of Lancelot, son of Arawn, and his great quest (that he'd forgotten) to free Annwyn of tyranny.

AKA depose Gwyn ap Nudd.

'But tell me,' the Lady says, brushing back a golden strand of hair, 'what did the Oracle set as the terms of your quest?'

She knows already, of course.

If she knows the Oracle set terms, then she must know the details.

She must know all about meeting the Heart's Desire.

Or reaping the Heart's Despair.

Thirty-Four

Best not to second guess her, though. Best to trust her. Best to tell her everything.

'The Oracle set the terms of the quest as the Heart's Desire,' I say, a tight feeling stretching across my chest. 'Maybe because it knew my Heart's Desire is to free Henry.'

'The terms must apply to all those who ally themselves to this quest.' The Lady waves her hand at the crystals. The cavern goes dark and the blackened face of Gwyn ap Nudd appears. Even though I know these crystals are simply scrying, my heart races. I feel blood draining from my veins.

'I will have my Heart's Desire,' hisses Gwyn, *'or you will all burn in hellfire.'*

Images of the Twrch Trwyth appear, its tusks still red with Lance's blood.

'NOOOOOOO!' screeches Rhi.

The tableau changes and there's Gran's cottage going up in flames with Gran screaming and screaming.

'Please stop!' cries George.

The crystals zoom in on the face of the Pookah child released from its chains and laughing.

'Gwyn ap Nudd has a Heart's Desire too,' whispers the Lady. 'He sends his demon creatures to aid him in pursuit of it.'

'What is Gwyn's Heart's Desire?' I ask.

The Lady laughs. 'You are wise, my child, to ask that. Long has Gwyn sought to punish someone he desired and could not have. Since then he seeks in every way to break her heart.'

I think I know who.

'And though he burnt up all of these Fae Lands, though he sends his fires to destroy the Mortal World, he can never have her.'

'But why not?' asks Rhi.

'Because these acts are unlovable,' says the Lady simply. 'And because she loves another.'

'But why is he after *us*?' asks George.

'He has heard that ancient saying: "Long is the day and long is the night, and long is the waiting of Arawn."

266

He fears the return of Arawn. Gwyn knows there will come mortals who will stand against him. And he must destroy any who do so, any who would aid Arawn's line, any who threaten him, any who would put a stop to his burning.'

'Lance is one of Arawn's line, isn't he?' asks Rhi, trying to brush tears off her cheek.

'Yes, he was,' says the Lady. 'Lance had his destiny laid on him a long time ago.' She puts her arm round Rhi to soothe her.

The Lady waves her hand again, and before I have time to work out more about Lance's quest, Sheila appears in the crystals. So lifelike! It's almost as if she's in the cavern with us!

'OMG!' shrieks Rhi.

She's aged somehow since I saw her last. She looks just as chavvy, though (sorry, I don't mean to be like that, but she does).

Sheila looks directly at us. Her eyes narrow. All the smudged make-up around them glitters blue-black. *'I will have my Heart's Desire,'* she hisses. *'Henry will choose ME. And you, Ellie, will be sorry you ever crossed my path.'*

I reel backwards. *Can she see me?*

'COW!' shouts Rhi.

Is this what drives Sheila to hate me so much? That I challenged her right to have any boy she wanted?

'She is the witch who called Gwyn ap Nudd with a blood sacrifice,' says the Lady. She waves her arm again. The crystals reconfigure in swirling lights to show Gwyn ap Nudd and Sheila on a high place among dark clouds; between them is a cauldron suspended over flames. Sheila throws a flower into the cauldron.

'What are they doing?' I ask.

'Preparing a potion,' says the Lady.

'What's it for?' I say.

'To enchant Henry so that Sheila can gain her Heart's Desire.'

'She can't have him!' I scream.

'We will stop them,' says George.

'It can only be done by the Heart's Desire,' the Lady warns. 'Perhaps it is actually Henry's Heart's Desire to vanquish Oswald. Perhaps he does not desire to choose either Ellie or Sheila, nor care at all about Gwyn's flames.'

What does she mean? That's rubbish. How can she even mention Sheila in the same sentence as Henry and me?

'Oswald's desire is definitely to kill Henry,' says George. 'But I've never heard Henry say he wanted to kill Oswald. I think he just wants to be free from the endless battling.'

George is so lovely.

Thank you, George.

The Lady smiles. 'So you can see into the hearts of dragons?'

George blushes. 'No, I cannot. I can only relate my truth as I know it.'

'And you do so boldly,' remarks the Lady.

Rhiannon raises her large brown eyes, as if she's had a Eureka moment. She looks at the Lady of the Lake, full of wonder. 'OMG,' she says, 'you've got a Heart's Desire, haven't you?'

'Should I not have one?' asks the Lady.

I'm almost sure she says 'or two?' under her breath. I'm not really paying attention … I'm thinking of Henry and his Heart's Desire, and Sheila and hers and the potion.

I straighten up a bit. I must listen more closely.

'B-but,' stammers Rhi, 'surely you must have everything – you're beautiful and you've got lots of magic. And can't you just wave your wand and get whatever you want?'

'I wish it were that simple,' says the Lady sadly. 'But sometimes beauty and magic are not enough.' Her eyes seem to focus on something very far away. 'Long ago I loved someone, and if any of you have ever loved, you will know that the heart can never be truly happy until it is with the one it loves.'

'I know,' I whisper. I swallow hard to ease the sudden tightness in my throat.

'I know it too,' says George. He looks at me, his eyes filled with a huge empty hunger.

'I know it as well,' says Rhiannon, and glances at George.

'Then I need not explain,' says the Lady.

'I've been in love with someone,' Rhi goes on, 'for like yonks, for like *ever* really. But he doesn't really rate me, not like that. However hard I try.' She stares away from George in the direction of the Hopeless Truth.

Poor Rhi. It must be really hard for her to say that. She's always been so determined to win George's heart.

I should have helped her more. I've been so mean and possessive.

The Lady takes Rhi's hand. 'Never abandon hope. The future is unknown. Many unlooked-for things can happen there.'

'I wish,' says Rhi in a broken voice.

The Lady smiles sorrowfully.

George looks awkward.

'I will give you Caledfwlch for the duration of your mission, if you can stick to the Oracle's terms,' the Lady announces. 'You will need to fulfil my Heart's Desire to begin with.'

'If you would be so good as to tell us what that is,' says George, trying hard not to look at Rhi, 'I for one will do my best.'

Rhi doesn't say anything because she's sniffing into a bit of her gangly sleeve.

'I will do whatever it takes too,' I add.

'My Heart's Desire is to be reunited once more with Merlin.' The Lady smiles at the thought. The walls of the cavern light up, as if the sun is quickly rising and spilling golden light all around us. The images on the rocky walls flicker and change to grassy banks where wild thyme grows, and the Lady is sitting with her head on Merlin's shoulder. Over them woodbine fronds twirl, and sweet musk roses intertwine to form a bower around them. As we watch, the vista unfolds and takes us to a beach with stretching yellow sands. And there they are, two lovers walking hand in hand beside a wide blue ocean, palms swaying, footprints in the sand.

I stare at the Lady. *So it's true. All the old tales about Nimue and Merlin. The paintings of them and the poems. It's all true.* I pause and think … *Be wary … if the legends are true, then it may also be true that she tricked him and locked him up.*

Which seems an odd thing to do if you love someone.

And a very tricksy thing too.

So why does she need our help?

More tricksy things?

Why can't she just free him to get him back?

'So if you can reunite me with Merlin, then I pledge to you that I will loan you Caledfwlch, for it must be so, if the Oracle has spoken.'

'Oh-kay,' says George slowly.

'But be warned,' says the Lady suddenly, 'you must fulfil *everyone's* Heart's Desire, for such are the terms of the quest. And I no longer know what Merlin's Heart's Desire is.' She sighs as she finishes.

'But like *where* is Merlin these days?' asks Rhi. 'Where's this tree he's stuck in?'

Aw, bless Rhiannon!

Totes awks, but exactly what we need to know.

'I can only set you on your path. You yourselves will have to find him. He may not wish to be found. You may search in vain. But be on your guard and know that if you do find him, I quarrelled with him a long time ago – just a lovers' tiff, but I was proud and strong in those days, and he would not do as I desired, so I imprisoned him in a cavern and sealed it within a cleft tree in a hidden grove. The magic I wrought was of the highest order, and I threw the spell book and the key away, so that I could never undo the curse upon him.'

'Wow!' says Rhi. 'That was like a bit HARSH.'

The Lady does not take offence but smiles at Rhi. 'Yes,' she says. 'I was passionate and rageful.'

'I get like that too,' says Rhi, 'but I'm trying hard to deal with it. You should try mindfulness. It's really cool and you get to calm down. It's helped me not to do noodle stomps.'

'For many a long lonely year, I have regretted my rage,' says the Lady.

'But surely,' says Rhi, 'where there is true love … there must be a way?'

'I believed so, but as the centuries went by, I feared that even if I *could* undo his imprisonment, he would not forgive me.'

'CENTURIES?' cries Rhi. 'THAT IS LIKE MEGA MAJOR NOODLE STOMPING!'

'Perhaps you have all been sent to me by a higher power; perhaps the time is at last right for Merlin and me.' She smiles.

The unseen sun on the cavern walls sets and covers the rocks in a rosy glow.

'OK,' I say, 'so we have to find Merlin, break the spell over him, convince him to forgive you, plus wield the sword for us and kill Oswald. Anything else?'

'There is something else,' says the Lady. 'But that Heart's Desire is already fulfilled.'

'Should be a walk in the park, then,' George whispers to me.

'Shush,' I whisper back.

The Lady laughs. 'It will certainly test you,' she says, as if she knows something that we all don't.

The Lady of the Lake stands up and bows to us.

Our time with her is over.

Our mission is set.

'Do not forget,' she says, 'return Caledfwlch and his scabbard to me when your quest is won.'

'We will remember,' says George.

The Lady holds up her hand in a gesture of farewell. Her sleeve of white samite falls away from her arm. She blows gently across her flattened palm, as if she is blowing us a kiss. A great wind rushes from her open hand.

A hurricane surrounds us, and I spin. Wind rushes past my ears in a funnel of energy, yet I hear the Lady say, *'Do not be surprised at anything, Ellie. These are the Fae Lands where all things are possible. You sacrificed seeing Henry again when you used the last shard of my charmed mirror to save the dignity and honour of my darling child, Lance. Your act was selfless and noble. You shall be rewarded for that.'*

I feel myself picked up, spun and squeezed, as if I am

being shunted through a very narrow passage and stretched out. It's kind of weird and very, very cold.

I should be hanging on to the others, as we did at the roundabout, but it's too late. We've forgotten to join hands. *Maybe I won't find them again. Maybe the Lady has separated me from them on purpose.* The spinning reaches a crescendo. *I'm going to be sick.* All the air spins out of my lungs. I start to panic.

What's happening?

Thirty-Five

In Which Ellie Finds Herself in a Realm That Is Not the In-Between Place

I am standing on the winding path leading to Dinas Emrys from the National Trust car park. Why am I here? This isn't Merlin's Grove.

This is near Henry's resting place.

The Lady said I would be rewarded. *Maybe I'll get to see Henry?* I set out for the top of Dinas Emrys. *Maybe he'll be there waiting for me.* I make it to the slopes above his buried cave. I pause. Catch my breath. Breathe in warm air.

I look up towards Snowdon. I think it's Snowdon. I can't be sure. Everywhere is so thick with brilliance, but through the blinding sunshine, blurred by the shimmer of heat, I'm certain I see a figure.

Rhi? George?

No. It's a young man poised on the edge of the mountain.

Henry?

I rub my eyes. *Oh I wish.* But how can it be? *Please let it be him.* My shard of mirror is broken. There is no way I can get back to the In-Between Place. Maybe it's just a trick of the light? *Or maybe it's my reward?* I squint to see better. Rays of sun dazzle me. I can't see anything. My heart starts pounding. Please let it be Henry.

'Henry, is it you?'

I check around me. No one. I exhale, twist up my lips, swallow hard.

'Remember this time and place,' says Henry.

OMG! I nearly jump out of my skin.

It is Henry!

I tremble all over. I'd know his voice even after death!

My pulse starts dancing. I wheel around. 'You're here!' I shout, looking wildly around for him.

'Yes, I'm here,' he says.

And suddenly there he is. *Right beside me!*

It's all very weird, but I don't care. I throw my arms around him. A lovely shiver runs right through me. Electric. Awesome. This is just where I want to be. Always. Always. Anywhere with Henry.

'How did you *do* that?' I cry out. 'Just appear?'

'I'll show you,' he says.

'You know how to do everything!' I say.

'Yes,' he says simply. 'Dragons have skills.'

'Tell me,' I say, hugging him.

'You just have to focus,' says Henry. He hugs me back. I quiver all over. 'Focus with all the power of your mind. Imagine yourself in the place you want to be. See your hands, your arms, your feet. Feel your hair, your face – anything to focus on bringing yourself to the place you've set your heart on.'

'I've set my heart on being with you,' I say. I'm so happy. My heart pumps. Strange, half excited, half terrified. I squeeze my eyes tight, and then I flick them open. HE'S STILL HERE!

He laughs. 'It's not a random thing that brings us to Dinas Emrys, though. It means there's something new about this place we ought to understand.'

'Well, come on,' I say, 'Mr Dragon Skills, tell us.'

'I think I told you once that seeing into the future is not so simple. It is like the parable about the blind men and the elephant. Reality is relative. What I see may not be what another sees. If we act on such limited visions we may change what will be. We may bring our Heart's Despair upon us.'

I go cold.

Heart's Despair.

I'd been trying to forget about that bit of the Oracle's terms.

I squint up towards the summit of the mountain. But it's not there. All the brilliance has clouded over. My heart drops. I know what's coming. I glance over at Llyn Dinas. Its deep, shadowy, turquoise depths warn me.

Henry puts his arm around me. I stare up at him. His grip on my shoulder tightens. 'Over there,' he hisses.

I turn my face away from him and look up at the slope behind us. The clouds are closing in.

'Not that way.'

His grip on my shoulder weakens. I whip my head around.

HENRY!

He's fading.

All the fiery loveliness of him is evaporating.

He struggles to speak ... 'Look down there.'

If only I can follow him wherever he's fading out to. I see my hands, my arms, my feet, my hair. I focus on being anywhere Henry is. I stare at the place where he was sitting, willing myself to follow him, hoping it will work.

I close my eyes. *Let me see him.* I open them.

Instead I see SHEILA!

Just down the hill. Just a stone's throw from where I'm sitting. Storm clouds swirl around her.

'I will have your heart,' she mutters. 'You will love me alone, more than that minger Ellie. I will have you, Henry. You will see.'

She collects something from the hillside.

She holds it up to the light and shrieks. She drops it.

I feel myself fading. *Focus on staying here. She'll get Henry over my dead body!*

I close my eyes, focus on my feet and hands and heart. I steady myself and open my eyes, but Sheila has gone.

Then I look for what scared her. I pick it up. It's a little straw effigy.

And I remember. *I came here last Beltane, to do crogi gwr gwellt – hang a straw man!*

It's a tradition on May Eve that when a lover has lost their sweetheart they make a man out of straw and put it somewhere in the vicinity of where the lover sleeps.

The straw man guards the beloved from the one that seeks to take their heart away.

My straw man has frightened Sheila off. My straw man is powerful. I select a wide straw from over the straw man's heart and work it loose. I'm going to keep it. In my mind I imagine blowing down the heart-straw, blowing evil away from Henry. Blowing Sheila off the side of Dinas Emrys.

Then I place the figurine back over Henry's resting place. 'Stay there; you are needed,' I tell it.

I recite the words from last spring, as best as I can.

'By water and fire, earth and air,

Let Henry's enemies beware.

Keep him safe from those that plot

To take his heart from this spot.'

I use all my focus.

Done.

And then I feel myself fading again.

Fading out.

Thirty-Six

We're running. Fast.

In the dark.

On the dry acrid plains.

Back with the razorgrass. Back leaping the low, deadly spike bushes. Back to being torn to shreds by tiny thorn trailers. Back to the heat. Back to the fear.

Me, George and Rhiannon.

I'm sprinting. They're sprinting. Red faces. Breath laboured. Legs burning with the running.

They don't seem to have missed me.

'What is it?' I say. I've missed something important. Like why are we running?

Rhi shoots me a really funny look, her face strained in the stark moonlight. She mouths, '*Whaaaat?*'

George gasps out between chest-heaves, 'Can't you hear them?'

I listen, sides aching. Over the noise of shoes crunching charcoal underfoot, over the sound of rushing air, over the sound of my blood pounding in my ears, I hear them.

The Cŵn Annwn.

From Nimue's haven, we've re-entered the hostile world of the Fae Lands at a *really* bad time, then? Or is it always like this? Always hostile, always hunted, always afraid.

'I can't run any faster!' shrieks Rhi.

A long escarpment stretches beside us on our left. Craggy cliffs. Unscaleable heights ...

I scan them as best I can. I see a shadow carved out down a cliff. A way through, maybe?

'That way!' I yell.

'But that's UPHILL!' screams Rhi.

'There,' I point.

Closer up, we see it: a sort of creek, a pass, a narrow passageway between steep cliffs. Perhaps once a stream flowed there. Before this place became a desert.

It might work ...

'Get there. Battle ... of ... Thermopylae,' I pant.

If we can get through the pass, we might stand a chance. No choice. We can't outrun the Cŵn Annwn for long. But up there we could topple the overhanging cliff edge down on to the hounds maybe ... hopefully ... Or take them on one at a time? The whole pack can't squeeze into that narrow pass at one go. Can they?

'OK,' yells George.

Uphill, though, and a few hundred metres away.

Rhi is really slowing down. 'Come on, bestie,' I urge, 'we can do this.'

'I can't,' she pants. 'You go on … '

'Yes, you can.' I grab her hand. 'We can defend that place like the Spartans did at Thermopylae.'

'They lost, you IDIOT. The Greeks LOST at Thermopylae!'

Yeah. That's true. But they held out a while … 'TRUST ME!' I yell. 'GET THERE!'

Somehow the three of us make it to the pass. But it turns out to be only a long fissure through the hillside and a dead end. Not a pass at all.

'IDIOT! IDIOT!' screams Rhi again. 'I TRUSTED YOU!'

It's too late. We're trapped.

'We should scale the cliff,' says George. 'C'mon.' He kicks out a few toeholds and starts upwards.

'You next, Rhi,' I say. 'I'll push from below; George can haul you from above.'

'I CAN'T DO THIS!' wails Rhi.

I shove her up against the cliff face and shout, 'CLIMB! OR I'll RIP YOU TO BITS MYSELF!'

Rhi whimpers and finds the toeholds. George gouges out more for her.

And we climb.

We hold rocks. We shove toes into cracks. We scrabble. We slip. We push. We haul. We pull. We bully. We slide. We scream. We curse. We weep.

Fingers scrape. Blood smears. Nails break. Rocks fall. Toes bruise. Muscles strain. Lungs exhale. Sweat runs.

But we make it to a ledge halfway up, shivering heaps of jelly legs, jelly arms, jelly chests. We sit all scrunched up, shaking, breathless.

Beside us is a great rock balanced on the ledge. Rhi looks at it and whimpers. George looks at it and smiles.

'If I can dislodge that down on to them, it'll topple all the loose debris from those overhanging bits below.' He flexes his biceps and examines the rock, as if weighing up if he's strong enough to bring this section of the escarpment crashing down.

Rhi sniffs and wipes her hands on the inside of her dress. She catches sight of the soiled velvet and wails.

'They won't be able to climb up here,' I reassure her.

'What if there are Pookah?' she sobs.

'Let's not scare ourselves,' I say.

The baying in the distance has gone quiet. That's ominous.

'They're very close now,' I whisper. We peer in the direction where we last heard howling.

And there they are! Cascading towards us in a ghostly flood.

The lead hound is the hugest of them all – terrifyingly beastly, like some Otherworld demon with horns – and it's racing like the wind, heading straight for our narrow pass.

Rhi starts sobbing again. I hold her hand tight. 'It's OK,' I say. 'They really *can't* climb this cliff.'

'But what if they get up above us and drop rocks down like the Pookah did?'

'Two can play at dropping rocks,' I say.

I squint into the distance again. The darkness ripples in shadows; a night mist hovers over the plain. The pack glimmers and morphs. The lead hound, that strange monstrous creature, is much taller than the others, as large as a horse. It flickers and merges into the mist, all blur, shining almost silver in the light from the three moons overhead.

I shiver despite the sweat still streaming off me. The mist swirls around the pack. Such speed! Impossible to see clearly. Then I lose sight of all of them completely as a stony outcrop blocks my view.

'Get ready,' says George. He places his hand on the huge

boulder; then, realising it'll take more than a quick shove, places his back to it. 'You'll have to help me time it. I can't look and push.'

'What's the plan?' I whisper.

'We'll crash this rock down on that lead hound and smash it to bits. That'll make the rest of the pack think twice.' His voice is barely audible.

'OK,' I say. 'Rhi, you ready?'

George braces himself against the boulder. 'Tell me when to shove.' He starts rocking it back and forth.

'OK … about thirty seconds … ' I whisper. 'They're rounding into the pass … out of view now … I can still see moonshadows … '

'OK,' mouths George.

'Get ready … '

George nods.

Timing is everything. I see the flash of shadows racing across the far side of the pass. 'Ten, nine, eight … ' I say, ticking the seconds off on my fingers. But just as I get to 'three, two, one … ' Rhi shoves her hand across my mouth, so flipping hard it hurts.

'NOOOO!' she screams.

'WHAT?' George yells.

I rip her hand off. 'PUSH!' I shout.

We're out of sync.

We've missed the moment.

George pushes anyway. The boulder budges, rocks, teeters.

'WHAT THE HELL DID YOU DO THAT FOR?' I yell at Rhi.

'Because ... LOOK!' Rhi points at the racing moonshadows. The lead hound comes into view around the corner, and I see it is not a lead hound at all.

George heaves. Sweat breaks out on his brow.

And the teetering, tottering boulder tips in slow-motion ...

And rolls ...

And pauses ... rolls some more ... then crashes down.

Straight into the path of a racing, full-grown, fleet-footed, beautiful Unicorn.

Thirty-Seven

Down the boulder bounces, smacking the surface of the cliff, bringing with it showers of loose stones, soil, dust, debris.

Rhi screams.

On the Unicorn races. OhmyGOD!

OHMYGOD!

But the boulder misses the shining Unicorn by a flick of the tail, and instead hits the passageway behind her, blocking the path of the white wolves.

Rhiannon screams in joy. Then she starts slithering back down the rock face.

At the dead end of the passageway, the Unicorn slides to a stop, rears up on her hind legs and lets out the most piteous sound. She turns and sees the pass blocked behind her and then raises her eyes up – to Rhiannon, holding her arms wide and literally skimming down to greet her.

The white wolves begin howling as they realise their prey has got away.

By the time George and I have reached her, Rhiannon is standing beside the Unicorn, a look of rapture on her face.

The Unicorn's head is low and trembling. Her flanks heave, shiny with sweat; nostrils quivering, snorting in the moonlight.

'OMG!' shrieks Rhi. 'OHMYGOD! OHMYGOD! OH MY GOD!'

'Rhi,' I say, 'I'm sorry. I'M SO SORRY.'

'YOU NEARLY KILLED HER!' screams Rhi.

'I know,' I say. 'And I'm SOOOOO glad I didn't and I'm so, so sorry.'

The Unicorn reaches out her muzzle and gently nuzzles Rhi.

'OMG!' cries Rhi. 'OHMYGOD! OHMYGOD! OHMYGOD! I'm being nuzzled by a UNICORN!'

'We thought those hounds were after us,' says George to the Unicorn. 'How long have they been hunting you?'

'Ever since the beautiful maiden called me,' pants the Unicorn.

OMG! A Unicorn that talks!

'Called you?' asks Rhi, as if a talking Unicorn is normal!

'When a virgin calls to me with words of power ... in her love and need ... I will always come.'

'Wow!' says George.

'Virgin?' I hiss at Rhi. 'I thought you said ... ?'

Rhi scowls at me. Then glances at George.

'Oh-kaaay,' I say. So all her hype about *things* was fantasy!

'But the white wolves?' asks George.

'When I set out to find you, the Cŵn Annwn knew ... They heard the fair one calling to me too.'

I roll my eyes. (I can't help it.)

'They knew I would lead them to you ... ' The Unicorn gasps and heaves, clouds of air shooting from her nostrils. 'I have raced far and wide ... tried to mislead them ... so that you could be safe ... even risking my life ... When the Cŵn Annwn knew I was leading them on a chase ... they set their teeth to kill me ... '

Rhi shrieks.

'But the words of power held me ... I was obliged to find you.'

'Oh, I'm so MEGA happy you did!' says Rhi, flinging her arms around the Unicorn. 'I'd almost given up hope.'

'And ... thank you.' The Unicorn nuzzles Rhi again. 'Thank you ... for saving me.'

'Well,' says George, 'I'm not sure we did ... it sounds like we were the cause of your ordeal.'

The Unicorn stops quivering, lifts her head and looks at George with sad, knowing eyes. 'There is a wisdom in the universe,' she whispers. 'You called me and rescued me for a reason.'

'Maybe it was to ask you to help us put out the fires on Snowdon … ' I start.

'Of this I know nothing. And in knowing nothing, I know everything,' the Unicorn adds cryptically.

'But … ' I say.

'I can only tell you this. Three firestones there are and three spiritual wisdoms: As above. So below. So mote it be.'[1]

'Oh, it's a RIDDLE!' screeches Rhi. 'I utterly, utterly LOVE riddles.'

The Unicorn nuzzles Rhi again. 'There is something I must give you, little one, before we part. Look inside my mane.'

'Part?' says Rhi.

'I want to thank you for saving me by offering a precious gift, for that is the Way of the Unicorn.'

Rhi searches the tide of silver hair flowing down the Unicorn's neck. Woven inside a lock is a tiny, shiny white box, hardly bigger than an acorn.

---

1. I'll be rubbish at explaining this, but witches use those words when casting spells. They were written on the Emerald Tablet and are also used by alchemists. They explain the spiritual and physical duality of existence. 'As above' refers to the spiritual realm. 'So below' refers to the physical realm. The idea is that these two realms are linked, but not adjacently. Got it? Not sure how that helps us put the fires out? Me neither.

'That, my dearest,' says the Unicorn, 'is for you, for your love and for rescuing a Unicorn from certain death. Please accept a Unicorn's gratitude. It is a box made of fairy silver. Inside it are three tiny eggs. Protect them carefully for now, for from those eggs will hatch three songbirds and they will be known from this moment on as the Birds of Rhiannon.'[2] The Unicorn trembles and nuzzles Rhi again. 'You have always wished to see me; you have believed in me and loved Unicorns for so long. Such a love as yours is treasured.'

'Oooohhhhhhh WOOOOWEEEEEEEE,' whispers Rhi. 'All for me?'

'Guard the eggs well. Use them when your need is greatest and your hour darkest. And look for me in that dark time – call to me with the words of power. Whatever realm you are in, I will come to you. I am bound to come until I have saved your life in return.'

Rhiannon is sniffing. She looks as if she's about to burst into tears. 'Oh, thank you SOOOOOOO much,' she says. 'I'm so sorry for calling you, and making you all scared and tired, but I've always wanted a Unicorn. Though I know you're not a pet or anything like that, I've always wanted to plait a Unicorn's hair.'

---

2. The Birds of Rhiannon, the *Adar Rhiannon*, appear in the Second Branch of the *Mabinogion*. They are described as 'they that wake the dead and lull the living to sleep'. They are connected to Rhiannon, who is thought to be a horse goddess of Welsh mythology(!).

I close my eyes and roll them upwards.

Oh My Days.

Note to self 1: You Are Trying to Be Nicer (Good. Pat Self on Back).

Note to self 2: Try Hard Not to Die of Embarrassment (Try Very Hard).

Note to self 3: Try Even Harder Not to Think People (Rhi) Are Cringe.

Weirdly, though, the Unicorn seems genuinely pleased. 'I always know those that truly love us. You may braid my mane if you wish.'

'OH MY GOD,' says Rhi. '*OH MY GOD!*' and throws her arms around the Unicorn's neck all over again.

A gust of air sets little wispy twisters off in the dust. I shrug. Maybe I'm just too uptight?

I squint up at the cliffs. Dark, shadowy, blackened rock. Twisted, spooky, barbed bushes; dust, cinder, ashes. Moonlight and shadows. And behind us, the unseen, wailing wolves.

Overhead, huge menacing clouds climb upwards towards the three moons.

'Erm ... ' George looks at me and taps an imaginary watch on his wrist.

Rhi strokes the Unicorn and plaits away.

'We need to think of a way out of here, maybe?' I suggest.

'And the way back is sort of blocked,' adds George.

'And the way up is sort of high,' I say.

'There is another way,' says the Unicorn. 'For always when one door closes, another opens.' She nods her head, all Zen-like.

'OK,' I say hopefully, 'I guess the stream that carved this pass must have come from somewhere.'

'The sides of the escarpment?' suggests George.

I shake my head. I remember from geography that most escarpments are made of porous stone, with a harder, more resistant cap rock on the top. Rain doesn't pour off them much. It sinks through cracks.

'It came from underground, I think,' I say.

'How do you know?' challenges Rhi.

'Because I've been getting an A* in geography like *forever*,' I say.

George starts exploring the head of the pass.

I draw closer to the beautiful Unicorn. 'We're trying to find Merlin,' I whisper to her, hoping enemy ears won't hear me. 'You wouldn't happen to know the way, would you?'

'All ways lead to your destination,' replies the Unicorn inscrutably.

'OK,' I say, 'but is there maybe like a shortcut? Is one way quicker than another? We haven't got a lot of time –

the fires from here have got through to our world …
and … they're burning … '

'Only the pure in heart find that the way opens to them,'
says the Unicorn, bowing her head.

George makes a stifled whoop before I can press her more.

'Come and see!' He beckons to us, suddenly excited. He
points to some thick thorn bushes and gesticulates. 'There's an
entrance to some kind of underground watercourse up here!'

'Then that is your way,' the Unicorn says, nodding.

'But … ' I hiss, 'what if it has sheer drops, or there's a
raging river down there?'

'Well, I can't climb those cliffs again,' states Rhi. 'And
Uni says that's the way to go.' She rolls her eyes at me. 'So
unless you've got a better idea … ?'

I shake my head.

'I will leave you, then,' says the Unicorn.

'Oh!' cries Rhi. 'I thought you'd come too?'

'Your way lies under. Mine lies over.' She tosses her head
in the direction of the high cap rock of the escarpment.

'Must you really go?' wails Rhi.

'Look around you.' The Unicorn points to the shadowy
wasteland of the hills. 'This is what the fires of Annwyn do.'

It's true. We must go. And quickly. Those fires are still
raging on Snowdon.

Rhi sniffs and hugs the Unicorn tight.

The hounds howl at the moons. Rhi sobs and lets her go. The Unicorn inclines her noble head and then bounds her way – agile, effortlessly – up the cliff sides, like a magical mountain goat. We watch, breath held.

Then together (carefully) we hack aside the thorn bushes with axe and fingers and feet.

And step into the unknown.

Thirty-Eight

We're plunged into darkness. My heartbeat shoots into overdrive.

'Wait!' hisses George. 'Don't move.' He pulls out his phone and puts the torch on. 'Let's try to educate ourselves a bit, before it's too late.'

He pulls out his tattered copy of *A Study of the Fauna, Flora and Inhabitants of Annwyn*. He looks at the contents page. 'Underground creatures of Annwyn,' he mutters. 'That should do.' He flicks forward in the book until he finds the relevant pages.

'What does it say?' Rhiannon gets out her mobile too.

'We've got a bit of a choice,' says George.

'We should keep moving,' I say, glancing back towards the blocked pass. 'I'm not sure how long our rockfall will keep the hounds out. And we should conserve our phone batteries.'

Rhi flicks her mobile off.

'*Morgans are Welsh water spirits that drown people,*' George reads. '*They may lure victims to their death by their sylphic beauty, or with glimpses of underwater paradises. They can tempt you with treasure or riches or visions of your Heart's Desires. The Morgans are eternally young and beautiful.*'

'Oooh, like mermaids,' whispers Rhi. 'I love mermaids.'

'They haven't got your best interests at heart, though,' I remind her.

'Huh! Says you!' Rhi tosses her head at me. 'Who says they drown people? Maybe they actually give you your Heart's Desire.'

'And there's the Ceffyl Dŵr,' George continues. '*A water horse believed to shapeshift and even fly, it has fiery eyes and is dark and forbidding. The Ceffyl Dŵr likes mountain pools, waterfalls and underground rivers best. Even though it appears solid, it can evaporate into the mist. As a horse, it leaps out of the water to trample and kill travellers, though sometimes the Ceffyl Dŵr entices unwary travellers to ride him. Flying into the air, the Ceffyl Dŵr evaporates, dropping the unfortunate riders to their death.*'

Fabulous. Dying to meet one.

'What does the book say about finding Merlin?' I ask.

'Nothing,' says George, 'but it does say something about

Caledfwlch. Not that I suppose we shall ever get it now, if we can't find Merlin.'

'What does it say?' I ask, determined to stay positive.

'That the scabbard is as powerful as the sword and that those who wear it will not die from wounds inflicted in battle. It actually says: *The scabbard is worth ten of the swords, for while ye have the scabbard upon you, ye shall never lack life blood, however much be shed and however sore ye be wounded; therefore keep well the scabbard always with you.*'

'Handy,' I say, 'if one was a medieval knight in battle.'

In the dark shadows of the torchlight, I see George shrug. 'Oh well … ' he says, then pockets the book.

Rhi puts her hands together in prayer form. '**Imperium Magis** Merlin. Namaste. Please!' she calls. When Merlin doesn't instantly appear, she adds, 'Well, at least he knows we're coming.'

'And so do the Morgans and the Ceffyl Dŵr now,' I add.

Rhi shrugs and hisses, 'Well, we've got to TRY.'

I shake my head. I am pretty sure trying to summon Merlin with a two-word witchy spell might annoy him. After all, he is a great magician. On the other hand, I do not have a clue how we're going to find him – so any attempt is better than nothing, I suppose.

'Let's at least get going and put some distance between us

and the Cŵn Annwn,' says George. 'If we're lucky and we
hit water, that'll put them off the scent.'

The passage in front of us twists round a few turns, then
begins to descend. Down we go. Down for a long time
before it becomes level again. I'm worried. All twitchy and
super-alert. The air down here is hot, stifling, and we can't
see anything outside the gleam of the mobile torch app.
George leads the way and swings the beam forward into
the unknown, then backwards to light our steps.

The path stays mostly level and widens out. Very soon
we find ourselves faced by a swift-moving stream.

'Bingo!' cheers George.

'I really HATE water!' moans Rhi. 'My dress is going to be
TOTALLY ruined now.'

'Sorry,' I say, 'but we'll have to wade through it.'

'Along it, I think,' whispers George. He sticks his axe
into the flow to test the depth. 'It's OK – quite shallow.'

The air is fresher by the stream. But I suddenly feel really
thirsty. God, I wish we could drink it. But Gran's warning
pounds like a migraine at the back of my brain: DO NOT
EAT OR DRINK IN FAIRYLAND.

'Which direction?' I ask. 'Upstream or down? What if the
stream divides further on?'

'I've got an idea!' squeaks Rhi. 'I picked some leaves off

Merlin's Oak – let's say the summoning words and throw them into the stream! The magic should make them lead us to Merlin.'

'Brilliant!' whispers George. 'Inspirational!'

Rhi rummages around in her pocket and pulls out three oak leaves. 'Shine the light on them while I put them in the water,' she whispers. Then she bends down. **Imperium Magis!** Oak leaves from Merlin's Tree, lead us to Merlin.'

In the torchlight the three leaves swirl in spirals, leaving ripple trails like a triskele. They do not instantly float away, but seem to wait for us. I roll up my jeans as far as possible, Rhi hitches up her dress and we step into the water. (George doesn't bother.)

The leaves float ahead.

We follow.

When we flag, the leaves swirl and wait.

The magic is actually working! My heartbeat returns to normal. We will find Merlin. All will be well. He'll agree to help us defeat Oswald. He'll agree to wield the sword for us. He'll agree to get back with Nimue. We'll get the sword. We'll kill Oswald. We'll free Henry. He'll put out the fires on Snowdon. It'll all be easy-peasy. Simple as a pimple. And I can be with Henry forever because Merlin will let him be a boy again. We'll sit in the sunshine on the aromatic slopes of dear Snowdon. As I peer into the water, weirdly even without the torch beam I can see that wild mountain slope and the sun rippling across it ... and all the dust and cinder and scorched herbage has gone and there is HENRY and he has his arms wide and he's calling to me ... 'Come to me, come to me, my beloved darling Ellie ... Come and join me here in the sunshine ... '

... and all I have to do is wade in a bit further and I can be with him and everything will be all right ... and it's not so far to wade as the water is getting deeper anyway and I'm already up to my waist ... and what does it even matter that we haven't found Merlin yet? I can just be with Henry anyway ... just go in a bit deeper ... I don't even need Merlin to let him be a boy again ... he's not a dragon in this wonderful paradise under the water ... he'll never be a dragon underwater because his fire won't work underwater ...

HANG ON.

Dragon?

Fire?

THE FIRE ON SNOWDON.

OUR QUEST.

'NOOOOOOO!' I shout as I see George and Rhi up to

303

their necks, the torch beam held only feebly above the surface.

'RHI! GEORGE! IT'S THE MORGANS!'

I grab them. I shake them. I scream in their faces. 'GEORGE! RHI! STOP IT! WAKE UP! YOU'LL DROWN!'

But on they step like sleepwalkers. Deeper. Deeper.

What can I do? I must wake them.

Break the reflection on the water. Use something? *What?* I plunge my hand into the swill and stir. I splash water in their faces. But still they step on like zombies. Deeper. Deeper.

METAL!

That's it. Metal! Fae Folk hate metal. *My chain with its silver charm.* Take it off. Throw it into the water.

But then I'll lose it. Without my grandmother's protection, I too may be lost.

THROW. IT. IN.

I wrench off my chain and hurl it into the water in front of George.

The water seethes and hisses, bubbling up in spurts and rages. Rhi screams. George straightens up and yells, 'What the—'

'It was the Morgans!'

'But I saw Gran and the cottage and it wasn't burnt and—'

'An illusion!'

'I saw you, George, and we were standing beside a lake and holding hands and—' begins Rhi.

'They tried to drown us!'

'Holy smoke!' says George, 'Thank God for you, Ellie. How did you break their hold?'

'I don't know,' I whisper, 'but I had to use my charm necklace.'

'Oh Ellie, your lovely charm necklace … it was so pretty … ' says Rhi. 'But … well … Uni said only the pure in heart could find the way. It means we're pure in heart, I guess, as we've been tempted, but … well … ' Her voice trails away.

'Where are the leaves?' asks George.

And there they are, glowing golden all on their own, urging us to follow.

And we do. And somehow we *have* passed the test and as we round a curve there are banks and trailing honeysuckle and thick greenery all around us. We duck our heads, and pass through a wall of soft leaves and shoots and blossoms, and find ourselves just ankle deep in a tiny stream dazzled in pure sunlight.

Thirty-Nine

For a moment, everything is muddled.

There's a soft green light coming from above, and a darkness below.

I open my eyes again. Sunlight dances through greenery on to the grassy bank around me. I'm standing on turf bespeckled with primroses by the shores of a little stream.

Here we are in a flowery glade, with three moons peeping over the top of leafy woodland. Everything is lit in bright sunshine, exactly as I imagined Fairyland would be, with wild flowers, trees blossoming, streams flowing ...

No acid smell. No burnt-out landscape.

I rub my eyes. I try to focus. This must be it! Merlin's magical green glade.

I know I'm right.

We've made it to Merlin's glade.

Even better, I know I can now drink from the stream. This stream is OK! It's Merlin's! Gran's warning no longer throbs away at the back of my skull. *And I'm so thirsty.*

George seems to read my mind. 'Wait,' he says, then bends down to wash his face and drink from the palm of his hand. He gives us the thumbs up. 'Drink. I'm George and I'm on a quest to save the world from burning. See, I can remember everything.'

'Great,' I say. 'God, I'm so thirsty!'

Rhi finds a pretty shell and fills it with sparking water. She sips some and hands the rest to me. 'Use this. Don't mind George. He prefers slurping like a horse.'

'Like a Unicorn,' corrects George.

I sip the water. I feel the power of it race through me. I look into the shell. The water in it sparkles with a bright purity, as if it has caught the light from diamonds. 'Wow,' I say, 'I don't even feel hungry any more.'

'I know,' says George, 'me too. I think it must be the legendary Water of Life!'

I look at the stream. Could be. It definitely radiates.

'So if I bathe in it,' says Rhi, 'I'll stay beautiful for ever?'

'I think you'll stay beautiful forever, whether you bathe in it or not,' George replies.

I look at Rhi. She's smiling in a way I've never seen

her smile before – really happy, not needy, nor flirty, nor conniving; just happy – and she really does look beautiful.

I turn back to George. An understanding seems to dawn in his expression.

'It's true,' he says. 'You look lovely, Rhi. You *are* beautiful. You'll always be beautiful.'

Rhi anoints her arms with drops of water and rubs them into her skin.

'I think we should find Merlin quickly,' I remind them.

I look up. Despite the bright sunlight, one of the three moons has moved across the sky and is spinning like a top overhead.

'You're right,' says George, following my glance.

'But how?' says Rhi.

A wind starts to sway the treetops. A dark haze forms behind the spinning moon.

'Nimue said he was in a cave in a tree – did Gran ever say anything about that? Anything in the old stories?' I ask.

George scratches his head. 'There were two stories. The first one is that Merlin was actually happy to be in the cave, a bit like a hermit. The other story says he was imprisoned in a tree.'

'What does the book say?' asks Rhi.

'Nothing,' says George. 'At the moment it's too soggy and

will just disintegrate if we try to turn its pages.' He lays it out on a stone to dry.

'OK,' I say, 'so there's no cave here, but lots of trees, so let's look for a tree that might be big enough to hold a person … or if we do find a cave further off, then we investigate?'

We walk around the glade. There are many, many trees and many, many rocks, but no caves and no trees that look like they might have a cave or a person inside it. We find two rusty bits of iron railing and an old walking stick. We jump over the narrow stream and check the other side of the glade. More bits of railing but no caves or hollow trees. As we move up away from the river, the trees begin to look skeletal, the grass withers and the flowers disappear.

'We must stay beside the stream, I think,' says Rhi.

'I agree,' I reply. 'I think it's the High Magick of Merlin that's keeping this stream pure and the grass growing.'

'You're right,' says George. He stops and scratches his head again. 'So logically, we should find Merlin at the epicentre of this glade.'

He's right. 'So all we need to do is find the centre, and then we'll find the prison?' I say.

'Cool,' says Rhi, 'that's mathematical and awesome, but

without a tape or anything to measure with, how do we do it?'

I look up. The moon is spinning so quickly now that it's just a blur. The haze around it is thickening fast. I squint to see the edges of the glade. *Is it my imagination or is the withering grass out there closing in on us?*

'Let's hurry,' I say.

George stops and draws a kind of Ban the Bomb sign in the stream's sandy shore. 'So you,' he says to Rhi, pointing to his left, 'go to the edge of the glade, through the trees, to where the first foliage die-off starts, that way.' Then he swivels his arm round. 'Ellie, you go and do the same in that direction. I'll take the final angle. It's not exact, but we'll soon find out where the relative centre is when we walk towards each other. If any of us pass this mark before the other two, then we'll try again until we can pin the centre down.'

I climb up the banks, up, up into the woods, until the grass starts to completely die off. All is dust and cinder. And a bit scary. Now I am out of sight of the others, the trees around me stretch stark fingers out. I freeze. I listen. *Can I still hear them?*

It'll be OK, I tell myself.

It has to be.

'Hello!' yells George, faint but definitely him. I breathe a sigh of relief.

'Hellooo,' comes Rhi's echo.

I yell my hello out as loudly as I can.

'Start walking ... towards the centre as you see it ... normal rate,' hollers George. His voice is weak, but I catch it.

Above me, the thick haze spreads out. The spinning moon seems to whine.

We must hurry.

'START,' yells George again.

I begin walking, but it's not so easy to take normal steps. I'm going straight down a steep bank. I hear the others crashing about in the trees. *It is the others, isn't it?* I hear the crunch of twigs, crushed underfoot. My heartbeat shoots up. My palms go clammy. The air stirs with the shake of branches.

'I'm past the sign,' yells George. His voice is much louder.
Phew.

'Rhi, are you there?'

I hear Rhi calling back.

Reassured, I work my way, step-by-step, towards the apparent centre. I keep adjusting my stride so it's regular.

Soon I see them. George is past the sign and Rhi is walking towards me. I continue onwards until I meet Rhi. We are about five metres away from George.

'Right,' says George, 'if we imagine this as an inner circle – curving between this point that I'm on and the place you girls have met – we will have narrowed down the epicentre, hopefully. It's not exact maths, but fingers crossed.'

'I don't really get it,' says Rhi. 'Is it kind of like geometry?'

'Hey,' I say, 'look.'

Just beside us, right in our 'inner circle', is a tree I hadn't noticed before. A tiny slender tree, barely a metre tall and as thin as a wand.

'That's it!' says George.

'You're right!' I say.

'But it's ... like ... Way Too Small,' Rhi objects.

'Think Tardis?' I say.

The tree is growing in the middle of our circle space!

'Let's try it,' says George.

'But how do we get inside?' asks Rhi.

Good question. The tree in front of us seems hardly big enough for anything to be inside it, not even a beetle.

'These are the Fae Lands,' I say, remembering something Gran said: '"Nothing is what it seems."'

'We should do the same thing as we did at the roundabout,' says Rhi. 'It worked then.'

I shiver at the thought of the roundabout and the storm

and the sleek Mercedes and the ugly sneering face of Gwyn ap Nudd.

'We must circle sunwise, deosil,' Rhi reminds us. 'Then we must repeat "by air, by water, by fire, by earth". Come on.'

We form ourselves into a pattern, somehow like at the roundabout. As if in response, the spinning moon fixes itself directly overhead and starts to spiral down towards us, like a huge, sharp-edged corkscrew.

'Hold firm,' says George.

'OMG!' screams Rhi. 'Look at that moon!'

My heart races. My knees tremble.

We move as solemnly as we can – clockwise, holding tight, chanting.

'By air, by water, by fire, by earth,

We call on Merlin first.

By earth, by water, by fire, by air,

Please let us know if you are there.

By air, by water, by earth, by fire,

Please grant us our Hearts' Desire.

By air, by earth, by fire, by water … '

We can't think of anything to rhyme with 'water' until Rhi says, 'Let us in, you know you oughta … '

The moon takes aim.

And nothing happens.

Forty

The spinning moon picks up speed and corkscrews closer.

'Perhaps this isn't the tree?' says Rhi. 'Or perhaps he doesn't want to see us?'

'Something bad's going to happen,' says George. 'I feel it coming.'

'You could've just knocked, you know,' says a voice that seems to come from the air around us. 'I think that's the normal way to ask to come in, not with all that appalling poetry.'

The voice must be coming from inside the tree. Immediately I knock on it. It sways and bends. 'Sorry,' I say, 'for doing it wrong! May we come in?'

'Absolutely,' says the voice, and a tiny doorway opens up in the side of the tree, which seems to expand into a sizable gap filled by a wooden door with a huge cast-iron doorknob.

'Just turn the knob,' says the voice. 'I am sorry it's so ginormous and cold, but iron is the only thing those pesky Pookah can't get past, and I really hate being disturbed by them day and night.'

The moon takes aim overhead.

'They like to play in my glade,' the voice continues. 'But even though I'm pretty sorry about the whole Grey Lands problem, I am not going to encourage them into my home. You may have noticed the iron guardians at the edges of my garden?'

So that was what those bits of railing were!

With a whoosh that blocks all other sound, the moon rockets down towards us.

The door swings open.

'C'mon,' says the voice, 'get in quick – when those moons start flying, they're lethal.'

We all jump inside, fast, where we're greeted by a tall, thin, VERY old man. He's just exactly how I'd imagine Merlin would be after years of imprisonment. Long beard, mostly white, twinkly eyes, wrinkly skin, crinkly smile. Very Gandalf.

'I'm not *really* in prison,' he says, seeming to read my

thoughts. He shaking his beard. 'There's not a snowball's chance in hell that you could imprison a magician without his consent.'

'But,' says George, 'why do all the stories say you are?'

'Fake news, dear boy.' Merlin grins. 'Fake news! Ain't it the biz? I like the world to think I'm out of commission. It gives me a chance to work on some of the more interesting aspects of High Magick. Plus I must admit I got a bit weary of everything after Arthur died and the Age of Chivalry passed. I swore I'd embrace the life of an ascetic. Self-denial and all that.'

'Wow! So you're like REALLY MERLIN!' screeches Rhi. She flings her arms around him. 'I've *always* wanted to meet you! But I thought you only existed in fairy stories!'

'King Arthur and the Knights of the Round Table,' I say under my breath. 'Or the *Mabinogion*. Definitely not "fairy stories".'

Rhi ignores me with a dismissive wave. 'I've ALWAYS wanted to know if your beard really touched the ground!' She bends down to see how long his beard actually is.

'Wow,' she says again. 'It's longer than Dumbledore's!'

I cross my fingers, hoping Rhi isn't going to say something so cringe and gushing that it puts him off helping us.

As tactfully as I can, I interrupt. 'Sire.' (I'm not exactly sure how you address a high magician but 'Sire' seems to fit the bill.)

Merlin laughs. 'Please, I don't need any of that guff, just call me Merl, like you would any ol' pal.' He laughs again. 'You're all so refreshing! It's been way too long since I've had a yakka-yak with young people! It's going to be such groovy fun! Plus I'd ADORE to see a mobile.'

'OK,' I say, 'well … '

George hands Merlin his phone.

'Merl, we need your help,' says Rhi.

'Of course you need my help!' says Merlin, clapping his hands together in excitement. 'You wouldn't have taken the trouble to come across the grey plains in search of my old tree-cave-house unless you wanted my help. But that's OK! I'm used to that. Now, tell me the problem, and I'll sort it out tout suite!'

Rhi giggles.

Merlin does a few excited jumps and his eyes go all sparkly.

I feel at ease and immediately tell him all about Henry, how we first met up on the mountain, and how *he*, Merlin, created the spell that turned Henry turn into a boy and all that … and how we fell in love. Then I stop. I realise I'm talking too much and it's *really* embarrassing and George is shifting from one foot to the other.

I think I'd better go a bit slower on the whole Henry and me thing.

'Oh, don't stop,' moans Merlin. 'I love to listen to your voice. And I do know the history of which you speak. I keep myself up to date through my various scrying devices. I've watched all the developments on my beloved Snowdon, and especially on my own part of it, Dinas Emrys.' He waves his arm at an array of magnificent crystal balls and stone bowls filled with water. 'I'm afraid I have to use these – they are pretty much the standard thing in our Fae Lands – but they're definitely not as good as video calling on mobile phones, or so I hear.'

Rhi giggles again. 'You mean "facetiming".'

'Oh, absolutely,' says Merlin. He looks at Rhi. 'How do you turn this on?' He hands her George's phone.

She passes it to George, who keys in his pin.

'I'm rubbish at anything techie,' she says, laughing. 'Once I tried to programme the timer on our cooker … and well … '

'Ah,' Merlin says sadly, 'though I have centuries to spare, I don't believe we have time for a real chinwag about your cooking, Rhi. That is not why you have come, I fear … '

Rhi laughs again. 'That's OK. BTW, my soufflé was a DISASTER. It blew up!'

'No,' I say, 'we don't have much time. Even as we speak, fires are raging across Snowdonia and people are suffering.'

Merlin sighs. 'That Gwyn ap Nudd is a really unpleasant character. He has risen to power through absolute trickery. I never liked him much – far too brash. And a right pyromaniac. I would like to have put him and all his fires out aeons ago, but sadly that is not allowed under the rules of High Magick.'

'We need to free Henry,' I say. 'We've been told that dragon fire can help stop Gwyn ap Nudd.'

'Yes,' says Merlin, 'that's true. And I think using Henry's fire is a better bet than summoning a different dragon, though there's one I know, over in Germany, who might come quite quickly … '

A dismay sweeps over me. *It must be Henry.*

'But then again … I think Fafnir has rejoined Draco … ' Merlin crosses to a stone bowl to double check, 'Yes, my bad – Fafnir was killed by Sigurd, not that long ago … Pity … though maybe not … He was a miserly fellow and would have charged us gazillions in gold … So we'd better get Henry on to it.'

Merlin picks up a crystal ball and stares at it.

Seconds tick past.

George shuffles.

Rhi combs her hair with her fingers and arranges it using the tiny silver box as a mirror.

I wait.

'Oooh dear … ' says Merlin. 'It seems the fires have now gone down into some ancient mines under Snowdon and are burning through seams of coal, deep below ground. That's not good.'

'How do you mean?' asks George.

'Well, they'll burn forever down there. They'll burn out the heart of the mountain.'

My chest goes tight.

Fires burning below Snowdon. Llanberis a blackened heap.

Of course that's where Gwyn would send his fire!

Deep underground.

Right into the dragons' lair.

To burn Henry alive.

As he lies there.

Trapped by Oswald.

Forty-One

'We have to free Henry,' I say. 'Quickly.'

Merlin nods his head in agreement. 'Yes, this pesky business of those two quarrelsome dragons is really not helping.'

'Is there no way we can free Henry until Oswald has been defeated?' asks George.

'I thought I'd settled the matter between them, by allowing them to choose to become human or by burying them back under Dinas Emrys, but none of that worked. Those two big fellows are a big nuisance and it is high time their quarrel was put to an end.'

I flinch. 'That's so not fair,' I say. Blood rushes to my face. 'It's Oswald who won't stop. Henry's not at all quarrelsome.' I fold my arms and look directly at Merlin. 'Oswald started it – he keeps attacking Henry. He wants to destroy him. Henry has to do battle to defend himself.'

'Yes, yes,' says Merlin, smiling. 'You needn't be so defensive. I know all about that Oswald character. He was a bad egg from the start and should have been fried into a thousand omelettes. And yes, you're right, Henry is really just reacting. But *we* need to crack on, because those flames have already captured the heart of Snowdon and are moving quickly.'

I exhale, count to ten (under my breath) and mumble, 'Sorry.'

'So how can we get that Oswald out of the picture?' Merlin spins in a circle and a trail of tiny stars follows him, as if the air in his cave is like water, filled with bubbles. 'You want Henry freed from the curse … ' He glances over to me. 'And I'm guessing you'd like to have him back in his human form? I'll see what I can do about turning him into a boy … later on … but first of all, we need him as a dragon to breathe fire at our enemies.'

My heart cartwheels. *Henry as a boy again …*

'But I can't promise anything. You know some of my magical experiments don't work out very well … ' Merlin scratches his chin and strokes his beard. 'That business with the crystals should have worked fine, but Oswald found a way round it, wretched fellow.'[1]

George looks puzzled. 'I thought magicians controlled

---

1. In Book One, *Here be Dragons*, we learn about that spell.

everything, and magic was, well, foolproof?'

'Now that's entirely wrong,' says Merlin kindly. 'And just the sort of damaging propaganda that is put about. Magicians are in control of nothing. It is merely that we like to play around with reality. We are seekers of the truth. Detectives, really. Once you know how something works, of course, you can add it to your Book of Shadows and, bit by bit, you can have quite a compendium of useful things. But essentially we are just as ignorant of this vast cosmos, with all its dimensions, as anyone else is.'

That's not very reassuring.

Outside I hear a vague rattling, as if someone has found the door and is trying to pick the lock.

Rhi hears it too. She looks worried.

'For example, I've never been very successful at stopping those two dragons fighting, but I'm quite happy to try again. What do you think might work this time?' Merlin looks eagerly at me.

'OK,' I say, 'it's like this, Merlin.' I take a deep breath. 'It seems like we will have to be ready to kill Oswald for the battle to end.'

'Oh dear,' says Merlin. 'So it's come to that.'

'And we actually need you to help us get the sword to do it with,' adds Rhi.

I stiffen.

'So we really, really need you to get back together with Nimue,' she continues.

OMG. Way to be tactful!

Merlin's eyes widen.

Rhi shoots me a *stop it* look, and says, 'We met the Lady of the Lake and she'd like to get back with you.'

'Ah, the beautiful Nimue … ' Merlin murmurs, instantly regaining his composure.

'Yes, she's totally more beautiful than … than … ' Rhi looks upwards. She seems to be thinking of a suitable simile, but only adds, 'than she ever was.'

Merlin sighs in delight.

George holds his breath.

'And she said that she would give us the sword, Caledfwlch, to free Henry with, if you will be hers like forever … ' Rhi smiles at Merlin encouragingly. 'She really likes you, you know.' Rhi looks at George.

Awww-kward.

I bite my lip, wondering what Merlin will say.

George smiles gallantly back at Rhi.

I mentally roll my eyes. Perhaps Rhi and George *are* fated to end up together?

Rhi looks around, blushing, suddenly realising she's put

her foot right in it. She takes in a deep breath, like now she's started down this track she might as well finish. 'She fancies you like crazy and is really sorry she stuck you in a tree.' She makes a big hopeful grin at Merlin and makes a heart shape with her forefingers and thumbs.

Merlin seems to be totally fascinated.

'You know how it is when you have a quarrel with someone you love?' Rhi is clearly determined he gets the point. 'You stay apart for a bit and that's supposed to make you realise that you love them – More Than Whatever You Quarrelled About. But it shouldn't really last that long … '

Merlin looks sheepish and pulls on his silvery beard. 'Do you think so?'

'I totally think so,' says Rhi. 'I totally think you two are being really silly and you should get back together again, because she is not happy. And she is really pretty too,' Rhi adds. 'And you can't be ecstatic about being stuck in this tree, can you, with just a little bit of green outside your door and all that?'

Merlin's eyes widen all over again.

'Plus you are all alone, and she is all alone, and you two like each other. I don't know why it's taking you thousands and thousands of years to work that out!'

'You are so right,' says Merlin. 'Perhaps when you have

immortality, you can tend to let things slide a little. And it's true, I do really dig her. But I have a problem. I am, a bit, well, not sure ... '

'Not sure of what?' asks Rhi, hands on hips.

'I'm not entirely sure that Nimue likes me for myself and not my magical skills. Is it really mean of me to think that?'

'OMG!' says Rhi. 'Really? Like you are totally insecure?'

'Well, now you put it like that ... yes, I suppose I am,' says Merlin with some surprise. He looks at George. 'Do guys these days feel insecure around the girls they fancy?'

George looks at me. 'Absolutely.' I can tell he wants to say something about how he has always fancied me – but he can't, really – not after I just said how I love Henry. Not to mention the Rhiannon question.

'Look,' Rhi says to Merlin, 'it's not just guys who feel shy, you know.'

'You are quite a remarkable young person,' says Merlin. 'After millennia, I do believe you have brought me to my senses!'

'Well, love is one of those things that just *is*, isn't it? You can't choose it. When you meet The One, that's just it. So I think you should make up with Nimue and try and work things out,' finishes Rhi.

'Ah,' I say, 'that reminds me ... '

'Of?' asks Merlin.

'The standing stone set fulfilling the Heart's Desire as the terms of the quest. You and Lady Nimue need to fulfil yours.'

'Interesting,' says Merlin. 'I always thought the Menhir of Mawr had a heart of stone.' He chuckles a little.

The wind outside rattles the door.

'There is one other thing,' says George, 'You see, though Nimue has promised us the sword if you'll get back with her—'

'Two excellent outcomes!' says Merlin.

'But,' I add, 'that doesn't provide us with the dragon lord to use the sword to slay Oswald … ' I leave the problem trailing in the air. Nobody grabs it. 'So, we were hoping … maybe you could come along with us, to help with that bit?'

'Oh goodness me! No way, Jose!' says Merlin. 'My dragon-slaying days are long gone! Plus I'm a vegan and an animal lover. I'd have slaughtered that white monster myself, aeons ago, but it's just not in me!'

'What are we going to do, then?' wails Rhi. 'The fires will last forever and my dad's hotel will be burnt to bits!'

'Oh, solving that is uber-duber easy-peasy,' says Merlin.

It doesn't seem that easy to me, but I don't contradict him.

'As you now know, I'm an incy-bit worried about the

motivation of my beloved Nimue. I think she probably does love me, and this tiff has absolutely gone on long enough. But I think I would like to remove temptation from the picture, you know? So that Nim and I can enjoy a happy eternity without my insecurities becoming an issue and biting us in the butt. You get me?'

What has this got to do with Snowdon burning?

'What do you mean?' asks George.

I can't help but start tapping my foot.

'My spells. My Book of Shadows,' says Merlin. 'You see, the Lady of the Lake is a very powerful lady, and you know what they say about power. Anyway, if she were to get her hands on all my spells, then I think the temptation to use them would be too much for her, which might lead to another drama. And then I might have to spend another eternity in a tree. And it might not be this tree. It might be one of those uncomfortable prickly pear cactus trees, or a pine cone jobbie, which would not be much fun. You know what it's like once you vacate your spot – you never get it back.' Merlin pauses and strokes his beard.

I try to stay patient, wondering where this is going.

'So in order to enjoy a happy future with my lady and P'n'Q all round, I think I need to find a successor so I can retire properly. It's something I should have done a long time ago, but I could never find the right person.' Merlin sighs. 'It's difficult to find anyone, especially when you're a hermit living in a tree-cave. I'd have loved to run a "Be My Apprentice" trial like they do on TV cookery shows, but that was never to be.' Merlin pulls a long face. 'Anyway, it doesn't matter, for now the right person has arrived in my life! So all I need to do is pass on my Book of Shadows, my sigil ring, my staff and my hat to my chosen successor!'

I frown. *What has all this got to do with dragon-slaying?*

He goes over to some floor-to-ceiling bookcases that line the far wall. He counts the shelves and at shelf number three he pulls out a book and takes a tiny key from inside its pages. He crosses to another wall, waves a hand over it and miraculously a keyhole appears. Merlin pops the key into the keyhole and part of the wall magically falls away beneath his touch.

There on a podium, held in three golden clasps, is a huge book. Dancing across its vellum covers, in moonlight letters, are the words:

MERLIN'S GRIMOIRE ~ The Ultimate Epic Book of Awesome Shadows. Yo.

He removes the gold clasps and picks the book up. He takes off his sigil ring, picks up his staff and returns to us. He removes his hat and says, 'Sorted. Here you are, George. Grab a pile of that. It's all yours now.'

Forty-Two

'*Whaaaat?*' says George.

'Here you are. Massive Props and Big Ups to you. You know, it feels so right. Such a relief.'

'WHAAAT?' says George again, his eyes popping.

'C'mon, take them! Don't grow older; just be bolder!'

'Uh?' says Rhi.

'B-but,' stammers George, 'this is your life's work.'

'Granted,' says Merlin, 'but I think giving up magic will really help me to see my way back to Nimmy.'

'B-but,' stammers George again, 'you are the most renowned wizard of all time … you're a legend … you're an icon!'

'No worries. It was all standing in the way of me and Nim. So really, you're doing me a favour. You'll find the grimoire is pretty comprehensive. I don't think you'll be disappointed. And in its appendix is everything else that I mastered in my pursuit of the Art of High Magick, above and beyond the normal High Wizardry stuff.'

George looks confused, then worried. *He's not the only one!*

'It's got everything that you'll need in it. Hint: look in the sub-sub-appendix if you get muddled.'

George just stands there with his jaw dropped.

Mine too!

'You'll be all right,' says Merlin. 'I can't tell you how to cast magic, though – everybody must find their own way to do that. The path in magical life is just as the real one – you've got to live it, to walk the road yourself, alone. But you'll be fine …'

'But a magician? A wizard?' says George. 'I'm not a magician.'

'Well, you are now,' says Merlin and plonks his hat on George's head.

George still seems unable to take it in. 'Really?' he whispers. 'I never thought of myself as a wizard.'

'Oh well, that's your mistake,' says Merlin. 'You should've thought of this career path a long time ago. But we all make mistakes, my boy. Wouldn't learn anything if we didn't.'

'But why me?' George asks.

'If you think about it, only someone called George can kill the dragon. That is the way the legend goes, and legends are told for a reason. George killed the dragon and rescued the community and for that was made a saint. This is why it has to be you. I am merely conferring upon you your birthright: the right to be a dragon lord.'

George smiles nervously and says, 'Oh, OK.' He takes the book and runs his hands over it. Lights dance upon its cover.

'There you are,' says Merlin. 'It's responding to you already. It'll be a bit bumpy at first, but you'll get the hang of it.'

I sit there trying to take this in.

George, a wizard?

Merlin turns to me and beams. 'Happy?' he says. 'All sorted, tickety-boo?'

'I don't understand,' I say.

'There's your dragon lord,' says Merlin. 'That is the first and most obvious point: George the dragon-slayer, as in myths of yore. He's young and brave and agile, with a sword and the love of the girls – much better than me for dragon fighting.'

I look at George. *How can he go up against Oswald?* But then I see a sneaky grin cross George's face.

'I have always fancied a bit of a dragon fight,' he says, 'but I've only ever had an axe. Now, if I have magic plus Caledfwlch, I think I might stand a chance. Soon it might just be Oswald's unlucky day … '

Stand a chance?

Is George nuts?

I look around the room for support, but Rhiannon is clapping her hands and saying, 'Hero! Hero!'

I turn back to Merlin. 'But don't you want to give George a trial, to make sure you're making the right choice?' I ask. 'Or send him to Hogwarts or something?'

Merlin laughs. 'That's one good thing about being a master magician – you know your own mind and you can be very decisive. The Oracle already told me a hero called George would find me out, and so from the first moment I saw young George here, I knew that he was The One. And now, if you'll excuse me, I'm quite eager to get back to Nim and make up for lost time.'

Merlin turns round and does a quickstep shuffle across the tree-cave-house floor. Then he bows and says, 'OK guys, bye then, toodle-pip, good luck with all that dragon-slaying stuff. Let me know how it goes, and just make sure you put those fires out as soon as you can.' He steps into a mirror that I hadn't noticed before just to the left of the front door. He raises one hand and gives George back his mobile. He adds, 'Take one of my crystals to stay in touch – and if possible, see if you can find your way to sending me a mobile phone when you get the hang of my Book of Shadows.'

'Wait,' calls George. 'I don't even know how to open it.'

'Don't worry,' yells Merlin, 'it's all part of the fun. Now off you go; tempus fugit, so hurry up.' And with the first half of him having already disappeared through the mirror, Merlin waves a final goodbye and slips after it.

Forty-Three

The mirror reseals itself behind him, rippling closed like the surface of water.

We stand there in his tree-cave-house prison. George clutches the grimoire.

Rhi looks at George.

George looks at me.

I look at Rhi.

'What happens now?' I say.

George has gone a peculiar shade of grey. He looks as if he's about to be sick. Rhi puts her arm around him and gives him a little girly kiss on the cheek. 'I know you can do this, Georgie. I've always thought you were fantastic and wizard at everything.' She smiles at him. 'Merlin made a good choice,' she adds. 'And he's right about the legends. It was George who killed the dragon.'

George sits down on one of the chairs (a twisted tree-root-type thing) and nearly drops the Book of Shadows. 'I don't have a clue where to start.'

'Well, we'd better start soon,' says Rhi, 'because although time here may run differently from time back home, like Merl said, we don't want to hang about – you know my dad's hotel … '

I pull up another twisted stool chair thing and sit next to George. 'Look, you're Gran's grandson, right?'

'Yep,' says George, 'I'm pretty sure my grandmother is Gran.'

'Exactly,' says Rhiannon.

They both look at me with big question-mark eyes.

'And Gran is just about the nearest thing to a witch I've ever met. I mean a white witch, of course – a wise woman. A Good Person Who Understands Magic and all that?' I cast a look at Rhi, who scowls back at me.[1]

George looks unsure. I can see he's grasping the direction I'm taking. 'So if you become a wizard, that is absolutely as it should be. Sort of hereditary. Who knows, perhaps your dad was a bit of a wizard at something or other, or might have been if he'd lived,' I add as gently as I can.

---

1. Rhi 'trained' to be a witch in Book Two, *Here be Witches*, but all that came to a VERY sticky end.

'I think the gift tends to skip generations,' says Rhiannon. 'I'm absolutely sure I heard that somewhere. Or I read it in a book about pink fairies or something.'

'That's interesting,' says George, 'because when I was really little, after Mum and Dad died and I started living with Nan, she kept giving me these tests to see if I had the Gift.'

'And did you pass any of them?' I ask.

'Can't remember,' says George. 'All I know is that she gave me yummy Welsh cakes afterwards.'

'Ah,' I say.

'Well,' says Rhi, 'it appears that you *do* have the Gift. I don't think a magician like Merlin would give you his Book of Shadows and sigil ring if he didn't think so.'

'True,' says George, 'but I'm kind of scared, because I'd hate to let him down, and it all seems … sort of … a lot… ' He stops in mid-sentence.

His jaw drops open.

'What?'

He points to the back of the door.

I turn my head and look. A sword lies on the floor. *On the floor?* Just as if it's been posted through an invisible letterbox in the tree-cave's front door! *A sword, in its scabbard, on a wide leather belt.* I'm sure it wasn't there when we came in. We'd have tripped right over it!

Caledfwlch?

George springs across the space and picks it up. It could be. It looks exactly like the sword the Lady of the Lake showed us.

It *must* be Caledfwlch.

'Wowee!' says Rhi. 'Let's test it.'

She takes the scabbard in one hand and the hilt of the sword in the other and tries to unsheathe it.

It doesn't budge.

She pulls on it.

Her face goes kinda weirdly reddish.

Purple almost.

And the veins at her temples stand out.

A rivulet of sweat runs down her cheek.

The sword doesn't move.

'Oh BUM!' Rhi says.

She wedges the sword between her knees and holds it with one hand and pulls and pulls with the other, as hard as she can.

'It's not going to work,' she puffs, 'if we can't unsheathe it.'

'Maybe—' I start to say.

'This sword is no good,' pants Rhi. 'It's stuck.'

'I think it's probably just you,' says George.

Rhi walks over to George and says, 'OK, let's see you try.'

George puts one hand on the hilt. The sword trembles at his touch and almost leaps into his hand, as if it is unsheathing itself.

'Easy-peasy,' says George. 'You need to go to the gym more often,' he teases Rhi.

George holds the sword aloft. The blade shimmers as if it has caught moonbeams in its silver steel. Its hilt sparkles with chased gold. Strange Celtic designs flicker up and down the blade. George twists the sword in his hand. Light dances all around the tree-cave-house walls.

Suddenly the blade becomes unbearably bright. I clamp my hand over my eyes and peep through my fingers.

Two chimeras from the golden hilt breathe flames along the blade, so brilliant it's like looking at the sun.

'Hey!' yells Rhi.

'Put it away,' I tell George.

Just when I'm sure I'm going to go totally blind, George whispers, 'Gently; your time will come.'

The chimeras subside and fade. I open my eyes and blink.

'Look, there's something written on the blade,' I say.

George examines the sword. 'It says "Take me up" on this side.' George rolls the sword over. 'And "Cast me away" on this.'

'What does *that* mean?' asks Rhi.

'I don't know,' I say, 'but remember your book said the scabbard has powers too?'

'Yeah, you're right.' George straps the sword on. 'With this on I'm dragon-proof.'

I give George's arm a squeeze and he gives me a watery kind of smile.

'Think you can do this?' I ask. 'Finish off Oswald?' I pull a hopeful kind of face.

'Fingers crossed,' says George.

'We'll have to make a plan,' says Rhi.

~~I look at her in amazement. Since when did Rhi make a plan other than to put on some false eyelashes?~~

Note to self: correction. Rhi is capable of incredible things. She has proved herself. She is always proving herself. We Will Make A Plan.

George looks at the sword, deep in thought.

'Why not put on the ring too?' I suggest. Poor George. It's a lot to get used to. If we had time, he could absorb the idea, get in some practice with the spell book, maybe use the sword a bit.

But we don't.

George nods and slides the ring on to the middle finger of his right hand where Merlin wore it.

It totally fits. And it seems as if a change comes over him. He somehow grows taller, but not older, though weirdly wiser. Don't get me wrong, George is smart and clever and all that, but he's always been ~~immature and silly~~ funny with it. Now he looks kind of sad, as if he knows all the sorrows of the world and can't fix them. I draw in a deep breath and realise with a rush that makes my chest tight how much I love him. How much I'd like him to be really happy. How scared I am about him going up against Oswald.

George twists the ring on his finger. He picks up Merlin's staff.

'OK,' says Rhi, 'shall we plan the plan?' She gives George the Thumbs Up. 'You will be an awesome wizard. And a brilliant dragon-slayer. But how will we get Henry and Oswald out from under the hillside at Dinas Emrys?'

She looks at me.

Fair point.

I look at George.

'It will take a lot to dig them out,' says Rhi. 'We'll probably need an excavator – and will it be able to get up there, across the mountain?'

I think of the mountain and the fires.

'Plus we have to get home – I mean out of here,' adds Rhi. She doesn't add 'safely' but we're all thinking it.

'Ah!' says George.

We look at him expectantly.

He pulls off the hat. A sudden light twinkles in his eyes. 'I know *exactly* how we can dig those dragons out! I think I can produce *exactly* the right kind of excavator.' He chuckles (a bit too much like Merlin, actually).

I frown and wonder if he's going to open up the Book of Shadows and magic up some kind of tractor-driven-combine-digger thingy and beam it down on to the side of Snowdon.

'But how?' I ask.

'Guess?' says George, looking at me.

'Magically powered spades?'

He shakes his head. 'Idris!'

My mind whirls.

Idris?

Idris Gawr?[2]

'He's a giant and he has boots,' says George. 'He can be on Snowdon in three steps.'

'But—' I say.

'He'll come,' says George. 'I know he will. I've been thinking of him lots. Did I tell you, last month I climbed

---

2. Idris Gawr is a giant who loves poetry, astronomy and philosophy. He stargazes on the top of Cadair Idris, a mystical mountain at the southern end of Snowdonia, from his bed of stones. He possesses a pair of seven-league boots too and is immortally in love with Angharad Golden-Hand who was brutally slain by the nine witches of Gloucester.

Cadair and sat on his pile of stones and talked to him? I couldn't hear if he answered, but I know he was there and I know he was lonely. It'll take his mind off missing Angharad, and give him something to do. He would've stayed last time round to fight if only there'd been enough time.'

George is right. 'But how can we talk to Idris from here?' I say. 'We're in the Fae Lands. How're we even going to get home?'

'I think,' says George, 'we may need to use this.' He taps the Book of Shadows lying across his lap. 'And for that I *will* need help.'

'So,' I say, 'if we can figure out how to use the Book of Shadows, then maybe we won't have to go back to the roundabout at Carmarthen, which is probably (certainly) blocked shut anyway with that Merc. We could just create a gateway for ourselves right here.'

'Brilliant!' says Rhi.

'Except,' I add, 'there's something about that which feels a bit wrong.'

'Like?' asks George.

'I'm not sure we should just open up a new gateway between the worlds,' I say. 'All the portals to the Fae Lands have been carefully sealed shut … I'm sure there's some reason Merlin did that.'

George sighs. 'You're probably right. Probably to stop the Pookah getting out.'

'So if we don't create a new gateway,' I say, 'how're we going to get home?'

'I think we only have one choice,' says George.

We turn to look at him.

'I think we'll have to use an existing Pookah portal after all.'

Forty-Four

'USE A POOKAH PORTAL?' screams Rhi.

'Not. A. Good. Idea,' I say. 'Gran strictly advised against it. I think we should vote. And by the way, I'm with Gran.'

Rhi gulps, then looks up at George and flutters her eyelashes. 'If you think you can get us home safely, I'll vote for you.'

Groan. Pass the bucket.

Then she mouths at him, 'Hero.'

George looks at her as if to say, 'When was I ever not your hero?' (Plus big melty eyes.)

Really?

Double groan.

'So that's it!' says Rhi. 'Two takes the majority!'

I take a small breath. I'm not happy about using a Pookah portal, but it looks like it's decided.

George consults his guide book, which has dried out quite a bit (though it's lost some pages).'The old gates to Annwyn are at Ffynnone, Glaslyn, Llyn y Fan Fach ... ' George checks them off on his fingers. 'Plus Grassholm, Pentre Ifan, and on the Berwyn Mountains – bit missing in the text here – but they've all been sealed shut. Merlin's Oak is blocked, and there are no details of the locations of the Pookah portals.'

'Could be because they are time limited, or move around?' I suggest

'I can teach you the summoning spell,' says Rhi. 'It's really easy. I'm sure you can summon up a Pookah portal.'

She flashes me a Look.

I don't say anything.

Then Rhiannon turns her attention back to George. 'OK, so, you must prepare the way, I think, by pointing the sword in the direction you wish to go. I guess now as we're in Fairyland any direction could be every direction with fairy magic whizzing around all over the place, so in your mind hold the direction we want to go in.'

George does not reply, but lifts the sword and holds it out steady in front of him. 'What now?'

'I think you have to wiggle the tip of the sword around. I'm sure I read that somewhere.' Rhi puts a finger on her chin, then pinches her eyebrows together, as if she's forgotten what happens next.

'OK,' she says, 'once you feel you've got your sword tip in between the worlds, point your ring at it, from the middle finger of your right hand.' She bites her bottom lip and chews on it for a little bit.

I'm pretty sure she's making it up as she goes along.

I vaguely wonder how Merlin has got on with Nimue and if they are reunited and what was said, and how it will affect the High Magick in our world. Then I shiver. I hope we can go straight to Dinas Emrys without going through the Grey Lands again to find a random Pookah portal.

'OK,' says George. 'What now, Rhi?'

'Now you have to use the summoning spell.'

'Which is?' George asks.

'Use the grimoire,' says Rhi.

'But how?' says George. 'I've got both my hands full holding this sword.'

I step forward. 'I think you should hold the sword steady with one hand and knock on the book with the other, very politely, like it's a door.' I hold up the book to him. 'And ask it to summon the correct spell to show us the portal. After all, the book is magical, so it should be able to manage that.'

'Just what I was going to say, plus you need to speak the Summoning Spell Words of Power which are **Imperíum Magís**,' says Rhi. 'Then I agree with Ellie – ask the book to produce the spell.'

I'm almost sure George is going to ask, 'What happens then?' But suddenly it's as if he seems to know. He stands up straight, grows taller. His shadow gets wider and deeper, and for a minute I think I see Merlin and other powerful wizards whose names I do not know as shadows within shadows.

George transfers the sword to his left hand and with his right lifts up the staff. It's a real Gandalf-type walking stick thing. He pounds it three times on the tree-cave floor, knocks three times on the book with the staff's rounded handle and then points it directly in front of him.

There he stands, staff held out, sword held high. '**Imperíum Magís!** To Dinas Emrys,' he commands. 'Open up a Pookah portal. Open up a way through and let us pass out of these Grey Lands.' He raises Caledfwlch higher and twists it a little. He pushes gently with the tip of the blade, as if he is trying to slice into reality.

Around us the shadows lengthen. A strange blowing starts, and the temperature in the tree-cave drops. The blade seems to stick. The sword sings out. A low thrumming starts. I can almost hear the sword telling me it's cutting a way through.

George twists his right hand and aligns the sigil ring with the tip of the sword. A stream of light pours from the ring. It fills the tree-cavern first with a rosy glow, then with the blue light of a full moon.

On the wall, a glimmering portal appears, tall and thin, like the door to a narrow cupboard. Through it, I see the dark peaks of Snowdon, lit up by a star-bright evening sky. I hold the Book of Shadows steady as it starts glowing.

George points the ring at the portal, as if to fix it there forever. The portal opens wider. He knocks on the Book of Shadows again. I feel the book move under his touch. '**Imperium Magis!** Make the spell that will now transport us through this Pookah portal!'

I hold my breath.

'It's working,' whispers George.

Rhiannon takes one long silent backward glance into the tree-cave-house and says, 'Dear Unicorn, I am sorry to leave Fairyland without seeing you again. I've clocked everything you said, though, and I miss you.' She blows a kiss from the palm of the hand towards the mirror, which leaves a trail of sparkles as it travels through the glass and out over a barren landscape.

'Come on,' yells George. 'Rhi!'

She's standing gazing soulfully into the mirror, at the swirling dust of the Grey Lands. 'I will come back,' she says. 'I will try to help you again, if you need me.'

I am not sure who she's talking to, or what about, but when she turns round, tears are welling up in her eyes. I grab her hand and drag her towards the portal.

The Book of Shadows falls open in my hand and across the page I read:

Summoning Spell for a Pookah Portal
WARNING: Only use this spell in extremis

A Pookah portal may be opened up anywhere and at any time, but if a blood sacrifice is not to hand, BE AWARE the portal may seize on one at its earliest convenience.

Once a Pookah portal has been activated, it will remain open for one rotation of the sun to all Pookah and additional members of the Wild Hunt.

The warning comes too late.

We are already stepping through the portal towards Snowdonia.

Towards the mound of Dinas Emrys.

Act Three

Midsummer's Day Evening

She crossed him once, she crossed him twice,
That lady was so brave;
The fouler grew his goblin hue,
The darker grew the cave.

From *The Lady of the Lake*
by Sir Walter Scott

Forty-Five

It's a hot, lazy June afternoon. Everlasting summer seems to stretch across the countryside. High above, skylarks sing. A gentle breeze caresses the mountains, bringing the breath of the hills.

And smoke.

I roll on to my back and gaze up into the blue beyond.

George is standing tall beside me. Caledfwlch hangs, in its scabbard, from his belt. Underneath one arm, cradled by his elbow, is the Book of Shadows. Sparkling on his finger is the sigil ring. He's still wearing Merl's hat. I've never rated boys in hats much. But somehow here on Snowdon, that hat looks kinda cool on George.

'Hey Ellie, fancy meeting you here,' he jokes.

A rainbow aura radiates around him. He stands straight and strong in silhouette against the sun. I realise that even though I've known George all my life, I've never *really* known him. I look up at him in a new, impressed silence.

'George? Ellie?' Rhi's voice rings out from higher up the mountain. 'Helloooo, bunnies, are you there?'

And from over the brow of a nearby ridge she comes. Rhiannon in her velvet princess dress.

So beautiful.

And so out of place.

Rhi and George hug. Then Rhiannon hurries towards me.

'Oh my God, oh my God! WE REALLY DID IT!' she says and throws her arms around me too.

Gently, I disentangle myself from her gangly sleeves. I look at them both. 'Ready?' I ask.

George nods. Rhi looks worried, but gives the thumbs up.

We are ready to unearth Henry and Oswald.

My heart beats like crazy. I have a gnawing feeling at the back of my mind, though, as if we've left something unfinished, something undone. I remember the warning about the Pookah portal, but it can't be helped. And I'm going to see Henry *so soon*.

I scan the horizon. No sign of Pookah, or of Gwyn or any

of his hordes. Only smoke. It drifts up from charred slopes in charcoal-grey wisps. Christ, the smell of it. Almost like the Fae Lands itself.

But not quite.

'Let's go,' calls George.

We dash to the top of Dinas Emrys, through singed woodlands and over ashy, grey grass that crumbles at the touch. The flames have done their work here well.

'We must be fast,' George says. 'Midsummer's nearly gone and you know the balance of power is already shifting. The darkness is growing stronger.'

'Yep,' I say.

'It'll be light until after ten o'clock, but we have a whole mountain to excavate and we can't get that done in half an hour,' George adds.

'Plus a massive dragon fight,' I mutter.

'We'll never get it done!' wails Rhiannon. 'I'm hopeless at digging.'

'Don't worry,' says George with a grin. He points the sigil ring at the Book of Shadows and then I hear him order it. (He's getting the hang of being wizardly.) '**Imperium Magis!** A spell to summon giants.'

'Wait,' I say. 'There are many giants in Welsh mythology. Not all of them are friendly.'

'I just need Idris,' says George. 'He'll come quickly. And I trust him.'

Even as he speaks, there's a stirring in the air. The spell book falls open. The pages whir. They settle. A whirlwind forms over the peak of Dinas Emrys.

'Idris Gawr, by the undying pledge of our friendship, I call on you now for aid,' calls George.

Through the spinning air, I catch the glimpse of a huge shadow. It twists and re-forms itself into a towering figure. Beneath my feet, I feel the mountain move. Thunderous footsteps shake the rocks.

And suddenly the welcome figure of Idris Gawr, giant of Cadair Idris, is beside us.

'**We meet again**,' thunders Idris. '**Perhaps you will be good enough to tell me why you have disturbed my solitary vigil and called me from my bed of rocks?**'

Giants always seem to greet you like that. You know, High Fantasy and **Bold**.

George rushes to Idris and hugs him. Of course he only hugs Idris's kneecaps.

'How are you, my old friend?' says George, 'I came to see you. Did you see me?'

'I saw you,' says Idris. 'It was good to have you sit next to me. The day you came was a day I was especially

358

downhearted. Your visit cheered me greatly, for I realised there is always another day and always another hope. You lifted my heart. I had not looked to see you and yet you came. It helped me believe that I might yet see my beloved Angharad again.'

'Aw, excellent,' says George, 'that's exactly what I hoped.' He holds up the Book of Shadows. 'This, my friend, is Merlin's grimoire! If it has any power at all, then I swear I will use it to bring Angharad back to you! But first we must save Snowdonia.'

Idris stands there stunned. '**Can this be true?**' he bellows.

'It's true,' George assures him. 'I have Merlin's ring and Merlin's hat too. He chose me as his successor!'

Idris starts to laugh, a rumble of thunder that echoes down the mountain and out across the hills. Rhiannon claps her hands over her ears.

'So,' says Idris, 'tell me what task I am to do.'

We quickly bring him up to speed, explaining about Gwyn ap Nudd and Sheila and Nimue and Merlin and the Grey Lands and everything. We tell him about the trip up to the standing stone and how we must free Henry to save the mountains.

'I will help,' says Idris, 'for I smelt that fire even from my mountaintop.'

'That's bad,' says George. 'Then we must work fast.'

'It's totally utterly majorly bad,' adds Rhiannon, 'and even the Unicorn couldn't help put it out.'

Idris looks at her and speaks gently. 'You're very lovely, and if the Unicorn has told you this, then it is the truth. No Unicorn would speak an untruth to one who is so fair.'

He bends down, takes Rhiannon's hand and kisses it. 'Oh my God!' she squeals. 'Oh My God!'

'Erm,' says George, 'there's only one catch. The standing stone set the terms of the quest. It said that nothing can be achieved without the fulfilment of the Heart's Desire. Do I have to ask you what your Heart's Desire is?'

Idris looks down at George and smiles.

'Just testing!' George laughs. 'I think I can summon Angharad, but I don't quite know what magic to use to bring her back to life. I'll order this ring to find me the right spell … and maybe the book will respond … '

Idris says nothing. He looks doubtful, then hopeful. He waits. We all wait.

'Let me see what I can do,' says George.

Again George points the ring at the grimoire. Again he calls out, '**Imperium Magis!** A spell to summon Angharad Golden-Hand.'

Perhaps the wind stirs the bracken around us; perhaps

the ash of mountain flowers is lifted on the breeze. But no Angharad appears.

'**Imperíum Magís!** I summon you, Angharad Golden-Hand!' commands George.

Idris looks sorrowfully around. He stretches his arms wide to welcome Angharad.

But she does not come.

'**Come to me, my dearest one**,' Idris calls, his voice filled with hopeless longing.

The breeze stirs the grass with an unseen hand.

'Just to hope she is near,' says Idris at last, 'is enough. For I fear there is no magic in any Book of Shadows that can ever bring the dead back to us.'

Forty-Six

'We need to cave in part of this mountain.' George points out to Idris to the area around Dinas Emrys that must be excavated. 'We must unearth to about five metres below the surface on the sunrise side. That's where the Chamber of Crystals is.'

'That's where the two dragons are buried,' adds Rhiannon like she is suddenly an expert on dragons.

'That is an easy matter,' says Idris. And in one swift movement, he gouges out tonnes of the mountain.

Dust clouds billow upwards. Dirt. Grass. Sand and soil.

'Maybe do it a bit more carefully?' I say, coughing.

'And more slowly?' adds George, pale.

'We want to free them and confront Oswald, you see,' adds Rhi.

'I hope you have a plan for that encounter,' says Idris, 'for even I fear the White Dragon.'

'I have the sword, Caledfwlch,' says George, swiping the dust from around him. 'And a brave heart. I have to try. My cottage is burnt down, my grandmother is homeless, our ally Lance is mortally wounded and the fires of Annwyn are still raging. It's the only way, so I have to try.'

'I understand,' says Idris.

With his second armful, he scoops the rocks and soil out just about as gently as a tsunami over a sandcastle.

With maybe not quite so much dust as before, though.

Rhi watches, wide-eyed. I cast a Deeply Worried look at George. Idris continues to hew out the side of Dinas Emrys with a third MASSIVE cave-in.

I cough and taste sand and dirt.

'**Imperium Magis!**' George orders the spell book to open up and find Summoning a Soul from the Land of the Dead.

A wind whips across the slopes. The dust blows back in our faces. The scent of burning gets more pungent.

Idris completes a fourth landslide.

The horizon turns orange. *Is that dust or fire?*

The spell book pages flick open and stop at '**To Recall Our Best Beloveds**'.

There's a fifth wrecking-ball onslaught.

I rock dizzily on the mountainside as it quivers underfoot. It feels like some kind of dream. *That orange line on the horizon is definitely fire.* It's all happening too fast – and suddenly I realise why.

Sixth, a mini avalanche descends.

'Hang on!' I yell, spluttering, waving my arms.

Seventh, a stupendous sturzstrom.

The flames are now visible, licking their way towards us like a live snake.

'What?' yells George.

'We need to figure out about Oswald!' I scream. 'We've got to defeat him in a fair fight. Nothing can be achieved against the Heart's Desire. The stone said so.'

'Don't overcomplicate things, Ellie!' yells George.

Eighth, a crumbling cliff attack.

Dust. Dust. More dust. And now smoke.

How can those flames move so fast? Everything's burnt to a cinder already.

'Oswald's not going to roll over and say, "Go on, do it. You win, Goddammit! Kill me. Just make it quick," is he? A BRAVE HEART IS NOT MUCH OF A PLAN.'

George looks like he's thinking about that.

Ninth, an extraterrestrial rockfall. I put my hand over my nose and mouth.

Crikey! Idris is totally going for it.

Still no Angharad.

'*And* we've made another mistake … ' I add. 'The worst mistake possible.'

'What?' asks George.

'Oh no!' shouts Rhiannon, suddenly panicked by the tone in my voice.

'That!' I point in the direction of Clogwyn.

Through the clouds of settling dust, the shape of something huge and dark is forming.

Everything happens at once. The sun sinks faster than ever towards the horizon. The mountains loom upwards in huge dark shadows. The deep blue overhead turns to indigo. A thin pink wash of light sweeps down towards us. The orange flames soar skywards.

Footfalls shake the earth.

The Book of Shadows flicks its pages and falls open.

A shimmering appears high on the mountaintop. Idris looks up and yells, '**ANGHARAD?**'

The shape whirls and a thousand tiny lights sparkle off into the evening sky. Idris strikes the mountainside with three last mighty blows. Snippets of crystal glow through the shifting soil; shards of them shower the hillside, glittering in the setting sun. The rocks shake and one part of the mountainside slips completely away.

Half of the entire cavern of the dragons is revealed. And in a sudden rush of stone, the other half collapses in on itself, and is buried twice as deep.

Idris speeds up to the mountaintop, hoping to meet with his beloved.

'No!' I shout.

The cavern is only half open.

Through the clouds of settling dust, the skeletal shape of something white stirs. The features of a dragon, bone-pale.

No sign of Henry.

We've done this all wrong. Claw and wing and jaw emerge from the dust.

Idris has released Oswald and buried Henry even deeper, under unmoveable piles of rock.

Draco has played a last trick on us. This was not supposed to happen.

George, Rhiannon and I just stand there. The dragon uncoils, blinks and opens its eyes.

No plan and only one sword between us.

Forty-Seven

There is a rustling of dry leather, and a raw icy blast strikes out from the heart of the Crystal Cavern. Oswald, the White Dragon, unfurls his leathery wings.

My heart pounds. Chest tight. In horror, I watch.

There he is, stamping and slithering. *We need Idris back here.*

NOW!

'IDRIS!' yells George.

At first I think I hear Idris's footsteps as he returns from the summit, but then I remember he wears seven-league boots. Those boots hardly seem to touch the surface of the earth. It'd only take one stride. He'd be back by now, surely?

So why is the ground still shaking?

And how are we going to unearth Henry?

The shaking gets worse. The whole of Snowdon seems caught in a ferocious volcanic rumble.

Rhiannon screams, 'LOOK!'

She points back behind us, over the brow of Snowdon, to where a dark shape is rearing up.

Rhiannon screams and screams, her jaw dropped.

A head appears over the mountaintop. Small eyes glitter out from a sneering face.

A HUGE, *MONSTROUS* sneering face.

A face much bigger than Idris's.

The monstrous face is followed by a monstrous torso.

Like a storm cloud, a red hairy cloak billows from its shoulders. Instantly I recognise it from myth and nightmare.

Rhitta Gawr, the Red Giant of Snowdon.

The giant who fought with King Arthur. The giant who slew armies and wove his cloak, thick and heavy, from thousands of beards ripped from hapless victims. Beards stained red in bloody battles.[1]

Oh no! The spell has called up Rhitta Gawr too!

We don't stand a chance.

'IDRIS!' I scream. 'WE NEED YOU!'

---

1. The Red Giant, Rhitta Gawr, is the strongest and most violent of all the Welsh giants. He overwhelmed armies and took their beards as trophies of his victory. Then fashioned them into a cape for himself to brag openly of the fate in store for any foe. Charming.

But Rhitta Gawr has sighted Idris as well. He stamps towards his ancient foe.

Oh My God.

We are out-sized.

Out-classed.

Out of time.

And out of luck.

Inside the collapsed cavern, I see the tip of a red claw, covered in soil.

A claw, an ear, an eye.

An eye that flicks open.

Henry!

Henry will help us!

I run towards him. I must help him get free.

It's our only hope.

But as I run, it seems a great spear of ice enters my chest. My knees give way beneath me. I feel the ice encasing my heart. I fight to hold my balance. It hurts. I stumble forward, falling.

Falling.

And falling …

Falling …

And freezing.

'I WILL HAVE MY HEART'S DESIRE!' roars Oswald.

~~~~~~~

Where am I?

What's happened?

Where's George? Where's Henry?

I can't seem to catch my breath.

I can't seem to catch my balance.

My mind is all misty.

I seem to be looking down at myself.

Floating.

How can I be here and looking down at me?

I'm not moving.

I look like a statue.

An ice stature of a frozen maiden.

I'm sure it's me.

Me, frozen.

Me, lifeless and still.

Me, a statue?

George dumbstruck in horror. Henry's muffled howling wail.

Rhiannon SCREAMING.

I'm frozen.

I'm not moving.
I wait for myself to move.

~~~

The truth slowly seeps in.

~~~

This is me up here.

And yet not me.

For I am down there.

But there is something very wrong with the me lying down there on the blackened slopes of Dinas Emrys.

Why don't I move?

Why can't I feel myself?

What am I doing up here?

Am I dead?

Is this the afterlife?

I don't know. But I must stay here and watch.

I am somehow tethered to the scene below. Although I feel the Distance calling.

It is hard to explain. The Distance. It's like the In-Between Place. Perhaps it *is* the In-Between Place. Its call is urgent. Intense even. It is like the air hunger you get when you dive deep in water and hold your breath.

And yet I can't leave my body. Not there stretched out, frozen solid on the side of Dinas Emrys. I can't leave my friends.

I can't leave Henry.

I don't try to cry out. I don't feel the need for help. I see Henry, all submerged in that humungous rockfall. Trapped underneath half a mountain. Only his eyes are clear. His dear dragon face is covered. He wails, he howls, but his cries are muffled under tonnes of rock. The mountain has swallowed all his dragon flame. I see him struggle to turn his head and breathe gentle, warm air over me. But he can't.

My body stays frozen solid.

And even though I am weirdly anchored to it, I cannot re-enter there.

IT IS FORBIDDEN.

I try to float downwards, it to see if it will accept me.

The Distance calls ... Even. More. Loudly.

And I cannot get back to myself.

The evening halts, seems to stand still. As if time itself must pause to mark my death.

Henry lifts his head, just millimetres. Rocks shift.

I hear an underground rumble. Muffled words. 'A THOUSAND CURSES ON YOU, DRACO, FOR YOU HAVE SHONE OVER THE MURDER OF MY BELOVED.'

And I hear the music of the spheres for the first time ever. Then the voice of Draco, Great Star of the Cold North.

'This is not of my doing, Red One. It is the work of the wizards. They have brought about her end. Dragons do not love. Dragons live forever, even until they become one with the constellation of stars around me and an eternal part of the Great Sky Dragon.'[2]

Henry does not respond but screams. Such a scream. The hillside trembles. A wind stirs. The last of the singed ferns bend their tattered fronds, but his fire is still metres deep. Dinas Emrys seems to glow with a roaring redness. Henry shakes insane amounts of granite, and faster than a thousand arrows – faster than lightning, faster than light itself – a volcano of lava belches forth from Henry and landslides towards Oswald.

I float, watching, wishing I could run to Henry – shake loose the rocks that pin him down, that block his fire – and tell him I am here still.

Because Henry cannot see me. Even his dragon's sight cannot see beyond the veil of Death.

As best I can, I rush towards him in my ethereal form, but even though I call out his name –'Henry! Henry!' – he hears nothing.

I look down at my fallen body. George leans over it.

2. BTW, Draco is a constellation in the far northern sky. Its name is Latin for 'dragon' and it was one of the constellations listed by the second-century astronomer Ptolemy. I learnt about it when Time all went weird in my last adventure in *Here be Witches*. Draco is circumpolar (never setting), can be seen all year round and completely controls Time. No wonder he is so powerful!

Gently he picks me up, carries me to a great boulder near Henry's exposed claw and lays me softly at its side. He wheels around and I cannot describe the look on his face: thunder, sunlight, eternity, sorrow. It is wild, wild wind and parched desert.

'You will pay for this, you monster!' George yells at Oswald, and suddenly he towers up, like a great giant himself. Merlin's hat straightens and grows until it stands tall on George's head. The ring on George's finger flickers through a million colours of the rainbow. I see colours even beyond the rainbow.

George draws Caledfwlch from its scabbard.

Blinding light.

I blink.

It's like looking into thirty sets of oncoming headlights.

On full beam.

And I can't see a thing.

Forty-Eight

I feel a hand slipped into mine. I look round and see her sitting beside me. Most lovely of women, Angharad Golden-Hand.

'Welcome to the Land of Shadows, the Land of Lost Souls,' she says. 'Do not be afraid. I will be your companion. You do get used to it.'

A huge wave of relief sighs through me.

'Know that we are made of dust and snowflakes, of blossom caught on the wind, and we cannot help them now. They cannot hear us, and they cannot see us. It is hard to sit by and watch those you love struggle to live, or die, and know that you can do nothing. All the dead that stay trapped in the Mortal Lands are doomed to this. It takes its toll.'

I look at her; she is still beautiful beyond earthliness.

'Am I dead?' I say.

'Yes, you have passed beyond the veil and are separated forever from your body.'

I look over at my limp form below. I try to reach out to it, but I cannot. 'Try not to panic,' she says. 'I'm here. It is how it should be, and I am here. Together we will sit on this mountainside and watch what happens. Above all things, do not be afraid; everything has a destiny of its own, and what will be will be. We cannot change any of it.'

I follow Angharad's troubled gaze and look up to the summit of Snowdon. I see the Red Giant. I see Idris.

'**We meet again, old enemy,**' says Idris. '**Can we not resolve this quietly?**'

'**QUIETLY?**' returns the Red Giant. '**SINCE WHEN HAVE GIANTS BECOME QUIET?**'

'**We do not need to quarrel,**' says Idris. '**These affairs of men and dragons, do they turn us giants one against the other?**'

'**I WILL NEVER STOP MY QUARREL WITH YOU,**' says the Red Giant and swings a mighty cudgel at Idris.

'Can we not help them at all?' I ask Angharad. 'In any way?'

I won't accept it.

I will help.

Angharad shakes her head as she anxiously watches Idris.

The Red Giant is thickset and heavy. His massive cloak of beards sways ominously. His face is red, his nose large, but Idris — tall, slim and agile — sidesteps the blow.

Sparks fly, for Idris still wears his seven-league boots. He lands on the top of Glyder Fawr, but the Red Giant with three mighty strides is there on the summit too. With one hand he swiftly reaches for Idris's neck; with the other he swings his cudgel.

'No,' whispers Angharad, stretching out a ghostly arm as if to stop Rhitta Fawr.

Am I mistaken or does the air around her quiver — just a fraction?

'Angharad?' I say. I want her to raise her arm again, so that I can be sure. But she does not take her eyes from Idris, and it is my turn to put my arm around her. 'Try not to be afraid.'

And I ask, 'If he dies, then he may join us here, in this afterworld?'

'I do not know,' she says, her voice full of pain. 'Others have died, yet they have not found their way to this place. Here in the Land of Shadows we are handcuffed to the Mortal World because of our love. Sometimes, when others die, we lose them forever. Sometimes they wait for us in the In-Between Place. I do not know. I cannot bear to lose Idris.'

My heart sinks. So I am trapped here. Doomed to watch only – and yet to be grateful that I can. Maybe never to meet with my beloved again. Never to meet my friends. Only to watch them grow and live and forget me.

And what of Mum?

Who will take care of her?

I turn and look at Henry. Will he forget me too?

Oswald is laughing. Oswald is taunting my poor trapped Henry. Oswald is blasting avalanches of ice which sear across the valley and freeze all the midsummer flowers left. Even the flames of Annwyn, far away on the horizon, seem to die back. Their smoke grows thinner.

George tries to get near enough to strike Oswald down, but the sheer force of the ice blasts hurl him back. Then Oswald starts breathing ice over Henry's trapped body. Layer by layer.

Entombing him deeper and deeper.

Can no one stop him?

Blast after blast, George struggles back up on to his feet, trying to confront Oswald.

The lashes on Henry's eyes freeze solid. Soon he's imprisoned in a frozen hillside.

He too can only watch.

'Know that I have broken you, defeated you at long last, Red Dragon,' jeers Oswald. 'My heart is full to brimming to see your true love lying dead, frozen by my breath. Despair and despair, O Red One,' he hisses. 'I will keep you in your case of glassy ice for eternity.'

Henry trapped for eternity.

I sweep my hand through the air to see if I can affect any movement, disturb any dust particle. *Anything* that might let Henry know I am not lost forever.

Anything to ease his heart.

But there's nothing.

'Angharad,' I cry, 'is there anything we can do?'

Angharad tears her eyes away from Idris. 'I do not understand all the different realms that exist and I have no control over them,' she sobs. 'I have stayed a phantom for millennia, and found no way to ease the pain. You are doomed now to share the same fate as me.'

Angharad holds on to my hand. I hold on to hers. I watch Henry. She watches Idris.

And in between everything is George.

He shouts out, 'It is enough, Oswald! All this must end.

I have Merlin's book and his ring. Beware those of you who would defy his High Magick.'

With one swift movement, George raises Caledfwlch and steps forward. He holds the sword clenched in his ring-hand. Around him an aura of light forms.

He advances towards Oswald. And Oswald veers backwards. Even Henry shifts in surprise. The ice around him cracks, just a little.

There must be some way I can help.

Suddenly Angharad clutches my arm. I turn and notice that Idris has gone. Rhitta Gawr too.

'Idris has taken the fight back to Cadair where he knows the territory. Rhitta Gawr has followed. I must follow too. I must be there with Idris,' Angharad whispers, her voice troubled, urgent. 'I believe just being near him is helpful, just sending him my love and strength.'

'I understand,' I say. 'But I must stay here.'

'I understand too.' She kisses me lightly, such a soft, sweet kiss. 'I will return,' she says. 'I will not leave you alone for long in this Land of Shadows. But I cannot delay a moment.'

And in a swirl of summer blossom, she's gone.

O Snowdon, please protect Idris. Help him to defeat Rhitta Gawr.

And protect George too.

I cross my fingers. And I focus back on the scene below me. I send George my love and strength.

George marches towards Oswald. Rhiannon follows him. The aura of light moves with them. It expands into all the colours of the rainbow. The ring on George's hand beams out like a torch. Caledfwlch shines with the light of a thousand suns.

George motions Rhiannon to wait, and unbuckles his scabbard. 'Wear this for me, Rhi. It is too clunky and too heavy. Wish me luck.'

I see what he's doing.

I know that scabbard is not heavy. He is protecting her.

Brave, kind, gallant George.

'White Dragon,' calls George, 'you have done much harm. You have sought to overthrow the Red Dragon for no good purpose, and for too long. This hatred has taken you over, until you have no other desire than to crush and kill Henry and all he loves. Now you have done so! You have taken Ellie, broken Henry's heart and imprisoned him in ice. But in taking her, you have freed me, because I no longer care if you are a dragon or a dormouse. I have only one desire now and that is to slay you. And I will not stop – so repent now, or God help you!'

Oswald flaps his scaly wings, lets out a puffing laugh and

jeers back, 'Boy of the burnt building, do your worst. You have stood against me once too often. And now you will pay for it.'

George doesn't appear to care, but says, 'I command you: by all the magick of Merlin, by his Book of Shadows, by his ring that I now swear upon, by this sword that has the blessings of Nimue, Lady of the Lake, leave off your fighting. Go home to England. Plague us no more! Return to Wessex and never again put foot in our beloved Wales!'

The whole mountainside grows eerily quiet. I focus myself. I send love. I send power. *Stay strong, George.*

'This is your one chance. If you do not accept it, I will cut you down, as I might cut down a bunch of thyme to hang in my grandmother's cottage.'

'You! Cut me down?' screeches Oswald. 'Who are you? And look what has become of your grandmother's cottage! You are nothing but an old woman's skivvy, a woodcutter who has swapped his puny axe for a tin blade. You think you have the power of Merlin's book and ring, because you have somehow managed to dig out a sword? You lie! Those toys are relics from some ridiculous museum. You think that those will defeat me?'

'Have a care how you talk of Merlin's power,' warns George, his voice low and steely. 'Have a care how you insult

the sword Caledfwlch, for it does not endure insults lightly.'
The aura of light around George shines on, the blade of the
sword growing incandescently brighter.

The flickering blinding starts again. I squint my eyes.
I send my energy out. Love. Strength. Success.

'DEFEAT ME? Defeat the ancient worm of the white
hills of Wessex who has lived for millennium upon
millennium, and who will live forever, while your brief
candle flickers out? Your candle which will be extinguished
NOW!' screams Oswald.

In one massive blast, an ice hurricane rushes down on
George.

I cannot help it. I let out a cry. I shut my eyes. *George, my
best-of-best friend.*

I can't bear to watch him die. *NO!*

Not after we have tried so hard and come so far.

*George, who has always been there … A future where there
will be no George … whether I am in it or not …*

NO!

But George does not fall. He does not turn to ice. He says
something to the ring. The aura around him glows pink
then red. The ice blast rebounds off it and hits the slopes of
the faraway mountains.

I rise up. Too quickly. My disembodied self, as light as a

feather, shoots up into the clouds. I see that the coast and the sea beyond – right down to Black Rock Sands – has frozen.

But George has not.

He raises Caledfwlch.

Oswald's jaw falls open. A look of complete and utter disbelief transforms his evil face. He sees that George has not fallen; he sees that George is before him – within striking distance.

He sees that George has not lied.

Henry shifts again, trying to break free from his ice cave without success. *Oh Henry!*

'I came too close to you once before,' says George. 'I attacked you with my axe. I had nothing but my love for Ellie and a belief that love and a weapon were strong enough. You wounded me on that occasion.' He rips open his top to reveal a crosshatch of great scars on his chest. 'But now you have come too close to me, so by these very scars which you made upon me, I take the power to strike you.'

Oswald tries to skedaddle backwards, his great claws slipping on the compacted ice. He tries to flap his wings and twist away to gain some distance.

He blasts his worst. There are more frozen hurricanes. But nothing touches George. And Oswald trips and slides on his own ice.

Straight towards Caledfwlch.

George raises his sword arm.

Caledfwlch cleaves the sunlight from the shadow.

'I gave you your chance,' says George. 'I will not give it to you again, for I see that you have no desire to change. Even if you now beg me to allow you to return to the chalk hills of England, where you might live a peaceful life, I will not show mercy.'

Oswald tries to back off, but the hillside is far too slippery.

'Join the constellation of Draco and become a solitary white star – you are done with your time on earth, Worm of Wessex!' George brings Caledfwlch down.

The blade shears a line straight through the scales of Oswald's neck and his head is cleaved from it.

Forty-Nine

A blurred whirlwind, a torrent of great white ice. Oswald's body flashes and writhes.

Everything pauses. The White Dragon slumps down into the torn scar of Dinas Emrys. Time seems to stands still.

Oswald is dead!

George did it!

George actually DID IT!

I want to jump up and down and clap. I do jump up and down. I clap and clap. Nobody hears me.

Oswald is DEAD. The curse over Henry is over!

Everything stays paused, frozen, immobile.

Everything except one person.

One figure moves. A scuttling outline, running towards George.

It trips and stumbles on its uphill route between the

old twisted trees. But it keeps going. In view. Out of view. In view again. There's no mistaking who it is.

Sheila.

Sheila. Evil ~~bitch~~ person. She twists through more trees. We must free Henry quickly. *Oh Idris, come back, we need you!* Sheila reaches the top of Dinas Emrys – what's left of it, anyway.

And there is Rhiannon in her velvet dress. She looks as surprised as I am to see Sheila. Rhiannon confronts her.

Sheila tries to push past.

Rhiannon raises her hands and blocks Sheila's progress. 'You disgusting COW!' Rhi says and pushes Sheila backwards.

'Get out of my way, you DONUT!' Sheila yells. She punches Rhiannon in the face and her nose starts bleeding. Rhi flops back in surprise.

In a terrific sprint (which frankly I wouldn't have thought her capable of), Sheila races up to Henry, and stands directly above him as he lies imprisoned in his glacier. She raises a hammer and strikes out.

'Nooo!' I yell.

But she does not hit him. Instead she smashes the ice around his face. I watch in disbelief as she cracks great slabs of it off. *Is she trying to help him?* She clears an opening around his eyes. I notice she leaves his mouth (which could roast her alive) iced shut.

What is she doing?

Even George is confused. He steps away from Oswald and looks up at her from the debris around the hillside.

I thrash the air around me, willing the motes of dust to swirl. Nothing stirs. Or ... perhaps a tiny shift? I *must* be able to help somehow.

Sheila chips away at the ice.

I cartwheel my arms round and round. *Angharad moved the air. I'm sure I can do it.*

Round and round.

The air quivers, just a fraction.

IT QUIVERS!

It *definitely* quivers.

If it quivers even only a little ... it means there might be a way!

'Sheil?' George calls.

She turns and gives him a thumbs up.

Does that mean she's decided to be on our side?

I'm not sure. I seriously doubt it.

Be careful, George!

I try to take it all in. *Oswald dead. Sheila trying to free Henry. But why is she doing that?*

And George, best of friends, Wizard, Dragon-Slayer.

Sheila taps away with her hammer. But there's no way she can free Henry.

George calls out, 'It's pointless, Sheil. You can't free him. *Sheil?*'

She doesn't reply.

Caledfwlch is still smoking from the blood of Oswald. So by the side of the great scar, by Oswald's slumped carcass, just metres downhill from Sheila, George bends down and cleans its blade, still calling out, 'Sheil? Talk to me.'

I sit, teeth gritted, fingers crossed. If. I. Can. I. Will. Help.

On the far horizon, the flames of Annwyn recover, burning brighter than ever. Their smoke joins the storm clouds gathering overhead. Not good.

A rumble of thunder echoes across the range. Far out, somewhere towards Beddgelert, lightning strikes. It reminds me of the way the storm gathered around us in Carmarthen.

A wind whips down the mountainside. *Storm! I know who's coming!*

'Sheila?' George yells again.

'COW!' yells Rhi at Sheila, then, 'She punched me, George!'

George is not himself. He keeps sniffing and dragging his

sleeve over his eyes. I hear him whisper, 'Oh Ellie, I've done what you wanted, what we set out to do. I wish you were here to be happy about it. I don't know what to do now. Henry's trapped. There's no way I can melt the ice. Even Idris can't melt ice. How are we going to put out the fire if Henry is trapped?' His voice goes hoarse, and I think he's crying; except that boys like George don't really cry. They just sniff and chew their lip and stand around in shock.

George: stunned at what has happened; astounded at what he's done; unable to accept I'm dead.

All alone, desolate and broken.

Poor George.

I cry out to him. But he doesn't hear me. I tell him to get Rhi and get out – that danger is coming. That his arm bone should warn him – that he shouldn't be so sad, because I'm not dead.

No. I *am* dead, but it's not as bad as he thinks – *I'm still here.*

I can still see him.

'I'M STILL HERE, GEORGE!' I yell.

But it's pointless. Angharad was right. I'm doomed to only watch, unable to help.

Between lightning strikes and the thrum of thunder, something streams over the far horizon. The tempest blows. The rain slices down. *I knew it.* The storm whips up a fury.

He's coming.

Just like in Carmarthen.

George still stands there, wiping the blade of Caledfwlch. 'GET OUT!' I yell.

Too late. Into the valley under Dinas Emrys rides Gwyn ap Nudd, his wild stallion moving like the wind. Behind him, the hordes of Annwyn stream out. The Pookah, grinning evil goblins, catapulting, cartwheeling, back-flipping and prancing; endless armies of them. The white wolves of Cŵn Annwn, those evil hellhounds, their eerie wailing filling the air. And a fearsome hag that shrieks and cries and urges the hounds on.[1]

Gwyn ap Nudd leads the way, club in one hand, spear in the other, horned and with blackened face. King of the Otherworld, Dark Wizard of Necromancy. Riding fast. Whirling wind. Crashing thunder. Seated in front of him, small and pale, rides the changeling child, its tiny chubby hand twisted into the horse's mane.

Oh, if only there was some way to snatch that child, to free it from its captors.

---

1. She's called Mallt-y-Nos, meaning 'Matilda of the Night', or alternatively known in Welsh folklore as *Cŵn Mamau* ('Hounds of the Mothers').

Rhi sees them. 'GEORGE!' she screams. 'THEY'RE COMING! GWYN AP NUDD!'

It was the Pookah portal. We opened the way.

'GEORGE!' I screech. But George doesn't hear me.

'GEORGE!' Rhi's voice is hoarse with shouting. 'They've got the changeling! I'm going to try and snatch it!'

Brave, stupid Rhi.

But George, blissfully unaware, finishes cleaning his blade. He reaches for the scabbard, then stops as he remembers he gave it to Rhi.

'GEORGE!' I scream again.

Something, I hope it was me, makes George raise his head.

He looks up – so hopeless, so upset and then *so totally shocked* – as he sees the towering figure of Gwyn ap Nudd and the Wild Hunt bearing down on him.

Not a moment too soon, George holds Caledfwlch ready and shouts, 'By the power of Arawn! Come no further. Take your horde and go back to your Grey Lands.'

He is greeted only by laughter.

And the silence of the white wolves.[2]

---

2. Remember, their growling is loudest when they are at a distance, and as they draw nearer, it grows softer until they are silent. That's really reassuring, isn't it?

Fifty

Our only hope is Henry.

How can we free him?

Sheila taps away, cleans all the ice from his eyes. *What is she trying to do?* She straightens up and, flicking back her hair, opens her handbag and pulls out a small spray perfume bottle. A perfume bottle?

What is she up to?

Does it have some magic that can melt ice and stone?

'Now we'll see who you'll give your heart to!' she says, laughing.

Whaaat?

I knew she wasn't to be trusted!

But she's not going to spray perfume into his eyes, is she? For God's sake! I mean, how nasty and twisted can you get? But mostly, how plain weird.

Perfume in his eyes?

I mean, who does that?

But she does. She actually sprays perfume in his eyes! Poor trapped Henry closes them up tight. It's all he can do. I swear she must've lost the plot.

Sheila laughs and says, 'Go on, open them – and let's see who you love most then!' And she stands square centre of his line of vision.

It wasn't perfume, was it?

That's what she was doing when we saw her in Nimue's crystals. That's the potion she was brewing up. That's why she was clearing the ice around his eyes.

It's a love potion.

A potion to steal his heart away from me forever.

I can't bear it. I CAN'T STAND IT. I'm dead and now I'll be forgotten and unloved. I've given my life and accepted the deal of the standing stone and risked everything to stop Gwyn … but it was always about Henry, always about needing him, loving him. And now he will love *her*. My eyes well up.

I hate her.

I hate, hate, HATE her. Everywhere I go, every time I try to put my life back together, every minute I've spent with Henry, ALWAYS overshadowed, spoilt, RUINED by her.

Sheila laughs. She sprays and spays again, then tosses the bottle aside.

Henry keeps his eyes closed.

'OPEN THEM!' she screams. 'You can't keep them closed forever! Open them and look at me!'

But Henry just lies there encased in his prison of ice, his eyes tightly shut.

Sheila jumps on to his face. She tries to force his eyes open, but he heaves and struggles.

I watch. I try to breathe. Henry has dragon's vision. He doesn't need to open his eyes to see what's going on.

He's refusing to look at Sheila.

'Open your eyes!' she screams again.

But Henry strains, cracks ice in his struggle and keeps them tight shut.

Henry still loves me.

'Don't ever open your eyes for her, Henry,' I whisper. 'Not until she is long gone.' I turn my attention back to the valley below.

Oh George, be careful.

Dear Snowdon, protect him.

Gwyn rides tall. Taller than any person I know, and definitely a lot taller than George. His face is darkened, smeared with something that looks like berry juice. Horns

I've never really noticed before grow from the top of his head as if he is part stag. I shudder. *Is he part devil?* Right in front of him on the horse clings the child, his little face so woebegone and lost. That poor, poor, poor little changeling child. Like Rhi, I wish to God there was some way to help him.

Gwyn ap Nudd holds his hands out. He gestures for his hordes behind him to hold back. Then he steps his horse up closer to George, his shadow falling before him. 'I sent the best Pookah I had to betray you. And you weren't betrayed. I sent my demon flames against you and yet they burned you not. I set devil dogs to hunt you down, yet you escaped them; I sent the storm clouds at you and yet you fended them off. I sent the tusks of the wild Twrch Trwyth to gore you, and it killed you not.

'So I have come myself to settle the matter, once and for all, lest you evade me again with your cunning. My heart cannot be satisfied until I see you lying in the dust like your companion.' He waves an arm over at my body (*is that really me there dead?*), lying by the boulder where George so gently laid me.

George just stands with his sword held high. An aura of brilliant light shines all around him. 'Have you come here to bore me to death with your words?' he says.

Somewhere overhead a huge dark bird flaps low. Its cawing punctuates the silence with harsh notes.[1]

'If you think you can stand against me, then do your worst,' says George. 'But be warned, Oswald thought he could defeat me. Yet the gifts of both Merlin and Nimue are with me. Furthermore, I have been called upon by your nemesis, Lance, heir of Lancelot, the son of Arawn, to claim back his kingdom from you. For his blood has touched my hands and his ancestors' blood has anointed this blade. If you cross me, you cross him too. So have a care.'

George rolls up his sleeve and nicks himself on Caledfwlch. A trickle of blood darkens his wrist. A few drops fall on to the blackened mountainside.

'By the blood of Arawn, by the prophecy that haunts you, if you get not hence, this very blade that has shed my blood will shed yours.'

Gwyn laughs and all the Pookah cheer, then the Cŵn Annwn join in … until all the Wild Hunt howl in unison with their creepy hunting cries.

'So if you value your kingdom, turn back,' George continues. 'Return to the Grey Lands; call off your fire

---

1. The Adar Llwch Gwin are giant birds, similar to griffins. My Welsh isn't that good, but *llwch* means 'dust' and *gwin* means 'wine'. These birds understand human speech and obey whatever their master commands. I've only ever heard of them in scary fairy stories.

and your dogs and your Pookah and leave my mountain in peace and quiet.'

Behind Gwyn, the Pookah climb on top of wolves and kick them with their heels until the baying and the howling echoes up the hills and down again.

Gwyn raises his spear and yells, 'Let the Wild Hunt begin!'

Bows twang, arrows whistle, the wolves pounce forward. But around George no arrow falls; no member of the wolf pack dares break the aura of light to hurt him.

Gwyn raises his spear a second time and the advancing hordes stop. 'Badbh, companions of the Morrigan!' he calls.[2]

A darkness comes on. A black cloud covers the sky. A storm blows in. Thunder rolls. A wild wind roars up and whistles down the mountain. Lightning strikes towards George.

And does not touch him.

Beneath the thunder, another blackness whirls forward – a vast cloud of birds, so dense that no light can be seen between their wings.

Carrion crows ... ominous, evil.

---

2. In Celtic mythology, the Badbh is part of the trio of war goddesses known as the Three Morrigna. She is not good news. She is a war goddess who takes the form of a crow. She causes fear among warriors and swings the tide of any battle her way. With powers over carrion birds and wild hounds and with her sisters, Macha and Nemain, Badbh is a horrific foe. Oh George, take care! May the power of Merlin and the Lady go with you!

'No!' cries Rhi. 'NO!' And seeing George standing alone against such a dread army, she throws herself between him and the hordes of Gwyn ap Nudd.

'RHI!' shrieks George.

Oh Rhi – true, loyal, crazy, loveable idiot.

There she stands, bravely, defiantly: Rhi in her princess dress.

'Stop it, you DREADFUL PERSON,' she screams at Gwyn. 'LEAVE GEORGE ALONE!' She flicks out her arms as if to shoo Gwyn and his hordes away. 'BEGONE, SPAWN OF WHATEVER!' she shrieks, arms lifted, standing between the advancing ranks and the boy she's always loved.

'Rhi!' I yell. 'Get out of there. They'll mow you down.'

'Get back!' screams George. He tries to reach her, but the hordes of Gwyn ap Nudd surround her.

'And hand over that POOR little child!' shrieks Rhi. 'You PAEDO-PSYCOPATH!'

I cover my eyes, and yet I must still watch.

Gwyn lifts his arm. With one swift motion, with a flash like gunfire, with a sound like a whip cracking and one flick of his wrist, his spear flies free. It hits Rhiannon right through the throat.

A fountain of blood.

NOOOOO.

She falls, but as she goes down she reaches out. She snatches the changeling child from where it rides in front of Gwyn ap Nudd. *She snatches the child. Selfless love. Just like in all the legends. Brave, fearless Rhi.* The boy lands in her arms. She tries to speak, but the gurgle of blood drowns out her words. As she falls, she entangles the baby boy in the velvet of her gown.

Blood spurts, pooling on the ground beneath her. The boy lies protected by her fallen body. *Oh Rhi!*

Gwyn does not pause; perhaps he has lost interest in the child already. Perhaps once a child is snatched back into the Mortal World, he cannot reclaim it easily. Perhaps he is too intent on defeating George. He only bends to pulls his spear free of Rhi's limp body, while the Wild Hunt trample over her.

Rhiannon: playmate, best friend, stupid airhead, best of besties. Rhi. *I can't breathe.* I can't cry out. My eyes fill with hopeless tears. My chest caves in. *How can this be happening? Gran? Henry? How can it have come to this? How did you let this happen?*

Rhi, so brave and so scared all at the same time.

Rhi?

There she lies, all alone on the mountainside in her fairy princess dress, torn and bloodied.

And Gwyn and his Wild Hunt gallop on.

On towards George.

The darkness of the crows descends, intent on blotting out George's aura of light. The horde cheers in a dreadful cacophony of hate. They crowd forward, surrounding him. The wolves howl at the sky. The Pookah cry out in triumph.

George stands there, a lone light amidst a tsunami of gathering darkness.

'Come!' he calls. 'Come and taste the steel of Caledfwlch, for you have slain my friends, and I shall have my revenge.'

On one side of George are the Pookah and the white wolves of the Cŵn Annwn with their fearful hag, the hound mother; on the other, the towering figure of Gwyn. Above, the carrion crows.

Gwyn ap Nudd laughs. He casts his spear at the sky. He cries out in his foul language. *A spell. A curse. A hex?*

No. A command.

I start to recite the Druids' prayer. I don't know if it will help, but I've got to do something.

The sea of crows descends. Caledfwlch flickers into life. A thousand birds are slain in the speed of light. A dark carpet of blood and feathers forms around George. The first thousand are followed by thousands more and soon George is knee-deep in carnage – scratched, pecked, weary. And the pages of the Book of Shadows are torn and scattered to the wind.

All the time Gwyn ap Nudd laughs. 'Fight on, boy of the mountain. You cannot stand against all of us forever.'

Gwyn ap Nudd lifts his arm. The wolves of the Cŵn Annwn attack. Caledfwlch swipes from side to side, again and again. Up to down, a blur of light. Wolves fall. Yet more wolves replace them. Everywhere is thick and heavy with wolves and blood, fur and feathers. I bite my lip. I chant harder. *Snowdon, Draco, stars above, help George, protect George.* And still the crows swoop down and the grinning, gibbering Pookah cheer.

I can hardly see George for the press of the hunt around him. *Snowdon, Snowdon, protect your son. Let him survive.*

George disappears within the onslaught.

Then I catch sight of him again, tired, and moving more slowly yet still bravely fighting. *Ancient Ones, help George.*

On the edge of the struggle, next to Gwyn ap Nudd, a huge hound with gleaming yellow teeth and white fur flecked red crouches low. Gwyn ap Nudd laughs and laughs and points at George. 'Go, my faithful Dormarch!'[3]

The huge beast springs at George. High. Higher than high. His weird tail beating the air. Round and round cranks

3. Dormarch has one head, two front legs and a body that narrows from the chest, ending in three fish-like tails. He looked like the other creatures until he leapt in the air.

the tail, like a mad propeller. Up, up rises the hound. Flying, soaring, he twists and turns with agile speed. As Dormarch spins and falls, his jaws click to with a hideous clack.

And Caledfwlch is wrenched from George's hand.

NOOOOO!

Gwyn ap Nudd shouts his triumph then stretches out his arm.

With one blast of dark energy, he strikes George down.

Oh God, no. I cover my face with my hands yet again.

Unprotected now by Caledfwlch, George falls.

No, this can't be happening.

Like Rhiannon before him, George lies there while the hordes of Annwn tear over his body.

NO. NO. NO. YE GODS AND STARS AND MOUNTAINS ... HOW CAN THIS BE?

George?

Crushed in their wake.

Crushed with a thousand wounds.

Already the earth around him is dark red.

George. Rise up!

George?

There he lies broken and dying, while Gwyn ap Nudd leads his hunt on up the side of Dinas Emrys.

Up towards Henry.

Fifty-One

My heart pounds.

My breath is caught somewhere far away.

My eyes are wide, although I wish I could close them. I wish I could turn back time.

Why did we ever set out on this mission?

Where did we go wrong?

The Oracle said 'by the Heart's Desire' – was it only the desires of Gwyn and Sheila and Oswald that counted?

We were doing so well.

And though I have no heart, my heart is trembling. I have no eyes, yet I am crying; no voice, yet I'm sobbing. *Oh, my friends ... I'm so sorry ... It was not meant to end like this ...*

I look over at where Henry lies trapped. *Dear God, don't let them hurt Henry.* I bite my knuckles that aren't there and they hurt ... I hurt and hurt.

I should never have asked George to come. Never allowed Rhi to ...

OH GEORGE.

GEORGE!

GEORGE!

GEORGE!

It's hopeless, awful, beyond awful.

I'm powerless, trapped and dead.

And still the hordes of Gwyn stream up Dinas Emrys. They form a circle around Henry, lying helpless in his coffin of ice.

Not Henry too ...

OH NO.

DEAR GOD.

Draco! Stop it! Help him!

With superhuman effort, Henry struggles to break free. His eyes still tight shut, his head still encased under ice metres thick. Without his fire to thaw the great slabs, he's helpless too.

'Open your eyes,' shrieks Sheila for the umpteenth time.

Henry ignores her.

Dragons' second sight is sharp. He snakes out a great scarlet claw, through a crack in the glacier that traps him. He stretches it out, hooks up my fallen body and cradles my form close to his face … then raises me up in front of his eyes.

'NO!' screeches Sheila. But Henry ignores her.

And opens his eyes.

'NOOOO!' shouts Sheila. 'YOU WILL NOT LOOK AT HER!' She tries to pull my body away from his grip. 'YOU WILL NOT LOOK AT ELLIE!' She yanks at my poor dead arms. But it's too late. Henry *has* looked at me.

Sheila erupts in fury, stamping her foot, raising her fist and cursing the sky. She goes purple. 'You will pay for this now, you GREAT FAT SLUG,' she hisses at Henry. 'You would rather fall in love with a corpse than me?'

Henry, how could I ever have doubted you?

'YOU ARE GOING TO PAY FOR IT NOW!' screams Sheila. 'You chose to love her, even though she is gone and dead. YOU WILL NEVER HAVE HER BACK!'

She's beyond furious. She's explosive, toxic, volcanic.

I think it's pushed her over the edge. *I'm glad. I hate her. It's all her fault.*

She can't believe that SHE, Sheila, the girl from Llanberis corner shop, who could have any male she wanted, has failed to get the one person she's set her heart on.

I don't understand her, though. Is it pride? From the very

first moment she suspected I had a boyfriend, she swore to take him from me. *Why would someone do that?*

And now it has come to this.

Sheila turns to Henry one last time and spits at him. 'Even though I went to all this trouble – made a love potion, called Gwyn ap Nudd out of Annwyn to burn Snowdonia and destroy Ellie and George and that stupid braindead Rhiannon – even though I've eliminated *everyone* who stands in my way; EVEN THOUGH I DID ALL THIS FOR YOU, YOU PREFER TO OPEN YOUR EYES AND LOOK ON *HER* DEAD BODY!'

Oh George. Oh Rhi. You didn't deserve this.

'ARE YOU STUPID?' Sheila finishes.

Oh my friends.

Henry does not respond. He doesn't blink. He doesn't even cast a glance in her direction. He just looks at me and huge tears fall from his dragon eyes.

Hot sad tears.

'Well, if I can't have you, NOBODY WILL!' shrieks Sheila.

She turns to Gwyn ap Nudd. 'Here he lies, your ultimate enemy. The one who can quench your fires with one puff. My plan has failed, and if I cannot have him under my thrall, then you are at risk. He can use his fire at any time when the ice thaws. And it will thaw.'

'He will not quench my fire,' hisses Gwyn.

'Get real, you MORON!' yells Sheila. 'He'll breathe his flames all over this mountain and you won't stand a chance! His breath will go straight through the Cloggy cliffs and quench the fires in your place too. Wake up and smell the FLIPPING coffee, Gwyn! You'd better kill him now – while he is trapped in ice.'

'There are risks to slaying dragons.'

'OMG, are you CHICKEN?'

'Dragons do not die easily.'

'Yeah? Well, they do with the right weapon.' She points to the valley floor where George lies trampled. 'That sword of his can kill dragons. It killed our friend Oswald, didn't it? And there was no comeback to that, remember? You're a wizard, AREN'T YOU? So you can kill a dragon. Especially one trapped and unable to fight back. That's a NO-BRAINER.'

How horrible can you get?

I can see in Gwyn's face he knows she speaks the truth.

'Once he's snuffed it, I'll take his heart. I'll get it one way or the other. I'll carve it out of him by force, if it's the last thing I do.'

OH GOD, NO!

GREAT SNOWDON, PROTECT HENRY.

Gwyn waves a hand and a group of Pookah rush to George's side to collect Caledfwlch. It takes about ten of them, and even then they're too scared to get very close to George.

One of them touches the sword and screams. They cannot bear the touch of steel. All ten of them scatter and return to Gwyn. The wolves howl. The air trembles. But none approaches the body of George again. Instead, Sheila goes down to the valley floor, picks up Caledfwlch and trudges all the way back up to the top of Dinas Emrys.

'For God's sake,' she says, 'it's only a blinking sword!'

She holds it out, and Gwyn takes it.

He looks at it, weighing it in his hand. He smiles. 'So here you are, sword of swords,' he whispers, 'in my grasp at last. I begged you of Nimue and she refused me. Now, by my wizard's art, I will command you.'

Caledfwlch does not burn Gwyn or jump from his hand, but neither does the blade sparkle and glow in the way that it did for George. It just stays there, heavy, dull, like any other ordinary blade. There is so little shine on it that Gwyn has to turn it over and hold it up to examine it very closely before he reads the words engraved on its blade: "Take me up" and "Cast me away".

'It is the sword,' he says, satisfied, 'and therefore I will take it up and I will slay the dragon.'

I look at Henry, his hot tears slowly melting small pools around his face. I scream out, 'HENRY, SAVE YOURSELF!' But he is so totally incarcerated in the side of the mountain and the ice is so thick over him it's useless.

The hordes cheer. They crowd around Henry's buried shape. Gwyn flexes Caledfwlch. He tests the sharpness of its blade on the icy mountainside.

It cleaves through stone and ice alike, as if they were soft butter.

Gwyn positions himself and selects the spot under which Henry's great heart beats.

Henry's eyelids flutter, his great long lashes twitch. He looks up into the cosmos, as if in search of mighty Draco. One glance. His eyes are wide, unafraid, yet still weeping.

Just before Gwyn strikes, he turns to Henry and says, 'Did you really think you could ever put out my fires?' He laughs, then shouts for all the mountainside to hear, 'See this stupid creature! See his pathetic allies! See what happens to all who stand against Gwyn ap Nudd!'

'You talk too much,' says Sheila.

Gwyn doesn't stop. 'The sons of Arawn have failed! Their blood is weak! Annwyn is mine forever! None shall ever quench my fire!'

Gwyn ap Nudd raises Caledfwlch, and with a terrible tearing and scraping and screeching, brings it down.

Straight through the ice.

Straight into Henry's heart.

I cover my ears.

I close my eyes.

I cannot look.

Fifty-Two

Oh Henry, beloved Henry, beautiful dragon-boy, kind, honest, wise Henry.

They slaughtered you, while you lay helpless.

My heart is broken.

The Menhir of Mawr warned me.

All Must Be Achieved Through the
Meeting of the Heart's Desire.
All Else Will Reap the Heart's Despair.

We have failed in some way and now I must accept the penalty.

But I cannot accept this defeat. I must do something. I must try.

Our enemies will not go unpunished.

It is not over, not yet.

I open my eyes. *I won't let you win, Sheila. I swear by the Menhir of Mawr I will be avenged.*

As Gwyn ap Nudd draws Caledfwlch from Henry, a fountain of the brightest red blood sprays upwards. The skies dim. The air storms. A veil appears in front of my eyes and for a moment I see Henry not as the Red Dragon lying there trapped and dying, but as a boy standing on the side of the mountain – just there, just near. I call out to him.

'Henry? Henry?'

And suddenly, like through a warp in time, I am back there on the mountain, on the morning I first set eyes on him …

A bank of cloud is above the valleys. Everywhere is thick with driving snow. Through the haze, I see a figure. He stands in front of Garnedd Ugain on the very rim of the great knife-edge way above Llanberis Pass. That dangerous place that Mum and I call the Devil's Bridge. I rub my eyes; a new bank of mist has swirled down.

Through the mist, the boy steps towards me. He's impossibly beautiful: dark eyes, thick auburn hair. He's laughing.

Time seems to stand still again. Perhaps this is the way it must always be.

And in losing each other, we have found each other, in a way that was not possible before.

For Henry is here with me.

Now.

HENRY IS HERE!

'Ellie?' he whispers.

I float into his arms. 'It's OK,' I say. 'Don't be afraid. We are together at last.'

But even as we hold each other, I feel the Distance calling.

Yet I know it's going to be OK. I know that the In-Between Place is waiting for us.

'Come,' says Henry. 'We can be together forever now. The In-Between Place is calling us home. There will be no more dark shadows to spoil our time there.'

I sigh in delight. What in life we could not achieve, in death we have been given. An eternity of being together.

And I know it's true.

My Heart's Desire has been fulfilled, though I gave my life to have it.

All the time, this was waiting for me.

But I've vowed two things. Firstly, to complete my quest, to save my beloved Snowdonia, to quench the faery fire. Secondly, I'm damned if I'm going to let Sheila get away with it.

She won't.

I'll avenge my friends.

'How can we use your fire now to stop the fires of Annwyn?' I ask Henry, hoping beyond hope that he really did preserve some of his flames in firestones as he promised.

'It is as I said I would do,' he replies.

I nod. That is good.

'I left three firestones in the cavern under Dinas Emrys.'

'OK,' I say. 'Somehow I will find a way.'

Henry holds me close. 'I can feel the Distance calling so strongly now,' he says. 'It wants us to go to the In-Between Place straightaway and begin our eternity there. Won't you leave this forsaken hillside and come with me?'

'Go ahead and wait for me.' I kiss his cheek. 'I'll come as soon as I can. There are still things that hold me here. I can't leave yet. I must finish what I began.'

Like all wronged phantoms, I am trapped here until my mission is accomplished. Until justice is done.

'I know,' he says. 'You are right to stay, for those things left undone will haunt us if we don't resolve them. I will resist the tugging and stay with you.'

'No. Much as I would have you with me for all of time, go ahead and prepare the way. Hold the door to the In-Between Place open for me until I can be will you.'

'Then I will be waiting. Always and always.'

I know he will.

I know that somehow, miraculously, I have found him forever. And my heart leaps with joy.

415

What is it that I must do then, before I'm free to be with Henry?

I look back down on the slaughter at Dinas Emrys, and a miraculous thing happens. Caledfwlch seems to quiver in the hands of Gwyn. It twists, turns and grows white-hot, so that even Gwyn cannot hold it. The sword rises up to a great height and shines out like a brilliant star, right over the spot where Henry lies.

As it turns in the air, an apparition appears on the mountainside. A phantom white knight in shining armour on a silver steed. Boyish curls flow from underneath his helmet and a red-cross knight kneels to a maiden on his shield.

LANCE!

Ohmygod! It's LANCE, HEALED AND WELL AGAIN!

There he is, translucent, wholly of the Mortal World and yet not of it.

'You have used the sword! You have brought the curse upon yourself!' cries Lance.

Caledfwlch turns all by itself in mid-air, and like an arrow plunges down at a terrifying speed. Lance catches it, and in the same instant sends it straight into the chest of Gwyn ap Nudd.

'Be avenged, my ancestors!' calls Lance. 'My quest is done! I take back Annwyn and claim my birthright!'

Caledfwlch dances in his hand, a deadly choreography of a thousand twirls. The blade flickers round and round. It slices and stabs and shears and cuts and shaves and shanks and carves and slivers, until Gwyn ap Nudd is shredded into a million tiny pieces.

Of course.

I remember what the Lady said: '*Arawn's blood stains the blade. Gwyn cannot use Caledfwlch without peril to his life, lest he summon the wrath of Arawn down upon him.*'

Sheila starts screaming. The wolves of Cŵn Annwn go insane, their cries blood-curdling, uncanny. The hordes of the Pookah shriek. Lance raises the blade high again and sets its aim directly at them.

All the Wild Hunt turn and torrent back towards Clogwyn D'ur Arddu. The air vibrates with their wailing. They sweep off the hilltop and down the slope, faster and faster. Back to the portal that stands open, chased by Lance in shining brilliance, until they are just tiny specks in the landscape.

Like a cold wind, I feel them passing. The ground shakes beneath their feet. Overhead, a flurry of foul wings fans the wild air.

And they are gone.

All the Wild Hunt.

All except Sheila.

Fifty-Three

The sun is setting. Golden rays spill down over Dinas Emrys and mingle with the blood of the fallen until the side of the mountain is awash with pink.

I don't think I've ever experienced anything as awful and hopeless as this.

It's so bad I can't breathe – even dead breathing. I can't cry. If I didn't know that an eternity in the afterworld with Henry was waiting for me, I swear I'd seek death for myself. RIGHT NOW.

All are gone, except for Sheila. There she stands by the dead carcass of Henry.

She pulls out a short blade.

She's going to cut his heart out!

I have to do something.

I won't let her. She will pay for what she has done.

What can I do?

I think back to happier days. Henry and me, here on this mountain. I think of the last time I saw him. Exactly here, actually. A memory flutters, nagging at me.

Something about this place.

I've got it. This is where I came after seeing Nimue, when Henry appeared so suddenly. Her reward. *What was it Henry said?*

'*Focus with all the power of your mind. Imagine yourself in the place you want to be. See your hands, your arms, your feet …*'

I flick my eyes open wide. Maybe I can apparate like Henry did!

Imagine myself on to the hillside, into the Mortal World. Become a proper ghost!

Confront Sheila; find the stones!

I choose a rocky tor just above Sheila. I close my eyes, and see myself standing there. I will myself to appear, so I can haunt her … It might spook her … stop her from desecrating his body …

'*Threaten the threatener and outface the brow of bragging horror.*'

I see my hands, my arms. I imagine my hair blowing in the wind.

Nothing. Well, not yet. *What else can I do?*

Angharad made the air around her swirl. How? She was very upset. Was that why?

'*Focus on bringing yourself to the place you've set your heart on.*' That's how Henry said he did it.

That's it. I must pour all my pain and need and hope into being here on this rocky tor in the land of the living.

I focus. I see my feet and my legs. I look down at the fallen bodies of my friends; I channel the horror and the sorrow and …

A tingling starts in limbs that are not there. I feel it … a pinching and a tickling. But nothing else. Nothing happens.

Below me, Sheila hacks away at the place where Henry's blood has melted the ice.

I just need some way to condense myself, to become channelled …

The straw!

The straw I took from the *crogi gwr gwellt.*

Blow yourself through it, Ellie; pour yourself down it!

I put the straw to my lips and pour myself through it, pushing myself, channelling myself into the spot I've set my heart on. I feel sick. I feel ill. It tingles and hurts and squeezes. It's scary like being pressed in a crowd.

Then I step down. (Don't ask me how, because it's like in a dream when you can be in two places at once. It feels normal and yet distinctly weird.)

And here I am, standing on the rocky tor above the great head of my beloved Henry.

I crouch down beside the dead dragon, trapped beneath the rock and ice. 'I won't let her maim your dragon form, Henry,' I whisper. 'I won't.'

Red blood drains out across the hillside like molten lava.

Sheila squats beside his great flank, still scraping.

She hasn't seen me. Not yet.

Perhaps she won't?

Perhaps my ghosting hasn't worked?

But already I know it *has* worked; I can feel the crossing of the veil like fire racing through my veins. I have only a very short window of time to stop her desecrating Henry's body.

Even if he's lost to me in the Mortal World, she shall not have even the smallest part of him.

She will never have his heart, never, never.

I need to frighten her. But what scares someone as evil as Sheila? Suddenly I have an idea! Sheila was frightened of my spell, my hanging straw man! My *crogi gwr gwellt* which protected Henry's resting place. I must find it.

I must focus myself, pick it up.

So I search while Sheila slices mercilessly at the ice with her dagger, trying to get at Henry's carcass. *Please, Nimue, if this was your reward, help me find my crogi gwr gwellt.*

But Sheila's dagger is no Caledfwlch. And the ice is as thick as the side of a building. She could slice all night and not break through it. She throws back her head and screams in frustration. I spot my *crogi gwr gwellt*, and set about picking it up.

Sheila's screams roll and echo off the side of the mountain. No one hears her. For who is left to hear? Dead or gone, all of them. Only me – my phantom self – to witness her hollow victory.

She raises herself up, turns her face to the summit. Above her, the air shudders. 'I will do this,' she shrieks. 'I Will Have His Heart. I Will Have My Revenge.'

She starts up an incantation:

'Lightning strike, rainstorm bite!
Melt all ice, this very night!
By darkest arts and deadly sin,
Let my unholy work begin.'

The wind howls. A fresh storm sweeps in with sudden vigour. Sheila steps back from Henry's head as a bolt of lightning strikes his solid coffin. There is a cracking, a breaking; a piece of ice shears away.

She calls again. A hurricane blows in – huge energies of air circle, faster and faster, overhead. A second lightning bolt hits the dead body of Henry and more ice cracks. Now a stream starts up around his face, like the meltwater of a glacier. It washes down over his lifeless body. Sheila raises her hands yet again, casts her eyes upwards and catches sight of *me*.

My phantom self, standing on the rocks above her.

Her face contorts. She screams, 'NOOOO, YOU'RE DEAD!'

I slowly raise my hand. I point a finger at her. I hold out my *crogi gwr gwellt*. My tiny straw man. 'Do your work,' I whisper to it. Then I call out in ominous warning:

'*By this crogi gwr gwellt I swear,*

Let Henry's enemies beware.'

Sheila goes pale. I take full advantage.

'Do not disturb the dead. Leave this fearsome work,' I say in a haunted tone (for effect). 'Let Henry rest in peace.'

She laughs like a maniac. 'You!' she says. 'Whether you are there or not, all this is your fault, YOU BACKSTABBER.'

Whaaat?

That is sooo not fair.

'YOU DON'T UNDERSTAND, DO YOU?' Sheila screams. 'I SHOUTED IT FROM THE MOUNTAINTOP, BUT YOU DIDN'T LISTEN.'

That is highly unlikely. Sheila is way too lazy to climb Snowdon.

'I WILL HAVE MY REVENGE. I WILL HAVE THE HEART OF HENRY PENDRAGON!'

What is wrong with her?

It's so sad. She's never moved on. And look at what it's brought us to. All her old mates slain. And she, crazy and cruel, trying to dig up a dead dragon.

It's almost funny.

She had *so many* boyfriends, wasn't I allowed to have even one?

NO. She had to prove a point. She had to have him for herself first.

Crazy. Cruel. Stupid. Sad.

She sold her soul to get him. She's the true backstabber.

And all of us have paid the price.

So horribly, unbearably sad.

And she wants to blame *me*.

I can hardly believe it.

I don't let any emotion show on my ghostly face, though. Instead, I whisper (hauntingly), 'BEWARE.'

'Don't look at me like that, Ellie,' Sheila screams, her face horrible, pale, ugly, yet weirdly beautiful. 'It *was* your fault. You refused to hand him over. You drove me to seek those far more powerful than you, more powerful than dragons, more powerful than love. IT'S ALL YOUR FAULT.'

All *my* fault?

'Nothing is more powerful than love,' I say. 'Leave Henry in peace, for you disturb him now at your peril.' I let out a long, low, spooky cry.

'You wish, you SIMPLETON,' she yells.

'You could've had *anyone*,' I say. 'Why Henry?'

Sheila throws her head back and laughs. Something evil and creepy in her cackling makes my phantom legs feel all crumbly. A bit like the last cookie in the jar.

Then she raises her head and screams at the dark sky, 'BECAUSE YOU HAD HIM!

Is that it?

Is that all it was?

'YES!' she screams.

It's no use trying to understand her or appeal to her. No use haunting her, or trying to scare her off, so I raise my hand again. I fill my heart with love for Henry. I hold the straw effigy aloft and say, 'SEND YOUR POWER AGAINST HER. PROTECT MY BELOVED.'

The *crogi gwr gwellt* twists in my hand.

Let the power of love defeat her.

She cackles, all hate, all venom. She raises her hand too. 'I'll strike you down, Ellie,' she shouts, 'IF YOU DARE TO DEFY ME!

'*Lightning strike, thunder bite!*

Perish all on rocks this night!'

'I'm already dead, Sheila,' I say. 'It won't work.'

'MORON!' scoffs Sheila. 'YOU CAN NEVER WIN AGAINST ME.'

She's lost it, she really has.

And with that she calls the lightning down.

The skies open up, the lightning strikes. The wind crescendos, and the bolt hits me full on.

I don't feel a thing.

The surge of power passes straight through me and hits the rock below.

There's a crackle of static. The rocks shake. A flash of light, then an almost instantaneous boom. My ghostly heartbeat shoots up.

The mountain shakes. Rain pours down. But I don't get wet.

Then, with a demonic explosion, the outcrop of stone I'm standing on splits in two.

SPLITS IN TWO! The air shudders. A boulder crashes down.

Oh my God.

And with a great cracking and a great splitting, another boulder falls.

And another.

An avalanche of stones.

And more.

And more.

And more.

One huge rock knocks Sheila down. She rolls and turns.

She pulls at bracken, the air shivering around her.

Her appalled shrieks rend the air.

The ragged breath of the wind tugs the screaming from her, carrying it into the hurricane.

She twists and howls and rolls towards the cliff edge at the side of Dinas Emrys.

The ground is smooth, treacherous. She's slipping and sliding, ten metres from the edge.

The storm rages. A booming. A shrieking. The deafening roar of a fresh avalanche; a new rockslide splits the evening.

Sheila skids out of control. Screaming, she shoots forward.

'Help!' she cries. 'Oh, somebody help me.'

But there is nobody left to help.

The earth beneath her gives way. Her body twisting, turning, down she plummets over the cliff edge.

Down the cliff …

Down. Down.

Hundreds of metres to the bottom of the pass.

Down beneath Dinas Emrys.

And there she lies like a tiny broken *crogi gwr gwellt*.

Half the upper side of the mountain slope caves away. It splits ice, cracks boulders and knocks the fallen bodies of the two dragons back together into the excavated cavern.

Burying them.

'Great Snowdon,' I call, 'do not bury the firestones too. Throw them free of the cavern so that they may help you put out the fires!'

I think the mountain hears. I hope so. I believe so. The whole mountainside heaves again, more wildly than ever, and a shower of stones flies up into the air.

I focus all my energy. I hold on to being in here, in the living world, as long as I can. I will try to find those firestones. I will. I will try to protect Henry. I will. Right to the last.

Sheila can't hurt him any more.

Stupid, mad Sheila.

Idiotic, envious, horrible Sheila. She brought her end on herself. I hate her, yet I'm sorry for her. Yes, sorry for her, despite everything. No eternity of love and togetherness is waiting for her. She is to be pitied.

The last peal of thunder rolls away to the east. It passes beyond the summit of Snowdon and a darkness descends.

I place the *crogi gwr gwellt* back over the last resting spot of my beloved.

I can hold on no longer.

I am so weak, so tired.

I let myself slip back into the Land of Shadows.

Just a little while longer, here in this ghostly realm.

A little while to watch over the bodies of my dearest friends, until they are claimed again by those who love them.

A little while longer to wait for them, in case by chance they find themselves lost here too. They should not be left to wander here alone.

And so, quietly, quietly, I set my watch.

My phantom tears fall.

My phantom heart breaks.

And as if I am the eagle's eye, I look on.

And eventually my phantom eyes close.

And I dream.

Fifty-Four

In Which Ellie Dreams the Dream of
the Adar Rhiannon, the Changeling Child,
the Unicorn and the Dragon-Slayer

Somewhere down on the valley floor in the hollow beside Dinas Emrys, an evening breeze tugs at the gangly sleeve of a velvet princess dress. The velvet is badly damaged, damp and bloodstained, torn to shreds in places.

Yet the wind pulls on the sleeve, and gently tucks the cloth around the form of a tiny child, which cuddles in sleep to a fallen maiden. The wind turns its attention to the maiden's hair, lifting a dark lock from her forehead and blowing back the damp strands that cover her face. Each lock of hair twists until it falls aside to reveal the closed eyes of Rhiannon.

The moon rises. Thin clouds pass across the evening sky. And so still lies the shape of Rhiannon, in her velvet dress, out in the hollow below Dinas Emrys.

The breeze stirs the wet scorched grass again and kisses her cold lips. It strokes her beautiful face and cries till the night is filled with mournful wailing.

All the little creatures of the mountain, the birds of the air too, cry out in sorrow. Cry and cry until they are silent again. And the child too moans in his sleep, such a sad lost little wailing.

In the darkest, loneliest watch of the night, a wild pony, dazzlingly white, makes her way down from the hilltops. She stops at the lifeless maiden, bends her neck and blows on the back of the girl's hand. The pony paws at the earth and positions herself carefully to stand on guard by the fallen body of Rhiannon.

There she stands. And when the hour is at its darkest, the white pony keeps watch. As the hours tick by, other kindly creatures come, and some keep watch too, while some cuddle their bodily warmth against the baby and soothe his cries with low murmurs.

All are lonely and hopeless, and all send mournful wailing up at the moon.

And so the night progresses, and all things get colder.

But at last the sky on the east side of the hilltops becomes a little less dark. Tiny movements start in the grass at Rhiannon's feet.

For the first time the white pony can see the face of the maiden.

The sky brightens. The stars get fainter, all except one very big star, low down on the horizon. And it is colder than it has been all night.

The shadows of dawn stretch out over Dinas Emrys.

And gently, so, so gently – so gently that even a butterfly might not feel its touch – the morning dew settles on Rhiannon's lips. Such lips! They look so perfect – so pink, glazed by dewdrops in pearly loveliness. A passing hiker might think she only sleeps.

Soon equally gentle drops of rain settle on Rhiannon's face, falling soft and sweet. They collect on her brow and form a haze of droplets down the sides of her cheeks. Slowly, slowly, the rain cleanses her face. All signs of toil and trouble and pain are soothed away, until she lies there free of all traces of blood, free of sweat, free of dust, free of cinder.

Beneath her, the damp earth has soaked up her blood, nourishing the soil. Tiny new shoots push skyward.

Does an eyelid flutter – or was that just a trick of the dawn light?

Can the eyes of the dead really ever open again?

But the maiden's eyelids do flutter, and she opens them. The wind stirs again and passes over her lips, and it is almost as if the maiden's chest, beneath the torn, stained princess dress, starts to gently move.

She is breathing. Can it be?

The white pony steps aside. She climbs to the shelter of an overhanging rock and lies down. She watches over the waking Rhiannon.

Dawn sends a pale wash across the sky. The shadows shorten. Minutes pass. Eyelashes flicker. Lips part; a gentle sighing breath escapes them.

'George?' Rhiannon whispers. 'George, where are you?'

Suddenly the maiden remembers. She sits bolt upright and looks around. She sees the child and holds it close and soothes its waking cry with words of comfort. Then she casts her eyes down at her hands. There are no bruises on them. She pulls the skirts of the princess dress up to her knees. Her ankles are whole and perfect, her skin unbroken. She pats herself gently around her waist. She feels her shoulders and touches her cheek. All is as it should be.

Finally, she runs her fingers over her throat where the evil blade of Gwyn ap Nudd's spear severed her carotid artery.

All healed. All well. All good.

She blinks in surprise or disbelief.

She adjusts the child, still holding him close, and straightens her dress. Her hand comes to rest upon the scabbard.

Of course – she is wearing the scabbard of Caledfwlch! Its magical powers have protected her! And with that realisation comes another.

'George!' she screams.

Where's George? she wonders. *What's happened to him?*

She remembers how George gave her the scabbard, told her to wear it for him, told her to guard it well and wish him luck. George protected her.

Oh George.

She sighs and screams, then cuts her screaming short as she soothes the child who sleeps in her arms. She pulls herself to her knees and then to her feet. She looks around. She sees only tiny shoots pushing up into the dawn's light, and shadows falling down the mountain slopes.

Then she catches sight of the fallen shape of George.

Hurriedly, she tears a strip of velvet from her skirts and wraps the child in them. She lays him carefully beside the shelter of a boulder, and half stumbling, half running, with her torn skirts tripping her, she races to the place where George lies.

'George!' she cries. She lifts his arm. It's limp and heavy.

She bends down. He's stone cold. She weeps over him. She wipes his face. She straightens his crooked limbs. She sets the sigil ring well on his finger. She fetches Merlin's hat and places it beside his head, all the while crying, and then she casts about for the lost pages of the Book of Shadows.

She tries to piece them together, but they are damaged and of no use.

No more tears are left and a sort of quietness comes.

There is nothing else to do.

'Oh help me,' she calls out. 'Oh Unicorn, help me now!'

The white pony picks her way down off the hills.

'Rhiannon,' says the pony softly, 'what was the gift that the Unicorn gave you?'

Rhiannon looks at her. She smiles and her tear-stained face is again beautiful. 'Is it you?' she says. 'It is, isn't it?'

'I come when I am needed. I come in many guises. All white steeds in the Mortal World are under my protection. Here on earth they call us "grey", for we hail from the Grey Lands.'

'Then it is you!' sings out Rhiannon.

The Unicorn – for she is one, although no horn is visible on her now – bows her head. 'Find the gift I gave you,' she prompts Rhiannon.

'Here it is.' Rhiannon removes the tiny silver box from the pocket in her dress.

'Open the box,' directs the Unicorn

Rhiannon obeys.

Three small eggs lie nestled inside.

'Do you know what these eggs are?' asks the Unicorn.

'Not really,' says Rhi. 'Sorry, I'm sure you told me ... but they call to me sometimes, and I hear them singing in my mind when I think about them.'

'These are the Adar Rhiannon, the birds of Rhiannon,' says the Unicorn. 'If you call to them now, they will break free of their shells and their singing will fill the air.'

'And then what will happen?'

'You have the power to direct their singing. For their voices can bring back the souls of the dead, and here you have two beloved fallen friends.'

The Unicorn nods its head in the direction of Ellie, where she lies by the newly fallen landslide. And at George right beside her.

'But,' says the Unicorn, 'you must choose who. The birds can only sing one soul back from the dead. That is their power, and then you must leave them to fly free.'

'Choose?' gulps Rhi.

'Only you have that power,' says the Unicorn. 'The birds belong to you, and they will only do your bidding.'

'Ellie would hate to be alive if Henry was dead,' says Rhi.

'That is true,' says the Unicorn, 'and George too may hate to live, if Ellie is dead.'

'Oh My God,' wails Rhi. 'I don't know what to do!'

'Nevertheless, you must choose.'

'How can I? I hate deciding anything. It's too much. I don't like responsibilities. Ellie's my bestie, but I love George, although he doesn't love me.'

And she sits down with a big frown.

'Can't you bring them both back? You've got magicky powers, haven't you?' she asks.

The white pony shakes her head sadly.

'Then it's really not fair! Everybody knows I can't do anything. I'm totally rubbish at things like this, and I can't make the right decision.'

The pony nods her head gently. 'But this is one time when you must.'

'No, I won't,' says Rhiannon. 'I would hate myself if I made the wrong choice, because I want to choose George, but Ellie deserves to live too.'

'Well,' says the Unicorn, 'in that case, we must refer to the Oracle. There is a greater good at stake here.'

'OK,' says Rhi, 'that's a good idea.'

Suddenly she grabs the Unicorn's fetlock. 'That reminds me of something. Maybe everything's gone wrong because we did not keep to the terms of the quest. The Oracle told us everything had to be by the Heart's Desire. So let me think.' She raises her fingers and counts off:

'1. Ellie: to be with Henry.

2. Henry: to be with Ellie.

3. Oswald: to destroy Ellie and Henry.

4. Gwyn ap Nudd: to destroy George and Henry.

5. Sheila: to have Henry's heart or destroy him.

6. Lance: to vanquish Gwyn ap Nudd.

7. Nimue: to get back with Merlin.

8. Merlin: to find an apprentice so he can be reunited with Nimue.

9. George: to be with Ellie?

10. Me: to be with George.

'All of those have been met,' she says, 'except George and me, I guess.'

'Perhaps there's a way,' says the Unicorn.

'It's no good,' says Rhiannon. 'I even looked for the pages of Merlin's Book of Shadows, but I only found this one.' Rhi holds up a loose page. 'And I'm not a wizard, so I can't magic anything with it.'

'Perhaps there is still a way,' repeats the Unicorn and nods her head towards Dinas Emrys.

'I can't see how,' says Rhiannon.

'You are not looking in the right direction.' The Unicorn hoofs the earth impatiently.

'I don't get you.'

The Unicorn pounds the earth. Rhiannon stands up and looks around.

Lying on the turf beside three round smooth stones with a curious Y shape scratched on to them, is a tiny phial of cut glass.

The love potion brewed by Sheila.

'Inside may remain a few drops,' says the Unicorn. 'You could use them.'

Rhiannon picks up the phial.

'George needs to see clearly where to love and be loved in return, then the terms of the Oracle can be met.'

'I can't spray love potion on George's eyes!' says Rhiannon. 'That would make me as bad as Sheila.'

'Why?'

'Because that's not right! It's not fair. It takes away his choice.'

'Was it fair that he gave you the scabbard of Caledfwlch to wear, so that you should live and he die?'

'Well … no … ' says Rhiannon.

'Then was it not an act of supreme love?' asks the Unicorn.

'Well … yes,' Rhi answers slowly. 'And no … because he was just trying to protect me.'

'And did you not try to protect him too?'

'Well … yes, I suppose I did.'

'Did you jump in front of Gwyn ap Nudd to try to save George?'

'Yes, I did.'

'Do you not think that true love was behind both of those selfless acts?'

'I don't know,' says Rhiannon. 'You're asking too many questions and making me all muddledy.'

'Do you not think it an act of true love, kindness and sacrifice to relieve George of his love for Ellie – who by the way never loved him as you do – now that she has died?' asks the Unicorn.

'Well, I suppose so.'

'And do you not desire his love?'

'DUH! Like, stupid question.'

'Well then, it must be a secret that you and I must keep forever. For the terms of the Oracle to be met, and all to end well, it is a sacrifice you must make, to know that you are loved beyond and above everything, even if you were not his first choice. Can you live with it?'

Rhiannon smiles a great big smile. 'OH HELL YES!' she says. 'I can definitely live with that!'

'Then help him to live and love, and help Ellie to know

that, at last, her two best friends will be safe and happy.'

Rhiannon puts down the page from the Book of Shadows, opens the little cut-glass phial and, with the last drops of the potion, anoints George's poor dead eyes.

The page flutters beside her and she catches sight of the words on it.

'To Recall Our Best Beloveds.'

She smiles and reads the instructions. Then she lifts up the open silver box and calls to the tiny birds inside their tiny shells.

Instantly, the shells crack open and the dawn fills with the most enchanting birdsong.

As their melody crescendos, Rhiannon sings out too in the sweetest of voices:

'Come back to me, George. I've sent my birds to find your soul and bring you home.'

George suddenly starts to look a lot more like himself again – his living, laughing, joking self. His poor dead face almost looks pink.

'Imperium Magis!' sings out Rhiannon, and throws her arms wide.

Light streams down over the peaks of the mountains and everything around Rhiannon and the Unicorn starts to wake up. Another bird trills out from the slopes behind them. It joins in with the song of the tiny birds. Another bird joins in too. Soon birdsong fills the whole valley.

The little changeling child gurgles and opens his eyes. He coos in delight at the morning.

The one big star over the horizon disappears. The mountains turn from dark grey to light. The sky awakens in robes of pink and rose and orange.

The birdsong reaches a pinnacle of harmony. A beam of sunlight from the rising sun escapes over the summit of the mountain and strikes out. It lights up George in a golden pool.

And he stirs.

His chest rises.

And rises again.

His lungs inflate, as the breath of the morning enters into him.

His eyelids flutter open.

And the first thing he sees is Rhiannon.

Fifty-Five

I jerk awake.

I'm sure George was here with me. I know I spoke to him.

But I'm still here. No George. Still out on the mountain.

Still dead.

All alone.

Just a dream, then.

I search the slopes for George and suddenly I see him.

And Rhi!

There they are.

THERE THEY ARE!

Alive and well.

ALIVE AND WELL!

It wasn't JUST a dream at all.

'RHI!' I scream. 'GEORGE!' Ohmygod! Ohmygod!

Can it be true? My heart jumps about in its phantom

ribcage and squeezes up tight. The morning becomes brighter. I shout and grin and leap up and down and grin and grin until my face aches and my ears burn. I shout and shout, even though they can't hear me.

'GEORGE! RHI!'

IT'S TRUE! IT'S TRUE! MY FRIENDS ARE ALIVE AGAIN!

And the changeling child is saved too!

O Snowdon! O Draco! O Ancient Ones and Nimue and Merlin, THANK YOU!

THANK YOU!

THANK YOU!

I look around. The avalanche has swept everything away. Feather and fur, all gone. Rock and rubble, soil and cinder. There's no sign of the dragons; they are buried metres deep under stone and ice in Dinas Emrys. The dust has settled. All traces of battle are gone.

Nothing remains.

Nothing except Sheila lying dead at the bottom of the gorge, and me stretched out cold beside it.

What will the world make of it? I imagine what the news reports will say.

ROCKSLIDE CLAIMS TEEN LIVES IN SNOWDONIA

Early this morning, a hiking group in Dinas Emrys came across the bodies of two teenage girls crushed by a freak landslide. Nearby they discovered two other teenagers, a boy and a girl, and a small child, all of whom had escaped the rockfall. The hikers were able to assist the survivors and summon help.

Sheila Powys and Arabella (Ellie) Morgan were pronounced dead at the scene. The survivors were taken to hospital and later discharged.

In a bizarre twist of fate, the child, a boy, is believed to be the sole survivor of a helicopter crash on Snowdon yesterday evening in which both the pilot and the child's uncle, a paediatrician, died. It is believed the baby must have crawled across treacherous terrain or been transported to Dinas Emrys by wild creatures escaping from the overnight fires. The teens had no idea he was there until after the landslide, when they heard crying and found him.

The child has now been reunited with his parents, who said, 'This is a miracle, a true divine intervention. We cannot believe our good fortune. He was so ill, even before the crash we had little hope; after the horrific accident we'd given him up for dead and here he is returned to us.'

The doctor who examined him stated, 'He is in amazingly good shape considering his ordeal, and there is no trace of the life-threatening condition for which he was being flown to Birmingham.'

This afternoon they will tell my mother.

Gran already knows.

Later on I will check up on them all.

One of the advantages of being a phantom is you can duck and glide through great distances in the blink of an eye.

So here I am, with Gran and George and Rhi.

They are sitting in Gran's hotel apartment. George and Rhi are telling her everything. Gran is preparing a lovely restorative tonic to give my mother, which sparkles with a strange glow. I can see its secret ingredient is stardust.

I'm so glad. I worry most about Mum. How she will feel. How upset she will be. The stardust will soothe all those painful feelings. It will bring calm and forgetfulness. She will never totally forget me, of course – but with the help of the stardust, she will be able to move on, to start her new life with Jeff. She will be happy again. Of this I am sure.

Rhi has told Gran all about the Unicorn, and now George is relaying a strange dream he had when he was dead.

I listen with interest.

'I didn't know where I was – well, not exactly. I was looking at me, but my body wouldn't move … I sat for a long time, trying to make it get up … I cried a lot, I can tell you that now – I'm glad you didn't see me. You, Rhi, were lying all crumpled up. It was horrible. But standing by you was a wild pony. At first I thought it might be your Unicorn, but it didn't move and neither did you. It was truly awful – I mean, really. I couldn't get myself to get up or do anything, so I wandered off to look for help … Everywhere was dark – and it felt like a hurricane had desolated the place … Then it was really weird – I mean, I saw Ellie lying down. I thought it was her … her dead body … but it wasn't – she was like me, in some sort of dream. She looked all light and translucent-ish and she was asleep. I sat down by her and I could tell she was dreaming, because every now and then she cried out or smiled.

"'Ellie," I said.

'I put my arm round her and she sort of half-turned to me in her sleep and murmured, "George?"

'And I said, "Yep, it's me. What's going on?"

'She sort of half sat up and said, "It's going to be OK."

'And then I just sat there while she slept and it was very, very dark. I think in my dream I fell asleep too. Because suddenly you were calling me, Rhi, and I could get back into my body again. So I sat up and tried to wake Ellie to say goodbye. I hugged her and she said, "George, go on, go back to her. Live long. Live for me. Tell them all I'm OK … Look, Henry is waiting for me." And sure enough, up by the Devil's Bridge

447

where the dawn was breaking, I saw Henry standing there.

'It was totally weird but not at all freaky.

'"There are stones," Ellie said, "marked by the sign of fire. It's like a Y. Find them and crack them open to close the portal at Cloggy – one above, one below, one in the middle." Then she put her arms around me and said, "Love you. I'm OK. I wouldn't want to come back, even if I could." And she pointed at Henry.

'"I'll miss you … it will never be the same," I cried, but the urge to re-enter my body was too strong to say any more.

'"It's all OK," she called. "It'll all be OK now we can put out the fire. Give Rhi my love – and Gran. Tell my mum I'll love her forever."

'And that was it.' George looks round sadly at Gran and Rhi.

Rhi starts crying. Gran looks weary and mutters, 'I warned her loving a dragon would come to no good …'

'She's happy, though,' says George.

I want to hug them. Tell them it's true.

I AM HAPPY.

Rhi nods and sniffs.

Gran smiles. 'Of course she is. We must remember this was her choice right from the beginning. She chose to be with Henry whatever the cost.'

'It's just SO MAJORLY SAD,' sniffs Rhi.

I leave them. I can't bear to see them grieving over me. And there are still some last things to do.

I am out on the mountain. But I am no longer anchored to the hillside. The Distance is calling. The anchor is broken. The kite can fly free. I can leave here and start my journey to the In-Between Place. Henry will be waiting there for me. For he once told me it is the only place where true lovers can always be together. The sun always shines there. The birds always sing. And no dark shadow will ever rise again to separate us.

I look up at the mountain. I see him there waiting, standing on the Devil's Bridge. He is not in a hurry. He will wait. He said so. He said he will wait for me for eternity. And I still have two tasks left to do before I can join him and start the next great adventure.

I turn away from Henry for now.

'Angharad,' I whisper, sending my call out on to the breeze, then I sit on the hillside and look out into the morning.

Angharad is soon here. She takes me by the hand.

'Tell me news of Idris and Rhitta Gawr,' I say.

'It was a bitter fight.' Angharad looks tired. Her eyes are red. 'Idris is grievously wounded, and I must go back to him. For even though he cannot see me, I must be with him.'

'And the Red Giant?' I ask.

'Rhitta Gawr was utterly defeated,' Angharad says. 'He has left these lands and fled to Anglesey, where he will find the Druids who can heal him. There are always Druids who will serve an evil being for a price.'

'Let us hope that Idris and he do not meet again.'

'It is unlikely, I think,' she says, 'for the Book of Shadows that called them to the Mortal Lands is destroyed. Merlin has returned to Avalon and the dragons are dead.'

'I have a gift for you,' I say. I press the straw into her hand. 'Take this. I've discovered something amazing and this straw helped me.'

Angharad holds it up and examines it.

'For those that wish to step through the realms and appear to their beloved ones,' I explain, 'they need only to master the art of pouring themselves with emotional energy through that straw, visualising their being in the next realm. The straw will channel them to where they want to be. Take it. You have more need of it than me.'

'But, Ellie,' she says, 'how can I accept such a gift? What if you wish to visit your mother or sit down again with your friends?'

'Take it,' I repeat. 'My mother will be happy again with

Jeff, and she will soon have drunk the stardust draft of easefulness. Then my passing will not be too awful for her to bear. Rhiannon at last has George, and George has found that his love for Rhiannon was there all along. He has so much love to give to her now. They will not need to see me. They both know I'm going to be with Henry, which is what I've always wanted. And that leaves Granny Jones, with whom I could have sat many an evening and told her things of the enchanted realms around us, but I am sure if she needs me, she will find a way to call me to her fireside. Plus I might find another straw. I'm not sure it's just the straw that makes the apparating work.'

I smile as I think fondly of the many afternoons by Gran's hearth, of her wisdom and her herbs, her mad velvet skirts and her record collection.

'But you will have need of this straw every day,' I say. 'For then you can be with Idris at all times. He will be able to see you, to talk with you, and although you will still be made up of dust and blossom and snowflakes, it will be a comfort to you both, for many an age. For too long have you been separated and now you can be together.' I press the straw into her hands. 'Go to him now and comfort him, for he is in pain and suffers.'

Angharad throws her arms around me. I feel her damp

tears on my neck. She tries to speak, but her voice is choked deep in her throat. I lift her head away from me and kiss her cheek. 'You do not need to thank me. You were there to hold my hand when I needed it most. Idris is a true friend … and look!' I point to the horizon, where the shadowy figure of my beloved Henry waits. 'I am blessed and I am happy. What once seemed my Heart's Despair has become the best thing that could ever have happened to me. I must go to him soon; the Distance is calling, and at last we can leave this Mortal World to be together forever.'

Angharad takes the straw. She is radiant. All tears are brushed away. The morning birdsong fills the spaces around us.

'Farewell,' I say. 'Give my love to Idris, until we meet again.'

And so it ends ...

23 June
Upon the Eve of St John's

'Had I known, had I known, Tam Lin,
Long before, long before you came from home,
Had I known, I would have taken out your heart
And put in a heart of stone.

Had I known, had I known, Tam Lin,
That I would lose, that I would lose the day,
Had I known, I would have paid my tithe to hell
Before you'd been won away.'

From *The Ballad of Tam Lin*
Anonymous

I stay and watch over my friends. The last task, the most important task, is yet to be finished and I know I will be held here until it is done. I must be sure – very, very sure – that the flames of Annwyn are put out forever.

Then I will be free.

It is afternoon and George and Rhiannon take the Ranger Path up towards the top of Clogwyn. As they climb, they point out my old farmhouse still smoking in ruins.

'I miss Ellie so much,' whispers Rhi.

'Me too,' says George.

They cling to each other for a while and I wrap my ghostly arms around them. 'It's OK,' I tell them. 'It's OK.'

They rally and climb on through the devastation caused by the wildfire. Gorse still smoulders. The air is still thick with smoke. The line of fire has passed down the slopes of Snowdon and is heading out into Snowdonia. Scores of people are still being evacuated at Blaenau Ffestiniog, and at Beddgelert, and on the Caernarfon road.

Hand in hand, Rhi and George look down towards the ruined cottage where Gran and George once lived.

'The insurance will pay,' George says. 'The rebuild money isn't massive, but I'll make it work.'

'You make everything work, you wizard!' Rhiannon laughs.

'Even if I have to build the cottage back stone by stone myself, I've promised Nan that she can go home before the winter.'

'I'll help,' says Rhiannon. 'And my dad has trucks and trailers and workers. He'll help too.'

George takes her hand and kisses it.

I'm so glad George will rebuild the cottage. Snowdon wouldn't be complete without Gran and George living on its slopes.

Over George's shoulder is a rucksack and sticking out of the top is a long tube of rolled cardboard, not unlike the containers posters are sometimes stored in. The bag looks heavy, but George has broad shoulders and does not feel its weight.

As the afternoon passes, George and Rhiannon climb to the top of the great cliffs of Clogwyn D'ur Arddu. They dodge outbreaks of fire and pick their way over cinder and blackened earth. Right at the centre of the clifftop, they stop and rest.

George unfastens the rucksack, passes an apple to Rhiannon and removes a stone from the bag. It's a round stone about the size of a grapefruit, and it's marked with a strange rune, almost like a Y. George places the stone carefully where it will not be dislodged by storm or winter frost and where no living creature will discover it. Then he takes his axe and with one hard blow cracks the stone open. All remaining outbreaks of fire burning on the clifftop immediately flicker out.

Oh thank you, Henry! Thank you! Thank you! Your firestones are working!

After they have shared the apple, George and Rhiannon take the Llanberis path down to Llyn D'ur Arddu. Together they make their way underneath the Cliff of the Darkness.

They rest again in Clogwyn's shadow, looking out at the lake. George puts his arm around Rhi.

'We'll crack the second stone here,' says George, 'and throw the last one against the rock face.'

'And the scabbard?' asks Rhiannon. 'Must we really chuck it into the lake?'

'We promised to return it. And I think it would be unwise to keep it a moment longer than we have to.'

'I know, it's just that it's really pretty – and it saved my life. I've taken pics of it – so we can remember how awesome it was, but that won't be the same ...'

Together they place the second stone under the cliff, and George breaks it open with his axe. The burning all along the bottom of the cliff blinks out.

Yes! I inwardly cheer. *We did it! We are doing it!*

Rhi and George move back a little from the cliff face and George takes aim with the last stone. He throws it as fast and as high and as hard as he can at Clogwyn D'ur Arddu.

As stone hits stone and cracks open, a deep echo rumbles out, almost like the boom of thunder. There is a flash of sparks, and the afternoon sun is reflected off the lake and on to the cliff front in dancing flames of light.

'OMG!' screams Rhiannon, as flames race up the cliff.

There is the smell of bleach and chlorine and then it passes. All the remaining fires are snuffed out as if by some unseen hand. Every last bit of cinder smoulders and dies.

The air is once more filled with the scent of wild mountain thyme and earthy bracken.

'Fight fire with fire,' orders George and points his sigil ring at the cliff face. As he says it, unbeknown to him, the flames burning deep in the coal mines under Snowdonia instantly quench. I know. I'm a ghost. I can check these things. The wildfire spreading over the furthermost mountains of Snowdonia, as far as Cadair Idris, dies out. Flames everywhere peter out into weak sparks and dulled embers. 'As above, so below. Close this portal. So mote it be!' commands George.

And the portal to Annwyn snaps shut.

'It is done.' George slumps down for a moment on a slab of slate.

Yes, it is done! NOW I am free to leave!

After a moment's rest, George rouses himself, putting his arm around Rhiannon again. 'Now for the scabbard,' he says.

Hand in hand, George and Rhiannon step down the blackened scree under the cliff towards the lake. The twisted remains of the helicopter still litter the lakeshore. George and Rhiannon pick their way around it until they stand at the south-western end of the llyn.

'Do you think this is the right lake to throw it in?' asks Rhiannon.

'The right lake!' George laughs and repeats what Gran once told him. 'There is no right lake. Everyone claims to have Ynys Afallach, the Island of Avalon, in their county. They are all correct and they are all wrong. For magic is not static and we cannot compare places in their world in the same way as they exist in ours.'

'Suppose so,' says Rhi, still looking a bit doubtful.

'Anyway, Nimue has such powerful arts, she'll find a way to receive it – I'm positive,' reassures George.

'Are you sure about the mobile too?'

George pulls the rolled cardboard out of the backpack. From it he takes the scabbard of Caledfwlch and checks the small package taped tightly to the belt: the latest iPhone loaded with every app imaginable.

'Just for you, Merl,' he says.

Together they check the note taped on to the bundle.

Dear Nim and Merl,

Thanks so much for the loan of Caledfwlch and all your help. We couldn't have done it without you guys. So glad Lance is better, and he was able to fulfil his quest (HUGEST sigh of relief - you know, that MONSTER G.A.N. obliterated and the Hordes of Evil vanquished!). BTW, Lance took Caledy back with him to Annwyn. We figure you know that by now, obvs, but we are returning the scabbard as promised (totally LOVE it - it SAVED RHI'S LIFE). We do hope to meet you both again. One day. Somehow.

Lots of love, Rhiannon and George (and Ellie - I guess you heard she is now with Henry)

PS Hope you are having a FAB reunion and LOTS of cosy catch-up chats!

Holding hands with Rhi, George stands by the very edge, where the waters lap the stone and sedge. He raises the scabbard bundle and takes aim. 'Here, these are for you, Nimue and Merlin,' calls George. And with one great swing of his arm, he hurls it out towards the centre of the lake.

The scabbard arcs high in the air, flashing in the afternoon sun. The reflection of light off that dazzling metalwork seems to strike something bright like diamonds in the waters of the llyn. Rays of energy bounce back in a rainbow of light and seem to mesmerise Rhiannon and George. For a moment, I believe the two of them see me and Henry, waving to them from some golden land – there, caught in magical crystals, in a wonderful cavern, deep down beneath the turquoise waters.

The scabbard twists and turns out over the water. As it falls, an arm rises up out of the lake, closed in white samite, wonderful, mystic. It catches the spinning scabbard. As the afternoon sun sparkles along its length, the arm brandishes everything to the sky, three times, and then draws it down, down under the water.

Rhiannon lays her beautiful head on George's shoulder. 'It's done,' she sighs.

They both sit there a while.

'Wish Ellie was here. She'd be so proud,' says Rhi. She sniffs a bit and buries her head in George's jacket.

I am proud. I AM PROUD!

George passes her a tissue and bites his lip; a sudden, lost, faraway look troubles his brow.

'I'm OK,' I whisper. 'I love you both. I miss you too and I am here ... and I am totally proud that we finally did it.'

A sigh of wind ripples out across the lake. The smell of burning is quite gone.

'C'mon!' says George at last, giving Rhiannon a big hug. 'Let's go home.'

'Guess what?' says Rhi, cheering up. 'I think they're doing a massive, humungous, death-defying curry tonight in the hotel restaurant!'

George laughs. 'Have I ever told you, you're the best person in the world, and I'll love you forever and ever?'

'Erm ... I think you might have mentioned that a few times!'

'Plus, if you don't mind me smelling of tikka masala, I'll give you the biggest snog ever, later on when we're alone.'

'Brush your teeth first?'

'Deal!'

Rhi smiles and looks up towards the summit of Snowdon, where for a brief instant the white shape of a wild pony is silhouetted against the sky.

'Thank you,' she whispers.

And together, hand in hand, they go down from the mountain.

I watch them go, until they are lost in the distance.

I blow a last kiss after them. Then, at long last, I turn to the mountain, to the heights of Snowdon, to that In-Between Place where my beloved Henry stands, with the evening sun glancing off his auburn hair, silhouetted in sparkling air, up by the Devil's Bridge. Up there waiting for me.

And I step out up the slopes towards the greatest adventure ever.

My heart dancing.

Fin

Acknowledgements

Huge thanks to:

Jon Barton

Margaret Bateson-Hill

Cameron Bonser

Catherine Coe

John Coefield

Joy Coombes

Matt Dickinson

Ruth Eastham

Emma Greenwood

Lorna Hargreaves

Sophie Hicks

Caroline Johnson

Kitty Kettle

Emma Lockley

Karen Owen

Chitra Soundar

Nathan Ryder

Susie Ryder

Ray Upstall

Google

Snowdon

Blaenau Ffestiniog

And all the books with magical worlds
that I have ever read.

Imperium Magis!

Author Biography

Sarah Mussi is a multi-award-winning author of children's and young adults' fiction. Her first novel, *The Door of No Return*, won the Glen Dimplex Children's Book Award and was shortlisted for the Branford Boase Award. Her second novel, *The Last of the Warrior Kings*, was shortlisted for the

Lewisham Book Award, inspired a London walk, and is used as a textbook in Lewisham schools. Her novel *Angel Dust* was the lead title on the Hot Key list 2012, and was followed by *Breakdown*. Her thriller *Siege* was nominated for the CILIP Carnegie Medal in 2014, and won the BBUKYA award for contemporary YA fiction. Her thriller *Riot* was longlisted for the Amazing Book Award amongst many others and won the Lancashire Book of the Year Award in 2015. This was followed by *Bomb*, published by Hodder Children's Books; *Room Empty*, published by One World in 2017; and *You Can't Hide* (Hodder) in 2019. *Here be Dragons*, the first book in the Snowdonia Chronicles trilogy, was published by Vertebrate Publishing in 2015; *Here be Witches*, the second book, followed in 2017. *Here be Wizards* is the third and final book in the trilogy.

Sarah was born and raised in the Cotswolds, attended Pate's Grammar School for Girls, and graduated with a BA in Fine Art from Winchester School of Art and an MA from the Royal College of Art. She spent over fifteen years in West Africa as a teacher, and now lives in London where she is the current Co-Chair of CWISL (Children's Writers and Illustrators for Stories and Literacy). Sarah splits her time between writing, visiting schools as an author and promoting creative writing for children. She also teaches English in a Lewisham school.